The Trauma Pool

JOHN KENNEDY

CONTENTS

Part 1: IMPACT
1 – 25
Part 2: AVOIDANCE
26 – 38
Part 3: FRACTURE
39 – 55

Part 1: IMPACT

The crags were blotted with rain and the line of towns they protected were black holes. Nothing much escaped; light, youth and kindness spending itself on these wet valley walls daily. But blame was wasted because he knew it wasn't the place. Not really. It was him and what he carried that blocked the light.

DI Will Ashcroft swung down into the valley and parked by the portacabin at the edge of the factory grounds.

Too many cars, he thought. Junior officers would spill brandy-laced tea from flasks and grind cigarette butts all over the scene. Later there'd be visits from at least one Superintendent and other seniors who'd do much the same. By the end of tonight, the chances of finding anything useful would be slim as a famished moor-rat.

He adjusted the mirror and put a hand through his unruly hair, trying to loosen his shoulders. He shut the car door, hauling his combat jacket over his wiry frame. The rain had stopped but it was cold for May. His eyes flickered upwards at the misshapen tower sticking out from the distant trees; a local folly, fashioned by a madman with too much time, too much love, too much something.

A sergeant and constable waved him through the gate and two reporters, one greying and bearded, another with a copper-coloured mullet, turned to check him out. Only a few hours since the body was found, so they were sharp for small-towners. Mullet raised his camera and clicked. 'Can you tell us anything?'

Will shook his head. 'I'm not the SIO.'

The rugged path wound round the cabin through the trees. He hunched, droplets catching his neck. The leaves gave way to a fence, graffiti covered; a muted yawp of the topical, *Keegan Rules! Save the miners*, and the less topical, from at least five years ago, *Up yours Argies! Falklands ours!*

Local kids had always hung out here, he remembered, shinning over to drink cheap cider or get stoned. But tonight, they'd stumbled across more than wilted condoms and discarded porn. Even off their heads, they'd been scared enough to report it to the night-watchman. They'd be in the portacabin now, finishing their statements, poor sods.

The coal-mound nosed up in front of him. Halfway up, two constables and an overweight, middle-aged, uniformed sergeant were trying to erect a frame, laughing, capering. Will watched a few seconds before clearing his throat. The sergeant stepped over the barrier, stumbled and slid down the mound, bloodshot eyes on Will, broken veins at his cheeks spreading along with a smile with no pretence at warmth. 'Bloody hell. Thought you'd moved down London years ago, Sergeant.'

'I'm a DI now.' Will watched one constable prodding the other with a tent-pole. 'Grundy, don't you think we'd be better off just laying a tarp over the body. No point setting up a tent on top of that.'

Grundy scratched his reddening ear like a pantomime policeman. He flashed yellowed teeth at Will and walked away, shaking his head, muttering, waving them down the coal mound.

Will did a full circuit of the stack, waiting for them to pick up all their rods and get out of his way. They took their time and he felt their glances, sharp as granite. Their talk was fast, clipped by choked-back laughs, Grundy filling them in, no doubt. Who Will was. What he'd done. He heard a 'That was him?' and one of the PCs stared now; a cold mix of awe and derision.

Finally they shuffled down and he climbed, hands outward for balance. He glanced at the sky, the fading light of a spring evening; not the best.

The body was face-up, arms spread wide; middle-aged, maybe late forties, a face that might have once been striking. Unshaven, maybe four days' growth. A beefy frame gone to flab. Medium length jacket over brown suit-trousers, torn in two places and a once white shirt, grimed almost to grey.

Like he'd been put through his paces.

The arms were interesting. It would have taken some extra effort to place them like that; spread wide to the skies. Will glanced back beyond the trees. It was good the Press hadn't been let in. All kinds of meanings could be attached to the positioning, but 'take me with you' would really stir up the crazies.

He leant in closer to the trouser legs. There were purple specks caught in the weave. Heather? He glanced up past the dark valley walls towards the moor.

He leant back on his haunches. The SOCO had looked already, of course, heart attack as apparent cause of death, the word *misadventure* already filtering through the radio to Will as he'd driven over from Leeds. Still. It was all in the detail. He grimaced, bent forward, manoeuvring himself so that he could lift the head with both hands. Too early for Rigor so no resistance, but something slippery spread on his fingers. Jelly? On the underside, untouched by rain. He squinted down the collar, easing the head up. The neck was raw and pink and scalp was showing, a fair portion of the hair having fallen from blistered skin in two-inch circular patches. Coal dust coated the pink flesh, and he tasted sudden bile and sucked in some air.

He pulled at the shirt collar. The circular marks continued onto the shoulders. It wasn't acid. More like he'd been held, tied against something hot. Really hot. Severe burns or scalds, maybe third degree. But not the cause of death, or not straight away anyway. The blisters weren't fresh. Will sniffed at the sticky substance on his fingertips.

'Any of you touched the body?'

The two constables shook their heads. Grundy smiled. 'Not my type. You been transferred back up here from London then? For this?'

Will stared at him and then back down at the head he still cradled. He let it rest, rolling his fingers. Coal dust in the jelly was like grit in an oyster. 'I've been over in Leeds a few months now. So, where's the night-watchman?'

Grundy was gesturing one of the constables towards the portacabin where Will had parked. 'Suppose things didn't work out in London, then, Ashcroft?'

Will grinned. If Grundy had any idea what had really happened to him in London, he'd shit his pants and choke on his next whiskey. He stood. 'Before you and your two monkeys climbed up here, did you notice any signs that someone had carried this poor bastard to the top?'

Grundy sniffed. 'Nah, don't think there was any.'

'But we'll never know for sure, now, will we?' Will surveyed the coal around him. Of course, it wouldn't have mattered if Grundy had set up a chimps' tea party. Coal was virtually impossible to track through, anyway. Too hard. Impermeable.

Grundy had coloured. He pulled out a cigarette and lit it, tossing the match into the coal. He took a few drags, probably so he had some ash to flick in Will's general direction as he turned and stalked away.

Will smiled, massaging and stretching his neck. But there was the faintest tremor in his hand and he stared at it, then at the hills and the rocky expanse around him. The old tower on the hill looked like a crow, the wind in the trees was full of menace and he had the sudden urge to walk back to the car and just drive out of here.

A cough from the bottom of the mound. The night-watchman's eyes were dark pits, his movements twitchy. Will nodded, took a single deep breath and picked his way down to him. 'I'm sure another officer has spoken to you already but there're a couple of things. What did you do when you first saw the body?'

The man scratched his cheek and glanced towards the mound, looking down again quickly. 'I phoned you lot.'

'I reckon if I'd seen someone lying up there, I might've felt *compelled* to have a closer look.' Will stared at him until he shifted his balance.

'Yeah, okay.' He paled. 'I went up there. But I didn't touch him. I shouted first, like, to see if he was drunk. Thought maybe he'd got in here and fell asleep after a skinful. Knew that wasn't it though. Wish I hadn't got so close, as it happens.'

'How would anyone have got in, anyway? Don't you lock up?'

'Course I do.' He gestured at the fence. 'But the coal-yard's not even part of the factory. Not my job to watch it. Though I try to keep an eye out. Anyway that fence is easy. Bloody kids always in here, smoking pot and God knows what –'

'Yeah, they're being questioned.' Will traced the line of wooden struts and wire mesh. There was a spot where the fence

4

looked damaged, where it backed onto woodland that stretched up to the edge of the moor. He turned back to the watchman, gesturing up at the body. 'Ever seen him before?'

A shrug. 'Nah. Never. Don't think he's local.'

'How come?'

'Dunno, really. Maybe he is.' He gave a sad smile. 'But he looks about my age and I've lived in Spinnerby all my life. Mind you, he could be with the fezzy crew.'

The upcoming festival in Hebden Bridge, a few towns further up the valley. There'd been workmen earlier, putting up scaffolding in the park as Will had driven through. He made a mental note to send a constable to see if the work crew was missing anyone. It hardly fitted with how the body was dressed though.

'It's weird.' The night-watchman squinted, shaking his head. 'Laid out like that. Looks like he's been *dropped* here, dunnit?'

'Don't let's get any silly ideas.' Will gave another glance towards the reporters near the gates. Paranormal tales and rumours were rife in this valley, always had been.

Eyes narrowed, he stared up at the starfish pose again as the night-watchman walked away. Had he died in situ or been carried? They'd have to wait for a lividity test to be sure. Except the soles of the shoes were clean; no coal-dust at all. Just possible the recent shower had washed it off, but the way the body was left on the mound's slope, the soles were facing downwards, sheltered.

He turned and made his way back up to the top, losing his footing twice on the wet coal, trying to imagine carrying 14 stone of middle-aged and half-burnt flesh, and that was after getting it over the fence. More than one person? Or just one very strong man?

Will stood on the mound and watched the last slivers of sun. He could feel Grundy and the others looking up at him, still sniggering. He wasn't even sure why he'd come back up here, something was wrong though. With what? This scene, the body? The way it had been placed? Maybe. Maybe to all of those. But something... something else. Something wrong with... himself? He stumbled suddenly, the ground, the air, the whole landscape shifting under him. His right hand shook again, legs locking, his head a roar of sudden noise, the coal-yard blueing out.

'Ashcroft? What the fuck?'

Will raised a hand as if to ward off help, finding he couldn't even tell where Grundy was. He could see rain, now, slanting through that wash of blue light, even though he knew it wasn't real. Water, in his eyes, in his nose. He shook his head and spat. Didn't matter. He'd count to ten, close his eyes. When he opened them it would all be gone. The blue, the rain... there'd be just the coal-yard around him and a bunch of coppers staring at a weirdo in their midst. One, two, three...

2

Funny thing was, the blue light and rain softened into something else as he stood there on the coal-stack, his balance reeling back to him. A simple memory this time, not a violent insertion. A forgotten moment.

The hospital. The one in Hackney where they'd taken him and the Havilland boy.

He'd taken off the oxygen mask and sat up. They'd flapped around him, saying he had to stay close, in case of respiratory failure. He probably told them to piss off. Or worse. Stupid really. Just doing their jobs.

He'd calmed himself, told them he had to see the boy. They said no. 'Course they did. He stood up. A bit woozy, sure. He'd been lying for hours. They mentioned hypothermia and he laughed at them. 'Not you. The boy.' They said it not unkindly, considering the prick he was being.

More toing and froing. Him folding his arms and telling them jokes to prove he wasn't delirious. Them laughing, though he didn't think their hearts were in it.

In the end a couple of the nurses steered him along the corridor. He didn't shrug them off. One of them was pretty and he thought he'd mentioned it once or twice. It wasn't that they'd given him anything, no sedatives he was aware of, just that… the world was different now. He didn't see why he had to pretend about things, soften what he meant with politeness. He was alive and every leaf on every tree was his to pick.

They got to the room. There were some flowers in a vase. The boy's parents? Why were they not here?

Because it was five in the morning, pretty nurse said. Anyway the mother was in a state herself and the father was asleep on the bed next door. Not to be sneezed at either, a spare bed for a visitor with all the cutbacks and everything…

He nodded. So why were they walking him around if it was so early, giving him what he demanded?

'Because you're an absolute bloody hero,' she said. She kissed him, full on the lips, the other nurse's laughter tickling the air around them like confetti.

He should have enjoyed it. Would have. But it wasn't him she was kissing. Just an idea of him.

They left him alone with the boy.

There was water, in a jug, on the table. Water. Tamed, life-giving. But he'd had enough for a lifetime, doubted he'd ever drink it again.

It started leaking from his eyes when he saw the boy though. Wouldn't stop. Like he'd absorbed half the bloody stinking pool and now the only way out was through his tear ducts.

He looked at the boy, wanted to pull the tube out of his mouth and pick him up. He didn't feel right without him on his shoulders. Symbiosis.

Then a line of golden sunlight, almost horizontal, caught the rise and fall of the boy's chest and Will's tears dried right up.

Every breath from now is a gift, he remembered thinking. Every breath...

3

A headache stalked him from the coal-yard to the incident room.

There was bustle at the door. Grundy came first, then DCI Ronnie Price. The DCI moved in bursts, overtaking Grundy, cigarette flashing. Pinched face, nose hooked, grey hair at the temples, the glare Will remembered. There was a glance for him – no change of expression but a slight nod. Price sat on the front table. 'Okay, lads and lasses. Eyes front.'

Price's use of a plural had Will glancing around, but though he'd seen several WPCs on his way up to the incident room, there was only one female officer assigned to the response team. It was hard to miss her. For one thing, the wave of tension in the room. For another, Detective Constable Samira Byrne, as she'd introduced herself earlier, was a single non-white face adrift but buoyant in a sea of Caucasian ones.

Mid-twenties, he figured. Great face, high cheekbones, just this side of *Vogue* striking, saved from it by a mouth that wasn't quite perfectly even. Her large brown eyes softened the severity of the tight pony-tail and arched brows.

Grundy, Will couldn't help noticing, had been giving her a dull-eyed stare since he'd come in; the kind of look belonging on men in betting shops, the slightest sparkle of longing in a glaze of bitterness. Then again, it could as easily have been indigestion.

'Right, okay.' Price was pinning up more pictures. 'Not much from forensics yet. We're still going with heart attack, so this is not a murder enquiry. Misadventure still pretty likely. Kind of thing we'll never be able to suss out. Got drunk, walked into a pylon or summat.'

The headache gnawed.

'But it's just possible some random nutter picked up this poor bastard, burned him, did whatever it took to get his jollies, then left him on a pile of coal for ET and his mates to –'

'Beam me up, Scotty!' Grundy laughed, most chorusing, DC Samira Byrne notably not among them.

'I've already contacted all local funny farms, just in case. You never know. Some mental case might've done a runner. Any further on the vic's ID? Turner?' Price was looking at a brawny constable, neck like a trunk, ears rugby-battered.

'Nothing yet, boss.'

'Someone must have known him.'

A voice in his head was telling Will to stay quiet, but he just couldn't do it. 'What about the jelly, boss?'

Price's grin dropped away and he waved stiffly at Will. 'Aye. This is DI Ashcroft, on loan from AMIP in London. Come to show us how it's done.' He softened the last with a laugh. 'What jelly?'

'The stuff coating the wounds on his back.' Will kept his tone even. 'If it's ointment, it could be somebody tried to help him. Or that someone wanted to keep him moving despite his injuries. The state of his clothes as well.'

'Maybe…' Samira cleared her throat. 'Maybe he got away from whoever burnt him. Ran over the moor.'

The room was silent. Will looked at her. Her thinking was close to his own.

Price's glare had gone up a notch. 'Anything else?'

'The burns.' Will held Price's gaze. 'Maybe we should be looking at factories. Could be our boy worked somewhere like that. Those circular shapes could be from something industrial or –'

'Or he fell onto his barbecue!' Price rolled his eyes. 'Or a hundred other things.'

Will shrugged. 'We could do with seeing a burns expert.'

'What's wrong with the labrats? Booth's mates in white coats can suss it out.' Price rolled his eyes at the owlish looking SOCO. Booth blinked, gave a nod to Price, but without much gusto.

Will took a breath. Burns were a specific field of expertise; even the path-lab might need to consult. He wanted to mention HOLMES too, how they should be using the integrated system, flawed though it was, to look for similar unsolveds nationally, but the headache was thrumming at his temples, the room seeming to flicker blue, and the voice in his head was telling him he'd pushed enough.

Price had turned away. 'Okay. That's that then. Let's get this poor bastard named. Grundy, keep monitoring missing persons reports. Someone'll come forward. That's if he had anyone. Benson, keep workin' through locals with any previous. Sturgess, we'll consider the factory angle. Ashcroft.' Price grinned. 'You can co-ordinate the door-to-door in Shockley Beck.'

Bastard. Will curled his lip.

'Turner.' A wink for the burly constable. 'You have the statements so far, not that there is much. Residents might be more forthcoming with a couple of...' he glanced at Samira and Will, '...*different* faces.'

A choked ripple of laughter in the room.

'OKAY!' Price boomed it out. 'Let's name our vic, if he was a vic, and wrap this up.' He came close to Will. 'My office!'

Will followed him in, feeling the eyes of the room boring into his back.

'Close it.' Price half-disappeared behind strewn papers, coffee cups and folders. The hooked nose was sharpened and Will thought of a ratting terrier let loose in a cellar.

'Let's cut through it. You were *golden boy* for a while down London. The way I hear it they're even thinking of giving you a fucking medal. But I know there's some shite hanging over you. Don't know what it is yet but I can smell it.'

Will stared straight ahead. The Queen's Gallantry Medal. Of course, they'd have heard about that up here. Made the connection. *Didn't he start out in Spinnerby? Well, la-de-bloody-da!* But AMIP had kept the detail of the Creasey case pretty dark so far.

'You probably reckon the Super's sent you because he thinks we're a bunch of gawbies who can't handle a serious crime. Personally, I think it's cos he knows you're washed out.'

The headache was spiking now.

'I'm sure you'd like to turn this into some drama to get you back in the brass's favour but let's face it, really we're talking about some poor silly bastard who fried himself, then some joker came along and stuck him on the coal-stack for shits and giggles. Just to stir up the nutters, give them a headline.'

There was something in that, Will thought. Not in the way Price meant though.

'Now, I don't want you here, but you're here. So I'm gonna use you as I see fit and if that means going door to door, that's what you'll bloody do.'

The headache was flaring blue sparks on the edge of his vision, Price and the office fading. Will could almost see slanting rain again. He felt his hand threatening to quake and he stilled it with his other, clasped in front of him.

'Go on then. Off you trot!'

He turned, groping for the door. But then he stopped, turning to Price with a real effort, hand against the wall. 'He's heavy, our vic. Fourteen stone or more. Dead weight, to the top of a coal-stack, just for shits and giggles?' Will shook his head. 'I wouldn't fancy it. Would you?'

4

Samira slowed at the eggs and bacon, shook her head, went for the wholemeal toast option. Maybe with jam? She took a strawberry carton as a raucous laugh went up behind her in the queue. Her back stiffened; no reason for it. Might have nothing to do with her. Except it did. Something about the brashness; there's laughter because you find something funny, and there's laughter because you want people to think you do.

Spinnerby nick's canteen was airy enough to lose yourself in the corners, as she'd managed this past month and a half. But the counter and serving area was a bit tight; it made her personal bubble less than inviolable – it burst right now as someone brushed against her arm. Turner. She stared up at him.

'That all you're having, like?'

She glanced at her tray.

'Not gonna put much colour in your cheeks is it?'

A choked-back laugh deteriorating into a bronchial cough from Grundy behind him. A grin from Turner. 'Hey Bev!' His eyes stayed on Samira but the waitress leant in over the counter at him. 'What's the difference between a naked white woman and a naked black woman?'

Bev did an *ooh you're incorrigible* look. But she leant in further, fake-tanned breasts squashing against pastry display-glass.

'One's on the cover of *Playboy* and the other's on the cover of *National Geographic*.'

Lovely. More coughs from Grundy, more eye-rolling from Bev, though Samira seriously doubted either of them knew what *National Geographic* was. She put the jam on the tray, pushed it along to the till and ordered a coffee, pleased her voice was steady. But from behind her, a few phrases took flight; 'take a joke' and 'stuck up jig' being two of them. She turned.

Options. Tell him a magazine cover was the closest he'd ever get to a naked woman, black or white? Tell him he was a complete arsehole? She looked at them both. Overweight, faces the colour of gum, gurning with tin crown confidence and foreheads that made her seriously concerned for the future of the species.

She was opening her mouth to speak when the mood shifted, a slim shape inserting itself into their little drama. DI Ashcroft, appearing from somewhere, moving between her and the two men. Not particularly tall or imposing, his build wiry if anything. Self-possessed in his movements though.

His eyes were flinty as he faced up to Turner. 'The statements from the petrol station near Shockley Beck –'

Turner did a shrugging kind of sway, trying to budge the DI out of the way with sheer size and proximity, something you could tell he was used to getting away with. But Ashcroft didn't move and the PC stopped, thinking better of it, shuffling back.

'I need you to go and get your notes from upstairs.'

'Aww! What, now? I'm on –'

'You've missed something important, Turner. Better get your notes.'

Turner's head was down, forehead thrusting. A glance at her, another at Grundy, who'd turned away. Then his big shoulders dropped and he turned, moving toward the door with that rolling swagger that men of his size couldn't or wouldn't seem to avoid.

The DI turned to her. 'I need to see you as well. Got a drink, yeah?'

She moved to a side table. Not that it mattered. Already on the fringes of this little squad. Could coffee with the DI from London do any more damage?

She stretched and cricked her neck, eyes on Grundy. The gathered glut of tension in her dried throat and belly was fading, and she helped it with a deep breath. Because, yes, these snide morons bothered her. She hated admitting it, but they did. But that didn't mean she needed some white knight in leather jacket and jeans swooping in to save her. White or any other colour.

They never tell you this bit, she thought. The recruitment drivers with their ad campaigns and their *broadening participation*. Yeah, come join up, but be ready to spend your time choosing between bristling silence or playing along. She'd done it, at first. Grinned like a fool, been one of the crew. Canteen banter. Harmless. Except it wasn't.

She let out a breath. Why wasn't she like Mum? Mum who

just sailed above it all, who like so many Jamaican women had this incredible ability to just accept. Samira was more like Dad with his Irish hot-headedness.

As the DI got his drink and came over, she watched him openly. Good face, pale but not pasty under unruly dark hair. Something careworn and easy in it, though the eyes were harder. 'I was thinking...' he said, planting himself opposite and sweeping some salt from his half of the table-top. 'You went to check on the festival crew over in Hebden for missing people, right? We should probably do a quick check for previous as well. They'll have been around a few days and –'

She nodded. 'I already did. Just minors, a driving offence, drunk in charge, the usual.'

His eyebrows arched. 'Okay. Nice work.'

She let herself smile and he joined her, seeming awkward for the first time. She leant in. 'You're not happy with the misadventure angle are you, boss?'

A measuring look, then a shrug. 'Call me Will. No, I'm not. Are you?'

She shook her head. Emphatic. Pleasant afternoon chat over coffee. 'I've read about some killers inserting things. Grass, stones, whatever, into bodies.' She winced. Why did she feel like a true crime enthusiast instead of a detective? 'That's in, well, sexual cases, obviously.'

'Their moment in the sun,' he said. 'Their moment to say *hey, look at this! Look what I did.* No sign of that here though, no obvious symbols. I mean, other than the coal-stack and the arms wide open, which could have meaning, I suppose but...' He spread his hands, then looked away like a boy too old for Top Trump cards, caught playing with some.

'But the torture?'

He nodded.

She sipped at her coffee and noticed he hadn't touched his. He was looking over in Grundy's direction now and she wondered what the sergeant was making of their sharing a table. Nothing good.

'Surely we haven't got so many black female DCs.' He said it easily. 'How the hell did you end up here, anyway?'

A bit soon for gripes, she thought. How could she put it? Say she'd applied for promotion after nailing a couple of nasty Moss Side bastards, and they'd rewarded her by sending her to this butt-shaped crack in the Pennines? She literally bit her lip and glanced out at the day. 'Got transferred from Manchester about six weeks ago.'

He gave a slight nod, looked like he might have been about to ask more, but then the warmth swept from his face. Turner was back in the room, heading for their table.

'Here's me' notes.' He slapped the pad down.

The DI was staring down at his own hands, touching the fingertips of one with the other. 'Why didn't you interview the night-worker from Saturday?'

Turner's face was blank. 'I spoke to the manager. He said –'

'I know what he said. The night-worker hadn't seen anything. And he's been off yesterday, sick.'

'Aye.'

'So, you didn't follow it up. Find him at home and talk to him personally?'

There was a sudden scatter of blotches up that thick neck.

'What about the cameras?' The DI looked up for the first time, leant forwards, hands spread on the table now.

Turner's head slotted from side to side in its turret.

Samira leant in, clearing her throat. 'CCTV installed. Recently, by the looks. State of the art, so maybe VHS recorded.'

Turner blinked at her, like he'd forgotten she was there. No, worse than that; she was interrupting *man's talk*. 'Don't see how that's –'

'The camera probably covers the moorland path down to the coal-yard?' She waited for the DI's nod, turned back to Turner. 'Our vic had some heather on his clothes. Likely he crossed the moor Saturday evening. Possible the camera caught him.' She watched Turner, despite everything a vague sense of sympathy stirring. Her earlier thoughts of Mum came back to her. Acceptance. She coughed, looked back at the DI. 'Sir, why don't Turner and I sort this? We'll go get the footage. Then talk to the night-worker.'

DI Ashcroft looked back at his hands, nodded, then gave her a quick smile. 'Okay.' His expression changed as he looked up. 'Hope you appreciate it, Turner.'

Whether he thought he did or not, they never found out. A gruff shout, heads around them jerking in unison like broken soldiers as DCI Price nosed around the canteen door. 'My lot upstairs in five. Our vic's named and claimed!'

5

Slate skies and mist collapsed the light on the M62 over articulated trucks and coaches; a wall of drudge and spray. He'd used the beacon a couple of times to cut through it.

It was sheer luck that someone in Liverpool had matched a missing person's report from three days before with their unclaimed corpse. Evie Smiles had been shipped over to the valley to ID her husband, courtesy of Merseyside Police, and then driven back home. Evie the ice-queen. She was a well-kept woman, mid-forties. *Just about doable, warmed up a bit*, had been the station consensus.

Price had gotten nothing. Her husband, Peter Smiles, had been unremarkable. A woodwork teacher. No reason she could think of why he should have wound up on a coal mound 70 miles from home. He had no connection with the valley at all.

So, as soon as the door-to-doors were done, Will had pointed his car at the hills. An hour and a half to Liverpool, but even with the weather, he made it in an hour and fifteen.

He knew a couple of people at the Liverpool nick, so getting some background wasn't too difficult. Of course, his visit was unsanctioned, so no doubt he'd face the wrath of Price tomorrow. So be it.

Merseyside police had got zilch from the school, the headmaster a *right sanctimonious little prick*. Either Peter Smiles, already *Smiley* to their incident room, had been as boring as he seemed or the headmaster had done a quick whitewash; so many headlines lately, neglect, abuse, cruelty, it wouldn't be that surprising. 'But what did your gut say?' Will had asked.

A well-seasoned DI Will had never met had raised his hand, letting it waver along with a wide-lipped grimace. Universal signage for *something a bit iffy*.

Good enough. Will had thanked them and headed for Smiley's allotment near Sefton Park.

He wandered a while between the lines of veggies and then hoisted himself up, bracing between shed and wall. There was an old track snaking up from the rear of the shed and into the treeline. Was there room for a car or small van further up? He pictured Smiley lured out, dragged off and hustled into the boot. But that only made sense if the shed had a back door, because the track was unreachable from the front of the allotments, brambles and overgrowth long since having corralled it.

He eased himself down, feeling only faintly ridiculous and opened the lock. Smiley's keys had never been found but the spares from the caretaker worked fine.

It was dim in here. Woodworking tools, gardening equipment racked and a woodwork-table central with a lathe off the other side. There was a turned table leg, a lamp, and some picture frames. It was a woodwork teacher's hobby space, alright. No back door, he noticed. But something was wrong.

He walked outside again and partway down the path, thinking lengths and distances. A slow grin spreading, he went back in.

He moved around the bench and to the back wall. He crouched under the shadow of the lathe. There! A hatch. About four by four. You'd really have to be looking for it. He pushed, crawled through.

Darkness, but the light from the window of the main shed was diffused into ribbons around his feet. He stood, hands brushing something. A cord? He pulled, blinking at the single bulb.

'Come on, Smiley. Don't be boring.' His voice was flattened by the small space as he stared around him. There was camping equipment, some torches and an air-rifle. A clutter of tin cans too; peaches, tuna, meat. A water container and an army sleeping bag. Stacked boxes. He lifted them down. More tins. No stashed porn, no cameras, no ropes and chains. Why build a secret room and fill it with cans of Spam?

Maybe Smiley had held someone here. Or been held here himself? Doubtful, though. No signs of struggle, no blood. There were no power points, either. If Smiley's injuries were caused by something electrical, the killer, if there was one, would have needed a generator, or an extension lead. This space was tight, airless. Sweat trickling down Will's neck even now, and that was without any machinery or a burner or whatever in the name of home improvement had caused those burns on

Smiley's back. A dark laugh in the back of Will's throat.

Okay. He bent to his haunches. Nothing else to be done without calling in the SOCOs. He shuffled around; an about face from the wooden flap he'd come through. Opposite was another one, leading to the outside world, an unlocked padlock dangling. He pushed it open. got up and stared around him, gulping at welcome fresh air.

He walked up the track, the light low and hard on the gravel. Tyre-marks proved nothing, but they were there. A Transit, from the wheel-base width. Cigarette-stubs or food-wrappers would have been too much to hope for. No obvious signs of dragged heels or a scuffle either.

There was a low wall and a fence directly behind it. He sprang onto it and heaved over, buffeting into wilder grass, gnarled roots and stooping branches. There were twin orange lines long and rusting behind shrubs; a disused railway line, overgrown. But from here, a perfect view of Smiley's shed. Cigarette butts this time. Quite a few. He bagged a couple, for the brand more than anything, his thoughts going to the ongoing rape-murder case in Leicestershire where people were being screened for blood samples. A day might be coming, if one or two of the lecturers he'd seen at AMIP were right, when something as simple as saliva from a cigarette might even secure a conviction.

He went back to the car. The sky was a spreading ink-blot and he had another call to make.

Smoke was rising from behind the house. He got out of the car and stared at it a few seconds, then at the street with its neat leafed edges and fancy coving.

He opened the gate, something making him jog around to the back. It was a little bonfire at the end of the spacious lawn in a purpose-built brick barbeque space. But the flames were crackling yellow with blues and purples thrown in. He could see books, magazines and videos. God knew what else.

'Oh shit!' He glanced around; nothing to douse it. He grabbed a pair of burger-tongs, leant in, heat on his face, everything swimming. He closed them on a wad of smouldering magazines and pulled them out. He stamped on them and went back to it, shielding his eyes.

'Who the hell are...?' Evie Smiles was behind him, another box in her arms. Her hair was wild firelight, eyes sparkling and cheeks wine-flushed. Her dressing gown was open, nightie silky and clinging. She put the box down, covering herself.

He flashed his warrant card and gave her a glare. He walked past her, picking up the garden-hose and scanning the wall for an outside tap.

'Oh, for God's sake!' She shook her head. 'For god's sake! Here!' She took the end of the hose, threading it through the kitchen window. She disappeared inside and the hose begin to straighten. He walked it down to the barbecue and pointed at the base of the flames.

She didn't come out again for a few minutes and by that time it was a sodden clump. She'd put a jumper on. Her perfume was strong, almost overpowering the smoky dregs.

'They must've told you not to do this.' His tone was reasoned. 'The other officers today. To leave all his things alone.'

She snorted.

'You being widowed, it would take quite a bastard to actually follow through on obstruction charges.' He let that hang for an instant. 'But then you've met my DCI, haven't you?'

She did a quick double take at him. Then slumped a little. 'Okay. Okay. But you don't have to worry. There's nothing. Not a sodding thing. I've spent the whole of tonight going through it.'

Will gestured at the mess. 'So why this?'

She picked up a smouldering magazine, held it up. 'Because this! This! This is what he was into. Books, meetings, trips with other little saddos.' She held what was left of the cover out to him. From the browned edge of the top half, the shape of a rifle. She passed him one from the box, a guy in a bandana, face paint and camouflage jacket with what looked like a man-made spear, a huge bowie knife sharpening the point. *Real Survival.*

It explained the food-stockpiling. Smiley, not planning a kidnapping, after all, just prepared for all eventualities.

'Was he always into this stuff?'

She cleared her throat. 'Our honeymoon was a camping

holiday. Should've told me something.' She shook her head. 'Most people crap themselves at the thought of nuclear war or whatever. The end of civilisation. I swear, Peter couldn't wait! Everything revolved around his little game.'

'What game?'

She glanced at Will like she'd forgotten he was there, then at the smouldering clump in the barbeque. 'Survival. What else?'

He put the magazine back in the box. 'So why didn't you tell my DCI about this today?'

She shrugged, seemed to be thinking about it. 'Didn't see why anyone should know our business. But tonight, looking through this crap's brought it all back. It's pissed me off!'

Will let her have a few seconds. He thought about Smiley's thickened waist, flabby arms and jowly face. 'So, was he any good at it, his game?'

'Not the last few years. Sad really, someone can't admit they're over the hill.'

'These shared trips he went on. What about names –'

'I told you, there's nothing.' She swept a hand at the barbequed mess. 'And it's not like he introduced me to anyone. Same roof, separate lives, last ten years or more.'

He ran a hand over the stuff she hadn't burned. It was conceivable Smiley might have met someone dangerous. Some disappointed army-dreamer. Someone not just playing. The magazines might have personal ads worth checking.

She offered him wine, he settled for tea. He was looking at the framed photo on the mantel when she came back in. 'Your daughter?'

She nodded stiffly. 'Juliet.'

'Away at school, right? She been sent for –?'

'Your boss wanted to, I said no.' Some tension crackling under her voice. 'She'll be back at the weekend. No need for her to know about all this until then.'

He frowned. Stared at her a few seconds. 'How long she got to do at boarding sch–?'

'No. She's done. I'm pulling her out. She's my daughter and I want her with me, now she'll… now I've got nobody else.'

He nodded. Understandable sentiments. Probably even true. But not what she'd been about to say. He put the photo down, walked closer to take the tea mug from her. He waited until she'd passed it and said, 'So, did he hit her? Or was it more than that?'

Her eyes widened and her lips drew back. A sudden dog-bark echoed between houses and the wind swished the trees out there. Evie's breath hissed out to join it.

She could throw him out, of course.

For the first time she seemed unsteady. She put out a hand and he took it, sat her on the edge of the sofa. When the tears came, they were scudding, awful and soul-deep.

Not what he'd expected. Not sexual. Not even violent.

Evie had been ill. Hospitalised for two years with pleurisy. When she'd come home, Juliet was four years old and changed. Cruel.

'He turned everything into some challenge she had to complete. At first, I thought it was great, you know? Building her confidence. But if she didn't perform, he'd give her forfeits.'

'What kind of forfeits?'

'Standing for an hour with a book on her head. Shovelling in the coal shed. Standing in the cold in just her jammies.'

Will put down the tea, stared at the unlit fire.

Evie told him she'd been bedridden after the pleurisy. Depression, bad. Eventually, she'd snapped out of it. Given her husband an ultimatum. He'd have as little to do with his daughter as possible and keep his little bloody game and his family separate or kiss them goodbye.

She breathed deep, looked at Will. 'I know what you're thinking. Why didn't I just leave him, right?' She shrugged, then looked around her. 'Nice isn't it? Neighbourhood watch. Coffee-mornings.' She shook her head. 'Told myself I'd get out when the mortgage was paid, when Juliet grew up a bit more. But somehow, the years just get away from you, don't they?'

'No one's judging you, Evie.'

'Yeah, sure.' She tilted her wine glass, lips stretched taut to meet it. Then her eyes flashed at him. 'Looks like somebody judged Peter though, doesn't it? In the end.'

6

Samira wiped her forehead with the back of her hand and took a deep breath, regretting it instantly. One of them, either Vardy or Turner, had a BO problem.

The garage's small back room had a couple of screens hooked up to video. It was clammy, its air pent-up with nowhere to go. Vardy, the garage manager was probably mid-fifties, belly hanging over his belt like an old punchbag. His face was flushed at the exertion of loading and replacing cassettes for the last five minutes.

She coughed. 'So, are you saying the tapes for Saturday night have gone?'

'I don't get it. Really.' He looked up, but not at her. A *poor-me* roll of the eyes for Turner, Turner's shoulders answering in a motion of sympathy. Vardy grimaced. 'I always use the blue labelled ones, then red, then green. Tape over them when they're full. But it's only me who changes 'em. Typical it's the ones you're after. I'll try this lot again, maybe third time's a charm.' He started shovelling cassettes out of the box.

'Mr Vardy, they're not there,' she said.

Vardy stopped, blinked, again looked at Turner.

Classic, really. Vardy hadn't answered her directly in the ten minutes they'd been in here. No eye-contact. Not a race thing though; she had pretty good radar for that and Vardy's reactions were too bland for anything so passionate as hatred. No, it was simpler.

Vardy would defer to the other man in the room, even if Samira were Chief Constable.

She shook her head. 'Can you tell me about Tony Wilkinson.'

Vardy glanced again at Turner. 'Tony? Well, he's worked here a few months. First job after leaving school, he's twenty-two. He's alright. Bit absent-minded, but there you go.'

She leant forward, touched his arm. 'Isn't he a bit young for looking after a petrol-station on his own at night?'

Vardy paled a little. At last, he looked at her. Criticism then, was that what it took? 'It's not all night. Just until eleven.'

In other words, Vardy wouldn't shell out for a shared shift.

She gave him a long, hard look and then took in the surroundings; the moorland road winding upwards, the village of Shockley Beck to their left. The station was well-placed for catching trucks and vans cutting over the moors to and from Manchester, but otherwise isolated.

She looked at Turner's dampening tunic and the sweat dribbling down his meaty neck. Not Vardy with the BO problem then, for all his exertion. 'PC Turner, why don't you take Mr Vardy, see if you can find an address for Tony.'

Vardy shuffled out and she tried not to hold her breath as Turner passed. She said, 'I wouldn't mind another look at the range on the front camera. Which tapes –?'

'Box on the right,' Vardy mumbled.

She fanned the air, grabbed a tape, stuffed it in the player and pressed play. She squinted at the scene. The range wasn't brilliant, but as well as the garage forecourt, the distant moor was just about visible beyond the main road at the edge of Shockley beck. To the east, about a quarter of a mile away, was the coal-yard where Smiley had been found. So, if Smiley had wandered down from the moor, coverage from the night in question could have been useful. It was a good call then, from DI Ashcroft.

So where were the tapes from Saturday night?

She was half-watching the footage, ready to press stop, when someone, presumably Tony Wilkinson, drifted on camera, tugging some bin bags out back, a nightly ritual according to Vardy, who trained his staff to clean up before it turned dark. Then they would lock up, sit behind reinforced glass and deal with any late custom through the window. Wilkinson's head was down, eyes darkened pits, body moving slow and relaxed. Nothing unusual there. But there was something, wasn't there? Something Samira was seeing that she wasn't quite seeing.

She hit rewind and then paused.

The white sliver behind Wilkinson's ear had looked like a flaw in the tape, especially at full speed. But frozen on screen, it was plainly something three dimensional. A pencil? No. Too white. Too squat.

It took a few seconds, but then she breathed a quick laugh.

She stuck her head out and called for Vardy, half expecting him not to answer, the little woman out of sight, out of mind. But he bumbled over, managed to raise his eyebrows helpfully.

'Is this Wilkinson?'

He glanced at the screen. 'Aye, that's him. That tape's a few weeks ago though, not the one you —'

She walked past him, went to the boot of the car, grabbed two pairs of polythene gloves, and headed round the back towards the bins. Turner was watching and she rolled up a pair and threw them at him. 'Come on. Time for some police work.'

7

Sleep was as patchy as the threadbare quilt Will had tossed aside in favour of his coats. His hotel was nasty and draught-ridden with mustard décor and dark ceiling-stains that defied but demanded explanation. He'd woken, lain rigid, the dull throb in his head buzzing like a business of flies. A few bites of something on something like toast hadn't helped

He'd actually set off for the station half an hour ago. It was the strangest thing though… he could barely remember the drive down to the nick. And it had taken him twice as long as it should have.

Exhaustion? He took some Ibuprofen from the car and glugged a couple with some water from the tap in the gents, forced himself to take the stairs to the incident room.

Nine-thirty. He was late and expected an atmosphere thick as PC Turner's neck. But no. Instead, bustle, but a weird kind of bustle. Frenetic, wide eyed. The team were mostly here, along with some officers he didn't recognise. Price was twitching around a map spread over the table, a stubbed cigarette budding from his lip like a growth. Will glanced around for Samira but couldn't see her. Did they have her on something else or was she following up on the garage CCTV? Rugby boy wasn't here either, so maybe.

But something had happened, clearly. An arrest?

Price broke off from what he was saying to the officers, directing his sharp features at Will, with a quick wave of his thumb towards his office. 'Super's here. Wants to see you.'

Will nodded. What was this? About him dicking around in Liverpool?

Superintendent James Stratham's steely grey buzz-cut fizzed over the crisp black uniform. Probably early fifties, but it was hard to nail. Spry, expensively bought tan, lip curled as he glanced up at Will. 'Against my better judgement I sent you over here in the first place.'

Will focused on Stratham's polished epaulettes.

'Totally straight now, Ashcroft, do you want out?'

No answer for that one.

'No shame in it. Not after everything in London.' Stratham's eyes lost some of their hardness. 'Get behind a desk. Somewhere the most serious crime's tax fraud or kerb crawling. Somewhere quiet.'

Headingley? It rolled right to the tip of Will's tongue. The unofficial top retirement spot for northern police, also where Stratham lived. Will glanced at the window. 'This *is* somewhere quiet.'

'Not at the moment.' Stratham frowned. 'Seriously, Will.'

He'd known Stratham a few months; first name terms was undiscovered country. He gave a headshake as emphatic as he could make it. 'Doesn't appeal, sir.'

'No?' Stratham leant forward. 'Then get this team on side and stop playing lone wolf. I've spent a bloody hour smoothing the feathers of a pissed off DCI in Liverpool who failed to notice Peter Smiles' shed had a secret room. Well done for that, by the way. Sterling police work. Next time though, try going through proper channels instead of swanning in like Dirty bloody Harry –'

'They can have all the kudos. I just thought I'd take a look, as I was there.'

'Not the point.' He held his hand up. 'Look, I don't get you, Ashcroft, I really don't. I mean, you started out in this town as a PC, right? You know how things work up here. Far cry from AMIP but this lot get the job done too. In their own way.'

Will gave a slow nod.

'But they're tight up here. They keep it close. Outsiders don't last very long. I know you're used to more autonomy…'

Will was about to say that actually he'd always felt everyone had his back in London and he'd never really thought of himself as an outsider, but Stratham was rallying now. 'Somewhere like this, without backup, you'll wind up bleeding your life out in a bloody ditch.'

He had nothing to say to that either, though the thought had occurred to Will too.

Stratham leant back. Lecture intermission. He stood, walked to the window, clasped his hands behind him.

'I did pick up some interesting stuff on Peter Smiles in –'

'Bollocks to Peter Smiles.' A shake of the head. 'Simple misadventure. Merseyside can wrap it up.' Stratham's tanned neck was rigid as any procedure manual and Will's thought of protest died on his lips. Stratham turned his face. 'We've got a missing kid. It's a bit early to be sure but… looks like he was snatched from school yesterday. Some complications too. He's adopted. Pretty well-to-do family.' Stratham's mouth turned downwards at the edges. 'Oh, and he's black.'

Will's brow must have betrayed his thinking. 'What difference –'

'Every difference and you know it. You can multiply Press interest by ten, and if we seem like we're dragging our feet, or we fuck up, in any way…'

Both were unavoidable with this crew, but Will steadied his indignation.

'Price will fill you in. But it's right up your alley and I need you on it, immediately.'

Stratham had turned back to the window, as clear a dismissal as Will was going to get.

His hand jittered like a teenager's first dance as he left.

He sat in his car near the school, wondering if he was up to conducting the flood of nervous energy thrumming through Spinnerby nick.

Missing child cases cut through stations like shit through a sieve anyway. Junior officers would pray for the best, the more hard-nosed grafting to avoid the all too probable, paddling like hell for the vaguest island of hope. Only around 20% of missing children are not found alive; pretty promising. But of the 80% that are found, the vast majority are found within the first 48 hours. And Ryan Byford had already been missing for close to 20.

Noticeable how Ryan's being black had thrown it all into sharper relief. Some of the gallows humour had dried up, even the bigots floundering. Turner and Grundy were quieter than a couple of librarians, for instance. For now, anyway.

But all of this was academic. The question wasn't whether he could handle this case, but whether he should.

Because something was wrong with him and had been for weeks. Nightmares. His little blank-out this morning. Freezing up on the coal-stack the other day. Memories jemmying in... but not like memories... different. Like he was there, Docklands, three months ago.

Not just seeing it all. Reliving it.

On top of that, *he* was different. His personality had... well, changed. His attitude, resentful at having to prove himself to a bunch of old-school coppers. He could have played it differently at the briefing yesterday, making suggestions to Price on his own, later, instead of making him look a prize cock in front of his team. The same with the task force in Liverpool. It was like he'd lost a layer of social savvy. Like he wanted to be on the outside, looking in.

Something was happening to him. Something big. No point ignoring it and hoping it would go away. In fact, it would be criminal to do that.

He flexed his hand, resting his arm on the steering wheel. He should drive back to the nick, tell the Super he wasn't up to this. That would actually be the responsible thing to do. Give it to Price and this crew, or better still get someone drafted in from Leeds or Manchester to head it up. Only coincidence Will happened to be here anyway. Lying low. So much for that. He could go and get himself some counselling and then...

And then what?

He pulled a grim smile.

There was a phrase, and as soon as you heard or thought it about yourself you might as well apply for that job in security, or somewhere your greatest risk is a paper cut.

Burn-out.

Seniors would rant on about the support available but in the end it would come down to an overworked counsellor, a few weeks off and some sleeping pills. Then, the talk would start. *Thought he was up for a medal! For what? Shakin' like a shithouse rat?*

No. It wouldn't do.

But what if he messed up? Had one of his little... episodes... at a vital moment and some innocent paid the price? Like this missing kid, Ryan Byford.

He knuckled his eyes, then glanced up just as the red and white arrived, one of the Fiesta *jam-sandwiches*. Grundy got out and opened the back door. A delicate ankle flexed in an expensive shoe. Cathy Byford was late thirties, but Will only knew because he knew; she looked ten years younger. Slim, an exquisitely long alabaster neck, pillar to a short tousle of blonde hair. There was something elegant in her stance even thrown into the bottom half of a trouser-suit and a woolly beige jumper. It was almost as telling as the dark half-rings under un-made-up eyes; desolate. And as he closed his own car door, they turned and fastened on him.

He wasn't sure what he'd been expecting. *Posh hippies* had been Price's take on the Byfords. *Who else would adopt* a *half-caste kid?*

He gave her a nod, walked towards her.

Just for a second, her stare at him was everything he expected it to be. The look. The one he'd seen on every desperate parent he'd encountered, and there'd been quite a few. Her need for someone to say: 'I can help you,' so inscribed over her body that she staggered under its weight like a doe in moorland snow. But suddenly it slid off her, replaced by something more brittle.

He looked at Grundy. 'I'll take it from here, Sarge.'

There were no smartarse comments and no mumbles, Grundy on best behaviour. He sloped away.

'I'm DI Ashcroft. Sorry to bring you out here. Chances are I'll repeat things you've already been asked. I don't like relying on other people's notes, so apologies in advance.'

She shook her head, ruffling her hair with two fingers and thumb.

'Your husband's away on business?'

A glance at her watch. Armani. 'On his way back. From Bern. I couldn't get hold of him until late last night.' A tut, a slight shake of the head.

He narrowed his eyes. Jarring; the words and body language of someone who'd lost a kitten they weren't that fond of, not a son, even adopted. Just a hint of flirtatiousness in there too. Yet a moment ago, her entire body had been a cry for help. He cleared his throat. 'Other family? Anyone with any reason to take Ryan. Even if –'

'Nothing like that.'

'Okay. What about Ryan's birth parents?'

Another tousle of her hair. 'Killed eleven years ago. Accident, here in Yorkshire. He was orphaned.'

'Could any of their relatives have –'

'No. Not unless they came all the way from Malawi just to find him.'

Still something that would need checking on. But he nodded. 'Either of you married before?'

'Sean was. He's quite a bit older than me.' Her lips stayed parted. 'No previous kids, before you ask.'

'He and his ex on good terms?'

She gave a shrug that turned into a nod. Like she couldn't care less, but yes.

He asked questions as they walked, some he already knew the answers to; others she'd have already been asked. She answered automatically, the same bored monotone.

'Okay.' Will massaged his eyes. 'So, in these cases, nine times out of ten, the child comes home within 48 hours. Took off somewhere by himself, run away or –'

'No. No way. No arguments. Nothing like that. He wouldn't... just wouldn't run away...' She spread her fingers like a popped balloon.

'Okay. Close your eyes.'

'What?' She laughed, lashes beating.

'Close your eyes. Please. Think of yesterday.'

'Next you'll be swinging a pocket watch.' Will raised his eyebrows but she shook her head and closed her eyes. 'Okay. Eyes closed, officer.'

Flirting again. He felt like telling her it wasn't necessary. Even if, a few minutes ago, Will had considered handing this over, the sight of Grundy leading this woman from the car, desperate even if she didn't seem to want to admit it, had been enough. Decision made. Will would stay on this case until whatever end.

But her attitude was seriously starting to bug him. And he'd seen enough shock to know that wasn't it. A change of tack, maybe. 'You were a little late to pick Ryan up, right?'

Eyes flashing open, she let out a low howl. 'Yes. I was. Ten minutes. I've thought about nothing else all bloody night.' A glint of steel through candy floss. He liked it better. She shook her head. 'If I'd been on time –'

'So, why weren't you?'

Blinking. 'Just something at work. A mess up.' She shook her head, words tumbling. 'You think this is some pervert or…?'

At last, some normal reaction. 'Pointless speculating. We just don't know enough yet.' He looped the topic. 'That happen a lot, you arriving late?'

'Now and then.' She frowned. 'But Ryan's not stupid. He waits inside the main building. I made sure of that. Soon as we moved.' She gestured at the school. 'I mean, we used to live just up the road. Ryan's twelve. He'd walk home with friends all the time. Nothing ever happened. We moved further out, near Gallerton, more than a year ago. And now this –'

'Mrs Byford –'

'It's Cathy, for God's sake.'

'Cathy. Close your eyes.'

She blinked and then did as he'd asked, minus the flirtation this time.

'I want you to think about dropping Ryan off yesterday morning. Go over every minute of your drive here. Anything out of the ordinary. Anything he said or did. Anything you saw.'

A quick nod. Will went to the gates, looked over the school grounds, the portacabin classrooms, main building and extensions. He turned slowly, taking in the slope down into the valley, the moor above. Nothing striking. He turned back to Cathy.

Had to admit, he couldn't quite work her out. Flirtation out of desperation he could understand; probably not even aware she was doing it. And that helpless deer in the snow thing wasn't an act, exactly. But there was something else under the soft pelt.

As he watched, her eyes fluttered open.

'Anything?'

She shook her head, but something in her manner had

34

changed. She briefly touched Will's arm as if in thanks, but chaste, eyes a smoulder-free zone now.

'Drive from work to here, same time you would normally this afternoon. Drive from home to here at the same time tomorrow morning. That's if... if we're still looking by then.' Will winced, half expecting an outburst, but instead she was nodding. He continued. 'It might shake something loose.'

'I can do better than that, with Sean's help.'

He frowned, thinking of her comment about the swinging pocket watch. 'What does your husband do, anyway?'

'Thought you knew. He's a psychiatrist.'

Will gritted his teeth. Stratham and Price had given him chapter and verse on known sexual and racist offenders in the region, but that little nugget about Ryan's father, they'd never unearthed.

'He can bloody well hypnotise me.'

Will nodded and gave her a smile, because she needed it. But her husband's profession, he thought, was interesting for all kinds of other reasons too.

8

Samira had Turner park near the garages, not that it would make much difference. If they got back and his Fiesta was on bricks, Price would have *her* on traffic.

Haughton House was one of the high-rise blocks in the Craven Estate a few miles North of Spinnerby Bridge. A 'right shit-hole', was the consensus. Samira, who knew a little something about social history, might have called it a misguided experiment in modernism held together with plasterboard, spit and best intentions. Then again, maybe 'right shit-hole' was more accurate.

'Hey, you heard?' Turner was gum-chewing loudly. 'The other night. Paki shopkeeper, North end, not far from here. Some lads scared the piss out of him. Baseball bats, masks, the works.'

She thought about challenging the constable's nomenclature, settled for a sigh instead. 'Lovely. Robbed?'

'Nah. Just a right good kicking.' Turner smiled. 'Hey, they'll have you involved won't they? Get you liaising with the Paki community. Keep things calm.'

She'd been about to open the door but sat back in her seat. 'Why would they want me involved? I'm not Pakistani.'

He shrugged, mumbling something.

'Sorry?'

He grimaced. 'I said - you're black though, aren't you?'

She stared at her reflection as if to check.

Technically, she thought about saying, I'm mixed-race. Dad's Irish, Mum half Indian, half Jamaican. So, what does that make me? She looked at her new partner, reached for the door handle. 'Come on.'

Turner's large frame unpeeled itself from the Fiesta, his dull gaze on the tower block beyond the carpark. Sad thing was, he was probably right about her being reassigned. Building bridges in the community was common practice after Toxteth and Brixton riots last year. Of course, Samira had no more affinity with the Asian community than her Caucasian colleagues, but Price and maybe even Statham wouldn't grasp that. In truth, even if the crime had been committed in an Afro community, the assumption she would have some sort of natural kinship would have been just as ridiculous. Would a white copper have a special empathy with a victim just because they were white?

She looked at the graffiti-scrawled doors, a hundred gleaming windows above them. Turner's uniform was a target. Her own round shoes, slacks and officey blouse under navy jacket weren't much better, really. Curtains were twitching already.

'How we gonna do this then?' Turner asked.

Should they thumb all the intercom buttons in the hope someone would buzz them in? She was ready to suggest it when a young woman trundled her pram out. Samira grabbed the door, held it for her. They stepped inside.

Two girls, maybe six or seven were playing in the hallway, near the lifts. One was in denim dungarees, another in a *Garfield* T-shirt. They stopped and looked up.

'Hello, there.' Samira glanced over their heads at almost unreadable flat numbers on a brown plaque, grime-covered arrows giving a choice of stairs or a urine-smelling lift. She frowned and did a quick bit of mental arithmetic, considering the flat number they were after and the number of flats per floor.

Suddenly, the taller of the girls ran to Turner and embraced his knees. The other one shuffled through the double doors.

There was a squeal above Turner's waist. 'What do ya want, mister? What do ya want, uh?'

Turner looked at Samira helplessly as the little girl squeezed his big thighs. Samira enjoyed it a few more seconds. 'How come you're not at school then, eh?'

A dull hollow tapping began in the heating shaft above their heads. Repeated, it swelled to an echoing clang. Clever! Every tenant likely had their grilles removed and ready to bang against the shaft at the first sign of *Babylon*, maybe any outsider.

Samira ran for the back doors, craning her neck to see the lower floor verandas. Sure enough, two figures dangling from the third, their legs stretching for the second-floor balcony. They found their footing, turned to face outwards. They took a jump of about twelve feet and she heard a sharp, surprised 'Ahhh!' The other one was into a roll, coming up on his knee.

Both turned, flicked some Vs at her before heading up the slope, the limping one dragging behind and shouting 'COCONUT!' before the oinking and monkey noises started from above her head.

Something made her jerk back just as a long slosh of murky amber liquid spattered down. She glanced again at the two figures heading into the surrounding estate. No. Neither looked like Tony Wilkinson. Anyway, if her maths was accurate and he'd decided to jump, he'd have more than a twisted ankle.

Turner had one hand on his truncheon, the other on his walkie-talkie and a *love me, I'm clueless* face. Both girls were playing with their dolls as if nothing had happened. The block was quiet. How many toilets were being flushed right now? She moved to the stairs, 'Why don't you take the lift? Then we've covered both –'

'Out of order.'

'Course it is.' She pushed the stairs door open.

Breathing was hard by the seventh floor but she felt pride in hers being less ragged than Turner's. So much for all that rugby. The climb hadn't done much for his BO either.

Wilkinson's door. She stopped Turner from knocking and knocked herself. She gave it ten seconds before trying again. She dropped to her haunches and cautiously opened the letter box. A single pervading aroma, hardly surprising. 'Tony, it's the police. I know why you took the security videos.' She gave it a few seconds. 'I'm on my own.' She glanced up at Turner, shaking her head and putting a finger to her mouth. 'If you let me in, we can talk about it, just you and me. But if you make me come back here, it'll be different.' Something. The sound of a breath? She stared at the letterbox. 'We'll drag you in. Withholding evidence pertinent to a possible murder enquiry.' Another few seconds. 'And Tony, it's true what they say about Armley, by the way. You'll be shower bait.'

There was movement and the flush of a toilet, then something like a low groan and the rustling of clothes. She stood. Turner was shaking his head. She pointed at the corridor, gave him a nice Cheshire cat grin and mouthed 'Piss off!'

His jaw dropped. But he shuffled around the corner just as the latches slid back. The curtain behind the door moved and it opened.

'How long you been getting stoned at work?'

They were still in his hallway. Wilkinson's bottom lip hung. 'I never –'

'Don't bother, Tony.' Samira shook her head. 'Found some roach ends in the bin bag from the other night. Your shift. Lucky your boss wouldn't know one from a rolled-up bus ticket.'

Slow blinks and a shake of the head. 'Yeah but three or four of us work shifts there. Anyone could be smoking up.'

She let out a breath. 'I looked at a recording from a different night, just to see if the moorland road is within range. It is. But, know what else I saw? You wandering across the screen, a joint stuck behind your ear.'

The lip retracted itself. Tony looked at the floor between his feet. 'You haven't told him? My boss?'

She said nothing, ushering Tony into the murky innards of the flat, scanning around her as she went. There was that resin-sweet dope scent again but nothing evident. 'Sit down there.' She pulled an armchair close to the settee. 'I'm really hoping you didn't throw the tapes out the window before you flushed your stash just now.'

Tony's black-centred orbs widened. He dropped his gaze, shoulders slumping. 'Been trying to jack it in. The ganja. I mean, I know I'm lucky to have a job.' He raised his head. '*You* must know how hard it is, right?'

She blinked. 'What?'

His hands were up, his eyes anywhere but on her skin. 'No, I just mean... well, you're cool, right? You must've hung out. I mean –'

'Tony, probably best you shut up now.' She took a breath, glanced around the flat. The trappings. Loose rolling papers here and there, paisley throw over a box probably with a bong inside, battered tobacco box where a little cannabis baggie would have been until a few minutes ago. Che Guevara on one wall, Pink Floyd on the other. The thing was, Tony wasn't that far wrong. Samira had kept herself mostly clean, but she'd partied just a little too. Teenage rebellion. Then there was her brother Darren.

She hardened her eyes. 'The tapes?'

He pointed at the TV cabinet. 'There. Next to *Back to the Future.*'

'Okay. One from the forecourt and one from inside, right? Let's have the forecourt first. Then you can go make me a coffee, white, no sugar. And Tony...'

His eyes widened again.

'Don't gob in it.'

He shrugged. 'I wouldn't. Even if you weren't threatening to arrest me.' He walked to the cabinet and inserted the tape. 'It's... on the right bit. Just play.'

She glanced around again, thinking of her brother, last she'd heard, getting fairly cosy with some scumbags from Salford, ironically a couple of white boys she was pretty sure got off on having him as their black mate. Not dealing, as far as she knew. But stoners, weekenders, working to finance habits they didn't even realise were habits.

Idiot. After landing that job as a legal clerk too.

In Dad's eyes, he could do no wrong. Mum knew better but just went along. It pissed Samira off no end. Darren the enterprising one who always wound up on his feet, Samira... great results at school, a first from Leeds in History, yet somehow the disappointment. Dad hadn't spoken to her for almost six months when she'd joined up.

Not that surprising really. The hassle he'd had over the years for marrying a Jamaican woman. Then again, him being an Irishman living in England, one who liked getting drunk and spouting about the Guildford Four and the Maguire Seven might have played into it. Yeah, Dad had no love for the constabulary. Understatement.

They'll call you a bloody coconut, he'd said.

Black on the outside, white on the inside.

She snarled her thoughts away, settled back with the remote as Tony clunked around in the kitchen. Her thumb idled over 'play' but she pursed her lips and pressed rewind. His instructions had seemed a little forced. Sure enough, there was the tail-end of some TV programme about microchips. Didn't quite seem Tony's line. He came in, balancing a tray.

'No biscuits?'

'I could get –'

'Why did you tape over the start of this, Tony?'

The widened eyes again. 'Ahh… err… I just –'

'Truth.'

'Okay, okay. At first, I was gonna tape over all of it. But then I thought it might not be a good idea. Look, I'd decided to give it to you lot, honest! I was just trying to figure a way of it being found at work. Misfiled or something.'

Samira narrowed her eyes. 'So, the bit you taped over wasn't important? You having a little toke, maybe?'

A pained look, cheeks sallow.

'Sit down.' She hit play.

It was black and white and the swishing heather on the distant moor was muted to a darker grey than the grass and scrub. It was raining, but not so heavily as to obscure everything.

'There's a couple minutes of nothing. You could fast-forward –'

'You like your movies, don't you?' She waved a hand at his video collection. 'Me too. Let's let the tension build.'

The monochrome scene was static apart from the wind and rain. When movement came it was a flicker at first, amongst the distant long grass; a figure, moving fast with a ragged run that broke down as it reached the road. Now it was heading straight for camera, she could make out the features; the spare look about the face, the teacher's clothes put under strain.

Peter Smiles stood, hands on thighs, panting, then passed to the front of the garage's shop and pulled the door open, staggering in and out of the camera's range.

9

Torchlight frightened memories into shadow. The oak beam, the epic fireplace and chairs under dusty sheets were less substantial than the versions in his head, so that for a second, Will wondered if he was in the right house. The stone floor was bare. The two-year-old sack of plaster in the corner was still ready for the skim he'd never quite got around to. Because this would never be his place, whatever the deeds said, always Dad's.

A few hours to set up in his old room; the master bedroom a boundary he wasn't ready to cross. He cleaned the floors, aired out the matrass a little. He sat on the floor by the space heater and opened a beer.

Today had been a bastard. After Cathy Byford, he'd spoken to the school; the head, Ryan's form tutor and classmates. The kids had been reticent and the WPC he'd been assigned, Clarke, hadn't been much help. He'd felt the lack of Samira Byrne. The one officer he thought he might be able to work with, hijacked.

Some locals with previous convictions for flashing, indecent assault as well as a few race extremists were being brought in. Will dipped into questioning to make sure Grundy and the others weren't getting silly. Coercion was too easily sanctioned with sex offenders.

He'd waded through a barrage of red tape to trace Ryan's natural parents' family, as far as he could. No one living in or currently visiting the UK so the idea someone might have travelled from Malawi to snatch him was less and less likely.

He'd gone back to the incident room, its attentions now securely transferred from Peter Smiles to Ryan Byford. There was a small package on his desk, Marked *from DC Byrne*. He thumbnailed it open and removed a single note of A4 wrapped around two VHS tapes.

DI Ashcroft,
I've been put on a different case. Mr Shafiq Ramir, shopkeeper, currently in hospital after being terrorised. I'm flattered by the unswerving faith of my superiors in my ability

to foster community empathy in PC Turner, my partner.

Sorry to say I won't have the pleasure of your company, sir.

I know the Peter Smiles case is being dismantled. Just thought you might want a look at the tapes enclosed from the petrol station, before passing on to Merseyside, obviously.

Best of luck finding Ryan Byford, boss. For what it's worth, I'm really glad you're on it.

Will destroyed the note. It was great that she trusted him after a single conversation, and she was right to, but he'd learned long ago that irony, however well-meant, didn't go down at all well in CID circles. Things written in jest had a way of being found and used against people. It said something about Samira though; she took risks. She'd have to watch herself with this lot.

He took the tapes down to one of the interview rooms and watched them.

Now, Will was thumbing through the box of survivalist stuff rescued from Evie Smiles' bonfire. Distraction? Maybe. But he'd known from the moment Stratham dismissed the death as misadventure that he wasn't just going to leave it alone. Everything about Smiles was wrong.

By ten-thirty though, he was pretty sure he knew all any human being could usefully know about non-perishables, bow-hunting and essential knots. He rubbed his eyes and switched off the camping lamp. The *Survivalist Special* cassette and the two *Bushcraft Survival* videos could wait.

There was still nothing connecting Smiley with Crag Valley. Why had a middle-aged woodwork teacher from Liverpool wound up on a coal-stack in West Yorkshire?

It didn't matter for now. Ryan Byford was in far more need of his attention. There was just one thing he had to do before he could sleep.

He made a face at the space heater and rustled out of the sleeping bag. He walked through the hallway, loitered at the door to the master bedroom, as if there was a museum-exhibit rope barring his way. He grinned down at his bare feet and pushed it open. The old double divan with the mahogany

43

wardrobe behind it. He padded over and turned the little brass key. An obliging creak. The smell of wood, mothballs, old cloth. Two shirts and a baggy jumper. He pushed them aside.

It hung right at the back, its shoulders narrower than he remembered, the high collar less imposing. The pockets were baggier than on the tunic he'd worn himself several years ago and the 1960s weave was less tight. The constable's number glinted from the shoulder as he pulled the rough material towards his face and sank his nose into it. Dank from so many years unwashed, but beneath the musk, there was something, wasn't there? He closed his eyes.

Tobacco, sweet and deep in the weave. A thousand times Will fetching the old tin and rolling papers with a mug of tea, then Dad's triphammer fingers filling and rolling with unlikely skill. Feet up at last, potatoes steaming. Something medicinal; rubbing ointment, back and shoulder pains that were maybe the beginnings of worse to come.

His own voice, loud in here, Dad's words. 'There's life after a life in blue.'

Well, there had been, for a time. It was as if the cancer had negotiated after taking Mum, just enough time to raise Will before it doubled back for Dad.

Gooseflesh spread along his arms and he pulled his head back. Rain was just starting, a spray on the window.

He headed back to his room, dousing the heater, settling into the sleeping bag.

The heather, blue in the moonlight, was rippling down from the nearby moor and breaking around him like a wave. He was shaking, combat jacket fastened over suede making no difference, because it wasn't the cold making him shake, or his jeans damp at the bottom and slapping against his ankles, grass wet under his trainers.

He rubbed his eyes. Ten minutes ago, he'd been asleep. He'd thrashed awake but whatever danger he'd dreamt… hadn't stopped.

Still there, now.

No sound but the wind and the steady roar of the water

winding down to Shockley Beck. His arms were rigid, legs too, like every muscle was tensing, fight or flight. But there was nothing to fight, nothing to run from! He pressed his hand to his heart. Thumping fast.

He reached the wall, hunkered, peering over. Moors grey and dim, the serrated teeth of the dry-stone wall that skirted downwards. The strangest feeling of being watched, of some impending threat. A sudden crushing certainty that he shouldn't be seen. Every nerve in his body rang with it. Danger. Danger. Danger! But from where?

He crawled, the wall for cover, elbowing rough grass. Jeans drenched, long blades swiping at his face. He slowed, the wall curving away now. No choice; he'd have to stand.

A half run, stumbling down over divots and long grass clumps, out of control for the last ten yards until he spilled onto the winding black river of tarmac. He stood, panting, hands on his thighs, almost laughing in the darkness of the moorland road. What was he doing? What the hell was he up to, really?

The sense of danger, still here.

He started at a run, wind lapping around him, fine rain at his face. This was crazy. There was nothing here. Nothing but the night. But even that felt heavy, hanging over him, bolting him to the asphalt, his feet slow like magnets. He passed the corner, the white and orange lights of the petrol station a few hundred yards below him and he thought suddenly of the VHS tape from Samira. He stopped, panting, looked back up to his left at where Smiley had crossed the field onto the road, stumbling, hunted and panicked. Not so different to Will right now.

Chest heaving, muscles knotted, rain pummelling his forehead. Hydraulics and wet tyres swished upwards from the garage and he turned to watch a truck pulling out and heading up towards him. Every instinct was telling him to hide, to duck down in the ditch until the truck had passed. But why? He shook his head, rooting himself to the spot. It picked up speed, the driver's head barely flicking towards him over the spray of the tyres, Will nothing but a minor distraction in a long-distance vigil; a cut over the tops to the Motorway slip-road. No threat. No danger at all. Why had he thought it was?

Just… the environment, the world around him, seemed wrong. Everything stark, jagged, pitched against him. The way the light from the petrol station glistened on the wet road, the way the grass swayed, the baleful swell of the skies. It sickened him. He tried to remember his dream, but it slid away like… like water, actually. He shivered, wiping rain from his face, pushing his sodden hair back out of his eyes. Somehow… the water had started him off. The sound of it, pattering rain as he'd slept, the scent of it in the air, cloying at him.

Just like the pool, of course. That rusted hole on the London docklands where he'd found the boy. The last place on earth he wanted to think of… but somehow the only place he couldn't really forget.

His hand was doing its thing now. He raised it up; a shaking salute to the steady drizzle. The sense of danger was gone, though. He'd traded one for the other.

Body shaking, he walked off the road, leant over and lost the contents of his stomach on the coarse grass. Sweat joined the rain on his forehead and his hand twitched away of its own accord. He blinked. Took some breaths.

He walked, deliberate and slow; down past the garage. He was on the verge of turning into the forecourt when he stopped, glancing down the hill. On the corner, just before the village houses of Shockley Beck looking from here like adornments on a broken cake, the phone booth stood at the end of the low wall.

He thought of the black and white footage of Smiley in the garage. Mouthing something, presumably asking for change. Threatening to jump over the counter had been enough to scare the attendant, Smiley scrambling around for tossed coins like a street-beggar.

Will walked down to the phone booth, pace quicker now, more his normal gait though his limbs were stiff, every muscle aching. He pulled the door and stepped in. Rain-diluted urine. His shoes slid on something. Scattered coins. Smiley's? Leftover coppers, dropped in haste to make a call? Maybe. Or they could be anyone's.

He stared around him, rifled the phone book.

Who had Smiley called?

It wouldn't take long to find out, of course. After the telecommunications act of '84 regarding malicious communications, Spinnerby's force intelligence officer could get a list of numbers called from here in a couple of hours. Okay, it wasn't related to the Byford case, but… but his instinct was telling him it was important.

He thought of the pale face on the video, the stretched features, the stagger of the body pushed beyond its limits. For the few seconds they'd been visible on-camera, the eyes had been desperate.

Was this where Peter Smiles had realised he was going to die? Or had he already known?

10

The 48-hour window was closing, without even a sliver of promise.

Will was in the incident room by 6.30, on statements and interview notes from yesterday. He had to wait for something like a reasonable hour to call on the Byfords, though it was doubtful they'd be getting much sleep. Around 8.30 he took the Gallerton turn off. The long steep moor road was tree-straddled, the Byfords' cottage just visible half a mile up the rise. Above it, the craggy edge of hillside and the unfinished tower presiding over the valley like a big broken bird. Gallerton Folly.

A flash of his dad and him; a trip out, when he'd been about twelve. There was a small network of caves under the crag, sealed off now after a landslip. Back then, it had been popular. Will had loved it. Wobbling around in a torch-helmet too big. First time he'd ever done anything like that. It was one of the few times he remembered Dad happy too, after Mum and the cancer.

Sometimes he thought he could demarcate his whole life that way. Before Cancer, After Cancer. Before, golden, even though he knew his memories were probably half-fantasy; he'd been eight when she'd died. After, everything… fine. Just somehow drained of all colour.

He pulled up near the cottage and did his best to put his memories away.

Cathy Byford opened up. There was a spasm of hope in her questing eyes, but no sign of that flirtatious intensity he'd seen in her at the school. 'Nothing yet,' he said quickly, one hand up. He watched her crumple and studied her. No redness or puffiness around the cheeks. It would be better if she just cried. Time enough though. Unless they got lucky.

'We were just trying to eat. Would you… like coffee?'

Will shook his head and followed her through.

Byford was tall, loosely put together, a fair paunch around his middle, but piercing eyes made him look a little less than his fifty-five years. He had a brittle frown that needed to be taken seriously.

He'd got back from his business trip last night about Ten. which had given Will far from his first twitch of unease. Will had never had any children, but he was sure, flight delays notwithstanding, an abducted son, adopted or otherwise, would have him move a few mountains, or at least charter a plane to fly over them.

'Inspector.' They shook hands. 'I've been putting that list together.'

Will had left instructions with Cathy yesterday to pass to her husband.

'I've covered most of my private practice, but I'm afraid my time at the hospital and everything else is too far back. So many patients. Isolating those with a history of abuse or racial hatred... needle in a haystack. You'll have to check with NHS records.' Byford made to stand, presumably for the list, but Will's hands were up.

'It'll wait.'

'Will it?'

'A few minutes, yes. While we talk. I also want to have a look at your son's room, if I may.'

Byford nodded, waved Will towards the chair opposite.

Cathy was wiping absently at washing up splatters on her blouse. She came over to a third chair, then stood bolt-still, looking at the chintzy upholstery desperately.

Byford's forehead crinkled above the strong lenses of his glasses. 'What are you...?'

Will got up from his chair and pulled another stool over. 'I'm sorry. Sit here, please.'

Byford's jaw still hung, so Will decided to help a little, his tone gentle as he could make it and focused on Cathy. 'That must be where Ryan always sits. Completely natural. Things like that catch you by surprise.'

She avoided the chair like it was plague-ridden and sat instead where Will had been.

'Cathy.' Byford was shaking his head and Will couldn't work out if it was *let's not do this in front of the policeman, dear* or disgust that something so mundane as a chair had set her off. 'It's alright,' Byford said.

'What's alright? What is?' Her hand came away from her husband's and both of hers were over her face. Then she stood, looked at them both and moved out of the kitchen. Still no tears, Will noticed.

A strained smile from Byford. 'Suppose I could've handled that better.' Then he shook his head, the defensive veil dropping again.

Will gave it a moment. 'Tell me about Ryan.'

A breath, deep, 'He's a perfectly normal twelve-year-old boy.'

'What's he into?'

'What? Oh, I don't know. Star Wars. Collects figures, comics and so on.'

'You don't approve?'

'Harmless fantasy I suppose. Certainly better than last year's obsession. Army this, army that.'

Will tilted his head. 'Better, why?'

'Well, I don't imagine Star Wars will get him killed...' He winced, clearly realizing what he was saying. 'I just meant... he wouldn't end up with a bayonet in his guts on some island in the North Atlantic.'

Will chewed on that a few seconds. 'There are twenty-eight kids in his class. Twenty-six of them are white.'

'No problems with that.'

'None at all?' Will made a face. 'It might not be overt bullying. You know what kids are –'

'Yes, I do.' Byford's smile was probably the kind he used with clients. 'Generally, kids are far more accepting than we credit them for.'

'Some are.' Will nodded. His interview today with Ryan's classmates hadn't thrown up any obvious bigots, but none of them had been able to say what Ryan was into; sport, movies, pop stars, whatever. The boy the teachers had put forward as Ryan's closest friend hadn't offered much more. 'I get the impression Ryan's quite withdrawn.'

'He's independent. Does his own thing. Anything wrong with that?'

Will let out a breath. 'We asked your wife this of course but, what about drugs?'

'No.'

'Sure? Wouldn't be the first twelve-year-old to try some weed.'

A firm shake of the head.

'Booze? Cigarettes?'

A laugh. 'No way. He had a sip of beer at Christmas a few years ago and nearly vomited.'

A few years can make all the difference, Will almost said. 'Okay. What about girls? Any particular interest there yet?'

Byford shrugged. 'I don't think he's sure what girls are about yet, Inspector.'

'Me neither.' Will said. 'Doesn't mean I'm not interested.'

'Well, no crushes yet that I know of. Girls or boys before you ask.'

'Teachers?'

The strong lenses glinted at Will. 'Not that I'm aware of. You could ask Cathy as –'

'I already have. I just wondered if you'd seen any signs of anything. From a professional point of view.'

'What you mean abuse?' He blinked. 'No. Definitely not.'

'The photo your wife's given us. She says his hair's cut shorter since then. But on the snap Ryan looks a little bookish.'

'Bookish.' Byford gave a sad smile. 'Is that a euphemism?'

'Actually no.' Will frowned. 'I was bookish. And bullied, at one point.'

Byford glanced at Will's longish hair, Will suddenly aware of his own wiry build against suede jacket and baggyish suit trousers. 'You must fit in really well with your department here,' Byford said with sarcasm that so captured what Will had been feeling since coming back to the North he laughed, almost warming to the man for a moment.

Byford studied the chintzy chair that had caused his wife's meltdown. 'No. Like I said, no bullying. And I think I'd know.'

'Anything else unusual? Falling out with classmates?'

A shake of the head. Byford stared at the chair again, and Will had to admit he was starting to recycle questions.

He cleared his throat. 'I saw a statistic the other day, said

51

almost ninety-three percent of adults have absolutely no idea what's really happening in interactions between children. What we see on the surface bears no relation to what's going on underneath.'

Byford's eyebrows rose again. 'Then there's the one that says ninety-nine percent of statistics are made up.'

They looked at each other for a few more seconds before Will glanced at the doorway. 'I wouldn't mind a look at your son's room, now.'

Cathy intercepted at the bottom of the stairs with a quick press of Will's arm. Her eyes were dancing again, flicking away but not as far as Byford as she spoke. 'I'll take you up.' There was no reference to earlier. More than that, no recognition of it in her movement, her body language. She was smoking, cigarette held high between delicate fingers, head to one side, basking in the blueish haze like some 1950s diva. She turned and slinked up the stairs.

'Well, if you're sure…' Byford lingered at the bottom.

Will followed her, eyes fixing on tasteful prints and mahogany bannisters.

Ryan's room. Blue walls, a single Star Wars poster and a large collection of figures and spaceships on a long table. Neatly posed, almost regimental, jarring with the rest of the room, with clothes hanging off chairs and a few books and magazines scattered. 'Do you tidy up for him?'

'Usually.' She waved vaguely at a strewn t-shirt. 'Your officers told me to leave everything as it was.'

He nodded, wandering over to the Star Wars table. Her change of attitude had him rattled and he was trying like hell to focus. 'How long's he been collecting this stuff?'

'Oh, years.' A wistful smile. 'Though, he put it all away last year. Boxed up in the attic. Said it was too young for him. More interested in soldiers and army.' The smile again, wrong somehow. Like her boy was away at summer camp. 'A few months and then he lost interest in that, got all this out again. But boys go through phases like that, according to Sean.'

He reached for one of the Star Wars figures, thumbing the dust off it, lifting it to check underneath. A visible patch where dust hadn't collected. The same with everything on the table.

'He doesn't like me... cleaning around his collection.' Cathy pursed her lips around her cigarette.

Will nodded. It wasn't cleanliness or lack of it he was interested in. Why get out a bunch of toys from storage and set them up neatly but never play with them, never even pick them up, by the look of it? Could it be a need to convince that this harmless celluloid fantasy was the only thing Ryan was obsessed with?

Because there was something Sean Byford hadn't mentioned downstairs. He was a card-carrying pacifist. Will had done his research. Could his only child's army interest be something the liberal but not so mild-mannered psychiatrist wouldn't tolerate?

'What exactly happened last year, when he decided he was more interested in soldiers than space heroes?'

She blinked. 'Oh, I dunno. You know kids. Sean says –'

He stepped closer, quietened his voice a few notches. 'But what do *you* say, Cathy?'

Her eyes darted around her. Was Byford listening? This was a well-made cottage with good walls, but Will supposed it was possible. It was more telling though that she thought he might be. But it was all too easy now to paint Byford as some small-time tyrant, even after Cathy had cuckolded him at the bottom of the stairs. Will moved closer again, within touching distance, but simply looked at her, face blank.

The Diva act seemed to spend itself along with the last of her cigarette smoke. Her eyes clouded with distant pain again, as if reality had just walked into the room and sat in the corner. 'There was a new boy, last year.' She sniffed, 'From a problem family. I think that's where the army thing started, to be honest. Ryan trying to impress his new friend. Anyway that boy's gone now. Didn't stay at the school long.'

'What was his name?'

'Can't remember. Brandon... someone or other.'

'Did Sean get involved? Talk to the head?'

She gave that *startled doe* look again. 'I think he might've said he would've liked to. But... I mean, it's not like you can get someone removed from a school just for being a bad influence on your son, is it?'

No, Will thought. Not unless you happen to be Chairman of School Governors.

Which Byford was.

11

There was a clamour of laughs and whoops from the supermarket canteen.

'Our frozen-food man's leaving do.' Halford's moustache twitched. 'Promotion. Going to the Salford branch.'

Samira followed the small-framed deputy manager down the corridor, the dull thud of Turner's Doc Martens keeping time behind her and then buried under bass and synth from the doorway at the end. The stage was strobe-lit. There were two figures, one dull in his blue *Presto's* outfit, standing, another kneeling and rocking back and forth in front of him. It took Samira a second to figure she was seeing a police uniform; black skirt stretched taut as it would likely go on a woman bent on fleshy knees, her head bobbing to the rhythm of Frankie's *Relax* rattling through speakers clearly better equipped for staff announcements.

The woman took her over-glossed mouth from the truncheon pressed to the handcuffed frozen-food man's crotch and tossed a wink at Samira and Turner in turn.

Halford looked at the kissagram girl, but pitching his voice for those near the front, said, 'Careful, luv. These two are the real thing!'

Her bottom-lit face was cherubic, its eyes flashing all the way to Turner's toes and back, and then flicking over Samira. 'I bet they are, luv!' She offered the truncheon's spittle-covered end to Samira. 'Wanna take over? This lot wouldn't mind a bit of ebony.'

Turner's laughter was pitched for everyone but himself, most of the room joining in.

Samira let out a pained smile and opened the door at the back of the canteen, hoping like hell it wasn't the broom cupboard or something. She held it open for Halford and Turner. Both had slowed, clearly happy to stay out here and watch the entertainment, but Halford's smile froze at Samira's intense look and he trotted to the door. Turner followed with a sigh. Behind them, the frozen-food man's face was disappearing into the strippagram's mountainous veined bosom.

'The show goes on.' Samira said quietly.

Halford shrugged as he walked. 'Here we are.'

The second room was smaller, a few people scattered; hardcore *Sun* readers finishing lunchbreaks and threads of blue smoke accumulating around a single gasping ceiling fan like desperate migrants. Samira could see Denise Owens from here, her hair bleached and straw-like over a face just this side of orange. Denise's eyes were fierce slits. She stared over the top of her paper at Samira's trouser suit and skin with disdain bordering on relish and looked at Turner. 'Hope you're in charge, luv, cos I'm not talking to her.'

The Owens family had a bit of a rep in the valley. Full-on, swastika-wearing nut-jobs, was another way of putting it. Two boys, one under 18, one 20, the elder with enough form to sink a North-Sea Ferry, which had brought Samira here. A work-visit rather than home might have rattled their mother, Samira had figured. Anyway, Denise's part of the Craven estate was about as discrete as full-blown syphilis. But Denise's scowl right now was loaded with pride, for the room, for her boss Halford. She'd wear a visit from *Babylon* as a badge of honour. And a 'coconut' copper, one she'd refused to speak to, a bonus. Samira had been planning on taking Denise to a private room, opened her mouth to request it now... but something told her to let this play out.

As she watched, Turner grinned and Denise returned it. Redneck solidarity or more? Samira shook her head, real anger stoking itself. Her superiors were just as prejudiced, in their own way, as this woman in front of her; putting her on this case based on some misguided PR agenda when Ryan Byford was out there somewhere, in God knows what pain or distress. And it was nothing to do with his being black. Samira could help, if they'd let her. She knew it the way she'd known how to nail those dealers in Manchester. In the way she knew right now her career was hanging on the edge of the toilet.

She knew it, because she was a good copper. So, if they wouldn't give her a chance to prove it, she'd just have to work harder.

She looked at Turner. 'Leave us.'

'Again? You're kiddin'…?' The smile died in his eyes. He preened a little. 'Fine. I'll go watch the rest of the show then.'

She moved her chair close, much closer than necessary. Layers of make-up were flaky in Denise's crevasses, like a talentless painter had spent two minutes smearing an overstretched canvas and then given up.

Samira spoke quietly, almost intimately. 'A few days ago, four males in masks terrorised and beat a shopkeeper from the north end. He's in intensive care.'

Denise was fixed on her *News of the World*.

'I know,' Samira smiled. 'You don't have to talk to me if you don't want.' She leant back, cricking her neck. 'I hear Lee's doing well with his A Levels.'

A few seconds, then the paper rustled and dropped. 'You're a bloody amateur, luv! Think you can mention my boy and I'll just roll over?'

Samira just smiled, letting *Duran Duran*, or a cheap cover version more likely, buzz over the ruffling newspaper sounds for a few seconds, before Denise raised the paper, then dropped it again suddenly.

'He was with me Saturday night. Both my lads were.'

'Really? That's helpful.' She took out her pen and notebook. 'Thing is, I never mentioned it was Saturday, did I?'

A tight grimace, eyes darting. Then a grin. 'That proves nowt. It was in the paper.'

Samira nodded. But something under Denise's overwrought face-paint was flickering, she thought. Whatever her politics and her hard-bitch act, Denise was a mother.

'We have a description that matches Lee –'

'Bollocks!' A hardening of the jawline again.

Samira couldn't help a smile. Their one witness was a pensioner, Bridie Watkins, who'd risked the estate with dusk falling to get herself some cigarettes and a pint of milk. She'd seen them leaving, got a fairly good look at one of them, mask off. Her description could have been of Lee Owen, then again, just as easily some other pale 15- to 17-year-old with sharp, aquiline features.

She reached out and pushed Denise's newspaper down flat

onto the table. Denise blinked hard a few times, arms tensing visibly under the blue check of her uniform, and Samira held her own hands ready. 'Saturday night, one of the lads hung back and was sick near the newspapers. Him throwing up made the others stop the beating.'

Denise was still, features maybe paling, though it was hard to tell. She reached another Benson & Hedges from her pack. 'So? Must of been a right pussy!'

'I spoke to Lee's school. They said he's –'

'That bunch of pinko commie bastards can say what they frigging like!'

'Well, they spoke very highly of Lee. Said he's got a promising future. Just one thing holding him back.'

'Yeah? Fuck's that?'

Samira leant in, butting distance again. 'His family.'

If Denise was going to move, it would be now. They stared at each other a good twenty seconds until a sneering grin spread across the woman's sunbed mottled face. 'Shouldn't you be out looking for that kid that's gone missing. One of *your* lot, isn't he?'

'Yeah, Denise, I probably should. While we're on the subject, what were you and your boys up to on Monday?'

A laugh. 'Jesus! Reaching aren't you?' A level look now. 'Sam was over in Huddersfield, with his tosser dad. Easy to check up on. Lee was at school, then home with me. Alright?' She shook her head.

'For now.' Samira nodded. She leant back, dredged her mental notes. Husband gone fifteen years, Denise grafting, food on the table, determined to pass her little empire of chintz, leopard-skin rugs and union flags to her boys. So, what a surprise Lee must have been. Sam on the dole and would likely stay there. But Lee? Predicted straight A's in all subjects. Exceling in History and Art. Clever, always asking questions. An apple having fallen not just far from the tree but into a completely different orchard.

Would Denise joke with her National Front mates about the prodigy in her midst? Probably. *Don't know what to do with this one, lads! He's got ideas!*

But would she secretly be proud as hell at the same time? Was that what was flickering under all that slap and bravado?

'Denise...' Samira's voice was soothing. 'Lee threw up, not because he's a pussy. He threw up because he knew what they were doing was wrong. He worships his big brother and he wants to please you. Only reason he was even –'

'Fuck you know about what my boy believes?'

'Nothing.' Samira smiled. 'But I know this much. We'll nail whoever beat Mr Ramir. If we have to go through Lee and Sam to get to the big man of their little crew, we will. But I'd rather not.' She shook her head. 'I'd rather see Lee sit his A Levels. That's why I've come to you first. Sam's made his choices already, but it's not too late for Lee.'

Denise was chewing the inside of her cheek. She said nothing, but she glanced upward, pointedly.

So that was how it would be. Even in this small canteen, there'd be someone who knew someone whose cousin's mate knew someone... Samira's visit would get around.

Samira slid the card with her direct contact number under the newspaper, saw Denise notice it. Under her breath she said, 'I just need a name. Think about it. I'll keep Lee out of it. Can't promise the same for Sam.'

A glare, a long breath laced with sausage and nicotine. The slightest of nods.

Samira flicked her eyes towards the rest of the room, her voice quiet. 'There's probably a few things you'd like to say to me. Aloud. Now's the time. Just don't force me to arrest you.'

She stood and turned, and the tirade started. She tuned most of it out, but enough got through, just for a few seconds, of monkey noises and *this bloody country going to the dogs* and of *coming here and dissing my family* and *bloody jigs and coconuts* to make her wonder if she should have stayed outside with Turner to watch the entertainment.

12

It was the second school Will had visited in as many days. But this one was inner-city, underperforming, underfunded, with failure writ large on every graffitied window. The young teacher in front of him now, mouth corners folded like idle wings, was probably figuring how he could get through the rest of the day without being embarrassed, threatened and verbally or physically assaulted.

Will had left Gallerton pretty riled. Sometimes, intelligent people were a liability, deciding they knew what was and wasn't important. Whatever his wife's seismic personality shifts, at least Cathy was forthcoming. Byford had mentioned nothing about Ryan's loss of a mate.

But his son was missing and Will had asked for information on anything unusual.

His son! Adopted or not.

That could be it right there, of course. No matter how hard you'd try, adoption papers might never equate to blood ties, he supposed.

But if Byford had held back about Brandon Conrad, what else? The list back in Will's car could be useless if he'd overlooked someone to cover something else he didn't want known.

Maybe he could just go back and shake Byford by his ears until he stopped being a prick.

He looked at the young teacher. 'So, where's Brandon likely to be?'

Another glance at his watch. A shrug. 'Dolling off probably. He was in assembly. But he's had RE this afternoon. It's easier to slip out than most lessons.'

'Why's that?'

'Usually a fight breaks out or something. Big groups, so it's impossible to keep track of who's in, who's not.'

'Ok. Where do they go?'

He blinked and rubbed at the side of his nose.

Will touched the teacher's arm just above the elbow. 'You've heard there's a boy gone missing from Crag Valley? Brandon knew him when he went to Shockley Beck Comp. I need to speak to Brandon. It could be really important.'

The eyes still held a dull look. A shrug, but Will didn't let go of his arm, putting on just a little pressure, touch becoming grip, enough to force eye-contact. 'I bet you wanted to change the world when you started, right?'

He gave a shy look downwards with a slight laugh.

'But that's all gone already. Just live for the summer hols now.'

The young teacher's face turned back upwards, a darker look in place.

'You wanted to change lives. You found out there's too much stacked against you. Yeah?'

A grudging nod.

'Help me find Brandon Conrad. Can't promise you'll change a life, but you might. You might even help save one. Imagine that.' He let go of his arm.

The young teacher looked at Will, then nodded and motioned him towards the window. He pointed to the ravaged wire mesh of the basketball courts, billowing like a broken sail. Behind it, just visible, the trees of the local park and the recreational grounds.

The rec had its share of uniforms, alright. Getting close enough to check faces was tricky; they scattered as soon as Will drew near, not running exactly, just spreading out and changing direction fast like a herd of jumpy gazelles. But in every pack, there's always one who hangs back. This one had a limp.

'What happened to your leg?' Will asked him.

The lad shook his head and tried moving away. Will blocked him easily and showed him his warrant card. 'Police officer.' Will passed him the leather-backed card. 'What's your name?'

The boy studied it and made a grimace. 'Jason.'

'Okay, Jason.' Will held out the photo. 'I need your help. Know this lad?'

'Seen him.'

'Today? Is he around here?'

Hesitation. Then a nod.

'I'll do you a deal. You go find him and bring him back here.' He held out a couple of pound notes. 'These are yours.'

He straightened with a spur of pride. 'I ain't a narc, like.'

Will nodded. 'I know, Jason. But this lad's not in any trouble. I just need to talk to him about something.'

His lip was out. 'He won't come back here with me.'

'He will. Tell him there's a copper wants to talk to him. And listen, this bit's really important. Tell him it's about Ryan Byford.'

Jason screwed up his eyes. 'That lad who's missing –'

'Yeah. You got it. And tell him I know why he had to leave his last school. You got that? Repeat it.'

He did. Will gave him the notes, nodded and walked over to the roundabout.

Brandon Conrad's face was well-formed. The first throes of adolescence had pulled the jaw a little tighter than on the one-year old photo. He stood at a distance, head cocked to one side as Will showed him the warrant card. 'My little brother got one of them in his *TJ. Hooker* set.'

Will let out a laugh. 'Why did you have to move here from Shockley Beck?'

'Thought you was gonna tell me.'

'Okay.' Will stretched the tension out of his neck. 'For bullying Ryan Byford because he's black.'

'You what?' He accompanied a disgusted look with a hawk and spit in the grass. Then a shrug. 'He's alright, Ryan.'

'You and him were mates?'

'For a bit.'

Will nodded. 'Bit too soft for you though, right?'

He screwed up his face, like adults knew nothing at all about anything. 'Nah. That's what they said on the telly, last night. Like Ryan's a swot or summat.' He spat again. 'Bollocks!'

'Well, his grades are pretty good, Since last year anyway.'

The hard face cracked a little. An inward look. Then a stare at the school buildings behind the fence. 'Ryan were a right laugh. For a while anyway.'

Will glanced around at the rec. 'Did you two used to skive

like this?'

A grin. 'A bit.'

'Where did you go?'

He shook his head.

'The moor? Anywhere special?'

A tight-lipped grin. There was nothing so sacrosanct as a den.

Okay. A different tack then. 'Wherever you used to go, just think about this for me. Was there ever anyone hanging around, watching? Someone who looked wrong?'

Brandon's eyes opened a little wider. He walked towards the roundabout, sat, pushing his body until his back was to the central spoke. He looked down at the wooden slats, picking at one with a fingernail. 'What did them lot say about why I got kicked out?'

'Behavioural issues. You were missing classes, giving teachers a hard time. Then you hit Ryan in the playground. The board of Governors recommended you be suspended. Your mum and dad decided to move you here, instead.'

He could have swaggered at that, Will thought. But he didn't. Just shook his head.

Here it came.

'Wasn't the moor. Well, not after we found the den. Down by the cut, near the caravans. It's an old mill or summat like that. Well cool. But you can only get to it by walking a high wall, right on the edge of the canal. Well dodgy with trees sticking out. So this one time, there was a bloke watching us on the wall. But we didn't want him to know about the den so we backed up, went back along the ledge. This bloke were daring us. *Oh, you can't do it, black boy, you're gonna fall.* He put Ryan off and –'

'He fell in?' Will was dimly aware of his hand beginning its tremor.

A nod and a gulp. 'I couldn't... get him... too far down. I wanted to jump in but I couldn't do it.'

'You'd probably both have drowned if you had. So, what happened?' His left hand was over his right.

Brandon breathed hard. 'The bloke got a branch and pulled Ryan out.'

Okay, Will thought. Then, he looked at Brandon's face. Back in the chasm between childhood and adulthood, where so little is easy to articulate. 'That's not all, is it?'

Brandon's head shook, slowly. 'The bloke, he... he didn't just pull Ryan out straight away. He kept jerking the stick away... like... *come on darkie boy, reach for it.*'

Dull anger quietening the shake in Will's hand.

'Then, after he'd got him out, I don't know. I don't know what he said, what he did. By the time I'd got back over the ledge and circled over the footbridge it were maybe five minutes. They were gone!'

'What did you do?'

'Well I didn't wanna just go to Ryan's house. I mean, we were skiving school and his dad's a... prick! So I waited 'til later. His dad answered. Said Ryan was okay but I shouldn't call round again. That was it.'

'Ryan tell you what happened with the biker bloke?'

A shake of the head. 'Didn't say nothing.'

'Not even next day?'

'No, I mean, he didn't say nothin' ever again. Not to me. He were out of school for a week. Then when he came back, he just wouldn't come near me. The teachers separated us. I were put back a year. At break, he'd just walk away if I tried to talk to him.'

Will let out his breath.

'I... didn't mean to hit him. I just...' An exasperated shake of the head. How do you articulate affection with only pre-teen swagger and rage to work with?

'Can you describe the bloke by the canal?'

'Course.' Brandon gave Will a measuring stare; taking in his shoulders and arms. 'Big bastard. He'd have you, easy. Biker jacket, head shaved like a skinhead but big beard. *Like Z-Z Top.*' He shook his head, eyes darting over the rec. 'I heard it on the news about Ryan. I didn't think of that bloke though. Dunno why.'

Will said nothing. Maybe Brandon hadn't consciously made the connection, but it sounded like the event was pretty close to the surface. All the same, he could understand why he hadn't come running to tell anyone about the incident from a year ago.

When the system has given you nothing but flak, it takes either an idiot or a real hero to stick up their hand to go back in the firing line.

This lad was too smart to be either.

13

This was a mistake, he thought.

It wasn't that it was hard to find. From Brandon's directions, once past the caravans and down to the Canal's edge, the rest should have been easy. Over the footbridge and along to the wall, then a quick scramble up and shimmy along. But there was water. Lots of it.

Will would have to be fairly stupid not to have worked it out by now. The sound, the smell, the sight of water in anything like quantities to cover a body was enough to start him off. His head had been pounding as he'd reached the footbridge and by the time he'd climbed the wall, images were flooding around him; the dank swell of the docklands pit, russet flakes of corrosion on every pipe and jagged strut. Him stretching ever upwards, to nothing, shoulders giving with the weight of the boy, heart hammering, water lapping at his neck. More intense now, his body tightening, his self, that auto-pilot part of him crushed down in water. London Docklands. The stinking awful bloody pool…

The sky was darker. He was curled atop the wall like a limpet, hands and knees raw on stone.

Ten minutes? An hour? More?

He straightened, dragged himself to a kneeling position, pain in his head, his jaw, even his teeth. Nausea.

He was still for a good minute, not trusting his body for movement yet. Finally, edging along, inch by inch, bending his body outward around outreaching branches. At last, rough stone and the lip of a window, the glass long-since gone. An annex to an old mill or a grain store possibly. He hoisted himself up, feet dangling over the canal and his heart hammering again as he sat on the lip and tucked his legs in, spinning his body and squirming through.

Exhaustion. Body aching inside and out. He lay, breathing, just breathing.

There was just enough daylight to see by. The wall curved

around a single door with a well-rusted lock. Whatever building this was annexed to was likely derelict. A forgotten space; probably hundreds of them lining the waterways.

He blinked. Army stuff. Some helmets, model tanks and jeeps, some carrier bags, one with what looked like magazines.

Ryan's? Abandoned here by him and Brandon? Had he never been back to pick anything up, after being pulled from the water by the big biker? Too scared to return, even for his gear.

He moved in towards the stash, unsteady, groping for the bags, pulled out the magazines. Will stared, just to be certain. The top one was dated April, this year. A month ago.

Somebody had been here recently.

Had Ryan carried on using this place as a den after his little dip, after all? Will thumbed the mags underneath, less glossy, pages yellowed and curled after being left here to the elements. He focused on their dates, taking his time, to be sure, because numbers… numbers right now were tricky…

He sat back, closing his eyes. There was a fair gap between the dates of the older magazines and the ones on top. Suggesting Ryan, if it was Ryan, had stayed away about six months, then started coming back here again a few months ago.

Will dragged himself to a crouch, muscles jelly, clanging headache but so what?

Concentrate.

Something glistening and he stretched for it. An empty *Marlboro* packet. He thought of Byford's certainty his son didn't smoke. Had Ryan found some new mates? Might explain the newfound courage to come back here after so long. Then again, this place might be used as a den by lots of different kids.

His eyes adjusting. A cluster of beer-cans in the corner with some take-away cartons, a few torn newspaper sheets; page-three breasts crumpled out of shape, several paper bags, screwed up tinfoil. Something stale and cattish. He pulled at the foil; flakes of dried tuna, white bread blued.

Another bag though, and now he looked at it, the paper was cleaner. Inside, wholemeal bread, quite fresh. He peeled the slices apart and sniffed at it. Pastrami?

Will's blood coursing again.

Cathy's first statement had detailed what Ryan had had with him on Monday; a full description of his packed lunch. Pastrami sandwiches, suitably exotic for his mum, Will had thought at the time, despite the fact that at 12 anonymity is everything; white bread, a cheese triangle if you're lucky. Had Ryan brought his lunchbox here just so he could eat somewhere his pastrami sandwich wouldn't have gotten him a good kicking? *Little black boy, with your posh scran!*

Nausea again, Will putting a hand to the stone and breathing deep. His thoughts fogging up. But something... something important... the time... the time it would take...

He straightened, eyes swimming but thoughts clearer. The canal was over twenty minutes' walk from the school, and that didn't count shimmying along the wall. Lunch break was only 45 minutes. So, if Ryan, with or without some mates, had come here on Monday lunchtime it was a fair bet he hadn't gone back to school for the afternoon, or at least not on time. Which raised a worrying question.

According to the register, Ryan hadn't missed or been late for an afternoon or morning in four months.

So, either someone else entirely had sat down here gingerly poking at their Pastrami sandwich, which he had to admit was possible, or...

He had a hand to his head now, pain in waves. *Come on! Finish that thought!*

...or the school were telling porkies. Or at the very least, incompetently keeping registers.

He blinked.

He stared at the beer-cans and the crumpled cigarette pack. His breathing was fast, his head and body gouged out, almost feverish now. His imagination could well be running away with this, but...

He swallowed. The implications were huge.

Of course, Ryan could have run away. It was still a possibility, whatever his mum said. If he was in the habit of coming here, truanting, then there was plenty already she didn't know about her little boy.

Or, and here was the worrying bit, Ryan could have been

snatched alright, but from right here, or from anywhere between the school and here, rather than from the school itself.

He stood, swaying, holding onto the wall, thinking what he had to do next.

Because it was just possible this entire investigation so far was an almighty fuck-up.

14

The Caretaker's flat was No. 1. Convincing him to open up took a while and when he did, it was a matter of two deadbolts, a Yale-lock and chain.

Collins was shortish, overweight, around fifty. He nodded at Samira's ID card and gulped as his eyes tracked up to Turner's six-foot whatever frame.

A seedy smell, literally seedy that is, and Samira heard the trilling of a budgie before she saw the standing cage in the corner of his murky room. 'We're looking for Kenny Macfarlane.'

'He lives in number–'

'I know where he lives. That doesn't mean anything with Kenny though, does it?'

Collins stepped back, jittering a 'come on in' gesture. They followed him, Samira shaking her head to the offer of tea, a disappointed shrug from Turner.

It wasn't the same block they'd found Tony Wilkinson in, but the same estate. Craven Tower itself, dominating the village with size and reputation. In her six weeks in the region, Samira had managed never to set foot here. But here she was, second time in as many days, this time on information extracted with all the ease of a cheap gold filling from Denise Owens in that greasy supermarket canteen.

Denise had left a message on Samira's answerphone, only a few hours after Samira had left her. 'You know who this is. Can't believe I'm... okay. Okay.' A breath. 'Kenny Macfarlane. Little Kenny, he goes by. Better keep your word, coconut copper.' The last was said with some deliberation, like Denise had meant to say something else, then thought better of it.

Whatever.

Kenny Macfarlane.

According to two hard-nosed coppers on the drugs team, Kenny Macfarlane, AKA Little Kenny, was a vampire. Not literally, she assumed. But amongst some other equally useful snippets, they'd told her that pinning the bastard down at night was only close to impossible. During the day; no chance at all.

So here she was, the sun sinking, the one place in this town where people shouted *rape* for a joke, with only Rugby boy for backup. She looked up at his sweaty neck and wondered whether, worst-case scenario, he'd be up for a scrum. All fifteen stone of him.

The caretaker's chin gurned up a little, and she realised he had no top teeth. 'I don't really know what –'

'Kenny runs this block, doesn't he?'

She watched his Adam's apple bounce once as if to nod at her. From what she'd already sniffed out, much bigger and tougher men than Collins had given in to Little Kenny. Intimidation, low-level extortion. His official flat here, he rarely used. He mooched around the block, sometimes into unoccupied flats, sometimes crashing with 'friends' (people who owed him money or favours) and occasionally with law-abiding residents waking up to a surprisingly scary bloke, Nazi tattoos and bulldog stare, on their sofa.

The drugs team had given up on nailing Little Kenny about a year ago. Even apart from the difficulty of getting hold of him, he was pretty small-time. He supplied the block and the surrounding area and that was it, no ambitions beyond his fiefdom.

'Where is he right now, Mr Collins?'

His eyes widened.

'Ok.' She leant forward. 'The nasty truth. At some point, we know Kenny has gotten into a lot of the flats. Most likely scenario, he's scared you into giving him access to your utility cupboard, where I'm guessing you have spares and skeleton keys?'

Turner chose that moment to chip in. 'We could nick you for that, eh? Misuse of... I dunno. Municipal property or whatever.'

She closed her eyes. It was like being one half of a dysfunctional good cop, bad cop routine. She opened them again. The blood had voided from Collins' face.

'Does he put the keys back?'

Collins nodded. 'He's... he made a copy of the cupboard key. Can get them any time he –'

'Okay.' She nodded at Collins. 'Kenny will know we've come and talked to you, so he'll probably come back at you for it…'

Collins cringed.

'…but, he can't really complain you took us to the utility cupboard, can he? We're police, and we're asking to see your keys.'

Collins was gurning again like a cud-chewing cow.

She stood. 'Either that, or I let PC Turner here arrest you, like he wants.'

He chomped a bit more, then he was up, nodding, making the most of what must have been a shitty night.

In the end it was easier than it might have been.

'What goes on that top hook?' She pointed unnecessarily.

Collins swallowed. 'That's the roof.'

'The roof?' Turner's voice was just a little quakey, and perversely Samira found herself enjoying it. 'What would he be doing up there, like?'

Collins was ghost-like in the basement light. He was shifting from foot to foot and Samira put a hand on his arm, just below the shoulder. He blinked at her. 'There was a bloke here earlier, asking for Kenny.'

'Aww, right!' Turner's voice boomed in the tight space. 'You could've bloody mentioned it earlier!'

For once, something sensible from Rugby boy. She glared at Collins. 'Who?'

That was it for Collins. It was like watching a sack collapse, sand spraying out of it. He gave them a description, someone educated, not Kenny's usual type of visitor. Collins had given the signal, banging on the ventilator grille, and Kenny had come down from wherever he was laying his hat. Collins, gulped, looked at the missing roof-keys. 'Kenny only takes people to the roof to show off, or scare someone –'

'How long ago was this?'

'About half an hour.'

Samira gestured upstairs. 'Which is the most reliable lift?'

'Closest to the steps.'

'Right. Shut the others off!' She moved, stopped, looked at

Turner. 'You ready?'

Turner breathing heavily. His voice was quiet, pitched for her alone. 'We could do with blowing in for backup. This is –'

'Except our walkie-talkies won't work in here. Or even outside.' It was true. The surrounding hills, the moor, the tower blocks themselves. One reason this place was avoided whenever possible. Even the car would need to be driven half a mile up the road to get a signal. 'We're on our own, Turner. You in or not?'

His eyes were everywhere but on hers but he stood a little straighter and manoeuvred his truncheon-belt. 'Okay. Okay.'

On her way out, she turned to Collins. 'Who was it? The bloke who's come visiting Kenny?'

'Ah.' A shake of the head. 'I been trying to remember. Bryson or Buford or something like –'

Samira felt her eyes widen. 'Hang on, not Byford?'

'Yeah. That's him.' Collins' nod was definite.

Samira pinched her lip and then looked at Collins again. 'Get back to your flat and phone our station, tell them DC Byrne and PC Turner urgently require assistance, a possible assault in progress. Byrne and Turner, got it?' She was out the door and running for the lift.

She was bouncing on the balls of her feet; the lift with another ten floors to rattle through if the soiled light display meant anything. Around them, Crumpled *Kestrel* and *Special Brew* cans, red and green graffiti scrawls on beige breezeblock; an art-installation no one would pay to see. *Eau de cannabis* everywhere urine wasn't. She looked at Turner. 'Makes Haughton House seem pretty tame.'

Turner blinked, a lopsided grin, eyes not really in it. 'Awww. you bricking it?'

She made a face. The more time with him, the more she saw through him. Yes, she was scared. This estate's crime stats were the worst in the North. Most housebreakings (around the affluent edges) per year, almost as many muggings as Manchester's Moss Side, and more than its share of sexual assaults, though likely three times that amount were never reported. Also, the highest number of heroin and crack addictions in the region.

Two other stats that fell close to home; more racially connected violence originating or orchestrated here than anywhere else in the valley, and the icing on this shitty little cake; more assaults on police officers than anywhere in the UK per population. So, all in all, Turner could take his *brickin' it?* and shove it where he normally kept his head.

The rattle of lift-doors. Turner glanced at her but she didn't make eye-contact as they creaked and whirred up fourteen floors; he'd had his chance for a pre-scrum huddle and blown it.

A judder and the doors rattled open. The corridor colder than the basement and she zipped up her leather jacket. She thought she could feel the sway of the building; the slightest yield under her feet, her inner ear swirling. A sudden sound, a creeping twist at her guts and a spike of alarm running up her spine.

Hard to tell at first, through concrete walls and high whining wind. But a second burst was clearer. A moaning, plaintive scream, with a depth only a man could manage. Out there, beyond the big blue door at the top of the stairwell. She shook her head, walked to it, checking the handle. Yes, unlocked. She pushed and stepped out into a blast of wind that almost yanked the door from her hand and sent it slamming against pebble-dashed brick, but she held onto it, barely keeping her balance. She twisted herself, looked over her shoulder.

Turner was gone.

'Bastard!' Under her breath, because there wasn't much of it to be had out here, wind whipping around her.

That scream again, shrill now, but no less male. Byford?

She moved from the door, out onto the roofing, sharper gusts tugging. She turned again, two figures half silhouetted by the russet and grey evening sky, one of them big, bigger than Turner certainly, rushing towards her from the edge of the outbuilding.

15

The track through the field was crusty, the suspension not built for it; every judder had him snarling until he was back near the canal. He switched off, stared at the irregular line of caravans just beyond the hedge. Two statics, one largish mobile.

Earlier, he'd been in no shape for a look around. Now, entire body throbbing, head sluiced-out, he was in no shape for a look around either. But it was quite possible that Ryan's 'rescuer' a year ago when he'd fallen in the canal, the big biker with tats, lived here.

Already it was getting dark. He grimaced for the officers and civvies soon trudging home after covering the moorland, hill road and Shockley Beck. He thought of the headmistress's face a few hours ago as she'd admitted it was possible the register from the afternoon Ryan had disappeared might have been inaccurate. A fare-thee-well look, he thought, for her career.

Price's reaction? Predictably Price. Thundering, baleful, flinging blame around like paintballs and then calming enough to begin reorganising the search plan for tomorrow.

The wind dropped, the quiet of early evening closing in. He got out, gritting his teeth, hands sweeping the long swards.

The third of the caravans, the mobile, was most secluded, its grey and white roof peeping over the treeline. The grass to the side flattened with two indentations – a bike parking spot, for a big one, judging by the depth.

He stopped dead. A noise. Scratching just under the rising breeze. From the caravan.

He went into a crouch so the tips of the grass were at eye-level. Pointless though. If he'd been seen already there was nothing he could do. He stood, moved to the caravan's window, peered through. A gap between the curtains into gloom.

The scratching again. Not quite distinct. From the back, he thought, near floor level. This time, something accompanying it. A muffled whimper.

That was enough really. He'd been thinking about jemmying the door, a phrase flashing at him: Fruit of the poisoned tree. It was a term UK barristers would use about illegal searches. In the US, a case could easily be thrown out. Luckily, in the UK, juries and CPS were far more interested in quality of the evidence than in how it was obtained. Nine times out of ten, the poisoned tree defence would be ignored if the evidence found was strong enough. But the image of Ryan Byford lying trussed in this caravan was enough to blow all of that away anyway. Will had more justification than he needed to take a look inside.

He took out a *Leatherman* multi tool from his jacket pocket, glanced at the door. No, back to the window. He could smash the glass but he had a feeling he wouldn't need to. Caravans were easy; basically boxes made of wood and plastic. If this had been a static, it might have been a tad harder, but no, every component here was designed to be as light as possible, including windows and latches.

It actually took less than a minute. The locking blade on the glorified penknife was slim enough to get between window-rim and panel, strong enough to let him lever the window out. He slid the blade along, finding the latch and snapping it away from the wood. He stood back, closed up the tool, eased the window outward, got his head between the curtains and squirmed his body in, working his leg up until he could hook it over. His foot touched down on a table and he dragged himself through.

The air was sweaty with carburettor oil. There were engine parts on a greasy towel in front of an orange cupboard unit and a small sink. Flyers, photos and used tickets from Rock gigs pinned to a corkboard. To the left, crumpled beer-cans and an empty cut-price whisky bottle. Filling an inside door, there was a poster of a girl straddling a chopper, front wheel impossibly distant from rear, breasts spilling from unzipped leather.

He stepped down and it wasn't until he was at floor level that the growling started, from behind the poster. Deep and ravenous. A dog? Suddenly the scratching made sense. The hairs on Will's arms stood up, a cold stab of primal fear in his guts as the door the poster was on skittered wide open and it charged out, right at him; squat, muscular, a pit-bull or something close, shoulders hunched, legs quivering.

16

'Police Offi –!' Words snapped away, wind roaring into her mouth. Her hand was on her warrant card but the smaller of the two men was almost on her and she made a snap decision; went for the telescopic baton instead. He was close, a waft of sweat and cheap aftershave. A stocky arm grabbing for her wrist and she flashed the baton outwards, hard edge blocking his forearm, point of her boot catching his knee, foot turning to scrape his shin and stamp downwards. A stumble and hop but she'd spun away to the shadows behind the outbuilding.

Dumb enough to move on her. How likely was it that they'd stop if they knew she was police?

She needed higher ground! She reached up for the outbuilding's edge, a drainpipe, a quick testing pull and she heaved, boots scraping brick, the struts holding the pipe. She scrambled and was up, dragging herself onto the flat rubber roofing, tucking her legs in quick.

The highest point of the tower block now, wind roaring around her, rain pelting the black surface, about ten-foot square. A seething flash. *Fuck you Turner!* She pulled her legs in close, grabbed her walkie-talkie. Pretty sure she had a signal; nothing above her but cloud and stars, so why not? Call-sign and position. 'Officer in distress. Need backup, quick!' She repeated it, glancing behind her, round the edge of the black roof. A hand was questing over the edge, feeling around for purchase just as she had, tensing to pull its owner up.

She thrust herself forward, wind snatching at her clothes, kicked out at the fingers, catching them with her heel, a sharp cry as they were jerked back. But then the hand was back again, dark laughter from down there now. She kicked again, another hand appearing, and the first was reaching, fingers snapping at her heel like a crab, a face appearing behind it, hooded, but a glimpse of a flat forehead and small eyes.

She drove her heel down into the other hand. A muffled yelp. Both hands shrank away and the face dropped out of sight. She pulled herself back, scanning around her. The wind dropped its pitch a little and she shouted, voice cracking and hoarse. 'Police officer! You'll be banged up in Armley by tonight!'

The laughing again. Then another voice, quieter, pitched not for her. She swallowed in a dry throat. Okay then. They'd be coming. From two sides at once; it was what she'd do, if she had someone with her. Another second or two pummelling the imaginary face of PC Turner. She hunched down, the baton extended fully. She'd give them all she could. She'd done some kickboxing, knew some moves that weren't in any police self-defence handbooks. She'd just have to hold out until some sirens sounded over that bloody hillside.

The wind had dropped almost to nothing and a loud clanging slam made her rock up off her haunches. The door? Shut by the sound of it. She was still, head cocked to one side. Had they gone? Seen sense? Another sound, a low groaning. Maybe they were still here... but the moan repeated itself. Full of need.

She gave it another full minute, peering down over the edge of the rubberised roofing to the concrete of the tower's main roof. Nothing. No movement, no jeering laughs. And then, that moaning again, this time a barely articulated phrase lost amongst it: 'Help me!'

'Oh, Lord!' She shook her head. If it was a trap, so be it. Some things you just couldn't help responding to. The wind was picking up again, needles of water at her face as she found the drainpipe and shinned her way down, waiting for rough hands to grab her legs from the shadows. Nothing, though. She was on relatively solid ground now, glancing around her. She moved away from the outbuilding, headed for the rail at the very edge of the tower block. The moan again. She headed for it. The shape of something hanging down from the rail and she wiped at her eyes with the back of her hand. She'd have to lean out over the rail to see what it was, though she had a pretty good idea.

A tumble of nausea as she looked down seventeen floors at the toy cars and houses below. She held onto the rail; stupid really, no way she could fall, the rail almost shoulder height. She steeled herself, leant over.

Byford was directly under her, hands tied together, head just visible, facing outwards into the rain. Sobbing, she realised. She checked the rope; tight on his wrists and secure to the railing, but sodden wet. Would it weaken, stretch, slip off his wrists? God, he must be terrified. She shouted down to him. 'Mr Byford? Mr Byford?'

No reaction. The wind was still up but she doubted it was that. Shock. She reached down, pressed her hand over his cold wet fingers. What had the DI said his name was? 'Sean. You're going to be okay, but I need you to tell me. Are you hurt?'

Some movement, crabbing forward; trying to arch his neck so he could see her. Not possible, the angle he was at. 'It's alright, Sean. Look. I'm a police officer but I'm on my own just now.' She looked around her, back at the doorway. What if those idiots decided to come back? Still no bloody sirens. What about Collins' promised phone call? Probably decided police reprisals were preferable to Little Kenny's. She hoisted the radio, tried again. Crackle, lots of it. She shook her head, repeated her message. She looked back down at Byford, her hand squeezing the wet rope again. 'Sean, I'll pull you up, but I'll need your help. Are your feet tied?'

His head moved from side to side.

'Okay. I need you to use your feet as I pull. Try to take as much of your weight as possible, okay? Okay, Sean?'

A grunt. Good enough. She leant over, planting her feet against the concrete lip under the rail.

Strangest thing. She thought of Mum. Some moment, maybe the night before school sports day. *My g'yal*. Patois exaggerated with passion, or after a few wines. *Strong with strong roots becas' you're my g'yal, strong like a willow.*

You bend. You don' break!

Samira had both hands on his wrists. 'Okay. On three. One, two...' She heaved, the top of the rail digging into her chest and underarms. The ridiculous thought that Turner could have done this with one hand, which made her angry, which actually maybe helped, because Byford's arms were bent back behind his head. At the end of her strength now though. Up to him. *Come on! Use your feet!* Sudden, tearing pain at her shoulders, all his weight in her hands, her forearms surely breaking against the rail, his rope-covered wrists slipping from her, but then...

sudden relief. He must have found purchase again with his heels, and he was up, his bald spot at her eye level. She circled an arm around him, pulling him back to the rail and he managed to turn himself, hooking his arms over. A clumsy hugging stagger, one last effort from her and he was over, the two of them on the concrete, Samira rolling and lying flat and massaging her arms, trying to suck some life back into her body. For a few seconds, Byford out of sight and mind and she tucked her legs up, hugging herself, shaking her head slowly from side to side.

When she looked up, Byford was kneeling, head down, body rigid, rain dripping from his thinning hair and his nose. His arms were stretched rigid and the rope trailed, still fastened to the rail. Samira dragged herself up and walked, checking his eyes as she passed.

First things first. She picked at the wet rope until she could slip it off the rail. Then she turned back, positioning herself directly in front of him, her hands on his upper arms, maintaining eye contact as she spoke slowly, tone as gentle as the wind would allow. 'Sean, look at me. Look at me. Now take a deep breath. In and then out. That's right. Now let your body go limp. Like this, okay?' She let her own body visibly relax; harder than she would have thought. 'Now you try. Just let your body relax. That's it. Good, good.'

Byford was beginning to tremble. Samira nodded. 'It's okay. That's normal. Just your body releasing itself. Just let it happen, okay?'

He was breathing deep now, staring at her. 'I'm… I'm in shock, right? I know because I'm a…'

Whatever he was, he couldn't say it. But she nodded. 'Good, Sean. That's good.' She was unwinding the rope from around his wrists, picking at the last knot. He was looking at the rope, clearly perplexed at how it had got there. Probably best to leave it that way, for now. 'Let's get rid of this silly thing.'

'Psychiatrist!'

She gave him a smile. 'Okay, Sean. Let's get out of this rain, now.' She hoisted him up.

She walked by his side, putting her hands about his upper

arms, guiding. She felt something skitter away from her boot and she squinted into the rain-sodden concrete. There. She bent and picked them up. Eyeglasses, one of the lenses shattered.

'Just like mine,' Byford said.

She nodded and put them in her pocket.

His fingers were to the bridge of his nose now, feeling around there. Then he stopped, nodding suddenly. 'They knocked them off when they...'

She nodded again, manoeuvring him to the doorway.

He stopped, turning and looking back at the rail. 'They... I could've –'

'I know.' She tried to maintain eye-contact. 'But you didn't. You must've been terrified, anyone would be, but you're okay now.'

Still glazed. His arms were trembling again.

Samira tried the door, half-expecting it to be locked. But no. It seemed Little Kenny wasn't quite stupid enough to add false imprisonment of a police officer to reckless endangerment. She shook her head, pulled the door wide, checking the corners of the stairwell and then shepherded Byford through into the light.

17

Rain bashed the bonnet. Will blinked at the black strip of moorland road winding through heather and wounded crag. He gripped the wheel, staring. Oldsill moor? Maybe. Not far from the turn off down to the village and the Craven estate.

Okay great. Great that he knew where he was. Fabulous, really.

But how did he get here?

He squinted at the flashing red light on the fuel gauge. 'Got to be kidding!'

Should he keep going? There was a petrol station at Oldsill, he remembered, but if *here* was where he thought, there was a good two miles of ups and downs before the road forked down into the village.

A series of chugs from the engine, fuel pump sucking in crap, answered the question.

Tufts of grass and scrub broadened just ahead as the road veered right; not quite a layby or shoulder but maybe the best he'd do. He pulled over, buffeting over the grass, angling as far off the road as he could without tipping into the ditch.

A dumb, frozen moment of nothing but wind-blown droplets zooming over the windscreen. How had this happened? He remembered… what? What did he remember? Seeing the fuel gauge as he'd left the RSPCA shelter, reminding himself to go fill up and then… nothing. Until now. A glance at his watch. He'd lost maybe half an hour.

But then, so what, anyway? He could just sit here and enjoy the rain.

Ryan Byford though. Duty tugged his armpits like a helium balloon, until he was up and drifting outside. Beats of water at his neck, a turn-up of his collar, he glugged to the boot, popping it open. He hauled out the waterproof anorak with POLICE emblazoned on the back. That would go down great where he was headed! He dragged it on. The hood smelt vaguely of engine oil, drops tapping at the plastic like a hundred shy visitors.

He slammed the boot, swished back around to the front, sat

and took the radio receiver, his thumb hovering over the call button. He shook his head once. Sort it later. Get petrol and a lift back up here. No need to call it in. He snapped the receiver back into place and locked up.

As he reached the road he crouched, kneading at his thigh muscles through stiff jeans with cold fingers. The asphalt was a wash of patters spitting upwards like silver-white sparks and he stood for a while, just watching it; nothing quite real, not yet.

He trudged along the edge of the moorland road that led down towards the village and its infamous estate, knowing he should be worried what the hell might be wrong with him. If he could just get past feeling he wasn't actually here, he probably would be.

The headlights went onto full beam and angled straight at him, though he'd already seen the driver's face. The Fiesta picked up speed and swerved away. Will stumbled back into the ditch, spray spattering the waterproof.

He clambered up to watch its tyres splash away into flowing blackness. Only one occupant; the rugby neck and protruding ears were a giveaway even from here. No sign of Samira though.

He stood. What the hell had just happened? With his hood up, he wouldn't have been known until the car was close, if at all; but the sudden acceleration seemed to mean Turner hadn't wanted to be recognised. Other than no love being lost, why would that be?

He stared at the ugly blot of Craven Tower. Hard to know what was going on but whatever it was he didn't like it. He stared around him, got back on the pavement and started jogging down towards the village.

Ramir's Off-Licence on the corner, the *offie*, was still operating. Was it the family stepping up while the owner was in hospital? Outside, three youths in trackie-bottoms and anoraks were sitting on pushbikes, sucking on roll-ups, at least one with a can of something they weren't old enough to drink. Will didn't slow, just kept jogging and by the time he'd passed there were a few jeers, not surprising with the lettering across the back of the waterproof. He glanced back; one of them was following, the others mounting up. Great. *Pied bloody Piper*.

By the time he'd turned onto Craven Avenue and was approaching the garages that serviced the tower and the smaller maisonettes surrounding it, two more youths had joined the procession, on foot. The cyclists were swerving around the road, not quite catching up or attempting to overtake, just keeping pace, occasionally darting in for a closer look, front wheels angling in towards his legs and twisting away at the last possible moment.

He was close to the tower block. He slowed to a walk, hands thrust in anorak pockets. He stopped, turned to the bikers and was about to say something, God knows what, when Craven Tower's main entrance doors opened and two figures appeared, one staggering, the other helping him. Samira and... Sean Byford?

Samira came closer. 'Glad to see you, boss.' She glanced around, lowering her voice. 'Not to be ungrateful but are you *it*? I blew in for backup.'

Will shrugged. 'There's just me. But I wasn't sent as backup.'

For a second, a pained look, quickly covered with an intense, focused stare.

Something had scared her. He turned to Byford. 'The fact you're here is...' Pointless finishing, he realised. Byford's eyes were fixed but not seeing much. Shock? Arms trembling, so that Will couldn't help glancing at his own hand. Jesus! Walking wounded, the three of them.

He turned back to Samira. 'Okay. My car's off the road, about a mile up that hill. If we can't find a working phone booth, we can at least get a signal from there. You can fill me in as we walk. Oh, and we might have an escort out of the village. It's alright, they're harmless.' He glanced at the bicycle gang. 'So far, anyway.'

Hard to say how consciously organised it was, but as a first line of defence, the bicycle gang was pretty good. All minors, for a start, which meant however hard they taunted, a response like pulling one of them off their bike, something that had occurred to Will more than once, was out of the question.

Parents, older siblings probably watching. One loss of patience and that tension could bubble up and spill-over; like Brixton or Toxteth last year.

The rain was drizzle by the time they reached the second phone booth. This one looked to be in working order. On the border of the village now, the gang dwindling to four, still in superior numbers though, and anyway, all carrion-eaters sense weakened prey. Byford looked awful, Samira world-weary and jumpy, and Will... well, Will was mostly what passed for normal these days, apart from the fact that his hand had started tremoring as they'd walked. he was aware of Samira's long look from the wall where she and Byford were perched as he fumbled with the phone.

He summoned an ambulance for Byford and a red-and-white to take Samira and himself back to the station. As he left the booth, one of the bikers was buzzing in close to Samira and Byford again and Will shouted, cupping his mouth. 'Backup's on its way, lads. You should probably call it a night.'

One of them came in close with a slit-eyed stare for Will. 'We're not doin' nothin'.'

Will shrugged. 'Okay. Stick around then.' He perched on the wall next to Samira.

They whizzed past a few more times, then, finally, as the distant sirens sounded, they turned and sped back to the village.

Samira was staring down at the tower block. 'You say you saw Turner heading back to town? What do you think his story will be?'

Will thought a few seconds. 'He'll say... you agreed he should take the car to the moor and call for backup. He'll say you agreed to wait for him, not his fault you decided to play hero up on the roof. Then he'll claim damage to the car-radio, smash it, loosen a wire or two. Say he didn't notice it until he got up there. Something like that.'

Her cheekbones were grinding.

'Sad part is, most people will know it's bullshit. But they'll claim to believe it.'

'My word against his.' She nodded. Glanced at him. 'What about Kenny?' Her voice was close to a whisper. 'He really scared me, Will. And as for what he did to Byford…' She shook her head.

Will held her gaze. 'I'll tell you about Kenny. I'm gonna bring the bastard in. Tonight.'

A smile. 'You'd need a full squad to find him in those flats.'

Will glanced at Byford and softened his voice. 'Missing child case. A full squad's no problem.' He looked at the tower. 'Might be a quicker way though.'

'Well, I want to be there.' She grimaced, looked into his eyes. 'See him get the shits up him.'

Without thinking, as the flashing blue lights came over the moor, Will drew out his hand to push himself off the wall. It was still juddering, and he stared at it like the foreign object it was becoming. Then he looked at Samira. Her lips were pursed, a frown framing those large eyes as she moved forwards. Her hand reached for his, just covering his knuckles and pressing gently.

The shaking stopped. Just like that. He blinked.

She let go. He half-expected the shaking to start again, but no. Turned his hand a few times, straightening and flexing fingers suddenly bathed in flashing blue light.

DCI Price had gone home and Turner was nowhere to be seen. Fair enough. Recriminations later. It meant there was only the night shift on in the station and a few of the response team pulling in overtime. Will recruited a few PCs from downstairs who looked like they could handle themselves. Then he checked a car out of the pool and told Samira he'd see her in half an hour.

'You bailing on me, boss?'

He shook his head. 'Just got to take care of something. A surprise for Little Kenny.'

'Oooh! I like surprises!'

It took longer than he'd thought, but as Will got back to the station, Samira was outside, on the bonnet of a red-and-white Sierra, three uniforms inside. As she slid into Will's plain car, she turned her head and stared through the grille at the back, eyebrows arching, grin spreading.

They pulled up at Craven Tower, sirens trailing an entourage;

bikers from earlier, a good few adults on foot too. They got out, Will opening the back and pulling the lead, the bulldog's neck straining, the wire mesh of the muzzle covering its pug face. He gave the lead to one of the PCs along with a nod.

About five minutes and the main entrance doors opened, Kenny, another man with him, able-looking but definitely not the second man from the rooftop, from Samira's description.

Kenny wasn't so small. Maybe five-nine and stocky. Was it a lifetime having to prove himself next to an oversized brother that earned him the *little* prefix? Or something else? Hair spiked and gelled, goatee, snide *Ben Sherman* shirt, smart jeans. Ruddy skin and a spatter of freckles on a flattened nose that the dead-eyed grin worked hard to nullify.

Will held up his warrant card, getting halfway into saying who he was before Kenny spat on the pavement. 'What you doing my dog?' Kenny spoke fast, ejecting unnecessary words, even the grammatically required.

'I found him in a caravan down by –'

'Caravan? Nah. Go to Tenerife, me.' Laughs.

Will smiled. So far, there'd been no trace on the caravan ownership. 'The dog was abandoned there and –'

'Abandoned, me' arse!'

'Not fed for at least a day. Nearly attacked me.'

'You must of broke in.'

Will shrugged. 'There's a picture of you on the wall in the caravan.'

'Fan club.' There was another slew of laughs, Kenny's mate joining in now.

'Pictures of your brother too. Ray, isn't it?'

The line of Kenny's shoulders twitched. 'Haven't seen him in ages.'

Will did a slow nod, walked towards the dog. He glanced at the entrance to the block, a few yards behind them, and spoke again, his voice pitched to carry. 'Because he attacked me, you could be prosecuted. Protection of Animals act. And the poor animal... what's his name by the way? His tag only had yours on it.'

A glance at Samira. 'Enoch!'

Will smirked. 'Not far off. We thought *Adolf.*'

'Someone nicked him a while ago. I'll be taking back now, thanks.'

'Dognapping?' Will did an intake of breath. 'Serious business. You never reported it though?' He put his fingers to the mesh of the muzzle. Enoch lapped at them. Will raised his own chin, all but shouting, 'Anyway, Enoch here might have to be put down! Shame!'

The doors were flung wide. Ray Macfarlane, arms working the air for passage, lowered head, tensed shoulders, teeth glinting menace from a flying-V beard, big hands clawing for Will's collar. Will felt his heels scraping the ground, but he'd had had the telescopic steel baton ready and he jabbed it up hard into the big man's guts, then again, lower. A blast of cider and nicotine breath and Will's feet were on solid ground again, his other hand on Ray's beard, twisting tight, swinging his head down, a uniformed arm appearing around his neck, another pinning one of his large arms back. A finger now in Will's hand and he twisted against the joint, did the same with the elbow, up and back, forcing the two meaty hands together. It was over. They had him.

Then they didn't. His arm pulled away, a faint crack of bone as Ray's finger snapped back. A low animal growl, the straightened arm flung at Will, knocking him backwards, another flailing blow grazing his chest, shoving him into a roll. The world inverted.

Laughs from Kenny, his mate and some of the gathering crowd.

Will was up, though, just as the PC behind Ray let out a strangled sound, Ray's hands on him, and as Kenny's voice roared a 'Behind you, Ray!' and Ray began turning. It was too late though. Will swiped both his cupped hands in at Ray's ears with as much force as he could muster.

Will had only experienced the double-handed slap himself, once. It doesn't matter how big you are. It hurts. And more than that, it disorientates.

Ray was stumbling like a toddler, hand to his head, handcuff ¹angling. Will grabbed it, the PC bringing his other wrist in and it was over. This time neither of them let go until he was on his knees.

Will was aware of Kenny, his mate and the other uniform and Samira all squaring off, so far; no scuffling. But Kenny's eyes flashed at him over Samira's shoulder. 'If you bloody hurt him…'

He looked at the big figure, writhing stupidly despite the cuffs, and couldn't help a laugh. Will closed on Kenny. 'I want you to come in and help with our enquiries too.'

'Fuck for?'

Will pitched his voice for Kenny alone, but glanced at the crowd, edgy, brimming laughs and jeers, a *come on, then* here and there. 'The missing Byford boy.' Up close, the bridge of Kenny's nose, broken in adolescence maybe, a face suddenly not so frightening. 'Your brother met him, a year ago. Scared the piss out of him.'

'So what?' But it was there, finally, the look Samira had wanted to see, the dead-eyed mask collapsing into darting glances.

Will glanced at the onlookers, then back at Kenny. 'Want to explain to this lot why his father was dangling from the roof earlier?'

Quiet now. Just a sneer.

Suddenly, he was walking, between Samira and Will, big grin for the crowd. They'd reached the Fiesta when he gave Will the stare, full-eyeball. 'Anythin' happens to that dog… or me' brother… you're toast, mate!'

Will smiled. In ten years on regular duties and at AMIP he'd had death threats from a couple of organised crime bosses, an armed bank robber and at least one serial murderer. But so far, none of them had been inspired by a pet and a sibling, in that order.

18

'Want coffee. Don't do tea!' Kenny stared down at the Styrofoam cup. 'Tea's why British Empire fell.'

'Coffee came from Ethiopia, apparently.' Samira glanced up from her pad, over at Will sitting opposite Kenny. She couldn't help checking his hand again, but he seemed to be on top of it, for now.

Kenny's head lifted and sought her out. 'Your neck of the woods.'

'What, Manchester?'

He lifted the cup and drank. Smacked his lips. 'Dark on that roof, earlier. All could see were teeth, whites your eyes.'

Samira flicked her head like an insect had momentarily annoyed her. Kenny stared at the blinds, the mirror and the open door in turn, where the three uniformed officers from earlier were hanging around, just in case. He looked back at her. 'Two-way glass?'

'No. You're not under arrest. You're helping us with our enquiries, that's all.'

'So, can go?'

She deferred to Will. He cleared his throat. 'Any time you want, but I wouldn't advise it. See, at the moment we're giving you a chance to explain your brother's connection to Ryan Byford. If you leave us guessing, we'll be intrigued.'

Kenny sniffed. 'Ask me' bro.'

Will let out a breath. 'Oh, we will. But first, we're asking you.'

'Can't help ya.'

Will shuffled a few papers and glanced in her direction.

'Here's the thing,' she said. 'Your brother doesn't have two CSEs to rub together. Whereas you, well, let's say you're smart enough to know what happens with cases like this. Missing children. Everything gets dragged into the light.'

A new look creeping over Kenny's forehead. Approaching artful.

Will leant forward now. 'About a year ago, someone matching your brother's description, right down to the tats on

90

his arms, pulled Ryan Byford out of the canal after he fell in.'

'Give him a medal.'

'Except he was part of the reason he fell in. And he didn't just pull him out straight away. He taunted him a bit first. *Come on, black boy.* That kind of thing. Then when he finally did get him out, he disappeared with him. What did he do to him, Kenny?'

A laugh. Headshake.

Will leant back. Samira cleared her throat, looking down at her pad as she spoke. 'Those photos in the caravan, Kenny. The ones of your brother with young lads. All over twenty-one, I wonder?'

Quiet. A good stretch of five seconds before his mouth moved. 'What you on about?'

'I happen to know one of those lads is Sam Owens. He's only twenty.'

'So?'

She looked up now. 'You know homosexuality's illegal for under twenty-ones?'

'What?' Kenny's chair scraped back. 'I'll…' His face had reddened, his head doing a slow shake from side to side. He stood up. He mumbled something, a basso rumble, might have been *no fucking respect*. Then louder, 'Bloody Coon!'

'You just used a racist slur against my colleague.' As Will stood, two of the uniformed officers moved into the room and Samira stood too. Will's voice had lost all trace of tone. 'According to part 3 of the Public Order Act of last year, we could arrest you just for that.' Kenny had turned but Will circled the table, putting himself smell-your-breath close. 'This is the first time you've even been questioned since your first offence as an adult, seven years back, right?'

Head down, a low growl, voice tight. 'Saying?'

'I'm saying you're clearly not a complete moron.'

Some light back in the eyes now, an adjustment.

But then Will's voice was a bellow: 'BUT THIS IS ABOUT A MISSING TWELVE-YEAR-OLD BOY!'

Samira was frozen still, just about aware that the other officers were rigid as her. Kenny's head had rocked back, eyebrows quivering, but Will leant in close and she felt a choked 'no' in

91

the back of her throat. He was begging a headbutt, just like she had today from Denise but... this was different... something truly reckless in it...

His voice was just above a whisper. 'If you're our prime, or even just brother of our prime on this, Kenny, you can forget your seventeen-floors, your connections in Amsterdam, your NF mates. Everyone will fuck you over, first chance.'

Kenny's eyes didn't waver from Will's for one second, his neck tensing.

She cleared her throat, going for a soothing tone. 'Kenny, we don't care what Ray's into sexually. Women and men, goats, whatever. But you can see how things look. Caravan decked out like a love-shack, bondage gear, and a possible interest in underage boys. Along with yours and your brother's... shall we say, *political* views.'

Will was still squared up, but his voice was less adrenaline tight. 'So, what happened that day by the canal?'

Kenny looked at the door for a few seconds, then turned and sat. Will followed suit.

'Ray's not like that. Not into kids.' For the first time, she noticed, Kenny was using close to full sentences. 'He pulled the lad out, but he was like in shock or summat. Couldn't just leave him. So, he got him back to the caravan. Tried to get an address out of him but no chance. Clammed up. So, Ray locked him in the caravan, biked to the phone booth and rang me.'

Will shook his head. 'Why?'

A grimace. 'Well, you've seen Ray, right? Scary big lad. Suppose he figured I'd have more chance with the boy. I can be a bit more charming, like. I got an address, trundled him up there. Nice place, posh. Classy people. Handed him over. End of story.'

Will made a face. 'Just like that.'

'Ask Byford.'

Samira smiled. 'So, speaking of Sean Byford, question one, why did he show up tonight? Oh, and question two, why did you decide to dangle him from a seventeen-storey building?'

That dead eyed grin again. 'He pressing charges?'

Will had leant back, thrumming the desk with his thumbs.

Samira had the impression Byford wouldn't, even if he didn't have a missing son to worry about. 'What if *we* pressed charges?' she asked suddenly. 'Reckless endangerment? We could, you know.'

Kenny shrugged. 'Chickenshit, and you know it.'

He wasn't wrong. A misdemeanour. False imprisonment of Byford and herself could get him a few years if it was treated as assault but they would really need Byford on board.

Will was doing that finger pinching thing of his again, a little vacant. She cleared her throat. 'Byford thought you'd snatched Ryan.' She didn't add a questioning intonation.

'Aye.'

'You didn't take kindly to the allegation.'

Kenny's lips drew tight. The mumble again. Sounded like *disrespectful*.

She leant forwards. 'Like pushing people around, don't you?'

The dead-eyed grin again. 'So, can I go get me' brother and get the fuck out of here or what?'

Samira got another nod from Will. She cleared her throat. 'Where were you on Saturday night about seven?'

His eyes clouded a second, but only a second. 'Ah. Home. With some mates.'

'The same mates you said were with you on Monday, watching videos? *Made in Britain* and *Meantime*?'

A nod and a grin. Samira had already pointed out both films were social commentary, not advocating racism but trying to understand it, but his eyes had glazed.

'So, what were you doing Saturday?'

'A few drinks. Game o' poker. No wait...' His eyes narrowed at her. 'Might've been *black*jack.'

She didn't react. 'Which?'

A few seconds of grin. 'Poker.'

'Write down their details.' She passed him a pen and paper. 'They'll corroborate for both nights, right?'

'Yeah, course.'

She watched him scrawl then put the pen down and pass her back the sheet. She let the quiet hang for a few more beats. 'Funny,' she said finally. 'Most people would probably have

93

asked why.'

His face blanched a little, but he recovered fast. 'Don't really give a shit.'

'The senseless beating of a local shopkeeper.' She smiled. 'I figured secretly you might be intrigued.'

'Sad. That it then?' He looked at the door. 'Cos I think if I stay any longer I might be needing to phone me' brief.'

Will raised a hand and leant forward. 'We'll be keeping your brother a while, see if he's got the brains to realise he's better off telling the truth. Personally, I doubt it, so it might be a few days.'

'Cocky shite, aren't ya? I'll remember that.' He stared at Will, eyes blank. 'No one... *ever*... talks to me like you did earlier.' Then he turned to Samira. 'And you, darling. A spade in a white deck. Easy to spot.'

She gritted her teeth. Threats, racist slurs and more than enough grounds to hold him a few days pending charges. It meant they could look into his holdings, so even if Ryan's disappearance turned out to be nothing to do with the brothers, they might uncover some of his dealings, get Drugs Squad interested and maybe, just maybe get him off the streets for a few years. Was it worth it? Too right it was. She wondered if Will was thinking the same thing.

Will smiled. 'Kenny Macfarlane, I'm arresting you on suspicion of kidnapping...'

'Aww what? You fuckin'...' The two officers moved in, had him by the upper arms quickly, snapped the cuffs on.

Will finished the caution, then, as they led Kenny out, shouted. 'Hey, Kenny!'

The officers stopped, turning him.

'You never asked about Enoch.'

A sneer.

'We'll make sure he's okay.'

The slow surprise edged across the low forehead. She watched as the look turned to satisfaction, and Will said, 'But we'll also make sure you or your brother never get near him again.'

Kenny paled, head thrusting down and forwards, an animal growl half choked by the burly officer's arm across him, spittle spraying and a couple of fake Ben Sherman buttons popping across the table, before they turned him and dragged him out.

19

'You what?' DCI Price wheezed on his Benson and Hedges and slapped the photos from the caravan of Ray Macfarlane onto the table, fanning them out like a winning hand. Ray with various lads, most in leathers or denim, some notably teenage. 'What you talking about?'

'I just think there's a good chance it has nothing to do with the brothers,' Will said.

Superintendent Stratham cleared his throat from behind the DCI. 'You brought them in. You arrested them.'

'There's clearly something going on between them and Byford. Maybe some low-level extortion. Doesn't mean they've done anything to the boy.'

Price's ratting terrier look was back. He pointed at the pictures. 'What d'you reckon big Ray did to him by the canal a year ago? Showed him his stamp collection? And what about these?'

'There's no evidence Ray's gay. I mean, as well as those pictures, there was a poster of a girl on a chopper and plenty of shots of Ray with girls too.' Will didn't ask why only the male-centred ones were here now; someone, Grundy or Price himself, had been a little selective when they'd searched the caravan. 'And even if he is bisexual, big difference between going with someone under 21 and abducting a twelve-year-old boy.' Will glanced between them. 'He might have just scared the kid a year ago. He is pretty scary.'

A grunt from Price. Stratham was looking at the lads on the photos, mouth curled in distaste. 'Could be they're all just part of some little Nazi club, I suppose. But the racist angle's still motive enough. We'll sweat them both, check out all their properties. Any haunts and lock-ups. So, what about Byford?'

Price let out a hoarse laugh. 'We could bring him in too, give him a fright. Cut through the bullshit. I mean for all we know, he's been doing the naughties with the lad himself.'

Stratham winced. 'I know fathers of missing kids usually get a first look from us but this is a respected psychiatrist. No…' He eyeballed Will. 'Unless you think he actually is involved in his son's disappearance?'

Will gave a shrug more towards the negative than the positive. 'Doubtful.'

'He's already had enough of a fright, anyway.' Stratham shook his head. 'Press him. Find out what's between him and the brothers. No need to drag him in though, not yet.'

Yes, there was. At AMIP, anyone withholding information like this, especially regarding a missing child, their adopted son, would have been downstairs by now no matter what their standing. But Will breathed it in. He'd need his indignation in a minute. 'There's a different problem.'

They both blinked.

'I've just come from the garage. The Fiesta that Turner claims was vandalised while parked up outside Craven Tower, and that's the reason he left DC Byrne in the shit –'

'Whoa...' Price's grey temples were stark against angry red skin. 'It *was* vandalised. He drove to the moor to get a signal but the engine packed in, left him stranded. I've seen the car. It's a right mess.'

'Totally,' Will said. 'Even the headlights are gone on the left.'

'Right then.'

Will left a beat of silence. 'Thing is, I saw Turner heading for the moor from Craven House. He nearly ran me over, as it happens. Both headlights on full beam.'

Price and Stratham's eyes narrowed almost in synch. Then, Stratham coughed, glanced at Price and said something under his breath. Price did a double take and Stratham said it aloud. 'I know it's your room but give us a few minutes, Ronnie.'

Price headed out, a grudging nod at Stratham, a 'you're in for it now' look for Will.

'What exactly are you saying, Will?'

First name terms again. Okay. Will took a breath. 'Turner's a lying sack of shit, sir. He left DC Byrne at the top of a tower block with a couple of maniacs. For no other reason than the colour of her skin. For all I know they're mates of his. Part of the same little Nazi club, as you put it.'

Stratham's hands were steepled.

'I saw him, and the headlights were intact. Which means he

smashed up the car and radio later to cover for the fact he abandoned her. So, it'll be his word against mine.'

The clock on the wall ticked away the seconds that Stratham's chin chomped. Will was an experienced police officer with a good record. So, he let the wall clock and Stratham's jaw and the daylight through the blinds do their thing and waited.

'I'll have a word with Turner and see what…' Stratham's eyebrows went up a notch. 'Hang on. What were you doing on foot, anyway?'

Shrewd, Stratham. You don't get to Super without some street-smarts. The quake in Will's hand started again and he got it under the table fast, but not that fast.

Stratham stared at him. 'Where was your car?'

'I forgot to fill up.' No point bullshitting. 'Ran out of petrol.'

The Super just looked at him. Will gritted his teeth, shoulders hunching slightly.

'An allegation against a fellow officer.' Price tutted. 'You need to be sure of your story, DI Ashcroft.'

So much for first names.

'Is WDC Byrne intending to make it official?'

Doubtful, Will thought, from the little he knew of her.

Stratham sat back, hands clasped across a whipcord thin midriff. He studied Will a few seconds more. 'I'll look into Turner's story. Send him on a few training courses…'

Will made a face.

'But not right now. I'm not losing valuable officers with what we've got on our plate.'

Valuable for what? Inter-station rugby? Will stood, his hand steady now. 'On that note, sir, it seems to have been overlooked, but DC Byrne is a really good copper. Having her on anything but the Byford case right now is a waste of material. In my opinion.'

Stratham's eyes were on Will's hand. But he nodded. 'Okay. She's with you.' Will was at the door when Stratham cleared his throat. 'What's your interest, Ashcroft? I'd have thought you'd just want to keep your head down.'

Yeah, you'd like that, Will thought. 'Don't like bullies. Never have.'

A message from the Force Intelligence officer was sitting on his desk, detailing numbers called from the phone booth where Peter Smiles had maybe spent his last coin. There'd been only one call between six and nine that evening. Will was just pissed off enough with Turner, Stratham and the whole crew to get some perverse enjoyment from following it up.

The reverse-directory took him to a four-storey house made into flats and bedsits at the bottom of the valley basin.

Mandy Riley was early twenties, small of body, hair dyed raven-black to her shoulders and eyes hard with experience. A worn *Black Sabbath* T-shirt, scruffy jeans. A baby boy, maybe ten months, was playing with blocks on the floor.

When he told her why he was here, she stiffened, reddened as if slapped and picked up her boy. To her credit though, she didn't deny the phone call on Sunday night, or try passing it off as a wrong number. Just as well; Will already knew the call had lasted two and a half minutes.

'So, who was it?' Will asked.

Her eyes narrowed. 'You know who. Smiley.'

Good. She was shooting straight. 'Who was he to you?'

She was bouncing her boy on her knee. 'No one. He knew my mum.' She glanced at the mantle.

There was something about the glance. 'Your mum?'

'Yeah. Died four years ago.'

'I'm sorry.' Will gave it a few seconds and then asked if Smiley and her mum had been close.

A laugh that almost liquified into a smoker's cough. 'Nice way o' putting it. Smiley especially liked being *close* to mum in the cleaner's cupboard. Or in the woodwork room when the real teachers had gone home. That's what she told me, anyway.'

Will kept his face straight. Gotcha! Smiley's connection to the valley. He'd worked here, maybe fifteen years ago. No, not worked as such. Student teacher? They'd checked his working history; he'd studied at Manchester. But his teaching practice – no reason that had to have been in the city. It would have meant he'd spent almost a year in Spinnerby, without actually being registered as living here. That's how they'd missed it.

'Your mum was cleaning in a school. Which one?'

'Junior and Infants up Shockley Beck.'

'So, what did Smiley say?'

'That someone was after him. Chasing him.' Her tone was flat but there was something playing under it. Guilt? 'I remembered mum saying he was into all that survival crap. But this sounded different.'

Will nodded. 'Mandy, when you saw it on the news, why didn't you come forward?'

Her face tightened. But then she looked at her boy, put her hands over his ears and leant forward. 'I was a kid, five or six when he pissed Mum about. All the time he was shacked up with some psycho bitch from hell. Dropped mum, in the end, for her. Smiley was a complete and utter piece... of... shit!' Took her hands away, bounced him again. 'That answer your question?'

She set the boy down and his arms and legs began to gyrate, sharp hiccupping cries starting in his throat.

But all Will could think was how desperate Smiley must have been, to make a call to a woman who could only have hated him, just because she was the only person in the region who might remember him.

If she'd still been alive.

20

Byford's head was hanging as they reached the top of the rise, eyes sallow, inward. The residue of shock.

Not that Will probably looked much better. Since his little… episode near the canal yesterday, he'd never felt so tired, his body a single aching mass but detached from him somehow; a vessel of flesh he had to lug along with him.

He stared out over the vale, the cottage a few hundred yards below. He tracked the line of rock up to the tower, a fine mist playing over roots and crags but everything above sharp, clear as a threat.

' 'Cold.' Byford offered.

It had been his wife who'd suggested he air her husband out up here. It was fine by Will. Meanwhile, Samira could sit down there in that chintzy kitchen sipping coffee, sussing out Cathy Byford. 'You want to head back down?'

'No… no. I'm fine.' Byford moved toward the edge of the path. There was a sheltered clump of rock and he sidled onto it. His paunch was pronounced in daylight and his movements seemed to bear the weight of every one of his fifty something years. 'Think I owe you an apology.'

Will perched next to him.

'I should have mentioned Kenny and Ray.'

Yeah, you fucking should have. Will breathed. 'Think they've got Ryan?'

'No. It was just a desperate idea really.'

'Based on what?'

He folded his arms, shifted on the stone plinth.

'Is Kenny into you for money? A reward for saving Ryan that's turned into some long-term protection thing?'

Byford's brow furrowed so much Will thought his glasses might fall off. 'No. That's not his pathology.'

Will made a face. 'You think Kenny's mentally ill?'

'At least borderline or narcissistic personality disorder, I'd say.'

This was why Will hated conversations with psychiatrists, not that he'd had many. Something about the whole idea of the science, if it was a science, made his brain scuttle. That tendency to rely on categories, everyone in a box neatly labelled. Or perhaps that was just the layman's view. Maybe when you studied further, it wasn't so simple. 'Go on.'

'Well, he's a bully, isn't he, for one thing. Lacks empathy. Exploitative. Runs that tower block like a gulag. Genuinely believes he's superior, and then the whole racist thing. Fragile, inflated self-esteem.'

Will let that roll around a little while. 'You think he should be locked up or treated?'

A bitter laugh. 'After last night, both!' Byford's hands came up. 'But I'm not saying he's any more ill than, I don't know... five percent of the population. Just happens to be a criminal too.'

'That mean you'll press charges?'

'Ah...' Byford's cheeks tightened. 'I just want my son found. Everything else is immaterial.'

Will nodded, let out a sigh. Something else he wanted cleared up though. 'Ryan falling into the canal. You assumed it was Brandon Conrad's fault, right?'

What sun there was threw a sparkle on Byford's glasses as he turned and looked at Will full on.

'Made a mistake there, you know.' Will said it mildly enough. 'Using your influence on the board of governors to get Brandon expelled.'

'He... he hit Ryan in school.'

Will shook his head. 'Ryan was his mate. He hit Ryan because he wouldn't talk to him.'

Byford looked down at the valley, a skirmish playing out across his brow.

'You didn't want your boy playing army, did you? Hanging around with rough kids?'

More staring at the landscape. There was the sound of something in the distance, feeding, scrabbling over something smaller and less able to defend itself. Byford took off his glasses and massaged his eyes.

'Carry on,' Will said. 'Last year. Kenny.'

Kenny Macfarlane had shown up at the door with a shivering

Ryan. They'd talked, he'd been his version of charming, he'd gone. But then he'd started appearing every now and then, inviting himself in, playing the lounge lizard. Byford looked pained. 'This'll sound a little pompous. You see, narcissists tend to want to be affiliated with people they admire. Socially accepted by groups superior to them. It's all about self-esteem.'

'And he never asked for money?' Will's brain scuttling again. There must have been something more tangible Kenny had wanted. A psychiatrist in his pocket? A sign off for diminished responsibility? 'What happened in the end?'

'He showed up one night when we had friends over and I had to ask him to leave. It was a nightmare.'

Had that pushed Kenny over the edge? Made him decide to do something bigger, like snatching Ryan? Will voiced the possibility.

'When I accused him last night, he was shocked, deeply offended. Could have been an act, but I don't think so.' Byford swallowed, chin jutting a little with clear effort at what he was about to say. 'He hung me from that… roof –'

'Just take it easy –'

'He hung me from there because he was disgusted with me. For even suggesting he might have taken Ryan. Because, I really think, on some level he thought we were friends. Well, friends is too strong, people like Kenny don't have friends, just people they use. But he thought we were affiliated.'

'Even after you'd asked him to leave one of your soirees?'

'Oh, he would've written that out of his script. He wouldn't admit to himself that I'd meant it.'

Will stood and they looked down at the cottage.

'Narcissists talk a lot about respect. What they actually mean is adulation. I disrespected him by accusing him.'

How many times had Kenny mumbled something about respect, last night? Will grimaced. 'Barking. That's my diagnosis.' He gave Byford a sour grin, gestured for him to head back down towards the cottage, trailing his lumpen steps with his own. They reached a sheltered spot and Will reached out, taking his arm, turning him. 'Why the hell didn't you tell us all this? Why go down to Craven tower last night and confront him alone?'

He coughed, looked at his feet. 'I just thought we could sort it out. Thought I could get Ryan back, without any more nonsense.'

'And what would you have given Kenny in return?'

Byford stared at the bird-like tower in the middle distance. For the first time, the absolute hell of his predicament seared his face in charring cracks. 'Absolutely anything.' He stumbled forward, Will catching him by his shoulders and steadying him. His voice was a low moan. 'Jesus…Jesus… find him, Inspector. Find Ryan!'

It was real, this sudden eruption of emotion, Will was sure. A relief, because it meant Byford did care, at least, that his adopted son was missing. But the temptation to give an answer, to be human, to reassure with a promise he knew he could never make fell on Will like an avalanche. With it, he felt his hand beginning to shake and he pulled away. Too late. Byford edged backwards, eyes flicking down and then up again, his own hand to his face, rasping at stubble.

It was a kestrel. Will could see it now, wind-hovering over the moor, holding its grey-blue head impossibly still to zero in on a vole or mouse sixty feet below. He watched it for a good half a minute, adjustments to tail and wings so minute they were invisible. Artistry, natural selection, who cared? The result was equally impressive.

He looked at the back of his hand.

Byford had got himself together now, so Will walked him down towards the cottage's expansive back garden. Silent all the way. The tension between them had reshaped itself, something new, that neither of them seemed to want to break for now.

Byford had only to say the word to Price, of course, and Will would be off the case. Not that that would be such a bad thing, but Byford's knowing of Will's problem, whatever it was, gave him power over him, and Will didn't like it.

He glanced back at the Kestrel, gone already, kill made.

Float. Take whatever comes.

Hand in pocket, he walked through the gate, turned to Byford. 'Tell DC Byrne I'm in the car, would you? Oh and…' Will pulled some crumpled sheets from his inside pocket. 'Now you know it's not Ray and Kenny, maybe treat this list a bit more seriously.'

Byford glanced at Will's hand with a thoughtful look, his mouth pursing to speak.

Will turned, headed for the car.

21

Turner was taking his time on the landing, sucking on a cigarette, as Will came up. The back stairs were a quieter way into the building, and Will was in no mood for fraternising. All the same he almost turned around and walked back down when he saw Turner. It might have been wise.

But Will kept moving, planting his feet a couple of steps below, Turner puffing up like a bullfrog and moving a step further down, probably making something of the fact it brought Will's eye-level to his chest.

'Dumb.' Will felt the adrenaline tightening his throat, vaguely aware he'd turned monosyllabic. Was he referring to Turner's position and the assumption of higher ground always lending advantage, or what he'd done to Samira, or both? He wasn't even sure.

A snorting laugh, arm swinging in towards Will, more shove than punch, more swipe than shove, but still. A school-ground tussle leer. 'Want summat, *sir*?'

Will had been a scrawny kid, with short hair that made his ears stick out, short enough to be noticed, just at that age when it's the last thing you want. But cancer was doing its thing with Mum, and Dad was preoccupied, to say the least. A once over with the clippers every few weeks from an ex-copper to whom the Beatles and the Stones might have been insects and things they hid under was the norm in the Ashcroft household.

Was the bullying because of Dad? It might have played into it. The classmates who targeted Will might have had parents who'd had some run-ins with the valley's constabulary and they might have taken it into their heads to give the ex-copper's skinny boy a hard time. Then again, they could just as easily have been middle-class boys railing against some or other perceived slight, because Will was bright even though he was scruffy. Or maybe it was just that he was smaller than them and that's the way it worked.

Will wouldn't have remembered which and it didn't matter now and it didn't matter then. What mattered was the six months

of private hell before he'd come home with a look on his face
that in one of those blessed moments that can turn a life, Dad
had noticed. He sat Will down and looked at him closely for the
first time in months.

Will had told him, in fits and starts, blubbering, mortified.
When he'd gotten his breath back, he asked the thing that
bothered him most. 'You ashamed of me, Dad?'

If anything, Dad seemed ashamed he might have played a part
in the reasons for the bullying, either by allowing Will's hair to
embarrass him, or through his ex-profession. He'd shaken his
head at the awful indignities of growing up and then he'd done
two things Will at first hated and eventually loved him for.

Will never had any more trouble from the boys in question.
Dad had waited outside school, followed them home and
'spoken' to them, 'spoken' to their parents too. What he'd said,
Will never discovered.

That wouldn't have alleviated the problem, of course;
someone else would have had a go, or Will would have just been
relegated to the ranks of loser nobody talks to for the rest of his
schooling, if not for the other thing.

Dad had a mate, Joe Farrell, an Irishman who ran a boxing
club in Spinnerby. Saturdays from then on, Will would clean
the place for Joe, sweep up, tidy up, do anything else Joe needed
doing around the place.

The genius in what Dad and Joe must have agreed on, was
that at no time was any pressure put on Will to step into the ring.
For almost the first three months, Will just got to know the kids
and older lads. The place was testosterone-heavy, but Farrell
kept it fair. No chance for bullying in a place where there's
always someone bigger and better than you, and the biggest and
best of all was Joe himself, who wasn't above teaching a lesson
to anyone stepping out of line. He rarely needed to, but
everyone knew that he might and that was enough.

When Will finally showed an interest in more than wiping
down the bags and mopping the canvas, Farrell let him spar a
little, always with someone just a little bigger and more capable.

Will would come home with bruises again. Of a different kind
though. These were educational.

Will reached out and grabbed the arm Turner had flung, throwing a two-knuckled swipe upwards into his crotch, then twisting his own body and turning him sideways, keeping him tilted as he coughed his cigarette to the floor. He edged him over the step, the bigger man's balance going, using his own weight to topple him. Turner tumbled down a few steps, Will moving with him, a push here, a kick there until he was a crumpled mess on the landing.

He brought his face level with Turner. Eyes were tight and the rugby neck was an angry red flush. Will's hand snaked down and grabbed his face, fingers dragging the head back so he had to look at him, Will's other hand poised to splinter his nose.

A low long grunt from Turner, a *no* buried somewhere in it.

Will stood, wiped his mouth with the back of his hand and walked down and out into the light.

22

'Just let me get this straight,' Samira was taking a crack at reasonable. 'You're saying there's no way of knowing for sure Ryan was in school the afternoon he went missing.'

The headmistress was generously built, every facial tick generating a ripple. 'As I told your colleague last night, Ryan's marked down on the afternoon register but it's… possible he slipped out after that.'

'How?'

'Most sessions, pupils stay in their form room with an allocated seat. But Mondays are a little trickier because they split for metalwork, PE and domestic science so –'

'Don't they take a register?'

'Yes, but…' A quick shake of the head. 'It's not infallible. I mean, these are teachers who see these kids only once a week. Big groups too. Mistakes do happen.'

'Mistakes?' Samira shook her head. 'But you've only got two black kids in the whole year, right?' She watched the eyes tighten at Samira's use of the word; never ceased to surprise her how people still thought it was the wrong word to use. 'So, how the hell could he not be missed?'

She sputtered a little. 'I… it's unfortunate.'

Samira leant forwards. 'Mrs Fletcher, when Ryan disappeared, our officers, not to mention his parents, assumed he must've been snatched from school at 3.45. You said nothing to suggest otherwise. Now, you're saying he might not have even been here after what, 2.00 pm?

A jowly nod. '1.15, most likely, if he did slip out. I'm not saying he did. But it's possible.'

'But we've got a bunch of his classmates who can't remember for sure if he was there or not for last lesson. How's that even possible?'

'Well, Ryan was a bit of a loner.'

'Was?'

Fletcher reddened, shaking her head and screwing up her nose. 'I'm sorry. Look I… I just meant that after what happened last year. You know about Brandon Conrad?'

Samira nodded.

'Ryan's been a bit withdrawn since then.'

Samira narrowed her eyes. 'Again though, that's not the impression you gave initially, is it? Not to the Press either. A popular member of the school community, great results, works hard, good attendance, star pupil.'

'That's…' Her soft face set a little. 'You can't blame us for that. You know reporters love to pigeon-hole. Ryan *is* bright, his results this year have been outstanding. But socially? That's a different story.'

Samira stared hard at her; put-upon mid-forties, baggage lugging down at eyes much younger. But more than a tint of awful awareness there too, of the seriousness of what she'd failed to disclose here. More than the head of the metalwork teacher would roll if it turned out Ryan had been snatched from somewhere other than here and the trail had grown so cold that he wasn't found as a result. Another near-seismic facial twitch, and Samira had an idea her thoughts had been read.

Samira leant in again. 'Mrs Fletcher, I'm going to ask something. Forget the board of governors, the funding council, even the Byfords for a second and think of Ryan.'

The headmistress let out a breath with the hint of a dry sigh.

'Is there one staff member here who knows these kids and what's going on with them? I don't mean grade profiles or who won the sports day. I mean the day-to day stuff they don't tell us. It might not be his form tutor. It wasn't with me.' Samira smiled. 'But there's always that one teacher who really *gets* you.'

A slow smile beating its way through the worry until her face was almost transformed. 'Sarah. You could try Sarah.'

Sarah turned out to be an English teacher. Painfully thin, likely subsisting on coffee, cigarettes and the occasional biscuit. Bleached hair cropped, dungarees, black and white striped top. Something shrewd in clear blue eyes, an angular face.

As soon as Samira mentioned Ryan's attendance on the afternoon of his disappearance, Sarah nodded and led her out to the corridor, a manila folder under her arm. They walked through the exit and took a winding path between the portacabins and up towards the cricket pavilion. 'This is how they slip out.'

No direct line of sight from classroom and staffroom windows this way, other than for a few seconds as they crossed the smaller field between the tennis and basketball courts. Even then, someone would have to have been deliberately looking to pick them out as distant specks.

Behind the pavilion, a Lilliputian village of scattered cigarette butts and coke cans, and the wall was low, scuffed and whitened in one place, the culmination of a thousand scraping shoes. Over the wall was the path down into the valley.

'I don't get it,' Samira said. 'Ryan doesn't seem the type. Grades good, shy, quietly studious. Why the skiving?'

Sarah unfolded her arms and perched on the wall, laying the folder carefully next to her and digging a crumpled pack of Marlborough Lights from her pocket. 'Mondays and Fridays probably. Metalwork and the dreaded Games.'

Samira chewed her lip. 'I used to love Games and PE.'

'You look like you would.' A smile and an admiring glance at her build that lingered just a little beyond the necessary. 'But the Ryans of this world?' She gestured at herself. 'Nerdy, different kids, we do anything to avoid it. Cross country runs, frost and snow, netball, hoping like mad you don't get picked and then dreading being left until last. Sharing a shower with a bunch of bigger, stronger, more developed kids. Bloody awful. I imagine even worse for boys. And for a black boy, one of only two in his year, of only four in the school…'

Samira swallowed. She'd had her own share of scrapes, but she'd been lucky enough to have some good teachers and to be in a school where the ethnic ratio was around 30/60. Anyway, the whole inner city vs. rural thing wasn't quite what people assumed, she thought, staring at the hillside. Ghettos might segregate but they also shape identity. Out here in the sticks, how would Ryan feel anything but the odd one out? She gave Sarah a smile. 'What do you think of his interest in the army?'

A tight grimace as she dragged on her cigarette. 'Doesn't

111

seem to fit, does it?'

'You think it was Brandon Conrad started him off?'

'Actually...' She looked down at the folder as if just remembering it was there. 'No. No, I don't. That's why I was pleased when Gwendy said you wanted to talk to me.' She invested her headmistress's name with something like pity. 'By the way, think my boss will still be my boss a week from now?'

Samira could only spread her hands.

'Hmm.' Sarah passed the opened folder to her, blushing a little as Samira got close to take it. 'I'm kind of fond of her you see. Not that she's got an inkling.'

Samira raised an eyebrow. 'Ah.'

'Married anyway.' Sarah's cropped hair glistened with gel, or whatever she used, and her blue eyes met Samira's. 'How about you, Detective Constable? Someone in your life?'

Samira glanced at their surroundings meaningfully. 'This where everyone cops off, is it?'

Another blush, eyes down.

Faintly ridiculous but Samira found herself giving some thought to an answer. 'Actually, I'm kind of in your situation, apart from the married bit. Far as I know, anyway. An officer senior to me. Complications. And he has no idea.'

'Right.' A shade of disappointment, another of camaraderie. 'Oh well.'

'So, what am I looking at here?'

'One of Ryan's creative pieces. Here.' She turned a page, traced down with a close-bitten fingernail. 'There. This bit, particularly.'

We reached Mount Longdon and the Argies hadn't spotted us. Then someone stepped on an AT Mine. Flashes, noise, mortar fire. I ran. Winding between shrapnel. Lost my section. My company too.

I found some cover. Don't know who I was next to. Someone from some other section. He whispered, 'I can see an Argie behind that bloody rock.'

I crawled around the rock, icy cold biting my knees and elbows. I found my spot. Shot him. A few times. Maybe five.

Maybe six times.

There's something about a body on the ground that tells you it's dead. I got closer. Just a kid. Catholic. Christopher's medal. Some poor Argentinian kid who'd done nothing to me, pissing his pants.

I don't regret it, though.

It just surprised me how easy it was. At the time, anyway.

Since then, it hasn't been so easy. Remembering it, I mean. Even when I don't want to. Like in the middle of the night or when I'm talking to someone or walking down the road or sitting on a bus or anything. And then I'm back there... fire from every side... voices of the dying... Argies and our boys... no difference... screaming for help... screaming for their mums... or just screaming... screaming... screaming...

All part of the game.

And the game goes on.

Samira had to read it again. Then she sat on the wall next to Sarah. 'Wow!'

'Yeah.'

'Twelve years old. Writing like that.'

'Eleven, when he wrote that. In terms of craft, he's a prodigy.'

Samira frowned. 'What about the content? Where did he get that from?'

'Yeah, that's the thing, isn't it?' She nodded.

Samira had a sudden flash of Will and his shaking hand. 'It's the attitude. The insight. From an eleven-year-old you'd expect something...' She couldn't think of the term.

'Boy's own?' Sarah deepened her voice and punched the air.

'Yeah. War's great, chocks away, all that stuff. But this –'

Sarah nodded. 'It's about war as it really is. And someone who's been traumatised by it.'

Samira sucked at her teeth. Five years since the conflict, virtually nothing in papers or TV she could remember about soldiers suffering. So where had a twelve-year-old picked up that idea? 'Did you ask him if he'd based it on anyone real?'

An uneasy shrug. 'He said he had an uncle who was a veteran.'

'But now you're not sure the uncle is for real, right?'

'Well, *is* he?'

Doubtful, from the profile of the family she had so far. Samira looked at the page again. 'We'll look into it.'

An unsteady breath from Sarah. 'I'm sorry. I should've…' She shook her head. 'I mean, if I thought he'd been abused or anything, I would've acted on it. Just a brilliant piece of writing from a boy thinking beyond his years, I thought. But then, last few days, I started wondering. So, I showed it to one of your lot and –'

'Hang on. You mean you've already showed this to an officer?'

Sarah blinked. 'Yeah. That WPC… Clarke, is it? She didn't seem that impressed.'

Clarke. Samira had talked to her a couple of times. She was a bit of a plodder. She'd probably not looked past the fact that it was a well-written story. *Gold-star* and *double ticks!* Samira shook her head.

'I was thinking of showing it to that other copper. That DI. Looks like he has some imagination, maybe.'

Samira put a hand over her smile.

'Oh. Right.'

They both laughed, Samira shaking her head, back in a time where boys, clothes and make-up were the only conversation worth having. It felt good.

'It's alright Detective Constable. Your secret's safe with me.'

She held up the file. 'Can I take this?'

'Sure.' Sarah's smile dropped away. 'I've kept copies of all his work. He's my best.'

The sun broke through and the field lightened as they stepped out from behind the pavilion, the kind of unexpected prelude to summer that belts out promise and renewal. But Samira found herself wondering if Ryan Byford, wherever he was, could feel its sudden warmth or ever would again.

Enright punched the bench. 'I still can't believe this. One of the others must've answered to his name.'

'I doubt it.' Will looked at Samira, and then back at the large-framed man in the grey overalls. 'He's not exactly mister popular, we're hearing. Wouldn't have thought anyone would stick their neck out for him.'

'No.' Enright grunted. 'They'd do it just to wind me up, little bastards.' He shook his head again and flailed out at the bench a second time. 'This'll have me out of a ruddy job.'

Will stared at him. 'When we've finished here, we'll join the rest of the officers from Spinnerby, along with fifty more regionals who've been drafted in to cover the area between here and the canal. An area we'd thought was irrelevant. We'll be at it until dark. Tomorrow, too, always supposing we don't find anything.' His tone was icy, just a hint of heat cracking the floes. 'So, to be honest, your job security's not exactly top of my list of concerns.'

Enright had straightened and was very still, arms drawn in by his sides.

There was just the touch of a smile on Samira's lips. 'Mr Enright. There are only two black boys in the year. Surely, it would have been difficult to miss Ryan not being here.'

Enright had paled. His chin bobbed a few times like a throttle-pedal before his voice finally caught. 'I must have…' He looked away. 'The other coloured lad. He was in, but quite often he wouldn't be. I must have looked around and… look, sometimes it's too rushed and they're all shouting and… I don't always actually call names, I just must have mistook him for Ryan.'

Samira was staring at him. 'So, we all look alike. That it?'

His head was down now, shaking from side to side.

She glanced at Will and cleared her throat.

Will spoke through gritted teeth. 'I was going to ask what Ryan's like in class when he *is* in. But if you're not sure who he is…'

'No, I mean I… know who he is now I've had time to think

about it.' Enright shook his head, perched on his bench. 'You know the kind of kid. Not very good at practical stuff. Happier with his nose in a book. Couldn't solder for the life of him, couldn't use a file properly, hopeless with a drill.'

Will's head was starting to pound again. 'So, you just let him melt into the corners? Embarrass him occasionally by showing everyone when he'd messed up his work? That sort of thing?'

Enright's eyes darted away. 'No. I tried to get him interested.'

Yeah, how hard, though? Will could feel his hand beginning to do its thing. He glanced at the window. It was quiet now, the sound of the playground muted by plasterboard and distance. He turned so his hand was out of sight. He'd already felt Samira clocking it, of course, but he just carried on staring out the window.

He heard her cough, about to ask something, when Enright spoke. 'There was one time when he showed some interest.' He nodded at the window, walked towards it, Samira and then Will following. 'Back when the new block was being built. Must be a year and a half ago.'

The brickwork was neat, the grouting pristine against the pointed rooves and railings of the Victorian building it was grafted onto like a new limb, functional, no thought to aesthetics. Still, in a few years, it would look as dark and awful as the rest. Or was he projecting? He winced at the daylight, glancing at Enright. 'What happened?'

'He'd been spending breaks and lunchtimes hanging around the builders. Gwendy asked me to monopolise, you know. See if he had any inclination towards technical drawing. So, I tried.' He shook his head. 'Not a glimmer.'

Will was trying to picture Ryan developing a sudden passion for construction. Could it fit with the army thing?

Enright was laughing. 'To be honest, I think it might've been the builders he was more interested in. Know what I –?' Will tightened his eyes and Enright's face was suddenly straight. 'Even if he did, like, whatever turns your crank, I suppose. I just –'

'Okay. Let's stick to the facts.' He let out a breath. Minus the bigotry, it was possible Enright had nailed it; worth checking which building firm the school had hired, he supposed. Ryan could've gotten friendly with one of them, or even developed a crush, but then what? Over a year later, the builder had decided to abduct Ryan? He shook his head. 'Anything else to tell us, Mr Enright?'

'No.' His chin was crumpled. 'I'll be out there too, you know, along with most of the staff. I mean, you lot have asked for volunteers, right?'

Will glanced at Samira and they headed for the door. 'Yeah. I'm sure Ryan's family will be very grateful.' He gave a last hard-eyed look at the metalwork teacher standing in his little empire of hammers, drills and metal files.

They were out through the main doors. Car-rooves and windshields gleaming in neat rows. He stopped near the Sierra a few seconds, jiggling his keys. 'Fucking unbelievable!' He muttered. He glanced at Samira, let out a breath.

'Negligent at best, I reckon.' She smirked. 'The other stuff… just the same old story.'

He nodded. The same crap she must have to put up with every day.

He leant on the car, a sudden idea brightening. 'Let's walk the route from here.' He glanced at his watch, other hand still quivering as he pushed up his sleeve. 'We can join everyone else, spread across the fields, get a lift back up here later, pick up the car. What do you say?'

One of the younger staff was passing; dungarees and striped top, short spiky bleached hair. Art teacher? She smiled at Samira and covered her grinning mouth with a hand. She didn't look at Will at all.

'That's Sarah.' Samira informed him.

'Oh. Okay.'

Samira looked at the ground, a smirk in place that he couldn't quite fathom. 'Yeah, I'm game, boss. About the walk, I mean. Let's go.'

They reached the pavilion and Samira stepped up onto the wall, Will joining her. He glanced at the field across the road at the narrow public footpath down through the trees into the valley. 'That snicket?'

She nodded and they jumped down onto the pavement and crossed. The old snicket was muddy, slippery at the best of times, Will remembered. Cobbles and flags mossy and badly kept, drystone walls on either side cutting down the hillside, to come out at the main road where you could slip through the factory carpark and down towards the canal. That would have been Ryan's route, chances were. But it was surrounded by fields and waste-ground further down, and every inch would need to be covered.

Again, there was a cold churn of anger in Will's guts. The school. Enright, the headmistress, the rest of Ryan's class as well. A balls-up that no one had sussed it sooner.

They had to watch their footing, but Will kept scanning the surrounding field where the wall and high grass allowed. Blue kagoule, navy school blazer and grey trousers. Drab, but at least the kagoule might stand out a little from grass, stones and scrub. 'Nothing doing.' He said it aloud just as he felt his boot slide and he put out a hand. She gripped it.

'Okay, boss?'

He nodded, drew back a little. It was his offending hand, the one she'd quietened with a touch last night. It was still now, but anyway he double-checked it.

'What's happening with Ray and Kenny, then?' She said it lightly, as if she'd wanted to say something else.

'Price is nursing the pervert angle on Ray and hoping Byford will change his tune and press charges on Kenny.' He glanced at her, shook his head.

'So, they'll be out by tomorrow.'

Will angled his head towards the valley bottom. The search would cover the area around the caravan and maybe, just maybe there'd be something. More than ever though, his gut told him the Macfarlanes were an unpleasant distraction and nothing more. He looked at her. 'There's always the attack on Mr Ramir. You can still nail Kenny for that.'

'Thing I don't get is, he has a perfect little set-up with the tower block. Why break cover? Beating an Asian shopkeeper into intensive care?'

Will stopped and scoured the slopes again. This whole area would be full of uniforms in an hour, but sometimes, you never know. Just a glint of something would be a gift. They stood for at least five minutes.

Nothing.

They walked again and he let his thoughts come back to Little Kenny, rolling over what Byford had told him. He told Samira some of it, the narcissistic personality disorder diagnosis. 'What if Kenny can't help himself? With the Byfords it was about being affiliated, apparently. Maybe it's the same with Mr Ramir. Don't ask me how, but in some weird way it could be about status.'

They'd reached the bottom of the ginnel and Samira sidestepped through the turnstile. She was lip-chewing, walking faster now they were off the cobbles. She turned and gave him a grin and a single word. 'Interesting.'

'By the way, I never really got your take on Cathy Byford.'

'Hmm.' She screwed up her face. 'Tricky one, alright. Can't decide whether she's living in absolute terror of her husband –'

'Or she's got him wrapped round her pinkie, right?'

She nodded.

'What about her reactions to all this? As a woman, mother to an adopted child.'

She pinched her lip again. 'Yeah. Something off. About both of them.'

'Think it goes beyond the fact Ryan's adopted? Not blood. I mean, I'd hate to think they're going through the motions and don't actually give that much of a shit he's missing.'

She shrugged. 'I think they're both hurting alright. Just not showing it.'

He nodded. Of course, it was one of the first things they taught you; people under stress don't always act like they're supposed to. But still, the Byfords seemed to be taking it to another level.

The factory grounds were close now and they walked to the edge of the bordering field. It was a natural vantage point; from here they'd be able to see the whole of the valley basin. Samira's body was taut against her medium length leather

119

jacket and slacks as she hoisted herself easily up onto the fence and peered over. Will dragged himself up beside her with nothing like her grace.

He swept the fields for Ryan's blue kagoule. It was a good few minutes before either of them spoke.

'Here we go!' He pointed at the field to the left of the canal; dark figures moving on the grass, bobbies' helmet-badges glistening like ant-armour. Maybe it was despite what they were about to be engaged in, or maybe exactly because of it, but Will suddenly knew he was looking at the wrong thing. He turned instead to the woman next to him.

Her tied-back hair was whipping in the wind, and he wondered what it would look like loose and wild against her tawny skin. Side on, her focused face seemed open and hopeful. She felt his gaze and turned. He coughed. 'When we're done here, I think we need a drink, you and me. To wind down and…' He stopped, aware he was about to blow it.

'Okay. Just not *the Lion*. Anywhere but there.' The nick's local, where Price and all the rest would crawl off to as soon as it was too dark to search anymore. It was the last place Will would have chosen anyway.

He got himself down and gave her a hand off the fence. She was close, her smile open, eyes playing with him like two sassy children.

Not the time. Not the time at all. He willed his mind back into neutral. Glanced up again: she was smiling still, but then she stifled a long yawn.

'Late one?'

She shook her head. 'Today was supposed to be my afternoon off. First in a few weeks –'

'Well, make sure you take it back.' He was trying not to sound patronising. 'With these types of cases, the frustration's unlike anything else.'

She nodded. 'I've only just started on this case though.'

'Doesn't matter. Take time where you can. Trust me.'

'Whatever you say, boss.'

They headed into the field, the thought of spending time with her lifting something from him. Even with what they were about

120

to be engaged in here, even if it seemed he couldn't get through a few hours without a shaking hand or losing twenty minutes here and there, he suddenly felt glad to be alive.

24

Dream on.

An hour into the search and Will was leaning, forehead to a tree, muscles in spasm. He was pushing hard, bark digging into his skin to meet the bone, the search-whistle out of his pocket but dropped somewhere, images of fox-torn remnants of clothing and flesh so putrid it was black littering the ground around him, so real he'd had to step round it, sweet offal colonising the mucous of his nostrils.

But it couldn't have, because it wasn't there.

But it had. Because it was.

His auto-pilot self, that part of him, remembered that the integrity of the search for Ryan Byford depended on everyone staying within range of eye-contact, so sooner or later, someone would raise the alarm and double back. Hopefully Samira. Even as he thought it, the shrill sound of a whistle off to his left. Then more distant whistles spreading outward like answering crickets, and that was it… the last of his awareness of now… of reality, being crushed down into himself… small body parts in chewed clothing all he could see or smell.

The vaguest awareness of a cool hand on his neck, of being drawn away from the trees now, walkie-talkie crackle as he stared at the grass around his feet. She had an arm under his shoulders.

Movement, her touch, seeming to bring him out of it a little, his head clanging like an emptied drain, only the occasional burst of imagery as they moved, and with a bleached quality now, no longer so convincing, so intrusive. But his body, still tensing constantly, like his muscles weren't his at all, flexing, flexing, that fight or flight charge running through them; couldn't switch it off, just couldn't.

They had to stop. Standing again, her hands rubbing at his rigid back.

How long?

On the move again.

Two figures near the treeline, one large and hulking, rugby neck and round ears. Turner looking at him and glancing away. But then Turner looking again, a new boldness and the slightest smile winking at the corners of his mouth. A coldness in the pit of Will's stomach. If Turner wanted a rematch, he was in no state to handle him.

Grundy's yellowed teeth forming words... something... about a dead rabbit?

Will's eyes were down; the ground in front of him, the detritus still there. Samira had his arm again.

They were at the gate, and through onto the road.

Two officers had just stepped out of a red and white Fiesta and Samira straightened, walked over to them. No inkling of what she was telling them, Will staring down at the gravel, flashes of offal still making it a patchwork of flecks. He looked up, blinking, as one of the officers passed her something, then both headed for the search with all the enthusiasm of condemned men. She jingled keys, walked around to the driver's side.

'... Grundy say...? Rabbit...?' His tongue was thick like a slug.

She was staring at him from the driver's seat and he wondered how long they'd been sitting there. Was the sky darker? Maybe. Then, with a jolt, he realised they were at the top of the valley, outside his father's... outside *his* house. Giddiness, like he'd just been picked up and dropped somewhere, and he put a hand to his mouth. How much time had he lost, this time?

She frowned, blinking, glancing at him sideways. 'Grundy assumed it was me that was sick. That I'd seen a dead rabbit or something. That *you* were helping *me* off the search.'

'Oh.' Was there relief in his tone? He wasn't sure. His body and head were a solid mass of pain now as his muscles loosened again, but he saw her stiffen. 'Sorry...'

She covered her eyes with long fingers for a few seconds and then her head snapped up. 'Right. I've had it with this. You refuse to go to the hospital...'

Had he?

'You want me to cover for you, and that's fine. You want me to make myself look incompetent in the process, well, I'm probably even dumb enough to do that as well.' She shook her head as if not quite able to believe her own words. 'But not if you don't level with me!'

He frowned, licked his lips.

She sighed, passing him a bottle of water. He took a drink and worked his tongue around his mouth. 'I've …brought you… up to speed on –'

'Not the case, Will! You!' She slapped her palm on the steering wheel.

He lowered his head, the now pouring back in around him. A sense of dread along with it, a sudden clarity, and memory, normal memory, of his last few months in London and the north.

He'd told no one, not in full. His superiors at AMIP hadn't even known all of it. And there'd been no one in his life close enough to give a shit; no, that wasn't the whole truth. He'd avoided getting close to anyone for months. How many people had he had a meaningful interaction with since he'd been back in the north, for instance? He could count them on the fingers of one hand, if it stayed still long enough. He'd withdrawn himself, avoided friends, family. Hadn't even had a beer with anyone at the nick in Leeds.

He looked at Samira's strong face. She'd be loyal. He wasn't worried about that. Could he talk to her? To anyone. But especially her, because… he liked her. Really did. Time to admit that, he thought.

'Will…' She let out a breath, the heat draining from her tone with it. 'When you talked to me the other day in the canteen… do you know what you were doing with your hands?' She demonstrated, pinching the fingers of one with those of the other. 'It's like you were making sure you were still there.'

He swallowed in a dry throat. He hadn't even been aware.

The silence hung there at least twenty seconds.

She put her fingers on the ignition key and looked at him meaningfully. 'I'm going back to the search, DI Ashcroft.'

He found his voice at last. 'This case won't turn on fifty coppers walking in a field.'

She frowned. 'Maybe not. But it's hard enough for me, the crap I take from Grundy and Turner and the rest. I don't need another excuse for them to put me on traffic.' She chewed her lip. 'I don't think you're in any shape for our drink tonight, and to be honest, maybe it's not a good idea anyway. But when you're ready to talk, maybe I'll still want to listen.' She turned the key, glanced at the passenger door.

Will stepped out.

He watched her pull away, certain he'd just said goodbye to a layer of his soul.

25

The scattered body parts had been a memory from a few weeks after the pool. That was the thing. For the first time a rabid storming of his senses from a time other than the stinking pool where he'd found the Havilland boy. Instead, three months ago, give or take, when James Edward Creasey had finally disclosed the location of the other children he'd abducted. The shallow ground of the disused train station near Chipping Ongar that had given up the first of its secrets by late morning.

Will had been present at the uncovering of murder victims before, of course. The smell was indescribable. Even after six months, bodies left under a few feet of earth would give off an odour, once uncovered, strong enough to knock you back. He always carried a stick of Vicks vapour rub and smeared some on his upper lip. It helped, but not much.

That day, it hadn't at all. He'd lost his deliberately light breakfast around the back of the old station toilets along with most everyone else on scene apart from one or two of the SOCOs. Then, he'd got back to it.

By 3.00, he'd had enough of Creasey's world for one day, the SOCOs would get along fine without him. The shallow grave and undergrowth had not protected what was possibly the corpse of 7-year-old Samantha Redditch from elements or small animals and the drive back to London with his DCI in London, Shelby, had been possibly the quietest 40 minutes he'd ever shared with another human being.

Later, standing in his flat, the smell was stuck on him even though he'd showered and changed twice. Armed with music he couldn't hear, whiskey he couldn't taste, Will had gamely soldiered on; just get through the night, he'd told himself. It'll fade. It'll all fade. Just like the pool.

And it had faded, sort of, to another *something* he just didn't look at. Until today, when the search for Ryan Byford had dragged it out into the light. That same terrible sense of futility, that this was a world where people could reduce the spirit and lightness of a child's life to truncated body parts in cold ground. Where these things actually happened and yet we carried on with our lives, as if anything could ever be important again.

Will looked at the bathroom mirror in his father's house.

This... all of this.

Killing his heart.

He gave himself one last glare and fumbled at his pocket for the plastic sealed essay Samira had given him. He'd scanned over it already, but no more than that. He moved through to the bedroom, his father's bedroom this time, his muscles like jelly, lugging them onto the bed. He read it slowly, forcing everything else from his mind but the neat blue ink between the faint black lines of foolscap.

He reached the last two lines and tightened his eyes, reading again just to be sure. His senses, after all, were hardly infallible these days. He lowered it, stared at the wall.

It was tenuous at best. The 'game' Ryan mentioned could be a creative twelve-year-old's figure of speech. But Will couldn't stop his thoughts going back to Peter Smiles.

He'd slept a few hours. The pain in his body and head had numbed a little, but he was far from back to normal. The phone to his ear was alien. A gauze of unreality was draped over the room like a camouflage blanket.

He shut his eyes, tried to remember how to talk. Face-to-face would have been harder though, somehow; requiring more connection. Small mercies. He cleared his throat, took some breaths and dialled.

'It's... Ashcroft. Anything?'

Byford's voice was fatigued. 'I've been through all past private clients, listened to session tapes. Nothing. Few have abusive histories, anyway. Impotence, inferiority complexes and general depression mostly.'

Sounded like the entire senior constabulary. Will fumbled for Byford's first name. 'Sean. Try and... forget Ryan's your son... a minute.' Tricky, balancing what he had to say with the live-wire tension humming between them. 'You know, well as I do... child goes missing, everyone thinks... perverts... so on.'

A tight swallow.

'Coppers are the worst... me...' A sudden flash of what he'd seen earlier in the field. He closed his eyes. 'No exception. But… what if this… isn't anything like that?'

A long breath. 'Christ, I hope.'

'Doesn't mean Ryan's not in danger.' Will massaged his jaw. 'Point is… you're not just looking for abuse histories but anyone who… could've had it in for you. For any reason.'

Quiet again. A stretched yawn of it. Then Byford coughed. 'You don't sound too good, Inspector.'

At last. They'd got to it. Okay.

Will took out his hand, laid it on the table, studied it, front and back. 'This may sound stupid, but what is it? What do I have?'

'Hmm.' Byford's tone was unreadable. Strange country they were heading into and he felt it too, Will thought. 'You have other symptoms? Memories intruding? Feelings of danger?'

'Yes.'

'Some might say PTSD related.'

'Thought that's something American soldiers get.'

'That's the common view. But *some* of my colleagues believe it can happen to anyone.'

'You don't agree?'

Byford's Voice was tight as a snare suddenly. 'Well it's in the literature now. The DSM III. Sorry. I mean the *Diagnostic and Statistical Manual of Mental Health Disorders*, though that's the US's bible really. Most of us in England pay more heed to the World Health Organisation's ICD. Look if you want to talk about it, it's not my field but I'm sure I could –'

'No.' Byford's barrage of jargon had said it all really. He was sure he could what? Condescend to keep an open mind when clearly he didn't have one? Will let out a breath, actually inclining his neck a little, picturing Byford holding a sword above it. Time to grab it off him and slice through the bullshit. 'If you want me off this case…' *Case* sounded wrong. 'Your *son*. Just say the word.'

Quiet. Maybe ten seconds of it. Finally, Byford sniffed, voice heavy. 'I do know this. People with all kinds of problems manage to carry on, with some adjustments. You and Constable Byrne, I want you both looking for Ryan. I think if anyone can find him…' The sentence trailed off like a broken streamer and despite everything, Will found himself trying like hell to think of something reassuring to tell this man. But what was in his mind wouldn't have done the trick at all.

Something's got to give, he thought. Just one thing, somewhere. Before I do.

Part 2: AVOIDANCE

26

The nurse was pretty, or would have been if not for the tiredness. Late twenties. Strawberry blonde. Freckled arms.

Maddie gave a quick wave from the doorway. 'Okay. Karen, this is Samira. Samira, Karen. I'll leave you to it. Drinks soon, yeah?'

Samira nodded, watching her old Manchester college mate swish back out into the busy hospital corridor, all blue and white fabric and black tights, clipboard in hand. Samira glanced at the Triage sign and the small room they were in. Maddie would be pushing it, letting them have use of the room, even for a few minutes. Samira turned to Karen. 'Hi.'

'Maddie says you're a copper!'

'Yeah, a DC. Not here about anything official though. Actually, it's my morning off.'

'Can't remember the last one o' them I had.' A pleasant enough smile.

'Okay, Karen. Don't want to waste your time. One of my colleagues... has a problem.' As succinctly as she could, she detailed what she knew of Will's condition, which wasn't much; shaking hand, vivid intruding memories and a reluctance to talk about it.

Karen sat on the desk's edge, legs kicking, glancing at her watch. 'Okay. Got about three minutes before I start my rounds. Here's what I know. If he's got what my hubby's got... my ex-hubby, that is, then I pity him. And you, if you're... involved.' A questioning glance.

Samira shrugged, asking herself again why she was even here, making enquiries on behalf of a man she barely knew and who probably wouldn't thank her for it. She looked at the overworked nurse. When she'd thought of asking Maddie if she knew of anyone with any knowledge of Will's symptoms, she'd been expecting she might suggest a specialist, not a colleague with personal experience.

'Okay,' Karen said. 'First off, when they have flashes, they're not just memories. It's like they're there again, reliving it, whatever *it* is, and they can't just switch it off. Then there's the

131

other stuff. Does he get like there's… danger around him, like paranoia? Or like he's watching himself, making sure he's still there?'

She thought of the finger pinching thing. Nodded.

'Has he talked about it to anyone?'

'Don't know.' Samira shrugged. 'He won't tell me anything.'

Karen gave her a smile. 'Don't be too hard on him. The weird thing is, even though they relive it, there's whole chunks they can't remember. Important bits too. And they get really good at avoiding what they *can* remember. Not all their fault, I reckon.'

Samira suddenly felt like a bitch. 'Well, we've got people he could talk to.'

Karen was laughing, bitterness not far under it. 'Would you go to your bosses and basically admit you're cracking up?'

'But it's not like that, is it? I mean –'

'It's classed as mental illness.'

Samira thought of a sergeant in Manchester who'd had time off with stress a few years ago. How long had he lasted? Six months at the outside. Not fired, just eased out. The consensus was he just wasn't cut out for the job. She nodded to herself. Copper's culture. Maybe even worse out here in the sticks. Not that different to the army, probably. She looked at Karen. 'Your ex, was he in the Falklands?'

'Ireland first.' A sad smile. 'Tell the truth, I think his problems went way back, anyway. Childhood. Falklands sure helped, though.'

'Did he find help?'

'Got some counselling, eventually. Useless, he said. By then, he was drinking like a fish, anyway. They treated that like a cause instead of a symptom.' She flashed a smile without warmth. 'The military! It's like they don't want to admit it exists. Want it all swept away.' She sighed, straightening her uniform. 'He'd have good days and bad. Bad days, he couldn't move, couldn't talk. Went far away. Really far away.' She raised her left hand, wiggled an empty ring-finger. 'In the end, I got out.'

Samira stood and Karen slipped off the table, eyeing her

watch.

'Thanks.'

'For what?' She moved for the door, then stopped. 'Is it early on, for your guy?'

'Think so.'

Her face straightened. 'Then get him to face it. Whatever it is. And talk about it. Sooner the better. And can I give you one more piece of advice?'

Samira nodded.

'Don't fall for him.'

She shook her head. 'He's just –'

Karen glanced at the wall clock. 'Your day off and you're here at half nine in the morning, for a workmate. Doesn't take a detective, Detective.' She shook her head, smiled, and held the door for Samira. 'Good luck.'

That was it, Samira decided. The rest of the morning was hers; she was going to relax if it killed her. She went home, packed her things for the sauna, not even having to resist the temptation to click on the radio in the car. Well, not much.

She'd thought of heading over to Manchester, seeing Mum and Dad. She tightened her eyes, shook her head. It was like all she wanted, even now, was sodding approval.

The sauna usually sorted her out; the mass of heat purging her skin, a plunge and a swim to tire her muscles, pushing her body and letting her mind float free, until finally walking out into the crisp air, a layer of stress sloughed away.

Not today.

For a while, it worked its usual magic. But then, somehow, that sense of ease was just that little bit out of reach; the sauna too sticky, the pool area too cloying, her muscles straining, her mind not allowing itself to be emptied.

Will?

It wasn't just about him, though. She wasn't so far gone. She kicked herself a little for how she'd reacted yesterday, true. But put next to the problems of the Byfords, it paled.

That was the thing though. Here she was, swimming and mooning over her DI, when a twelve-year-old boy was out there somewhere. In distress, or far worse. She suddenly swept to the side of the pool and surged out of the water, attracting more than a couple of looks from an oldish couple, disapproving, and some young exec types, quite the opposite.

Screw them all. She padded to the changing rooms and stuck her head under the dryer.

The air was all cold prickling drizzle and she felt better as she headed for her car. Coffee, something to eat, she thought. Somewhere nice. She threw her bag in the back seat, absently flicking the receiver on. Might as well have a listen, see if there were any developments.

It was the tail end of a message. WPC Clarke was stressed by the sound of it, dithering away from call-protocol. '… if anyone can advise. Anyway, I'll stay put here. Just thought I'd ask. Over.' Samira seemed to remember Clarke was on house-sitting duty, keeping an eye on the Byfords. She glanced up the hill, towards the leafy suburbs of Gallerton; as alien to this end of town as a spinning moon, but one whose orbit was close. In fact, she figured, she'd make it there before anyone else.

WPC Clarke looked frayed; fidgeting in front of her red and white Fiesta. The bird-like tower beyond the Byfords' cottage just to the right of her head seemed to be about to dip its beak in judgement.

'I've messed up.'

Samira said nothing, hands open.

'Don't know where she's gone. Mrs Byford.'

'Well, it's not exactly house arrest, is it?'

Clarke was pretty, and she seemed to try and use a little of that now, fluttering. 'I know. But DI Ashcroft said he wanted eyes on both Byfords. Nothing official but…' She winced a little.

A domestic officer assigned to stay close to the Byfords was standard procedure. But Will had clearly decided to up Clarke's remit a little. Samira tried not to make a face. She could have told him Clarke wasn't up to it. 'So, what happened?'

'She asked me to… to get some milk.'

Samira felt her eyes widening. 'You did some shopping for her?'

'I know I shouldn't have –'

'Well, you could've taken her with you.'

'She was so nice about it. I couldn't say no. I was only gone five minutes. I got back from the village and varmoosh!'

'Was she driving?'

A nod. 'Green Mini.'

Samira held up her hands. 'Okay. Let's get this in perspective. She's free to go wherever she wants and if she needs some time away from us –'

'Why? I've only been sitting out here, apart from when she's invited me in or if I've had messages to pass to her. Keeping those bloody vultures off, mostly…' She glanced over at a couple of cars further up the hill. Press, a skeleton group now compared to yesterday. 'I haven't been bugging her.'

'But it's still intrusive, isn't it? I mean, Christ knows what she's going through.'

Clarke was pouting. 'But she was so friendly, so nice. Then suddenly she slipped away. It's like she planned it.'

'She'll probably come back after a little spin… just wanted some breathing space. But I'll check around anyway.' She glanced at the Press. 'Hey, you didn't talk to *them*, did you?'

'No way. I'm not a total numpton.' Some relief in the pout now. 'Thanks, Samira. Owe you one.'

Actually two, Samira thought, if you count me not telling anyone about you missing the importance of Ryan Byford's little creative piece. But at least Clarke hadn't given the journos any headlines. She could see it: MISSING RYAN'S MUM GIVES PLOD THE RUNAROUND. Of course, they would have seen Cathy take off, no doubt the reason there were so few cars here; she'd probably left with a good few shadowing her.

On the bright side, Samira thought, about to trot over to the car, Cathy's Green Mini might be easier to spot with a cavalcade behind it.

'By the way…' Clarke was smiling. 'I like your taste.'

Samira shook her head. 'Uhh?'

A glance around, like anyone would hear them. 'Ashcroft. Well doable, I reckon.'

'What you talking about?'

'Come on, Samira. Why else would he have given Turner a going over?'

'Turner?'

A snigger. 'The big bastard's been walking like a cowboy since yesterday. Like he's had a good kick in the bollocks. He deserves it, anyway. Leaving you on that rooftop. Been laughing about it, Grundy even more.' She did a head-shaking tutting thing and then brightened. 'Still. You have your protector now, right? No one'll touch you. As long as you keep him happy.'

Samira was reeling, couldn't process. She was back to the car and in, no eye-contact with Clarke. No point saying anything. Different worlds. Different languages. But her fingers tightened on the wheel as she pulled away and she let out a groan that might just have shut Clarke up, if she'd heard it. It was hard to know who to be more pissed off at; Clarke, Turner, Grundy. The whole bloody station.

Or Will.

Samira had checked the file for Cathy's workplace. Dawson and Whilby's legal offices were in the centre, just off Market street. But she was so busy chewing over all the crap Clarke had spouted, she hardly noticed the commotion spreading out from the bend in the road near the canal until she was amongst it. She lowered the window and took it in, then pulled into a side street and straddled some double-yellows; from what she'd seen, this was starting to qualify as an emergency.

She took off at a jog, back around the corner. Traffic moved in fits and starts. There were knots of people staring at the green Mini squatting at the water's edge. Its back end was lifted, its headlights and grille saved from a dip by the barrier. A uniform or two were on their walkies; likely just arrived. A traffic warden was shaking his head. Samira flashed her card. 'You see it?'

A nod. 'Just cut out, right across the road, oncoming traffic, down to the canal. Could have bloody killed herself. And anyone else in her way.'

'Where is she?'

A shrug. 'She ran! Shot out of the car, down the towpath. Must've had a meltdown!'

Samira's thought of her one meeting with Cathy, Yesterday. Frail, on the surface, a little ditzy, a more upmarket version of Clarke, really, the kind of thing a lot of men would go weak at the knees and other areas for. But underneath, more to her, Samira had thought. A buried hardness, like flint in cotton wool.

She glanced again at the gathered crowd. There were a couple of expensive looking cameras and a few notepads. Press. She pictured it; Cathy's Mini roaring out and bumping over the traffic island's edge. The reporters drifting down with the flotsam of traffic to the end of the road before they found anywhere to stop. There was nowhere they could have jumped out and given chase. By the time they'd sorted themselves out, Cathy would have been off down that towpath.

Like she'd decided to lose them. But where had she gone?

Samira slung a look at the towpath. It led out of town, towards the Craven Estate. But then she turned, eyes scanning the footbridge and along the opposite path. An indirect route, but Dawson and Whilby's office was close. Three minutes at a jog, she figured.

Her guts tightened as she shouldered her way through the crowd. Cathy Byford had wanted away from a bunch of reporters badly enough to risk totalling her car and herself. If none of them had worked out that the offices where she worked as legal secretary were just around the corner, maybe they deserved it.

Samira waited until she was out of their sight to start running towards the office blocks. Something was happening here. Something important.

27

Will took the right fork from the Leeds road over the tops, back towards the valley.

The last of the listed names from Sean Byford had been a non-starter; two had died, three were in prison, three more still sectioned, and the rest had solid alibis. Interesting that despite everything Will had said about the non-sex-offender angle, six turned out to have been convicted or suspected of sexual offences, four involving minors. Once he'd cross-referenced with Price's roster of local offenders who'd already been pulled in and questioned, Will had spent the day chasing them up.

Spending time sifting through sad little lives was what he did, but being in the same room as the last one, whose only saving grace was his ability to recognise his sickness though not do anything about it, had made Will feel like his brain had been invaded by a million scuttling insects.

So, Byford's list had drawn an unmitigated blank, and the blank was somehow spreading under Will's nerves like a virus. Doubt, seeping in. Maybe this whole line of enquiry was off. Byford's being a Psychiatrist had seemed like it could be the root of some revenge motive, but no reason it had to be. No reason at all, other than Will having wanted it to be.

He let out a single curse muted by the drone of the engine. Why had he pinned so much on it?

Creasey. That was why. He just hadn't wanted... no, couldn't stand... to believe it was another child-killer. Some sick little bastard scurrying around, reshaping the world into the putrid image boiling away in his head. But why shouldn't it be? The simplest answer, after all. Occam's Razor and all that.

Another answer, darker, more personal, making his guts churn over; maybe he was just not seeing things clearly because... because... come on, Will, say it... *because you're cracking up!*

That it?

The car-radio crackled to life as he crested the highest point of the valley wall on the Bradford road; various voices, a traffic build-up and repercussions of some earlier incident in Spinnerby. Will tuned it out and tried to concentrate on his driving, something he was more than a little conscious of given his present state. He'd almost reached the turn off for the valley basin when a different voice cut through the static.

Tango Alpha. Samira, giving her location as Shockley Beck, the old orphanage. It was more specific than that, he realised, as her message ended. 'Can Whisky One-Five please deal? Incident is regarding *Willow*, over.'

Willow was the code-word for Ryan Byford. A bit theatrical but necessary. Some of the wilier Press made no bones about tuning into police signals. Will grabbed the handset. 'This is Whisky One-Five, received. What's the situation, over?' He waited ten seconds for a reply. Nothing but crackle.

Will spun the car into a barely legal turn and put his foot down.

28

The receptionist might have just been doing her job. Maybe she was even doing it well. But Samira was getting tired of her. 'Look. Either Cathy Byford's been in here in the last ten minutes or she hasn't. Which is it?'

'Mr Dawson will be out in a moment, I'm sure.' There was a light wrinkle of her nose and her lips turned down.

Samira leant on the desk so she could see the receptionist's pad, the obligatory photo, husband, two kids. Safe, ordered. She leant in further, put her hand on her wrist, the contrast between the hues of their skin stark in the office light. A flinch, a nervous smile.

'You probably think you're protecting your colleague, but actually you're being obstructive.'

'I... don't know what you –'

A door opened. Samira turned, but it was the door to the street. She saw a familiar face framed by a coppery mullet of hair; one of the reporters from yesterday outside the Byfords'. Samira looked away fast. No chance.

'Hello. WDC Byrne, right? Cathy *is* here then.'

Samira gave him a slanting smile. 'She is?'

'Well, you seem to think so.'

Samira heard the door open again, and quiet footsteps approaching. A couple, affluent, heading for reception but braking in unison like accident-voyeurs. They darted glances at the tense trio of Samira, receptionist and reporter. Uncertain smiles, a cough or two – wrong place? Should they come back later?

The receptionist dithered, held up a hand and picked up the phone. She said something quiet and nodded, blotches appearing around her collar bone. Her smile was tight. She stood, looked at Samira. 'Mr Dawson will see *you* now...' Her gaze shifted. 'But I've already told *you*... *three* times over the last few days actually... we're not talking to any journalists. I'm afraid you'll have to leave.'

He laughed, folded his arms like he might take root, head to one side, mouth open to speak.

Samira stepped closer and shook her head. 'Want me to make it official?'

He mumbled the beginning of something about the rights of the Press, then shrugged, backing off, giving Samira a wink. 'Be seeing you, Constable.'

The receptionist told the couple she'd be back momentarily, and motioned Samira to the double doors. Her movements were slow now and her forehead was quivering. They passed into a warm mahogany staircase. 'Okay. Just up here.' She didn't move though. Was she still flustered, or playing for time? Samira stifled the urge to reach out and nudge her forwards. Finally, she started up the steps.

At the top, there was a corridor too narrow for overtaking. Samira breathed.

Finally they reached a door, *T. Dawson* lettered on its bevelled glass. The receptionist gave a slow tap. 'Oh...' She funnelled a hand at her ear. 'I think he's on the phone.'

Samira nodded, then, movements suddenly fast, slipped very close and said, 'Out of the way! Now!' She flinched back, Samira pushing the door wide, ignoring her gaping mouth.

Dawson was fiftyish, bald, suit wide in the shoulder, face drenched in expensive tan. He was on the phone, fingers doing the *I'll be one minute* thing.

Samira closed the door, looked at Dawson, then at the partition door, presumably to Cathy's office. She headed for it and then stopped, looking at him again. Something about the way he was holding the phone, like a bad actor on *Santa Barbara*. She turned. 'Put it down.'

His face reddened, the dial-tone buzz apparent as he took the phone from his ear. 'I'm sorry... who are you again...'

Samira moved to the partition door, tried to slide it open. Locked.

Movements whip-fast now, she gave Dawson a snarl, her warrant card high. 'Keys?' He fumbled in his pocket, Samira shaking her head, moving close. 'Don't mess me about!'

He made to hand her the bunch. 'You really have no right. If she wants to be left alone –'

'Mrs Byford's already endangered several lives including her own, so I have every right.' She pointed at the door. 'Come on! Open it!'

He rattled at the lock and the door slid open. She elbowed past him, scanning the room. An opened parcel's brown paper, a cassette recorder, loader open as if a tape had been ejected, and a manila folder, a few sheets scattered on top of it.

Dawson spoke. 'She said the Press were hounding her. She just needed some quiet –'

'I'm not Press.' She looked at the corner. Cathy's shoes, heels high, splayed under the chair, classy skirt and blouse thrown, a large hold-all bag, empty. She glared at Dawson. 'Back way out?'

He nodded, pointed at the corridor.

Samira moved, grabbing the sheets from the opened file, Dawson beginning to say something, a quick glare cutting him off. She swept through the door and out onto the landing, the biting cold of this unheated staircase completely at odds with the mahogany and shag-pile affair at the public face of the building.

A window. She scanned the carpark below. There, walking fast, then running in short bursts, burgundy cap, jogging pants, trainers, denim jacket, a smaller hold-all over her shoulder.

Samira pelted down the steps, crashing around each landing, vaulting the last flight, shouldering the doors aside at the bottom. Cold drizzly air, clammy at her nostrils. At a full run now, straight for the road. She stopped, scanning one direction, then the other. A fleck of burgundy? There. At the bus stop, other side, further up.

The bus was coming. This direction.

Run back to the car? By the time she'd caught up, they'd be out of town, Cathy might have gotten off. Also, ginger-mullet journo might be hanging around Cathy's Mini.

Call it in, get some backup? Yeah, that had worked so well last time! Anyway, if she wanted to catch Cathy, she could do that herself, right now.

Better to see where she was going.

The bus had reached the stop and Cathy was getting on. The next stop was at least two minutes away, by road, over the bridge, past the market square.

Okay. Samira turned, ducked back into the carpark and ran, full pelt to the other exit, to the canal. On the towpath now, footbridge close. She skidded up the steps and over the bow shaped concrete, flashing down the other side, a jogger and his Labrador staring as she vaulted the railing back onto terra firma. She managed a croaky 'Police.' She cornered off the path and leapt the small wall. Back on the main road. The bus was just pulling into the stop.

She tried to keep to the edge of the pavement, turned her collar up, pulling her bobble and flicking her hair free with a headshake, turning away from the rest of the queue, coughing; sidled onto the bus.

She paid, walked to the back, no eye-contact with anyone. If Cathy recognised her, fair enough, she'd have to grab her before she got off. No movement for the doors though, bus starting to rumble along. She sat at the back, gradually surveying every head. Okay. Cathy must be upstairs. She had her. All she had to do was wait to see where she got off.

She pulled the sheets from her pocket, pored over them a couple of times. A copy of part of something, a tax-return? A page had been torn off at the staple. An address? The name was intact: Brenda Terrell. Could call it in, do a check, but she didn't want to draw attention. Eyes on her already; the tall black girl, hair everywhere, sweating and panting in her leather jacket.

The bus worried across the moor like a space probe. Not for a second was it welcome; as alien in these surroundings as Samira herself. This town, this department, this bloody job. Here she was, throwing herself in hell for leather with some vague hope of recognition. But there'd come a time, she thought, not too far away, when all her verve could boil down to bitterness.

Dad's face melted into view, acid disapproval. *I feckin' told you so!*

She shook herself, drawing her head back from the window. Someone had keyed the bell, was trundling down from upstairs.

Yes. Burgundy cap, the denim just that little bit too new to be lived-in.

Samira's head was down, hair covering the side of her face, feigning sleep. The swish of the doors as Cathy stepped out, the jarring as they closed and then a lurch forwards. She waited. The bus turned the corner, the junction leading down to the Craven estate, the houses beginning their decline into squalor. She sprang up, ran to the driver, warrant card up.

'There's no stop here, luv –'

'STOP, NOW!'

He saw the card, braked hard, doors springing wide with a hiss.

She was off, running back up to the corner, thighs burning with the gradient, tying her hair back again as she peered around the lamp post.

There, just heading down one of the side roads. Samira ran, slowing as she reached the corner.

Cathy was staring around her, pulling her cap against the drizzle like she wasn't so sure what she was doing. She dragged the small hold-all off her shoulder and put her hand inside it, took a few breaths, slung it back on and pushed at a gate, walking in along the path. Again, uncertainty. But then she hardened her face and straightened her back. She pressed the doorbell.

Samira hung back at the corner. She saw a face come to the door with a look that could have been surprise, could have been anything, from here. A woman, middle-aged. But Cathy had the bag in front of her, her arm out of sight, and the woman seemed to stiffen and draw back, Cathy following her inside.

Samira got the Walkie out. Surely there'd be coverage up here. 'Tango Alpha, request address check, resident, three-five Bartle Crescent, Craven Edge, over.'

She got an acknowledgement, glanced around her for a hiding place in case Cathy came back out. A low wall with some bushes. It would do.

Drizzle, her hair curling and frizzing, her neck cold. Being still was a true labour of will.

It was a few minutes before the crackle of a reply; Brenda Terrell. Okay. Samira requested a check for any previous. A few minutes later; nothing listed. But a little extra info; Brenda had only recently moved in.

Samira was in a crouch, peering over the wall when the door opened, the two women coming out. A few things wrong about it. Terrell was out first, for one thing. Do you do that, let a visitor close your door behind you? Then there was the body language. Distance, no contact. Wariness.

Silence as they passed her hiding place. She gave it twenty seconds and moved to watch their retreating backs. She vaulted the wall and followed.

About fifteen minutes' walk, not much cover, before they'd reached Shockley Beck, so she'd let them get well ahead.

She tried to remember what there was up here; an ancient graveyard and church, the old orphanage building, a row of cottages leading down to the village, a playground, small pub, the old Junior and Infants' further down.

She turned her trot into a jog, in case they turned off before she spotted them. No, there they were, looking like they were about to clamber over the dry-stone wall that ringed the grounds of the old children's home. She stopped.

The woman with Cathy, Brenda Terrell, presumably, put a foot to the stone wall and seemed to stumble, Cathy's hand out to steady her then retracted quick. But then Brenda flung her arm at Cathy, reaching for the hold-all, Cathy stepping back, her hand pulling something out and gripping it with both hands. From here, until it was levelled at Brenda, Samira found it hard to believe what she was seeing, heart thumping at the back of her throat. A gun. An automatic maybe.

Samira crouched lower in the heather, walkie-talkie out. The crackle gave her time to think and she chewed her lip; she knew the protocol, but this was Cathy Byford, mother of a missing son. Samira glanced at the blackened stone of the building. What if she'd found him, here, while they'd all been chasing their tails? Was Samira really going to reward her by bringing a bunch of armed response arseholes from Manchester crawling over the hillside with their flak jackets and their machismo and their worst-case scenarios? Cathy, maybe Ryan could end up bleeding out in a ditch.

No. She'd hold back any firearms mention, for now.

She needed some backup though, even if after the other night, she didn't care much for this department's notion of it.

She let out a tension-breaking laugh and hefted the walkie-talkie. The one person she trusted. As long as he didn't fall apart on her.

He was broaching the village, swinging into the pub carpark when Samira's voice crackled through again. 'Whisky One-Five, can you hang back with the car, please? Final approach on foot. Over.'

'Will do. Over.'

He grabbed the telescopic baton from the glove compartment and pulled his combat on over his suede. He nosed out into the rain, locked up and started jogging towards the old orphanage. He saw her as he crested the rise. Soaked, leather jacket collar turned up, arms folded across herself, squatting next to the wall.

'Enjoying your morning off?' He went into a crouch beside her.

'Every minute.' She glanced at her watch, then gave him a look. 'Your thing... your trauma thing. Doesn't have anything to do with firearms, does it?'

'What are you saying?'

'Cathy Byford. She has a handgun.' Samira's nostrils flared as she spoke. 'In there with another female, probably one Brenda Terrell. Forced her here more or less at gunpoint.'

Cathy with a gun? He rolled that around a little. 'Why didn't you –?'

'Thought the Manchester Macho squad would just make things worse. Was I wrong?'

She had a point, of course. Will inclined his head towards the building. 'Cathy? I mean, really?'

'She planned this, to some extent anyway. Change of clothes, holdall, gun. Crashed her car to shake off some bloody hacks. Got hold of this Brenda's address, new address, apparently, she just moved into the area a few months back. Walked her over the moor. To here.'

'Bloody hell!' He shook his head. 'What is it with this sodding couple? Like they're trying to out-crazy each other.'

'Marriage.' Samira's voice was tight, adrenaline-soaked. He checked her over again, thinking procedure. But her failure to follow regs wasn't bothering him half so much as the look in her eyes as she rocked from foot to foot on her haunches.

He held up a hand. 'Let's just take it easy. You might be right about Manchester armed response. I'd suggest calling it in to our lot but the only firearms trained officer in Spinnerby apart from me is DCI Price.' He grimaced a little, picturing Price blazing in with .38 and a Clint Eastwood swagger. Will looked at her. 'We can do without him or anyone else getting carried away up here.'

She glanced at his hand, a glimmer of annoyance at her cheek. 'What about you, *sir*? Feeling alright after yesterday?'

He grinned. Flexed his fingers and then put them on her arm.

Her breathing seemed to slow a little, her shoulders dropping. She gave a grudging nod and a grin flitted over her lips. 'Okay.' She flicked a glance around her. 'Maybe we should be asking *why come here*? Maybe Ryan was an inmate before he was –'

He shook his head. 'Closed about ten years ago. Ryan was orphaned when he was three. A year later.' He looked at the mullion windows and black stone left to gather moss; no idea what it had been originally, too big for a farmhouse; a grange, maybe. But it had functioned as an orphanage for almost a hundred years, as far as Will could remember from local history lessons at school, before being renamed Moorhaven Children's home in the 1960s.

'Let's see what we see. But no heroics, right?'

She gave him a *who, me?* kind of shrug. At least, that's what he thought it must be. He clambered over the wall, keeping his body low, sensed her doing the same behind him. They hugged the wall, working their way round the building. He stopped, voices cutting through an instant. He waved a hand toward the outbuilding further down the slope and they glanced at each other, moving towards it through unkempt grass. It hardly mattered in the wind, but he tried to keep the swishing to a minimum, his jeans sopping already.

Visibility was shit through the drizzle, the old stone barn revealing itself in hazy clots, ravaged, crumbling walls and a slate roof that might once have kept some livestock dry. The voice again, this time a repeated 'No!' with just an edge of desperation. 'No, no, no!' Cathy, he was sure.

He was about to motion Samira to stay while he worked

around the other side but she'd already set off, wading through the long swards. He shook his head, muttering and waving his hand, raising the walkie-talkie. He did a no-no gesture with his finger. She paused, then nodded. Last thing they needed was a crackling voice or beeping giving them away.

A sudden awful image of Samira splayed in blood-soaked grass.

Was this the stupidest thing he'd ever sanctioned? Okay, Cathy Byford had a gun, but still. He just couldn't square the idea of her having the will to use it. But did that matter? How many firearm injuries are accidental? Something like five percent. Enough. People not used to guns get nervous around them. Bad combination.

His thoughts swirled on as he moved closer to the broken wall, keeping it between himself and the two women inside. His face pressed to wet stone and he moved to the edge of the gap and squatted, peeping around the edge. If the day had been bright he wouldn't have risked it. But it was only slightly less gloomy outside than in.

Cathy's back was to him, the gun pointed at the other woman. A pudding-like face and a black slick of hair, bowl-cut.

He glanced at the layout. Another wall inside, originally to separate livestock maybe. He drew his head back. He could get in there, much closer if he could risk jumping this low wall, straight through the gap. If Brenda, if that was her name, would just turn away, he could do it. But the gun was levelled at her and she was stock still.

Cathy half turned so he had her almost-profile. Her blonde hair was dank with rain. The reddened eye he could see was screwed up tight and he saw Brenda stiffen. Then Cathy's head shook and she pushed forwards, gun up, Brenda backing away out if his line of sight. Now! He hopped over the low wall, landing on his toes and moving behind the stone partition, trying to still his breath.

A trough, rank with fetid water and God knows what else clogging its bottom was at the foot of the wall. The musk of dampened stone and peat was powerful, cloying. Two jutting, rusted hooks from the far wall, water dripping.

A sudden blur of images; Docklands, blue light flashing over corrugated pipe, the rancid pool a veneer over the dilapidated stone barn, reality, the now, receding. He heard Cathy's voice rising in sudden despair; floodtide passion from a mother at the end of reason, cutting through the clamour in his head for a second.

But then the roar and clang of water and iron swelled.

Samira stopped. She'd just taken it on herself to circle around, without even waiting to agree it with him. Not good. She glanced back over the long grass. He was out of sight. Okay. She looked down at her hands. Shaking? Just a little.

Shit! He had a point. She was hyped.

She raised her head and took some breaths, letting herself feel it. There was a gun in there, in the hands of someone au fait with hair diffusers and nail-polish but probably not much more. And this Brenda Terrell was an unknown quantity. Things could go bad. Easily…

For the first time, Samira felt it wash through her body. Cold, sharp, a knife of it in her belly. Fear.

She looked at the barn.

Why had she been so keen not to call this in? Because of what happened on the rooftop? A good enough reason, along with Cathy Byford being no more likely to shoot someone than Gandhi, but still, if she was honest, not her main motivation over the past hour, was it?

No.

She wanted to sort this out, herself. Something unequivocal, worth notice. She wanted to ram it in the faces of DCI Price and the Super. It was that simple.

Calm fell over her now.

She moved in, close to the back of the barn, grace coming back to her movements. Whatever her reasoning, here she was. She'd make this work. She was down on all fours, barely feeling the wet swathe of grass lapping around her. She slithered over near the opening. The voices inside were almost audible. She pressed her head to the stone, holding her breath.

'… talking about, you crazy twisted cow!' It was Cathy's voice.

A laugh in reply.

'Just tell me!'

Samira raised her head.

The side of Brenda Terrell's face was caught in a puddle of grey light as Cathy raised the gun and forced her back, closer to

Samira's position. Just a flash of a pudding-faced woman, seriously bad hairdo. But no fear in that face.

Samira got herself up on her haunches, toes clawing in her boots.

The change in the light was rapid, a blast of sunlight making her wonder when the rain had stopped; maybe a minute ago, maybe five. She saw Cathy glance at the doorway, ducked her head backwards. But then a grunt, the scuffing of feet and a small cry of surprise from Cathy. Brenda was on her!

Samira was up, had taken the corner, blinking, the murk of the barn, the two figures grappling. Samira sprang, left arm snaking round Terrell's neck, other hand aiming for her wrist, but the sudden elbow in Samira's groin was quicker, nastier than a woman of Terrell's age had any right to. Samira staggered, hissing air.

Terrell twisting with a swipe of the gun and a sudden tangle of denim limbs and expensive scent draped over Samira. They went down, Samira pushing until Cathy tumbled off her, a slack roll that ended in a crumple. Unconscious? Samira made to get up but found something cold prodding at her cheek. the oily scent of metal damping down Cathy's *Opium*.

'Face down, sweetie.' Terrell was grinning. 'Fold your hands behind you.'

A sudden strong urge to urinate; damned if she'd give this old bitch the satisfaction of that. She found her voice. 'Police officer.'

The muzzle was twisted up to her temple, hard. She turned, face to the cold stone.

'On yer own, Blackie? Doubt it. Always in pairs you lot.' The voice notched up its volume. 'COME ON OUT!'

No movement, no sound.

Terrell started humming, like a wander through unmarked graves, no melody, a few words forming: '… hmm, hmm… yes, sir yes, sir, three bags hmmm… Baa Baa Black sheep have you hmm hmm hmm…' The muzzle crept up Cathy's cheek, caressing her neck and back, the nape, then up into her hair. Her eyes closed. It came out of her hair and was touching her forehead, down to the bridge of her nose. 'Turn your head,

Blackie. Open your mouth.'

Samira was frozen, the fear in her so new and complete she couldn't fathom it. An image of Will; that moment yesterday when he'd turned from the tree, his eyes somewhere else. And she'd been so bloody clever, so cocksure, judging him.

When she heard his voice, she was half certain it was in her thoughts with the memory from yesterday. But no. It echoed short around the dull stone walls. 'Police officer. Put it down.'

The metal left her skin and she breathed.

'A wolf, is it?' The graveyard voice again. 'Nah! Kneel down here, opposite blackie.'

The steel at Samira's temple again, and that awful urge to apologise, to placate this woman, give her what she wanted, please her. Wetness in the corners of Samira's eyes and she screwed them up tight.

The wail was sudden, then another waft of *Opium*, a surprised grunt from Terrell, the Luger scraping away again... Samira surging up now, a jumble, Cathy's nails raking Terrell's face, Will at the other side, trying to get between them, Cathy draped on the gun arm, shouting something, hoarse, half-strangled.

Samira caught Terrell's other hand, ramming it up behind her, pinning her down into a crouch. 'Drop it! Drop it!'

But then Terrell jerked back her hand so that the muzzle rested against her own temple. Her finger twitched. A hollow click, another, then three more in quick succession, like a starter pistol in reverse, replacing the grunting, manic straining movement in the room...

Dead quiet, solemn, hanging between them.

As if they were all, Terrell included, trying to work out what the hell had just happened.

Samira forced the arm further up Terrell's back and a pig's grunt from that sweaty black head of hair beneath her. She found her voice. 'Drop it, now, or I break your arm.'

It clattered down, Will picking it up and standing, ejecting the empty clip. His eyes were vacant lots. Worse than she'd seen him. Even yesterday.

Samira put her cuffs on Terrell, glaring at Cathy. 'Why didn't you tell us it was empty?'

Cathy Byford's head was down, hair a tousled mess, the cap she'd been wearing thrown somewhere. She lifted a hand, all rabid fury and Samira wondered if this legal secretary would have known herself in a mirror. Cathy pointed. 'She knows where Ryan is!'

Samira turned Terrell, giving her a once over. Fresh red weals from forehead to cheek, pudding face white, graveyard smile still in place.

'Just… leave me with her. Look the other way. Ten minutes. She'll tell me…' Cathy looked at Samira and Will in turn.

Brenda snorted. 'What'll you do? Give me a manicure?'

'Couldn't have hurt you before. But now… now, I could.'

'Bollocks!'

Cathy's eyes were darting, tears coursing down her cheeks. 'See that… trough over there? I'll hold your head in it until… until your lungs fill up with shit… and you'll tell me… you'll tell me….'

Samira looked at Cathy Byford, for the first time really pitying the woman. Even if her words held no conviction, or her eyes just couldn't hold their fury long enough, that didn't mean she didn't have the right idea.

31

Will looked at the two women on the hillside and wondered where he was.

Every time he *came back*, he was further from recognising himself. More and more he was relying on that auto-pilot part of himself to make judgements because he couldn't. He thought, right now as he pinched the fingers of his left hand with those on his right, that he was here, back in the now, in reality, but he wasn't even sure he believed it.

The roughened walls and grass around him and the faces of Samira and Cathy were all less distinct than they should be, nothing to do with the drizzle that had started again as they'd begun their search.

Pain again. His head throbbing, whole body aching.

He closed his eyes.

A beach somewhere in the north. Whitby? Couldn't remember. Didn't matter. There she was. The woman with headscarf and dancing eyes, building sandcastles and letting him pour water around them, then burying him, later chasing him to the water's edge. Willowy and beautiful. Pale though. For the first time he realised the headscarf fluttering in the North Sea wind may have been for more than show.

Had she been ill, then? Already. He'd always assumed the memory older; him two or three. But no. Later, by a few years.

It was vivid now though. Almost as powerful as the flashes that seemed to be taking over his life. Why couldn't it be this? He'd gladly relive these moments every day and forever. His mother ankle deep in cold water, sweeping him up into her arms, touching noses with him.

He opened his eyes. Samira was looking at him from a little way down the incline and may even have been talking to him. She moved close enough for him to see the gung-ho flush was gone, the dark skin of her cheek a little ashen, if anything.

'Nothing,' she said. 'Not down there. How about the orphanage building?'

Will shook his head, more to give himself time to process what she was asking than anything. So hard to focus. But he'd spent twenty minutes trying every window and crack, only stopping short of climbing on the roof and up those gothic spires; he was in no shape for that. They would need keys from Social Services or whoever. But if *they* couldn't get in there, doubtful Ryan's abductor could have either.

'Maybe he's buried out there.' Samira flinched. They both stared at the moorland. 'I bet there's caves further up. Maybe crazy person in there does know...'

Will glanced at the shed. He'd fastened Terrell to the trough so she could contemplate the instrument of her intended torture by Cathy Byford, not that he thought that would soften her up at all. Someone who puts a gun to their head and fires five times isn't likely to be intimidated by the thought of pain.

'I don't know, boss... what if Cathy had the right idea?'

Ah, so that was it.

She was on the edge here, he thought, this fine young woman, this potentially brilliant copper. And because of that, even if his own sense of what was true and real was somewhere bleak as this fucking moor, he had to show her something different. 'Want to... stick her head in the trough?'

She did a quick double take, intense look softening to a grin. 'Felt like it earlier.' She sighed, shook her head.

'Cathy... said anymore?'

'Couldn't shut her up for a while. Practically catatonic now.'

Will breathed, trying to force himself to admit all of this was really happening. Everything still had that unreal quality; a shadow-puppet theatre. 'What brought Cathy to Brenda?'

Samira held up a cassette tape, in a polythene baggy. 'Delivered, I reckon, at the law firm.'

'She gave it to you?'

She laughed. 'Not exactly. There was an open cassette player in her office where she did a quick change. She claimed she'd destroyed the tape. I checked her rucksack while she was out here. Nothing. Well, just the bullets she'd taken out of the clip. But then I remembered Cathy sitting near the trough just after Brenda did her Russian roulette thing.'

'She hid it?'

'Under some loose stones.'

He almost smiled. 'Nice work.'

'You think Ryan could be hidden here? Or worse?'

He shrugged.

Samira scanned the hills again. 'She's convinced this guy's out there watching us. What'll he do with Ryan if he sees coppers crawling over this hillside?'

He swilled it around. So hard to see reality.

'Should we call it in? Get a full search going up here?'

She wanted answers. It was a shame he didn't have any. He looked at her. 'Need to hear the tape. She tell you how much this guy's asking for?'

'Nothing, apparently.'

He put his hands to his head and pressed his palms to his eyes. The last half hour had shifted his thoughts, or what thinking he could muster, away from a grudge against Sean Byford, to a kidnapping for money. Now he was spiralling back around again. He let out a breath. 'What about Brenda? Cathy know her?'

Samira grimaced. 'She says not.'

'The gun?'

'She claims it's her uncle's. He's a collector. Cathy borrowed it, without him knowing. Looks like her side of the family aren't pacifists.'

Cathy had appeared from behind the old well, head down as she trudged the field. Even from here, her eyes were dark empty pits.

Okay. He moved, trying to make it decisive. 'Listen, keep her from Brenda a while longer.'

He put the tape in the slot and turned up the volume. He closed his eyes and tried like hell to focus. Tricky; his head was still clanging. He had to stop and rewind, starting again twice.

The message was short, less than a minute. First listen, he couldn't get past the accent. Northern Irish, which could raise distracting possibilities, if real. They'd need a linguist, but Will found himself thinking of TV impersonations of the reverend Ian Paisley with exaggerated Belfast sounds.

Do exactly what I say. You don't wanna end up like Winnie

157

Johnson, do ya?

That got Will, putting something dark and nasty at the pit of his stomach. He could only imagine how it had made Cathy feel. Winnie Johnson, mother of one of the Saddleworth Moor murder victims, never found, Winnie still searching, trying to re-engage interest. Saddleworth about seventeen miles away. The shadow of Brady and Hindley's spree of child abductions and murders hung over every copper who'd ever worked this region, him no exception. Even Will's dad had been involved in the search back in the 60s, though he'd never talked about it.

Cathy would have recognised the name. Winnie had been in the news again recently, moves being made to get Brady and Hindley back to Saddleworth to help the Manchester Met find her son's remains.

Then, why a tape rather than phone call or letter? Undoubtedly intended to twist Cathy up even further, something she'd play and play again, even if she didn't want to. There was nothing more personal and intimidating than a voice, too; no escaping the reality of the situation. A person, a real person (accent fake or not) has taken your child.

There were some positives though. No mention of Ryan's ethnic background, and nothing to suggest this was sexual in any way.

Terrell's an evil old trout who needs putting down. I thought of asking you to do that for me. Not this time though. Just find her. She's just come back, so you won't have much trouble. Take her to the old Shockley orphanage. Get her to take you to what's hidden up there. She'll say no. You'll have to convince her. But feel free to smear her nose in pig-shit while you're doing it.

No mention at all of Ryan's being what was *hidden up here*. Cathy had joined dots that weren't there, letting her terror run away with her. Understandable. Her attempt to hide the tape equally reasonable. Because the last words on there were where some of the subtlety died away. *Don't tell hubby about this. Not yet. I'll decide when he should know. Oh and... take this to the pigs and I'll send you something of Ryan's. And it won't be his fucking lid. It'll be something wet and sticky.*

He took Brenda by the upper arms, gentler than he felt, and moved her out into the light.

Clear of the barn, he scanned around. Bushes shielded them from higher moorland. The only visible higher point was the familiar bird-like edifice on the other side of the valley some two miles away, close to the Byfords' cottage.

She was watching him.

'Head for the well,' he told her.

She turned and started trudging, Will letting her lead the way, giving no support this time to the middle-aged woman with hands cuffed behind her, not out of cruelty but with specific reason. As she took a left and crossed by the bird-dung encrusted sundial without a glance or a single stumble, he knew for sure that what the tape had implied was true. 'Used to work here, didn't you Brenda?'

A slight break in the rhythm of her steps. Something like a grunt.

'What were you, a cleaner or something?'

That made her stop, turn and spit at the long grass. Some of it caught her chin and it dangled as she grinned, staring over the fence.

He followed her gaze to the neighbouring field, the Shockley Beck Junior and Infants' sign just visible beyond it, the playing field's borders marked by a rough ginnel and a low stone wall. He hadn't realised how close to the school the Moorhaven orphanage was. Something clicking into place, Will allowed himself a small smile. 'You ran this place didn't you, Brenda?' He tried to imagine a worse choice of matron. Eva Braun maybe.

She shrugged, her stare at the school softening, almost fond, Will thought. Memories of green.

'Happy days, right? All those abandoned souls to take care of. You in charge.' His tone was wistful. 'On a related note, how long were you shagging Peter Smiles?'

The flash of the eyes was enough. She stepped forward; he had no doubt if not for the cuffs she would have been on him.

'Sorry, Brenda. I'm sure it was more spiritual than that.'

'Fuck you!'

'No thanks.' He glanced at the orphanage's dark walls. A chance meeting between two sadists. Was that how it had been? What was it Mandy Riley had said, her hands clamped over her infant son's ears? Smiley had used up her mum, two-timing and then leaving her for some psycho or other. At the time, he'd thought it just Mandy's vitriol. But now, looking at Brenda...

Suddenly whatever shred of pity he might have felt for a middle-aged woman trussed up and pushed around melted into the drizzle around them.

'Okay, I'm sick of this.' She grimaced at him. 'Either untie me, right now, or take me in. But remember this.' She jerked her head in the vague direction of the car where Samira was talking to Cathy. 'That manicured bitch abducted me from my home with a gun. If you nick me, I have every intention of pressing charges.'

Will's tone was flat. 'What about you holding that same gun to a WDC's head?'

'I don't remember seeing ID. You could've been two of her mates ready to ambush me. Anyone can shout Police.'

Tough to admit, but she could make something of that with a good solicitor. Samira had blown in there pretty fast and Will... well, he'd been a little out of it, to say the least. Flashing his warrant card hadn't been at the forefront of his mind. It was all bullshit and Brenda knew it, but there were other things in play here. Cathy Byford was in no shape to be arrested, even apart from how it would play out for DCI Price and the Super, never mind the Press, if Ryan's mother was charged with abduction while brandishing a firearm.

'If I let you go, what's to stop you sticking your head in the oven when you get home?'

She crowed a little. 'Aww, didn't think you cared!'

He said nothing.

'That were just... heat o' the moment.' She turned, stretching her arms up behind her. 'Anyway, I had a feeling that bloody gun were empty. Miss manicure would never have rushed me if it wasn't.'

It was quite a risk, based on a feeling, Will thought.

Her wrists were thrust at him again, and he held the keys

ready. But then she turned her head to him. 'And anyway...' A knowing smile and a glance at his hand. 'Bet your bosses would love to know how you went to pieces... shaking like a shiteing dog.'

Will stared at her.

She bared her teeth. 'Listen... I have no idea where her runt of a son is.'

He believed her. But that didn't mean she didn't know of something else hidden here... maybe for the last ten or fifteen years. Something Ryan's abductor thought important enough to get her panicked about. 'Funny thing, you know. I was just about to let you go. Not now though. No way.'

'Ahhh!' It was an angry whine. 'Come on!'

'No. You've blown it, Brenda.'

As he marched her towards the car, he heard again the thrill in her voice as she'd ordered Samira around, playing that gun over her head. He found himself grinning at her screeches and curses now; every other word a profanity.

But then she stopped all of that, drew her head back and gave a sudden howl, not particularly convincing, but something in it made Will's skin cold. She panted, tongue lapping. Finally, she quit it. Giving him the dead-eyed grin again. 'Poodle. You're a fucking poodle. When the wolfie comes... he'll tear you to pieces.'

She turned, shrugging off his hands, and walked toward the road with a horrible dignity.

32

Her eyes were diamond sharp. 'You look like shit, boss!'

He didn't need to check the rear-view.

They watched WPC Clarke shepherding Cathy into the cottage, arm over shoulder, clucking supportively. Samira turned to him again. 'I don't know where we're heading here…'

Did she mean the case? Or the two of them?

Samira slapped the steering wheel. 'Christ, Will. There's a bloody psychiatrist behind that door. Go talk to him.'

Will shook his head. One thing he was sure of. 'I don't trust him. Not completely. You shouldn't either.'

She leant back, face intense. She looked like she was making a decision. She really was beautiful, he thought suddenly. From somewhere, what was left of his battered soul reached his hand out to touch her arm, and she stared at him, hard as sandstone. He dropped his hand. But then she leant in close, languid now, eyes burning with more than anger.

Movement in the Byfords' doorway. They moved apart, Samira opening her door and getting out in one fluid move.

'I'll be a minute…' He watched her walk to Clarke, a finger touching her mouth absently. No look back, no giggle or flash of her eyes. Hardly surprising. Not the lightest of times for the buoyancy of an almost kiss. He was hardly even sure what he felt himself, his head a maelstrom.

Overthinking. Always overthinking.

He sat back, the scent of something rich and creamy from her skin still in the car. God, she was gorgeous.

He took that look in the mirror now, peering like a desk-sergeant at a procedure manual. Jesus! Face haggard, beyond his usual gaunt look. Skin not pale; pale he could handle, but greyed-out. The eyes the clincher, or what lay behind them – faraway, desolate… just… not… him. Like the clasping bleakness of these fucking moors had sucked out his soul, buried it in peat, seeped in as a replacement.

Like this world was no longer to be trusted.

He reached into his waistband and carefully pulled out the

luger. The glove compartment would have to do, for now. He took out the Ibuprofen tub while he was at it, thumbed a couple onto his palm, though they'd be as much use as a band-aid on a gunshot wound.

'She did what?' Byford was out of his kitchen-chair, cardigan sagging with his face.

'She's upstairs, settled.' Samira's tone was calming. 'Doctor's on his way. I don't think you should –'

Will shook his head. 'Actually, why don't you? Talk to her, I mean? If the two of you could actually communicate maybe she wouldn't have gone off and done something so bloody stupid.'

Byford flushed, blinking furiously. He put his hand on the back of his chair and slumped into it. 'But why? Why would she?'

Samira moved to the side unit, a questioning glance at Byford as she manoeuvred the ghetto-blaster closer to the edge, opening the tape-holder. Will wondered if it was Ryan's. Probably. It was sickening somehow, a message from his abductor played on his own tape deck.

Will watched Byford closely as the message played, eyes not leaving the psychiatrist even as he asked Samira to rewind and repeat. 'You recognise that voice?'

A hint of relaxation in his shoulders as Byford shook his head. Because it wasn't something he had to lie about? Surely it should be crushing disappointment; a voice he didn't recognise threatening to cut pieces off his adopted son. To be fair, Byford had blanched at that part, Samira pouring him a drink of water.

'You recognised the name Brenda Terrell, didn't you?'

Byford gave a grudging nod. 'Yes.'

'What can you tell us about her?'

'Nothing. Just rumours. Hearsay. Never met the woman. But I remember the name –'

'Rumours about the orphanage and what went on there?'

A shrugging nod. 'Technically, I believe Moorhaven was a children's home. Orphanages in England were closed down by the 70s. I heard some talk about the place but I don't really deal in –'

'Okay. The children's home.' Will didn't wait for a reply. 'Were you involved? Officially or otherwise, when it was shut down?'

'No. No involvement whatsoever. I was working on the ward at the time, remember?'

Samira's arms were folded as she leant against the breakfast bar. 'What about patients you've had since, Dr Byford? Any of them pass through Moorhaven?' Her tone was gentle, the perfect counterpoint to Will's. Except they weren't doing good cop, bad cop – Will was working hard to keep from reaching over and giving Byford a slap, and he wasn't completely sure why.

'No. Not to my knowledge.'

His head was pounding again. He knuckled his eyes. 'Please don't tell me this is some doctor-client confidentiality thing.'

'No. Anyway, I don't see how this has got anything to do with Ryan.'

Will was out of his seat now, face planted close to Byford's. He was jabbing the air, vaguely pointing at the tape-player. 'Because that bastard says it does!'

Samira coughed, turned to Byford. 'Why do you think he contacted your wife and not you?'

'Maybe… he wants to come at me through those I love.'

Will's blood roared, somewhere under it, a voice in his head telling him to shut up, that he was missing something important. 'You took an age to drag your arse back from Bern when your son had been abducted! You held back about Little Kenny!' His voice was shaking, the muscles in his arms bunched up, fists clenched. 'You're holding back now too… I just don't know what about!'

Byford had paled. 'I explained –'

'This is your son! Your son, you fucking –' His hands on Byford's shirt, bunching it up as he lifted him, the seat tipping, clanging down on the kitchen tiles.

'Easy, boss.' Samira's hand on his shoulder was firm, voice measured. His breathing slowed. Behind her head, through the conservatory glass, the early evening sunlight framing the broken crow of Gallerton folly, almost majestic. He let go of

Byford.

He had to get out. Moved to the kitchen door, turned, thought of telling Byford to stop protecting whoever he thought he was protecting… but the words just wouldn't come, his body tensing, adrenaline closing his throat, shrivelling his thought to fight or flight.

That gunmetal magnet stagger back to the car, shadows around the hillside deepening, rocks grinning like razor teeth. That encroaching sense of danger, close again – the kitchen he'd left, this house, the facade of middle-class safety melting to slag.

Nothing. Nothing was safe.

33

The mustiness she'd expected. The spacious sweep of gothic excess, somehow she hadn't. It would have sharpened the chill though, back when the place was inhabited. It was hard not to see Dickensian rows of shivering kids hunched over porridge and stale bread, even behind all the box files and stacked folders Social Services had left here in storage since the place had shut down.

It had taken what was left of the day to get the keys to Moorhaven. It was Friday afternoon though, so they'd figured it had to be done quickly or they'd be chasing paper all weekend. Will had insisted on coming with her. She'd begged him to go home and get some rest.

'You were out of order with Byford.' She'd told him.

He'd blinked. 'He's holding back about something and I –'

'Maybe. But that's got nothing to do with it. You lost it.' But there was more to it than that. She pinched her lip and looked at him. 'Know what I think? I think you want to believe Byford can't be trusted. It's the perfect excuse not to ask for his help with your… problem.'

Will seemed to take that to heart, quiet for a while. Then he shrugged, proving her right with a flick of his head. 'Look, I'm coming with you to Social Services even if I have to cling to the roof of the car.'

Avoidance. Probably wasn't even aware he was doing it.

No bad thing that he did come along, in the end. That murder-red glint in his eyes had scared the piss out of the council staff and got them moving. Got them talking too, eventually. About Moorhaven. What they remembered, surmised, had heard from so-and-so who heard it from so-and-so… and so on.

Sifting out the facts took some time. But basically, the Children and Young Persons Act of 1969 had been the start of the end for family or couple-run orphanages like Moorhaven. They'd either gone under or been absorbed by Social Services. Moorhaven had been one of the last holdouts in the region. Its owner, Seb Crawshaw, rich enough not to care about financial pressures and ill enough (bone-marrow cancer) to overlook the quality of care being given in his name, had appointed Brenda Terrell as proprietor and left her to it.

Thing was, Samira knew a little about Care homes. She'd been involved, strictly low-level, in one case of alleged abuse. A senior Manchester copper had told her he'd put money on a lot more allegations being uncovered across the country over the next few years, and he knew his stuff. *Powder keg of nasty shit*, was his take on the current state of UK children's homes. Male-dominated workforce on shifts; nothing stopping male staff taking jobs purely to get close to vulnerable kids. The old family-run system might have been quaint but at least staff had been mainly female and had lived on site.

The Social Services staff that she and Will spoke to were convinced that the opposite was true; the modern system was far safer; it was the privately-run orphanages 'back in the day' that had been dodgy.

Having met Brenda Terrell of course, it was easy to believe they were right. A woman who'd lived on site, and the very fact of her being a woman making it difficult to believe she could have condoned any cruelty. But Brenda was far from typical, that much was already clear.

Since arriving, she and Will had spent a while searching each room before reconvening in the hall. Will was accounting for all the keys on the bunch. 'This one. Doesn't fit anywhere.' He held it up, an old brass chub, then dropped it.

She bent to scoop it up, not even bothering to look at his hand. It seemed to be shaking more or less constantly now. 'Boss...' She shook her head.

'Call me Will, for God's sake.'

'I'll call you whatever you want, if you just go and get some rest. This is insane.'

The trace of a smile at the corners of his mouth. 'It's okay, Samira, I've made a deal with myself.'

'You've what?'

He shrugged. 'If we don't find Ryan by Monday, I'm... done.'

'What do you mean, done? You'll go see Stratham? Get some

help?'

The smile spread. Just not to his eyes.

She stared at him a few seconds, not liking the way he glanced at his hand, the way he was looking anywhere but at her. 'Okay.' She screwed up her face a little. 'Okay, so now you're gonna make a deal with me. When we're finished here tonight, we're going to talk. Properly. Somewhere away from all this.'

His smile changed a little and he looked at her.

Thing was, she knew what he was thinking now. There was nowhere away from all this, not for him. It was in his head and his body. She might distract him a while, but he'd always have to return to himself.

She let out a breath, held up the key. 'So, where can this fit? There're no more doors.'

'What about a cellar? Place like this has to have one.'

They passed through to the kitchen, walls grimed by a thousand steamy meals. Stacked box files and crates holding more of the same, some nearer the front, newer, less filmed with dust. Behind it all, an upended table, swirling mahogany legs jutting sideways into the room and behind that a stacked ping-pong table resting on a stained green curtain. If there was a door hidden anywhere, this looked like the place.

'Brenda?' Samira shook her head. 'I don't get it. If she wanted to hide something, why not just plaster it up?'

'Social Services took this place over a while before it was closed down. She couldn't know the council would just use it for storing all this crap. Probably just a rushed attempt at covering her tracks.' He started restacking the box-files further from the tables, Samira bending and doing her bit.

A few minutes, a sheen of sweat on her arms and forehead, their breathing faster and louder. Will dragged the table sideways with a grunt, Samira grabbing the other leg, lifting, shuffling. They slid the ping pong table aside. The key took some twisting around before it did anything, but with a creak worthy of any ghost story, the cellar door opened. Samira sniffed at the cooped-up air. She shrugged.

He reached around behind the jamb, looking for a light-switch, she figured. Surely the bulb would be gone after twelve years. She stood back, bent to rummage in the big hold-all he'd brought on from the car. Two torches. She handed him one, their eyes meeting, then flicking away. Her breathing was fast but nothing to do with exertion now, her tongue dry and the muscles in her thighs bunching as her toes curled. The sudden certainty they were getting somewhere. Maybe not close to Ryan yet, but close to... something.

Will had the torch in his left, she noticed, but his right was steady again. Adrenaline driving out the ghost of past threats? 'No matter what's down here, touch as little as possible.'

'I know.' Hard to keep the annoyance out of her tone.

She shone around their feet as they headed down.

'Oh no!' She felt herself saying, but under her breath. 'No, no, no!'

It was the hooks. Jutting out high from the walls. The cloistered archways, dark little crannies and the claustrophobic feel of the place despite its size she could handle, no problem. The mouldy smell was no more than expected from a cellar. But when she saw the hooks, spaced out along the walls, with a couple of crumbling holes where some had been pulled free, that was when she started quietly freaking, the part of her that wasn't logical wanting out of here. 'For meat, though right?' She knew she was jabbering. Couldn't stop herself. 'I mean, lots of places from this period have them, right? For hanging... carcasses...'

He touched her shoulder briefly, walked to the opposite wall, shining the torch over it, then passing it back again. He held the torch close, splaying the light along it at an oblique angle. He stretched his arm, staring head-on, keeping the torch in place.

'What?' An edge of nervous tension in her voice and she cleared her throat. 'What do you see?'

'Think there's blood on the walls, under a few layers of paint.' He motioned her over. 'Look.'

He moved the torch away, then put it back again, the oblique light making sudden sense of the large spatter of bumps.

'Could mean anything,' she said. 'Animals. Livestock.'

He walked to the side, crouched, flashed his torch over a pair

169

of woodwork tables. He leaned closer, passing the torch over one of the vices. He got up and tried another. He backed away suddenly, rocking on his haunches and steadying himself.

'What, Will? Come on!' She bent over it, shining the torch down.

'Blood. In the vice. Look. Wiped, not that well. Maybe some hair too.' He steadied himself and got up, skirting the tables, moving further back. A narrow passageway. She followed, him swiping a hand at his head, the touch of cobwebs at her own face making her shudder, blowing, pulling at her nose and mouth.

The mouldy stench was stronger in here. They stood, torches extending to sweep the room, Will from the left, Samira from the right. Where the wide beams of light met, just off-centre, was a black metal ring, three or four feet from the ground. She felt her breath releasing itself, the last of her denial going with it.

Samira pointed around it. 'It's been painted over too. Installed –'

'Relatively recently.' He nodded.

Twelve years, she thought. The hooks were equivocal, maybe there since this place was built. But this… this had been fitted for purpose. And what possible reason other than to keep someone, or several people, chained here?

Together, they did the torch thing again, one shining at an oblique angle, the other looking at the wall straight on, then swapping over, wordlessly. Spatters again, sprawling this time.

'Would Luminol pick that up?'

'Not under that much paint. Brenda would have been better using bleach though. Then there'd be no sign. Must've thought paint would be better. Rush job.'

She squinted into the light. 'It'll be difficult to prove that's blood. Let alone whether it's animal or…' Her voice trailed to a dull echo as something caught her eye. She hunched down, Will following her now. Near the ring, within reaching distance, under the paint, faint, but more apparent when she lifted the torch. Scratches, small. An *h* and a half-formed *e*.

'*Help*?' Somehow she needed to say it aloud. Of course, it

170

could have been anything. Just *he*, or the beginning of some other word, the rest obliterated. But it must have been etched when the plaster around the ring had still been fresh. A knife, a smuggled spoon. Somehow she hoped it had been something like that, not fingernails, though it didn't really matter.

The back of her throat was tight. 'We need...' She didn't know. Air. Water. Sunlight. Reality. A beach somewhere, standing at the water's edge, just him and her.

The sudden boom of a voice above their heads had them both standing. 'ASHCROFT! WHERE THE BLOODY HELL ARE YOU?' Some mumbling, familiar tones. Samira's shoulders relaxed a little, but she kept the beach in her head as they walked to the steps.

34

DCI Price was watching him from the driver's seat, chewing his sandwich. He pulled out a hipflask, swigged and offered it to Will, wiping the top absently.

It was closing on six, but doubtful the drink was the first of the weekend for Price. Will shook his head.

'Sure? Good stuff. I only drink the best.' Price took another gulp, screwed the top back on with a practiced hand and continued with his butty. It looked like sausage and bacon but so smothered in brown sauce it was difficult to be sure. A healthy, hearty dinner before the pubs opened, though to Price it would be 'tea'. Dinner far too middle-class a concept. When he'd finished his mouthful he looked over at Will again. 'You're not yourself are you, lad?'

Will glanced down at his hand before he could stop himself. Steady enough, he thought, right now anyway. And despite everything he'd seen in that cellar, no flashes at the moment. It had puzzled him at first but then he'd figured out why. Apart from a tint of damp in the air, the cellar was dry.

'That Terrell woman's made some pretty wild allegations.'

'I'm sure she has.'

Price's teeth, brown with sauce, showed in a quick grin. 'What were you planning to charge her with?'

Will winced, not liking the sound of the past tense. 'We can hold her for resisting a while longer without getting into –'

Price's head was shaking. 'Nah. Nah. I'm not bringing Cathy Byford into this, and that Terrell woman is saying she abducted her. At gunpoint. The Super will shit twice before breakfast.'

Will's hand swept in front of the windscreen, past his own car parked at the edge of the grounds, finishing on the orphanage. 'After what I've just shown you, what difference does it make?'

Price's eyes narrowed as he chomped away. 'There's nothing conclusive in that cellar, and you know it.'

'But there's enough to warrant a full search of the grounds.'

'For what?'

Will shook his head. 'I think she and Peter Smiles ran this place like a concentration camp. Had free reign with the kids here. God knows what they did to them.'

'Smiles?' Price's ratting terrier look. 'You have been busy haven't you? Smiles wasn't even working here.'

Will pointed at the school. 'Did his teacher training over there. We missed it. He was her boyfriend. Two sickos with a god complex. I think they went too far, got beyond cruelty, pain, torture, whatever. I think there are bodies here. That's what the tape's getting at.'

Price's hands were up. 'Woah! Woah!' He glared at Will, then licked his fingers. 'Right now, we've got a missing kid to find. How does this help?'

Will looked away. 'It's connected. We find out what happened here we'll –'

'You don't bloody know that!'

As they watched, Samira emerged from the building, carrying the hold-all towards Will's Sierra. Will was reaching for Price's door to get out and help her.

'She can manage.' Price was smiling again, sauce caught in the corners of his mouth now. He gave Will a side-long glance. 'By the way, you nailing that yet?'

A sudden coldness in Will's arms.

A mock Texan drawl from Price. 'Y'ain't a man 'til you've made it with a tan!'

The car, the hillside, the moor and the ruins, everything seemed to plummet away. Will stared at the granite horizon, his voice matching it. 'One more word on that and I'll kick your alcoholic arse around this carpark. Sir.'

A snorting laugh, but something behind it, almost satisfying. Surprise, just a touch of fear? A few seconds for Price to find his voice. 'You're...too easy, Ashcroft. Too easy.' A shake of the head. 'Can I be straight with you?' Price wiped his fingers with the paper bag his sandwich had come in. He scrunched it up, unwound the window and threw it. 'I know what happened to you down London. Stratham told me all about it.' He wiped the corners of his mouth with his thumb, licking the sauce off it afterwards. 'To be honest, you've been a pain in the arse since you got here. You're a good copper. A better one than me, anyway. But you just don't fit in up here. I know you were raised here but… this place just isn't for you.'

Will eyed Price. 'I'm officially requesting a full search of these grounds. SOCOs. Dogs, Methane probe. Are you refusing?'

Price opened his mouth but stopped, a mean smile on his face as he leant forwards again. 'I bet you have a good laugh at us down London, don't you? You and your mates at AMIP. Bunch of Yorkshire gawbies who couldn't solve a *Sun* crossword. That's us, right? But what you lot haven't got, with all your progressive thinking and racial equality, your little bits o' fanny shagging their way up to DCI… what you haven't got… is the balls to admit you've messed up.' He laughed. 'Like you did in London, Ashcroft. I know they're *thinking* of giving you that medal. But, way I hear it…they're not sure it's a good idea. You fucked it right up, didn't you?'

Of course that's when his hand started, making his fumble for the door even more noticeable, and Price's laughter harder to take.

That and the fact he was right.

35

The drizzle was slow enough for her to switch the wipers to a long interval, sharpening the Ramirs' Off-Licence from a clotted blur every thirty seconds. She'd parked up the side road between a Datsun Cherry and a rusty Volvo. There wasn't much chance of being noticed. She'd been watching half an hour, ranging between almost giving a shit and wild anger at being here at all.

Price. All this time she'd considered the man a typical backward-thinking moron. Not as bad as Grundy with his dog-with-two-dicks grin. But so dismissive this morning at the incident room. That broad Yorkshire drawl that didn't engage, didn't care. *Ramir case still not sorted. Redeployment.*

'What about Ryan Byford?' she'd asked.

'Ashcroft's off it. Not well.'

Wishful thinking or truth? Either way, it wasn't the question she'd asked.

'We're broadening the net with sex offenders. You can still help out with that. Some in Leeds, Doncaster and Wakefield worth looking at. But primarily, you're back on the Ramir case. Alright, luv?'

She didn't ask about Will, of course. Their plan of going on somewhere last night had been shot down by Price's appearance too. Will had stormed away from Price's car and got into his own, leaving her with a lift back to the station from Price. Yeah, thanks for that.

But the look on Will's face. It was the worst she'd seen him, in a way. Not quite there. Like he'd given up. She'd spent the rest of the evening resisting the urge to call around at his place. But she knew that whatever had passed between Price and him, Will had walked away from her for his own reasons. Avoidance, plain and simple. Hard on her ego, but so what. He'd taken the opportunity to side-step her so he could hold onto whatever was twisting him a little while longer.

Still, she probably would have called around anyway, if not for the phone call from her brother. The daft sod was on the

verge of losing his job and might lose the flat (as he called it –
a bedsit in reality) along with it. Bills unpaid. Could she help
him out?

She'd have to, of course. Even if not for him. She'd only just
got back on speaking terms with Mum and Dad. She couldn't
jeopardise that.

She watched the wiper do its thing. When was this drizzle
going to stop, anyway?

She tried to bring her thoughts back to the Ramir case. Sitting
here watching the shop had seemed like the thing to do this
morning. Why? Two reasons. Because coming back to it after
being away, something just didn't sit right.

The other reason. She couldn't think of anything else to do.

There had been several customers since she'd pulled in here.
Mostly older, calling in for loaves of bread, milk or other
staples. A few, mid-teens, had stayed in the shop for anything
up to twenty minutes each. Not that unusual. They could be
friends with some of the younger Ramirs.

As she watched now, a man, late twenties, lumberjack-style
jacket, red and blue check, was heading in. She half watched
him, thoughts straying back to Darren, to Price, to Will and
finally to Ryan Byford. Out there somewhere. Almost a week
now. In pain, distress, or worse. A flash of him as if tied to that
ring in Moorhaven's cellar, bloody fingernails digging into the
wall…

Red and blue check, through a crack in the upstairs curtains.
Above the shop, in the Ramirs' home. Okay. No big deal. Could
be friend of the family too.

She watched, brow furrowing a little. Three more lads
appearing over the rise and heading down to the shop.

Half an hour later, Samira was still there, jiggling with
adrenaline now, though.

It was dope.

The Ramirs were selling dope.

At first she'd thought maybe a knocking shop. But then
amongst the customers drifting in, two teenage girls, back out
in fifteen, passing close enough to the car for Samira to get a

look at their eyes. Black holes to planet shit-faced.

Now she sat, running scenarios across the misted glass.

There was an easy familiarity about the way the punters were arriving, trotting upstairs, sampling the wares, hanging around for a few tokes and a natter and drifting back out again. They'd been doing this a while. So, it was pretty likely Mr Ramir wasn't quite the innocent victim of a racist beating after all.

Turf war.

She blinked. Little Kenny had been protecting his territory.

It made sense of how the beating was reported too. The old woman braving the evening estate for her nicotine habit, no idea what went on at her local newsagents and tobacconists, seeing some hooded blokes running from the scene and finding Mr Ramir in a crumpled bloody mess. The family had been out; Kenny had chosen his moment.

Then Mr Ramir, banged about, under pressure from whoever interviewed him as he regained consciousness, had denied knowledge of his assailants but had stuck to the truth about Ray's size, the lad vomiting on the papers and so on. He'd probably figured there wouldn't be any arrests.

Samira couldn't help a low giggle. Lovely, all of it.

Price wouldn't give a shit, but the Superintendent would have kittens; the victim of a racist crime turning out to be a drug dealer. Not the kind of political points he'd been after, though he'd probably rally, turn it to his advantage.

It didn't mean Kenny wasn't going to go down for it though. She had a feeling she'd be having another little chat with those Drugs Squad officers pretty soon. Maybe a raid and the threat of the whole family arrested would be enough for the Ramirs to turn over on their rivals.

Enough. Samira shook her head, turned the key and headed for the motorway.

Back to Ryan Byford.

It would be two hours before she was due at the Doncaster station to meet Sergeant Naylor, who she'd been partnered with to interview a few assembled perverts without alibis for last Monday. So, without really thinking of it as an act of conscious rebellion, she took the Leeds turn-off and drove to Social Services' main office.

There'd been no records at all in the Spinnerby council office yesterday when they'd visited for the keys. Nothing on staff or children who'd been in residence at the children's home. Fair enough, she supposed. It was twelve years, and record-keeping for those kinds of institutions was notoriously bad, and Brenda Terrell had clearly covered her tracks best she could when the place was being closed down, and before then.

She looked the cold black-stone office block. It was Saturday morning. There'd be a skeleton staff here in Leeds, if that, the building not even open to the public.

A cleaner, cigarette dangling, mop in hand, blue overall too big, directed her grudgingly to the back office, where an elderly woman, fluffy cardigan, eyes drowsy and blank, looked at her Warrant card like she'd asked for the keys to the crown jewels. Samira glanced at the wall clock and inwardly screamed.

'You need to try the Spinnerby council office –'

'I already have. They have nothing.'

'Well then.' Finality in the intonation.

Samira let out a breath. She'd have to press now; warrant card or not, she was off her patch here, no official sanction. It would come to vague threats, allusions to incompetence. She'd have no good will from this woman and anything she did get would likely be a fraction of what was buried away in a creaky filing cabinet somewhere in this building. She'd actually opened her mouth to start when a shadow fell across the glass door, a largish figure struggling to open it.

Maybe mid-forties. Shuffling on a walking stick, laces slapping from one trainer, trousers flared over whatever the cause. His face was dark, more so than hers, full afro to her mixed origin. Could be a good or bad thing of course, no guarantees of brother/sister solidarity. But the smile he gave her was roomy and genuine, eyes shining with something his colleague seemed to have misplaced. Humanity. A face that had lived.

'It's okay, Lilly.' He somehow inserted himself between them without offense and, hand easy on Samira's shoulder, steered her into the office he'd come from, turning behind her and giving Lilly some small talk Samira couldn't even make out. Then, the funniest thing, Lilly's laughter, light petals of it trickling through the air.

'I'm Roland. How can I help you, my love?'

It was nothing to do with race. Some men used language to patronise. Others like a balm.

Samira introduced herself, took the seat he waved her into, watched him collapse like a barrage balloon into a cushion-laden high-chair, both he and it creaking.

In the end it wasn't even a decision, because that would've taken calculation. She opened her mouth and told him everything. What she and Will suspected about Moorhaven, what the implications might be. Risky. Social services would likely have to face up to whatever part it had played, and Samira had a feeling that would be considerable, somewhere along the line.

Roland listened, the light in his eyes dipping a little. 'Lord.' A low groan, doubt gathering at the corners of his mouth. There'd be self-interest, loyalty to his peers to contend with. Samira was gambling on his humanity. Would it win out?

'I'll get you everything I find. Might take a while.'

'It's alright Roland.' She said. 'I'll make time.'

She was half an hour late for Naylor, blaming it on traffic and not knowing the area. The pathetic female thing, shrugging, eyelids fluttering, letting his chauvinism fill in the gaps. Women drivers, female coppers in general, blah, blah, blah. It seemed to work, Naylor rolling his eyes and shepherding her through to the interview rooms.

Samira tried to keep an open mind. No sense dismissing the four assembled past or suspected offenders out of hand. At the very least they might spot someone covering up something else, she thought, or scare one of them into chemical castration. Yeah. Likely.

But three futile hours later they scurried out into the Leeds daylight and headed for their cars, certainly no more enriched with love for the human spirit and no closer to finding Ryan

Byford than before. Naylor was shaking his head. 'Fucking nonces. Do my head in.' He stretched his neck, cropped blonde hair sparkling with perspiration or gel or something. Not a bad looking bloke, she supposed, in that thickset freckly-armed kind of way. He coughed, clearly trying to voice something. 'Err, S'meera?'

She raised her eyebrows, fluttered a bit, smiled.

'Seeing as we're gonna be partnered up, let's go grab something to eat.'

She broadened her smile. 'Ah. Great idea but…' She did a disappointed eye-roll. 'I've actually got a few things to sort. Maybe tomorrow, instead? In fact, I was gonna ask you something. I could do with nipping home. Could you cover for me when you get back to the nick?'

He made a face.

'An hour. Two tops. Won't make a habit of it, promise. Wouldn't ask but err…' She did a kind of half whispering thing. 'It's womany stuff, you know?'

He reddened slightly. 'Oh. Ah right. Yeah, sure.'

'Cheers. Owe you one.' She trotted off to her car, giving him a grin as she got in.

'Hey S'meera.' He cupped his hands around his mouth. 'Follow me back. Don't wanna get lost again, right?'

'Oh, it's alright. Don't wait for me. I'll just slow you down.' A wave, the grin still plastered across her face as she pulled out of the carpark and took a left, then right, no thought for where she was going. She pulled into a side-street, keeping an eye on the mirror for a couple of minutes until she was sure he wasn't behind her.

She reached in the back for the mag-mount beacon and stuck it on the roof without ceremony. She pulled out, switched on the siren. She gave a little snort, lost under the Fiesta's climbing revs. 'No, you follow *me* mate, if you can keep up!'

There was no particular reason Price would hear about it if she buzzed in for some name-checks. But the station was insular, a lot of loyalty to the old-school DCI, so she didn't want to risk it. Doing it herself would be time-consuming, though.

She stopped at three booths before she found an intact phone book.

Even with the help from Roland, she didn't have much to go on. Some incomplete records pertaining to other staff, but nothing useful. But then Roland had hit paydirt, handing her some attempted adoption transfers for two boys and a girl from Moorhaven, run by an adoption agency called Right Choice (now defunct). All had failed to actualise; potential fosterers with cold feet by the looks of it. Or scared away by Brenda? Who knows? The girl's name was Smith, so not much possibility of a trace there. The first boy, Dan Taylor, a non-starter too; too many Taylors in Yorkshire by far. The second, more promising, was Jamie Longford, with only four Longfords in the region, two of those in the valley. Would he have stayed, though, after leaving Moorhaven?

A couple of calls and the ones out of the valley turned out to be too old. One of the valley-dwellers' numbers was answered by a wife; her husband away visiting his parents, which didn't sound like an orphan. It turned out his name wasn't Jamie anyway. Leaving one other number. A hesitant voice answered, male, maybe thirtyish. 'He's not here.' Then a 'Like we haven't got enough to worry about' at Samira's mention that she was police. It took a fair amount of reassurance before he finally told her Jamie was at work. Jamie. The forename was right, at least.

She pulled up at the garden centre and was directed to Jamie's department. A pale, wasted figure, unseasonably woolly hat, orange dungarees flapping around him, eyed her as she approached. She checked his name badge. What she could see of his hair was sandy, skin mottled. What she wasn't expecting was for him to turn after seeing the warrant card, walk to the edge of the enclosed garden area and throw up all over the hydrangeas.

She ignored the gathering staff and crouched with a hand on his back. 'You alright, Jamie?'

'Uhh... not so...great...'

Her fingers found shoulder blades, nobbles of spine through his shirt. A tightening of eyes as he stretched over the bucket one of the staff had passed him. His hat shifted forwards and almost tumbled off but his left hand found it, pushed it back into place, even as his body heaved again. Samira kept rubbing his back.

There was a flurry of activity around them, the store manager directing staff with mops, buckets, sawdust. Then he glanced at the hydrangeas and waved one of the female staff away. 'Just leave it. I'll take care of it.' A long look at Jamie; pity, annoyance, a tint of disgust. He shook his head at Samira. 'Second time this month.' He tutted, looked like he wanted to say more, cleared his throat and went to give Jamie a pat on the shoulder, his hand hovering for a second and then snatched away and examined almost furtively. He seemed to catch Samira watching him and reddened a little. He turned back to Jamie. 'Get home with ya, lad. We'll talk about this next week.' A harshness in his tone. But then it softened. 'You clock off in half an hour anyway. D'you wanna make a call? Get a lift or –'

'It's okay,' Jamie leant back onto his knees, eyes watering, back of his hand hovering over his mouth. He looked up at Samira. 'Reckon I've already got one.'

36

They drove to the rocks opposite Shockley beck. Wind buffeted the car, driving wild stems of rain over the glass. Samira had opened her window to a slit, enough for some cold air to circulate, giving him a carrier bag in case the car-ride set him off again. Actually, he seemed to have picked up a little.

'You're sure nothing has happened to Daryl.'

Daryl, presumably the man who'd answered her phone call. 'No. Like I said, nothing like that.' She winced a little. It wasn't like her, but she was finding it hard to start. She took in Jamie's blotchy gaunt cheeks, bony nose, the ill-fitting hat and stonewashed jacket. 'Does your boss know?' she found herself asking.

Jamie laughed. 'What? That I'm gay or that I'm…ill? Doubt it, either way. Probably thinks I'm on drugs. Well, I am, but not those kinds.'

She'd guessed the first part. Jamie's emphasis on the second didn't leave much doubt what the illness was. Samira tried resisting the cliché, found she couldn't. 'I'm sorry.' She thought of the Garden Centre manager's pulling back of his hand. 'Actually, I think you're underestimating your boss back there. You might want to think about talking to him.'

Head back. A gulp.

'Your boyfriend's sticking with you, right?'

'Yeah. Daryl's a good'un. I got lucky. Too late.'

She nodded. 'What about your family?'

He stiffened. 'I'm an orphan.'

Samira had parked on the promenade over the rocks, and the view was fabulous in its own rugged right even overcast and drenched, but almost directly opposite on the other valley wall was the road that led to Moorhaven and Jamie's eyes flashed that way as surely as a polygraph truth spike, or more so.

Okay. She tried to keep the excitement from her tone, given the circumstances. 'That's why I'm here. Brenda Terrell. Peter Smiles.'

Jamie's breath seemed to catch, a coughing fit that had her reaching for the carrier-bag but his hand was up. He shook his head, breathing, his colour draining out like an epidural. 'Christ! No one has said those names to me for...' He looked at her again. 'Had a feeling, soon as you flashed that card. You're a bit late though. Like fifteen frigging years.'

She grimaced. 'I know. I'm sorry.' She let him alone. Either he'd open up or he wouldn't.

Jamie had been an actual orphan, he told her, parents killed in a car-crash. Surprisingly few at Moorhaven were; most from poverty-stricken or abuse-prone families. His first years there, up until his ninth birthday, were idyllic in comparison to what came later when Brenda took up residence, her influence gradually making itself felt.

'You'd look up, scrubbing the floor, a smack over the head. Leather belt. Then you start wetting the bed. Beaten for that, wooden sandal, knees, elbows. Locked in a freezing room for days on end. One kid, not me... he was tied to a metal bed, electrocuted.'

Samira opened the window a little more, her hand kneading her abdomen. She didn't feel sick exactly, just somehow needed to touch the part of herself where she knew she would, with any luck, one day carry a child.

'Things changed when Brenda started bringing Smiley in for visits. More organised. More creative. They kept a frigging score sheet in the main hall, hanging over the tables. So, you'd never forget –'

'I don't get it. Scoring for what?'

'Everything. Cleaning up, putting our things out in the morning, getting in the milk, schoolwork, everything a competition. With punishments.'

'How much of it was sexual?'

Jamie sniffed, then let out a sudden choked laugh. His eyes flared. 'Moorhaven didn't make me gay, I've always known what I am.'

She shook her head. 'Not what I –'

'Sex was just... part of it.' A shy kind of look downward. 'Humiliation. Pain.'

'Peter Smiles involved?'

184

'Not in that.' Jamie was fixed on the windscreen, silently painting god-knows what patterns in his head. 'Not his style.'

'Day staff then? Their names?'

Jamie's skin seemed to tighten. 'Don't get it, do you?'

Samira frowned. What didn't she get? She watched the rain and they shared the noise of pattering for a while. Maybe time for a different tack. 'Why did you stay in the valley, Jamie? Afterwards. I think I'd have gotten out.'

'I did. Moved to Leeds. Tried education. Few other things.' He sighed. 'Suppose I came back to prove I could. Then I fell in love.' A smile, sad but radiant. 'It's just a place.' He wafted a hand around them. 'Anyway, there's no one left around here from those days.'

She thought of telling him Brenda Terrell was back in town. She sat forwards. 'If we can open a proper enquiry on this, would you be prepared to testify?'

A quick spasm around his eyes. 'Who would I testify against?'

'Brenda Terrell for one.'

'For what?' He seemed to deflate in the seat. 'She never touched us.'

Samira grimaced. 'What are you…?' She found herself going over everything he'd just told her. Had he made it up?

'Neither did Smiles. They just gave us a system. A game. Stood back and observed.' He was smiling now, so for a second Samira thought she was in the car with a lunatic, but then she saw it, suddenly, the awful logic of it. Jamie nodded.

'Oh my God!' Samira's hand was on her abdomen again. The older kids… no, not even the older ones, she thought. The stronger ones had their way with the weaker ones… torture… had them slaving for them. Hunting them.

'Wolves and sheep.' Jamie put an arm across himself.

Samira couldn't seem to stop her head from shaking, thinking of the cellar, the vices on the woodwork tables, the blood on the walls, the ring, then the tape and its message. She looked over at the hillside opposite. 'What's buried over there, Jamie?'

He was paler than he'd been, voice barely audible. 'Sometimes there were kids we wouldn't see again. Brenda would say they'd been adopted and we'd cheer for them, inside, be jealous as well but we never saw them leave. You'd expect a car or something. And… they were all *sheep*.'

She watched a single trickle of rain gather volume from the small drips in its path on the glass. Put her finger to it. Then she looked at him. 'Feeling up to a walk, Jamie?'

Samira reached out and took his hand.

He gave a thumbs up with his other, pulled his hat down a little and turned up his collar. Was this a bad idea? He was ill, after all. But she'd given him one of the Police waterproofs from the boot and he seemed to want some air as much as she did.

Once they'd passed down amongst the rocks, they had shelter. The wind's howl dropped away leaving that sudden privileged sensation of being dry and safe in a maelstrom; like being next to a log fire with rain smattering the panes.

She asked him if he'd ever met Sean Byford, thinking it was possible he'd had therapy after the orphanage. He shook his head, no hesitation.

'Jamie. This is important. Peter Smiles is dead. Sunday last week. Near here, even though he'd moved to Liverpool years ago. We think someone brought him back here and killed him.'

Shock she was pretty sure of settled in his wide eyes.

'Can you think of anyone, wolf or sheep, who could have done it?'

'Nah.' Eyes darting away now, for the first time.

He tried pulling his hand away, but she held on to it, pulled herself close to him. 'Jamie, I'm going to level with you. If this was only about Peter Smiles, I might take your *no* for an answer and leave it at that. But whoever it is, we think he might have kidnapped a twelve-year-old boy.'

'Ahhhh!' Jamie deflated again, head shaking.

'Come on, Jamie. Give me a name.'

He slowed his breathing. 'You don't want to know.'

'I do, Jamie. I really do.'

When it came it was choked by tears in full flow, so she had to ask him to repeat before she got it.

'Adam,' He said, calmer. 'It'll be Adam.'

Jamie was quiet all the way back up the path. She didn't break his silence. She was thinking of a book she'd read at school; a bunch of boys crash-landed on some island, gradually descending into chaos. But Brenda had given her prodigies a lot more than sticks and shells to play with. Samira shivered, thoughts drifting back to the cellar.

Adam had been one of the wolves, Jamie had told her. No idea of surname of course. Blonde, blue-eyed and bloody gorgeous. Enough to catch the eye of an adoption agency early in Brenda's tenure, until arrangements had 'fallen through'. Adam had changed then, become vicious. A survivor. Usually the one to lead the hunts over the moor.

She thought of Smiles when they'd found him a week ago, the heather in his clothes, the state of him generally. Put through his paces, as Will had said.

When they were back in the car, the waterproofs dripping into the boot, she asked him, 'Jamie. How did it end?'

'Smiley left Brenda to it. Dropped her. So, she just kind of withdrew. The games went on. Got worse.'

Brenda had finally crept from her pit and told them all the experiment was over, Moorhaven's owner was passing the property over to the council who'd decided to close it and if they wanted to be adopted '… or transferred somewhere *nicer*, we'd have to convince social services we were normal.'

'Lord,' Samira found herself saying, sounding like Nan back in Spanish Town. She reached for the keys, thought about asking if he wanted some music. No. Not right. She shook her head suddenly, frowning. 'I don't get why none of the staff reported anything. No one in five years?' She glanced over as the corners of Jamie's mouth turned up a little.

'Most day-staff only saw so much. Most of the bad shit happened at night.' His head was down, something flushing his cheeks. 'Actually, detective…?'

'Samira.' She said.

'I feel… really bad, Samira. Could you… take me to the hospital?'

She studied him between glances at the road and mirror. Collapsed, as if the last half an hour had bled him out. 'God, I should never have taken you to –'

'Nah!' He almost laughed. 'Love the rain… trees...'

She tightened her eyes. Rationally, Jamie had been careless, and now his body had turned, convincing his immune system it was worth nothing.

But that craving for love, for self-esteem that could never be answered, that was what Brenda and Smiles' little game had left him with.

She wound the car down into the rain-soaked valley, the wipers screeching on the window, inadequate and futile.

37

The estate was rammed. Flashing blue lights, uniforms and an ambulance were splayed around the house entrance. Curtains twitched and the locals were out in force, meaty tattooed arms folded, heads shaking at standing bobbies. A few older kids were playing around them on bikes, and everywhere, inert anger was hanging ready to spark.

He walked through it all quickly, knots in his stomach and pressure in his temples. He ran his hands through his hair and knuckled his eyes. The Craven Edge sign was graffiti-covered, swimming in his vision. There was a nod at his raised ID from a uniform he didn't recognise.

The door was open and Will passed through the narrow hallway, arms consciously pulled in to his sides though he wanted like hell to lean on something. A small living room, crowded. There was Price, Grundy, Turner and Naylor, two smoking, all rooting, touching, prodding around, and at least two more in the kitchen. Two ambulance men, too. No sign of Samira. No white-suited Scene of crimes officers either.

Price looked up at Will from his crouch over the settee and coughed, his cigarette raining sparks.

Will moved closer, seeing the slumped body of Brenda Terrell for the first time. She was on her back, laid out on the sofa. Her black hair fanned out above the kind of polyester jumper that smacked of indoor markets. Nylon trousers too.

A couple of the uniforms were laughing and Will caught a *you'd have to be desperate* from Grundy. Will grimaced and moved into the room, taking the Vicks vapour tube from his inside pocket, dabbing his top lip. The corpse smell was early stages, but death had already had its way with her sphincter, and under that there was a musty, old sweat stink to her that Will remembered from their scuffle yesterday. Probably just her.

Her left arm was cast outward, a syringe on the coffee table along with some dope, a leather belt, a spoon and burner.

Price gave him a sneer. 'Thought you were back down London, tail between your legs.'

He tried to concentrate on the older man's bloodshot eyes.

Should he ask him, straight out, what it was like to be a total arsehole? Or should he rant about the contamination of the crime scene and why Price hadn't thrown all the junior officers out? He could feel Turner's stare and thought of returning it but didn't have the energy. Another PC was coming in from the kitchen with a tray of coffee cups, raising his eyebrows at Will. Almost comical.

It didn't matter. Didn't matter now.

Instead he looked at the table, clearing his throat and finding his voice there, just. 'Is that… where the syringe and belt were, or have they been moved?'

Price frowned, then nodded. 'Aye. They were right there. Why?'

Will reached over, picked up the nearest cushion from the floor and turned it. He did the same with another one, examining it closely. He put it back but left it standing against the settee. 'So, Brenda was on the brown…'

'Aye. Bloody junky.' Price smirked. 'Never would've said it, looking at her yesterday. Middle-aged woman, not exactly your typical scag-head.'

Will moved closer, taking the dead hand. The tiny bruise fresh on her inner arm over older track marks. He focused on her face. Skin pale, not quite waxy, lips without any fullness but then they'd been that way yesterday, he remembered. But some discolouration around them and her nose. He lifted an eyelid, closed it again. Put a finger to the back of her neck. No sticky ointment residue and none of the burns that had marked Peter Smiles. But Smiles had been tortured over days, whereas this had been rushed. Different MO, unless you looked at it more broadly. Both could be seen as disorganised murders made to look like something else.

As he was about to let go, he saw a hint of whiteness around her wrist. As if she'd been tied, not at the point of death but a while before it.

'Accidental OD.' Price said it flat. 'Unless you think she did it on purpose.'

She'd pointed that Luger at her head yesterday and pulled the trigger five times, whatever she'd said afterwards. She could have come back here after Price had let her go last night and decided on bye-byes. Except... the side table was out of reach. She'd have had to shoot herself up, then get up to put the belt and syringe back there. Will pointed it out, watching Price's face fill with slow thunder. No point stopping now. 'And I've seen a few accidental ODs. Usually they fall asleep on their back and their body forgets to breathe. Brenda here, she has bruises around her mouth and nose and that cushion has traces on it.' He pointed at it, Price not bothering to even glance that way. 'Her eyes are totally bloodshot too, which doesn't fit with the whole *body forgetting to breathe* thing and –'

'Why d'you have to complicate everything? A druggy OD'd in her shitty little house. Who cares about the detail?'

Will held his hands open. 'The SOCO will bear me out. Where is he, by the way?'

'Off sick.' He held up a hand. 'Before you start quoting procedure, I've got a stand-in on his way over from Bradford. Traffic for the fezzie's probably bad.' Price's eyes were fixed on the cushion now, and Will wondered at its chances of still being here if and when the replacement SOCO turned up. Price shifted his gaze back to Will, smirk in place. 'You should be out looking for Ryan Byford, anyway.'

They looked at each other, Will pretty sure they each knew the other's thoughts. He glanced around the room; the uniforms all seeming to be getting on with something, clearly taking in every word. Turner and Grundy were openly watching, almost sneering.

Will looked at the cushion. He could pick it up now and take it to the car, bag it, insist on its being checked, along with the bruises on Brenda's face. She'd been smothered, he was sure of it; by whoever had put Peter Smiles through his paces on the moor, leading him to a heart attack that had probably saved him from worse. No way of proving the connection though.

All-out-war with this department. Was that what he wanted? He was already marginalised; another move in that direction and there was no coming back. He gave Price a lethal smile to match his own and the room seemed to crackle.

A voice, from upstairs. 'Boss! Err... better get up here!'

Price had actually said something like 'there's no need for you to stick your nose in' as he'd headed for the stairs but Will had just ignored him. Now, Price was quiet, staring around him with a face desolate with revelation. Welcome to my world, Will thought.

There were framed photos on the staircase so the fact that Brenda had had a darkroom wasn't a big surprise. The fact that the photos were really good was, somehow. Will didn't know much about art but Brenda had had an eye; that he could say. Not that any of them were easy to look at. Mawkish, something jarring in each one. Hardly surprising, after his one meeting with the woman; she hardly projected lightness. One shot of the moor almost threw him; at first glance a landscape he pictured hanging in some yuppie penthouse. Then, a closer look at the white blobs on the hillside; all sheep, all dead. Moved into place so they formed a vector shape. He wondered if Brenda had killed them to get the shot. Probably.

Others on the staircase were more blatantly dark. A rotting human cadaver, a gutted fish, a child's football squashed open with a tyre-mark running over it.

'Sick fucking bitch!' had been Price's estimation. For once, no argument.

The door had been forced, hanging off, splintered wood around the hinges. But it was the darkroom itself had quietened the DCI. The stench of bleach, for one thing. Slopped on the table, the floor, a bottle half-emptied. A tray on the side table, some ruined negatives, plenty more spread on a table, some envelopes torn open. But all of that was detail. What stole the senses was the collection of developed shots hanging up, drying out.

When Price finally spoke again his voice was different, flatter, the swagger missing. 'I don't get it. Why did she destroy the negatives and then develop these?' He gestured upwards.

Will glanced around him. 'I reckon she's in here, doing whatever. She hears noises. Someone's in the house. She locks herself in. Pours out some bleach, fishes out the negs and starts destroying them.'

'Why would she –?'

'Because she guessed who it was. And why he was here.'

Price subsided again. 'Why not just burn them?'

'Can't smoke in a darkroom or keep matches. She was a junky, but together enough to keep this little hobby going too. Because it was important to her.' Price said nothing, so Will carried on. 'So, she tried the bleach. Thing is though, it's not that quick. Strips off the coating but not instantly. And it looks like some of them she didn't have time to find. There are quite a lot. Meanwhile, he's working at the door hinges. He gets in, drags her downstairs, but not before he gets her to develop these. Or if he knows how, he does it himself while she's tied up.' Will glanced at the door. It wasn't so damaged it couldn't have been propped up to block the light. He nodded to himself. 'Then he hangs them up, for us to see.'

Price looked as pale as some of the faces on the shots behind him. He turned, head shaking from side to side as he shuffled out onto the landing. 'Need some air.'

Will followed, stood by Price's side. He looked down at the stairs, an odd sense of almost-camaraderie coming over him.

Without turning, Price said, 'Don't know how you handle it… seeing stuff like that all the time.'

'I don't.' Will raised the hand he'd been keeping hidden, shaking since he'd seen the string of photos.

Price nodded, something like a wince tightening his eyes. 'What I said last night about that case in London… I were talking shite.' He had a fresh cigarette to his mouth, lighter to it and snapping it back to his pocket quick as a salute. As close to an apology as Will would get, he supposed. It would do, though.

'One thing,' Price said through a lungful of grey vapour. He gestured down towards the living room. 'Why bother trying to make it look like an accident or a suicide? In fact, why bother injecting her at all? Why not just smother the old trout? We were bound to find that door caved in. We'll find out which window he forced to get into the house too. So, it's pointless.'

Will thought of mentioning they should have figured that out already instead of making coffee, but instead found himself saying, 'I reckon this guy doesn't really give two shits what we think. Suicide, accident, murder, whatever.'

Price sucked on his cigarette. 'Meaning?'

Will gave him a grin. 'You've been doing this what... twenty years, right?'

A *give or take* shrug.

'All that time, Ronnie...' Will's move to first name terms surprised him almost as much as it seemed to surprise Price. 'How many criminal geniuses you met?'

Price gave a sharp laugh that turned into a cough. He shook his head.

'Me neither. Don't exist outside of movies.' Will held up his good hand. 'Not that I'm saying our boy's an idiot. Probably smarter than average. He planned enough to get in here and through that door without getting us called out by neighbours or —'

'Hmm.' Price pointed at the wall. 'Old biddie next door's deaf as a post. Anyway... this neighbourhood, a door being bashed in of an evening's about as surprising as a dose of clap in a section house.'

Will nodded. 'Point is... he's made some effort to kick over his traces, fudge things a bit for us... just like with Smiles, laying him on the coal-mound, arms open for the UFO nutters.'

Price looked red at the temples, his sharp nose doing its ratting terrier thing again, presumably at Will's linking the two cases, but he took a breath, gave a shrug. 'Okay. So you think he's making it up as he goes along?'

'Not exactly. Think he plans in broad strokes. But basically he's a good improviser... makes the most of what's around him.'

Price nodded again and Will found himself wondering if he'd hallucinated the last few minutes. Had he just made an ally of an enemy? He glanced at the photos on the stairwell and then back at the darkroom. Nothing like a shock to drop the defences.

'Okay Ashcroft.' Price stubbed out his cigarette on Brenda's bannister. 'Keep working it your way. Not saying I buy it all... still not sure Smiles is connected... but we'll take that orphanage apart like you wanted. Dogs, methane probe, the works. But after we find that kid.'

It was good enough for Will. He watched Price heading down, steeled himself and was about to walk back into the darkroom when he stopped.

There was another possible reason, of course, why the scene here might lie somewhere between premeditation and chaos.

What if her killer had changed his plans? Quite a coincidence, wasn't it, that Brenda had yesterday become known to the police and then today showed up a corpse?

And how would her killer know she was in their sights? Unless they were in his.

What if he *had* been watching them on the orphanage grounds yesterday? Just as Cathy and Samira had thought.

Just as Will, for all his bloody cleverness, had failed to take seriously.

He was alone for the first time with Brenda's collection. The bleach was less cloying now, but there was a crackle of sweat on his scalp, the lights stark and unforgiving. He glanced at the developing trays, a fixer jar and a red lamp towards the rear. A council house, but it hadn't stopped her from plaster-boarding over the window and hanging blackout curtains everywhere. Expensive, especially when shared with heroin addiction, the two hardly going together, unless you considered what fuelled them. Destruction; of the self and everyone around it.

Will was no philosopher, but he reckoned he'd seen enough to be a fair judge of whether evil exists. People did good and bad things, and he was sure even Brenda Terrell had done some good in her life. But were some people so irretrievably twisted that what good they did counted for nothing?

The photos seemed to say so. Some were graphic; cruelty enacted one way or another, in forensic detail. The vice in the cellar being put to use, electric cables wired to an occupied bed, a close-up of skin, a girl's shoulder if the long comma of fair hair over it was anything to go by, being branded, then some flogging marks on another young back. Many more, much more blatant. But these weren't the ones Will had come back in here to look at again; they didn't resonate so much as those central.

They were portrait shots, several of them. Taken outside, the grey-hewn stone walls unmistakeable behind their subjects. The children of the orphanage. Winter shots; the crisp cold air accentuating faces stark and empty, despite their smiles. And the smiles were the thing that were twisting Will's equilibrium. Forced. How long had she waited, Brenda, for them to rustle them up, parodies of their own feeling, against the cold, against their suffering, against the bloody indignity of having to perform for the monster behind the camera? Awful empty contortions that didn't touch the eyes, one in particular so grotesque because the eyes, if you looked close enough, were streaming tears while the mouth below them curved upwards.

And then there was the other shot, the one central on the table, not hanging with the rest.

A single rip ran almost along its length, as if Brenda's killer had thought of destroying it and then stopped himself.

Will reached for it with the tongs and held it up.

The face was striking, a blonde boy, face already fleshed with an almost adult knowingness. The touch of a smile in an otherwise cruel mouth, but the striking thing was his expression, as if appraising Brenda as she'd pressed the shutter. Without fear. Without disdain. Just looking at her.

Will pocketed the shot. Not that he didn't trust Price's newly reformed sensibility, but he wanted to make sure this one was checked for prints as soon and thoroughly as possible. Not only that. He had a feeling the face might be one he'd want to remember. In his head, he'd already added twelve years to it. A face to conjure with.

Downstairs, things were a bit more business-like. The SOCO had arrived and Price had cleared out. Grundy and Turner were still standing around like spare pricks, but the rest of the uniforms were bustling. Will gave the two idiots a glare and told the flustered SOCO about the cushion, making sure he bagged it while Will watched.

That done, nothing more for him here. He headed for the car, hand kneading at his neck.

Most of the locals were gone; just a few at the edges of their gardens or yards, and some kids on bikes, the same ones keeping Will and Samira company a few nights ago. One of them swept close, eyes flashing over Will from under a red hoodie. Yes. The one who'd come in close last time. He shot past, turning down towards the distant behemoth of Craven Tower, swerving into the road and out again, repeating the movement, and again.

Will stopped at the car door, unlocking but not pulling it wide. He took a step back, staring around him.

Stillness. A weird quiet. All wrong for this estate, especially on a non-school afternoon. But then the air was split, shrill and awful, a wail, wracked with sudden pain. Deeper than a girl would manage, but young. From the verge of the estate where the crags overlooked the valley, he reckoned, an eighth of a mile away at most.

Real? His senses were hardly to be trusted these days. He glanced around for the burly-armed neighbours. All turned or turning away, heading for their doors. Something almost as chilling about that as the scream itself.

Kids playing, then? No. No way. Something in it; too distressed. He snarled at the disappearing neighbours, flung the door open and slid into his seat.

He pulled away, his thoughts flickering to Ryan Byford. No reason to think it was him. No reason at all.

38

'Proceeding into Craven edge –' The crackling swelled to a fuzzy yawn of white noise. This estate, this bloody moor. More chance of raising Space Shuttle Challenger on this radio than of bouncing a clear signal down into the valley. Will slammed the handset back into place and leant over the wheel. He wound the window down quickly, straining over the revs for another distant scream, but nothing doing.

The bike ahead did its swerve into the road and back again, so Will had to slow a little for fear of hitting him. Then, as they drew adjacent, the red hood turned towards him, a cocky smile playing from under it. The lad swerved away, the bike swaying under him as picked up speed, shooting from the exit and hitting the side-street, disappearing from view.

Will stayed with the narrow road that wound up past the rec, trying to listen over the rising whistle of the wind. A streak of crimson catching his eye, almost keeping pace, flashing between the rows of houses, bobbing along the path that must snake through the estate and up over the recreation ground and onto the crag that bordered it.

He reached for the handset; if he couldn't reach central up here on the moor, he should at least be able to get through to Grundy a few hundred yards back. A few wasted seconds trying to remember Grundy's call-sign. Not one he'd ever thought of using. Screw protocol anyway. 'Grundy. Ashcroft proceeding into Craven edge. Towards the crags. Possible minor in distress. Could be Willow, over.' Nothing but static. 'If you're receiving, please acknowledge. Could do with some backup, over.' He tried not to think of Stratham's comment about his ending up dead in a ditch.

A small graffiti covered power station loomed, wind gusting at the car. He snapped the handset back. He was over the rise and he slowed, a broken fence to his right, leading onto wasteland. The drizzle had finally given in but the sky was grey and baleful and the craggy edge of the estate rough and twisted. He edged the car through the gap in the fence, the track carrying him over a slight rise and then down. He stood on the brakes.

At least seven abandoned supermarket trolleys glinted from the bracken, stacked up, blocking the track.

He stopped, shoulders tensing, heart racing. Opened the window fully again, though it would take some set of lungs to get over the roar of the wind now. Should he get out? Something was telling him not to.

Then, as his head turned, a sudden movement, a flash of red cloth barely twenty yards to the left, over the clumps and divots of bracken and rough land. Biker boy was there. Not alone though. Another kid, podgy, pale, terrified face apparent, even from here. As Will watched, biker boy sent the portly kid on his way with a sneering flick of his head.

A creeping pang of doubt now, about earlier. Biker boy had swept in close as Will had come out of Brenda's place. Looked at Will. Recognised him. Then swerved all over the road... no, not all over the road, now he thought about it. More controlled, more deliberate than that. Like what? A signal? To someone ready to hurt an overweight, terrified boy for the sake of a scream to lure a copper up here. And maybe not just any copper.

Enough! He put the car into reverse, arm over the passenger seat, neck twisted back.

Another engine, revs increasing. A van. Just nosing up over the rise and down towards him. No way he'd get through the gap in the fence before it was blocked. He snapped his head around. The scrub of wasteland spreading past the trolleys to the edge of the crags was the only way to go. He changed back into first, edged towards the trolleys, intending to nudge them out of the way. Then, a horrible chill in his guts, he stood on the brakes again.

Glistening wet, two long chains snaking through the trolleys, stretching to the tree on the right, turning a flimsy stack into a barrier that would take more horsepower than he had to break through. He didn't need to look to the left to check if the other ends were tied to the fence.

In the mirror, the van stopping. A transit, its bulk sealing up the broken fence. No one getting out yet.

Not quite believing what he was doing, he reached for the glove compartment. Maybe it wasn't called for, and if he actually used it he'd probably be finished, but as a deterrent… a cold knife of fear now as he rifled through the compartment; the telescopic baton, some papers, the *Leatherman* tool he'd used to break into Ray's caravan… ironic because that was almost certainly who was about to step out of that van.

But that was it. Nothing else.

Where was the fucking Luger?

Oh, Samira, no. He felt his throat catch on a sick laugh. He thought of her carrying the stuff from the orphanage to his car as he'd sat and listened to Price's bullshit last night, and the way she'd stared at him as he'd told her about his little arrangement with himself. Had she thought he was suicidal?

You've killed me, trying to save me.

The van doors opened. Three figures. Masked, but not much doubt who the bigger one was.

No point wondering whether to stay in the car. They'd smash the windows or set fire to it, dragging or roasting him out.

He pushed at the door and dived, sprawling on the rough ground and then lunging up into a dash. He threw himself at the trolleys, clambering up the shifting structure, the chain not so tight they didn't heave and rattle, fingers wet, knees scraped, somehow finding his feet and balancing at the top long enough to make a tumbling leap for the coarse grass, landing and half rolling, up onto his feet and running again, a graceless lope towards the edge of the crag. The sound of the trolleys rattling behind him; they were close, but a grunting and jangling of metal gave him a little hope, and he glanced over his shoulder. Ray and Kenny not exactly agile. But the other one had gotten over quickly, was close at Will's heels.

Will came to a sudden stop and twisted his body as something swung out at him… a baseball bat? It split the air close to his head and he twisted, the baton extending as he thrust, going full on in a sudden flurry with it and his other hand, *nose, neck, nuts, knees!* Impossible to be accurate but something connected if the quiet choked grunt was anything to go by, the bat clunking onto the ground as its owner fell into a crouch, Will glancing up; the other two were over the trolleys and closing. He turned, sprinting forward again.

Near the edge now, a sheer drop of fifty feet, then fields and lights, scattered villages and hills leading over to Luddenden. He'd thought he might be able to scramble down there, but no way. He glanced along the edge; maybe from fifty yards further along where it wasn't so steep, but they'd never let him get there.

Will turned. They were walking towards him, unhurried, one limping slightly.

From here, between the two larger figures he could just see the main road he'd come from, snaking away back around to the estate. There, about three hundred yards away, through a gap in the overgrowth, a police car. Grundy and Turner? The car was still, as if checking something out. But surely they could see his Sierra from there.

The three of them had split and were converging on him now. Getting them away from the edge was the best he could do. He ran, making for the gap between the one he'd injured and the bigger one, Ray. Then, very last second he changed direction, tore straight at the one he'd put down earlier. All wrong, this time, and he felt it as soon as he was close, the man's readiness, arms wide, falling back, not engaging, just keeping Will here, dancing left and right as Will tried to get past him. Then, a sharp kick at the back of Will's knees that brought him down, from Ray, or Little Kenny.

They were on him before he could get to his feet, boots and trainers flashing, kicking, the whoosh of the swung bat. His baton was gone. He tucked his head. A hit to the meat of his upper shoulder but not much force behind it and he twisted away from the second, but then it caught him harder near his spine and he jolted, tried to grab it, managing to knock it away. A boot caught his side and drove the air from him.

Suddenly he was twisting and rolling, bucking and crawling, his movements random as he could make them. Kicks less powerful now because he'd confused them, but that wouldn't last. The baseball bat connected with his thigh but he rolled and squatted like a frog, crawling, half-jumping through a gap between them and he was up, on his feet but his wrist was caught, a kick to his calf sending him back down. They were crowded around him now, booting, stamping, blows vicious.

No strategy.

Roll up, take it, hope they don't have murder in mind.

Something blunt at the back of his head... hard... changing things...

... greyness, dragged, knees, feet scraping... ground... picked up between them, arms and legs pulled, carried... towards the edge...

They were going to throw him off. He heard a distant voice... his own? Somehow hoping it wouldn't beg or plead to these idiots. 'Stupid!' it said.

Greying out again. But now he was on his back, near the edge. One of them looking down, floating high above him at the end of a foggy tunnel, face shadowed by hoody, but that flattened nose just visible. Kenny.

Will's lips were stretched, his voice a wheezing creak. '... under arrest!'

Kenny looked at the others, bending and doubling up with laughter. The three of them now, creased up, shaking their heads.

Good enough. Will snapped open the short blade on the *Leatherman* and sliced the tendon behind Kenny's knee, the scream it produced higher pitched than the one they'd wrung from the portly kid earlier to get Will up here. Kenny fell forward, clutching his leg, the others clamouring around him. Will rolled and scrambled away, trying to get off all fours, not quite managing, trying again.

A sudden grip on his ankle, Will swiping madly behind him with the *Leatherman* again, but no contact. His foot was twisted so he was face down in the dirt and a boot kicked at his wrist, the *Leatherman* skidding out of his hand. A flurry of sharp kicks to his head, his forearms only taking some of them. Dizzy now, blood in his mouth. Grey patches of nothing, jagged movements...

Kenny's voice. 'Toss that... bastard over!'

Nothing left in Will now. Hands pawing at him, trying to pull him up. He thought of Samira. Gave her a smile even, or just a smile in his head.

Something cracked the air, distant but with a spattering, answering *phut* much closer. Familiar, though he'd only ever heard a few in reality; plenty on TV like everyone else. A second rang out across the valley, and this time the scattering of pebbles and dust was only a few feet away. Rifle shots.

The hands had left him and he was vaguely aware of grunts and scuffing, then hushed breathing and a 'what the hell?' from one of them.

It might have been a minute, though Will was probably fading in and out so it could have been five or ten, before he heard one of them start to move toward him again. The shot this time was frighteningly close, so even Will flinched further into the dirt.

'Fuck this!' He heard, something like a groan of pain or frustration from Kenny, presumably, and then they were scrambling, winces and grunts and the occasional 'Ahhh!' as Kenny was carried from the field of what should have been sure-fire victory.

Spiralling down, questions hanging, greyness like a blanket under Will that went miles deep… miles…

Part 3: FRACTURE

39

The nurse advanced, tutting, so close her round face seemed to swell up like a porpoise. 'Oh, God. I can't believe it.' Checking his eyes. 'Not supposed to sleep. Not with a concussion.'

He was on his side, not lying flat but propped. Warm disinfected air, unmistakeable, wafting down his back and buttocks. Christ! A hospital smock. He reached for his face but her hand intercepted his. She shook her head.

'Drink?' He managed. As she rounded the bed to fill the jug his hand made another dart for his head and he arched his neck. Pain, room swimming. He slowed, breathed, patting the dressing around his scalp and forehead. The skin around one of his eyes was puffed out and he winced as his fingers brushed it. 'How… long…?'

She tutted again, handed him a cup of water. 'Maggie and her bloody cutbacks. Not that Labour were much better. We just haven't got the staff.' She shook her head, held up her hand. 'You've been here a few hours. How many fingers?'

'Three. How'd I get here?'

She stood back, fixed on his eyes. 'You tell me.'

'Can't remember.' Not quite true. The hospital. A fuzz of misty edges. Faces hovering around him, yapping at him, this woman's tired one amongst them. Then, Will being stretched out and trundled down the corridor and… what? X-rayed?

What about earlier though? How had he gotten off that bloody hill? Had he found his way back to the car and driven here? No. He hadn't been in any shape for that. Had it been Grundy and Turner, showing up in their version of the nick of time? A sudden flash of scrubland; some vague idea of dragging himself down to the road. So unreal, like it'd been weeks ago, not today, surely not today. What then? A car stopping? Someone giving him a lift down into the valley. Dropping him here. No remnant of the journey, though, like who was driving. Some good Samaritan.

'Is it coming back?'

'A bit.'

'Good. Remember who beat you?'

'What did I say when I got here?'

Slightly perplexed smile. 'You kept asking us to check the hospital.'

Check the hospital. That didn't make any sense. Thoughts circling. 'What else?'

'Well, when we saw your ID we wanted to call your station but you told us no.' A brief sparkle in her eyes. 'My ears were turning blue. Said you didn't trust a single one of them fuckers down there.'

Will tried for a grin but it hurt.

'Apart from one. You kept asking for someone in particular.'

'And?'

'She's outside,' she said, her mouth falling into a smile. 'Just arrived. Talking to the doctor, now. Feeling up to a visit?'

40

'Aww Lord, Will. What they done to you?'

'Is there a mirror?'

She got an arm under his shoulders and helped him to edge off the bed. Together, they manoeuvred to the sink. He propped himself in front of his reflection. 'Oh, no!'

Samira backed away a little, the look of sheer wretchedness on his face actually making her feel sick. But then, without thinking about it, with a glance down his bruised body, the hospital gown flapping uselessly around him, she reached out and gave his bottom a gentle tweak, not even sure she'd actually done it until she had. Then she giggled. 'Actually, you look pretty good from this angle.'

A delicious flutter in her stomach and she choked back a sudden laugh. Nan again, zipping through her head, *Far from knowing yourself, g'yal.*

Okay. She fancied him. So what?

His laughter probably hurt, and his eyes darted to her in surprise but something else too, she thought, like a wolf long caged remembering its own nature. He turned, moved to her, suddenly not needing support, pulled her to him, hands on her waist. His voice had levelled too; less groggy, more certain. 'Got a thing for invalids?'

As they kissed she felt his body responding through the flimsy hospital smock and she let out a slow moan that made him break off, his head pulling back. She shook her head, pressing her face close again. He tasted faintly bloody, she thought, and though it should have been a turn off, somehow neither that nor his bloodshot eyes, bandaged face and bruised body could stop her from reaching her hand downwards.

They were that way for a while; it seemed a while anyway. Then Will eased her back onto the bed and she pulled her legs up around him. Thoughts flashing around now. Could they? Here? What if the nurse... shit, what about the doctor? But they'd be used to it, wouldn't they? She seemed to remember reading it somewhere; hospitals were actually pretty rampant. Staff thrown together, affairs left, right and centre, patients and visitors left to it, especially long-termers. But that hardly applied here did it?

Will was looking at her. 'Are we –?'

'Crazy?' she panted. She was so close to just hiking up her skirt and putting his hand on her... no, beyond that... lifting that bloody smock aside and pulling him into her. The strangest thing though, the strangest thought. Unbidden, unlooked for.

Not propriety, not duty, no fear of reprimands or embarrassment.

Ryan Byford. Out there somewhere. A week now.

Will slipped, his leg straining she realised, and she made a grab for him. He was on his knees, leaning on the bed, eyes fluttering a little. 'I'm... sorry... just need a...'

She was down by his side now, hand on his shoulder. 'You're concussed, Will. Don't know what the hell I was thinking.'

He grunted a laugh. 'Hospital gowns...lot to answer for...'

She helped him up, sitting him on the bed next to her. Both quiet now, breaths deep and measured. Her hand was still close to his lower body but she pulled it up and touched the back of his hand. Chaste, respectful.

'Nurse reckons I kept asking them to check the hospital.'

It wasn't exactly small talk, but it would do. 'Yeah. The doctor mentioned. Why?'

He shrugged, eyes tightening a little. 'No idea. Price been contacted yet?'

She opened her hands. 'Hospital called the station but asked for me. Just luck I was back there. But you need to report this properly. Full statement and description, right?'

'I will.'

Quiet again. Okay. If shop-talk was the only way forward... better make it useful. 'Will, I think I might have a... name.'

He blinked. 'Who?'

She told him something of Jamie Longford. Far from the full story though. Time enough later. 'Adam. Sounded like it could be him. No surname though.'

Will looked distant, even by his standards. Then he waved at the dresser. 'Would you? Inside pocket of my jacket.'

She reached inside, pulled out a torn photo, glossy, still

smelling of fixer. The thrill of recognition was so strong she had to catch her breath. The face was less full here, of course, more angelic. She shook her head, certain now. She'd seen him. In the flesh. And recently.

She'd actually opened her mouth to say it when Will put his knuckles to his head and made a low groaning noise that had her reaching for the bell-push to summon a nurse.

'It's okay.' He tutted, shook his head. 'I'm fine. Just remembered something. It wasn't *check the hospital*. That isn't what I was saying when I arrived here. It was *check the hospitals*, plural.'

'Why? Meaning what?'

'It was Kenny attacked me. Little Kenny, Ray and one other guy.'

She stilled a shudder. 'Okay. Can you prove it?'

'That's why we need to check the hospitals. And any dodgy docs and surgeons off the books we know of.' Will's eyes tightened again. 'Because Kenny's going to need some tailoring.'

Nothing like talk of violence to kill the passion. Not that she blamed Will for cutting Kenny's leg; his throat would have been equally fine. Well, okay… maybe not, but she couldn't help remembering that Kenny had threatened them both.

She looked back at the photo, checking again to be sure she wasn't crazy.

'Keep hold of it.' Will looked tired again. 'Maybe we can match up with a mugshot.'

They sat and exchanged stories; Jamie Longford's sad account of a ruined life and then Brenda Terrell's awful bloody gallery, torment tinting all of it like blots of exposed film. Somehow it made her wish they hadn't stopped a few minutes ago. What do you do when confronted by too much death? You make babies. Not literally, she wasn't so far gone, but the impulse is there.

And then she went and radioed in, told Price what had happened to Will and put out the word about Little Kenny. When she came back inside, he looked worse. He was sitting up, head down, breathing heavy but clothes out of the dresser. She sat by the bed and looked into his bloodshot eyes. 'Will. Do me a favour. Stay put a while.'

He grimaced.

Suddenly she knew something for a certainty. If she told him what she was going to check on first thing in the morning, he'd discharge himself before the X-rays came back. And he wasn't up to it. Not by a long way.

'Just hear me out. Price is on his way. They're checking on Kenny. There's an ex-medic on the estate who's been known to patch people up for a bottle or two. We'll start there.'

He wouldn't look at her now, his fingers pinching at those on his other hand.

She watched him a few seconds, then grabbed his hand and stilled it. 'Why don't you just wait for the all clear from the docs and then… if you'd like to, that is… you can come stay with me.' Now it was her turn to look away. But then she did a kind of shrugging *so what* thing with her eyes and he was almost smiling. Then the sound of the door opening made her lean back on the chair so quickly it squeaked.

She watched the tired nurse moping around Will and she had a sudden urge to forget what she'd just said, forget Price, forget what she was intending to check on, just grab him, get him out of here. They'd probably only advise him not to be left alone and not to sleep for a few hours anyway, and she could certainly take care of that.

But Price would put two and two together and it would be all over the station by morning. He'd be far less likely to sanction the manpower on watching that dodgy doctor on the estate if he thought Will was off getting shacked up with her.

Nice idea though, and she chased it around a little before letting it fade from *what if* to *if only* and heading for the car.

41

He stood naked, hands splayed on the tiles of the shower unit, a glob of blood, dark and stale, working its way out of him. His nose and mouth choked and then freed, his eyes filling and head shaking. It should have been nothing, would have, if not for the state of this cubicle, the rough finish of the tiles above him and the twist of overhanging pipes, dripping, dripping. Not like the Docklands pool, not really but… close enough.

He stumbled, limbs locking, hand beginning its rattle, out to the wooden bench. He could hear the nurses' chatter stop short in the adjoining room. 'You alright?'

He tried to hide his hand under the thick white towel, but that was no good, because he couldn't move properly when he was like this, muscles like old rope, and he dropped it, the two nurses peering around the tiled wall, one with a smile that creased with concern, the other alarmed, him knocking a trolley with his elbow, something metal jumping and clattering. He was on his knees. 'Fi… I…' he licked his lips. '…fine.'

The pool, the water crashing in, the corrugated roof and everything that went with it.

It was mercifully quick this time, though. A few minutes at most. Maybe it was the soothing touch of the nurse's hand on his back, the feel of towels being wrapped around him, or the painkillers in his system, or just the fact he was in a hospital. Safety. No threat here. Or maybe the beating and his physical condition had somehow jarred everything else further back.

When he'd come back to himself, the concerned looking nurse was helping him up, settling him back on the bench. He was suddenly aware of his nakedness, clasping his crumpled pyjama pants close to his crotch. The nurse smiled and shook her head.

Should he go and discharge himself, right now? It would get back to Price. Pretty bad form for a police-officer to be non-cooperative with medical staff, especially with every intention of pressing charges against Kenny and the others. He'd need evidence of his condition. His physical condition, that was.

Shit! He'd seen lesser things spoil a conviction.

The nurse was trying to help him into his pyjamas and he

brushed her off. 'I'm okay.' But his right hand hadn't quite got that message and he fumbled like an infant, only then noticing someone else in the changing room.

'...result of trauma... heard of it?' The doctor's Bengali accent lent lightness to what he was saying, but Will could barely make out the content anyway. He took a big breath and stared hard at the labouring mouth. '.... soldiers who've.... in actual fact... based on combat at all... anything... sufficiently stressful... can lead... even serious ... other... hallucinations, in some cases I...'

The words were fine. Putting them together was the problem. Because it meant focusing. Being here.

The doctor leant in close, examining Will's eyes. Then he backed off a little. Will could see his whole face now, could make out his expression. A smile under three-day stubble. 'I imagine... hard to admit to... within the culture of the police, for instance.'

Will felt his hand stop its shake, looked at it and rolled his eyes.

The irony was thick enough to choke in. He'd been concerned they'd think brain damage from the kicking he'd had, and this doctor had figured him out in a few minutes.

Worrying though.

Will was suddenly rational, thoughts firing. Up to now, he could have put his clothes on and walked out of here. The second he was suspected of having what could be termed a mental illness, he no longer had that power. They could keep him here, technically, long as they thought he might be a danger to anyone. And it wasn't as if could hold up has hands, vibrating or not, and tell them he absolutely wasn't.

'It won't be going away, you know. In actual fact... sooner or later you'll have to look at... whatever caused this.'

Will nodded. It was a different tune to the one Byford had played. Ironic though; this overworked physician seemed to know more about Will's condition than an eminent psychiatrist. Will tried for a reassuring smile, though all things considered, it probably came out more a gallows grin. 'I will. But right now, am I okay to go?'

The Doctor gave a long release of breath. 'Well, you were quite severely concussed and in actual fact there might be something else we've missed physically.' He pursed his lips. 'Tell you what. I'll be back in to check on you this afternoon. We'll review it then.'

42

The park's detritus was swampy. Two yellow-uniformed workmen dragged their rakes through it, trolley already brimming. Plastic beer glasses, bottles, ketchup smeared papers, decaying cones, cigarette stubs. Festival dregs. It would look far worse once the marquee was down, rides fully disassembled in a couple of hours, unless these guys were more efficient than they seemed.

Samira scanned their features, her shoulders tensing for a second or two. No. Wrong crew anyway. The ones she was after wore green.

The grass was dewy, boots swishing through it. She glanced at her watch, 9.15 on a Sunday morning. They'd all be on time-and-a-half, clearing everything away so the park and this little crack in the Pennines could seal itself up again and go back to sleep.

She turned, veering off towards a small cluster of vehicles where three figures were loading scaffolding. 'Okay,' she said. She could just make out the lighter green triangles on each of their darker green overalls, the same on the side of one of the vans. The logo was readable as she closed in: Apex Event Services.

The three men had stopped loading and she watched one of them move towards her, another stopping him and positioning himself in front, hardhat shining in morning light. The third, faintly ginger, full of smiles, seemingly viewing this as nothing but an opportunity for a break, leant on the truck and started on a roll up. The one who'd moved initially, skin-headed but with enough growth for black fuzz to bristle like filings under a magnet. He had a British Bulldog tattoo on his arm.

Alone again, she thought, fingers brushing her walkie-talkie uselessly. No backup. Will in that bloody hospital bed, waiting for her, waiting for confirmation of a simple concussion and nothing more.

'Can I help you, luv?' The foreman, she remembered, fiftyish, friendly enough. But bulldog stepped out, coughing deep and nonchalantly spitting what he'd trawled from a nicotine-lined throat, not exactly close to Samira's feet, but not that far away either.

'Nice.' She looked at the foreman, holding up her warrant card, which got a gravelly laugh from bulldog. 'Do you remember we spoke last week? We were trying to identify a body and I was checking if you had any of your workers missing.'

'Aye. So, what's up?' The foreman raised his eyebrows.

She glanced at the van logo. 'What kind of events do you work on?'

The foreman came closer, his hardhat glinting in the sun. 'All sorts of stuff. Rock-festivals, fairs, conferences, you name it.'

She glanced at bulldog and ginger. 'Where are the rest of your guys then?'

Something under bulldog's breath, sounded like *she's looking for a gang bang.* She grinned at him. 'Say something?'

He flashed a leery smile, putting out volumes of the same old story. *Don't like blacks, but I'd do you anyway.*

The foreman sighed, tutted, spoke without looking at Bulldog. 'Tim, why don't you stop being a dick and go and make yourself bloody useful?' Tim did a snorting laugh and sloped away. The foreman shook his head. 'Skeleton crew, supposed to be four of us but one threw a sickie. Enough though. Taking down's easier than setting up.'

She nodded, walked over to the van, this one without logo, just a battered and muddy blue Bedford. Bulldog Tim was messing with something, and she watched him. The skinhead turned, making some monkey noises, but Samira had eyes only for the contraption he was unfurling. 'What *is* that?'

The foreman stood next to her, taking off his hardhat to reveal a balding head that glistened almost as much. 'Industrial steam cleaner. For heavy duty muck and grease. On machine parts, like.' He stiffened. 'Old. Doubt I'll find receipt for it if that's what you're –'

She shook her head absently. 'Just show me how it works.'

As the foreman moved, Samira placed herself near Tim Bulldog, just a little too close, almost but not quite an invasion of personal space. She eyeballed him, hands relaxed at her sides.

This was usually the moment of truth, one way or the other. It happened quickly with Tim. The sneer turned into an insipid smile and he gestured at the cleaning hose. 'Why d'you wanna look at this, like?'

The foreman pulled the hose away from him and unfolded it, but Samira stopped him, taking it, tracing the end of the nozzle with her fingertips. About two inches in circumference. Same size as the marks on Smiley's neck and shoulders. She took a breath, thought of skin blistering.

She'd assumed, Will too, the grid-like sores meant Smiley had been held against something, or had fallen onto something with equally spaced holes. They hadn't envisaged someone with patience or strength of will enough to make the pattern using a single source of steam, applying it again and again.

Her heart was thrumming now. She could see the nozzle searing unprotected skin. Repeated agony from something designed for removing clogged grease from machine parts. Unimaginable pain, but it was more than that. The systematic cruelty of it. She felt cold.

'Stupid,' she said aloud. What was stupid? Some romanticised notion of Adam from Jamie Longford. And herself, for buying into it even a little. Anyone who could do this was… gone. Passed beyond.

She suddenly remembered she was being stared at.

'Don't wanna interrupt, like,' Tim bulldog said, giving her a wink as he eyed the nozzle. It was quite phallic, she supposed. 'I need to get that packed away so we can –'

'No, you don't.' She returned his wink and reached for her walkie-talkie. 'I'm impounding this gear. The van too.'

Bulldog laughed, his boss starting to splutter behind him. 'We've gotta get the marquee down and get all the –'

She shook her head.

She wasn't even supposed to be here. Price would shit, but in the end this was serious evidence and she couldn't let it go. Time to face the music. She waited for the crackle to settle and called it in.

She turned back to the foreman. 'So, just out of interest, the guy who called in sick today. What's his name?'

43

Will slept after the doctor's visit. Worries, injuries, his *condition*, Ryan Byford, the vague promise of something he couldn't quite see the shape of with Samira, all of it spooled away somewhere close but contained like a bottled storm. He slept deep and he slept heavy; no dreams he could remember, dark or light.

When he woke it was slow and languorous.

He was propped on his side to avoid leaning on his bandaged eye, but facing the door. Something wrong though. There was someone in the room with him.

The figure was slumped on one of the visitor chairs, feet up on the side of the bed. It grinned, shook its beanie-covered head and sat up a little. Well-built, something familiar in the face that opened its mouth to speak. 'Alright, squaddie?'

A cold prod of fear in Will's guts.

His visitor reached up and pulled off the hat, revealing spiky blonde hair, a little matted. Face and hands outdoor-labour-tanned so it was hard to tell, but possibly in need of a wash. Was Will hallucinating? He had to at least consider that. No. Too real. The face had filled out some since the photo, not quite in the way he'd have imagined. Something in that glint in his eyes that Will wouldn't have put there, too. 'How did you...?'

The smile dropped away, the slightest move of the shoulders that might have been a shrug, like Will had just asked the wrong question. Will's brain was firing, ten directions at once. Price had been here last night after Samira, then a couple of uniforms to get a statement off him so the hospital staff had already relaxed the *visiting time only* thing with him. In their heads, one more handy looking bloke with too much swagger and a combat jacket over jeans would be no one to question. Just another plain-clothes officer, always assuming he'd even been noticed.

But how had he found Will, here?

When it clicked, it seemed obvious. The gunshots ringing around the crags yesterday. Then the car journey he couldn't even remember. His good Samaritan. 'You got me off that hill. Brought me here, right?'

The grin widening. 'You did pretty well up there. Three of them.' His eyes were just a little glassy now. 'They would've killed you though. Or left you in worse shape than…' a wave at Will's bandage. 'In the end.'

Will nodded. 'I'm grateful, Adam.'

No reaction. A worrying gnaw at Will's guts. If Adam didn't care the Police knew his name… the call-button for the nurse was hanging from its cord on the bed-frame close to the side-table and Will, without glancing at it, put his hand to his bandage as if checking the swelling, throwing in a wince for good measure. Then he put his hand back down, this time closer to the cord. 'So, where's Ryan?'

There was a slight slackening of Adam's shoulders, like *that* was the question he'd been waiting for. But he said nothing, staring at Will, grin still in place.

A creeping coldness now. Something about this guy, genuinely frightening. Detached. No, that didn't do it… *disassociated.* That glassy stare, body language too, like he wasn't truly present, similar to what Samira had said about Will, but with this guy it was different because his body wasn't fighting it with twitches and shakes. He was at ease, and there was a readiness and strength about his hands and body that Will really didn't like the look of, at all.

Will swallowed in a dry throat and moved his hand a little closer to the cord. 'So, what's the plan, Adam?'

Adam stood to his full height, around six two, and stopped smiling. 'Barry Prudom. Remember him?' His face stayed straight. 'That's the sort of thing I'm aiming for.'

Will's blood was roaring. It was only five years since Prudom had gone on a spree in North Yorkshire, killing three people including a constable and a sergeant, inspiring the greatest manhunt the UK had ever known.

'Course, he was an amateur.' Adam winked. 'A STAB. Not even that. Reject from the STABs.'

'What the hell are…'

'Stupid Territorial Army Bastards. STABs.'

Will thought of the recording sent to Cathy Byford, the threat of something being sent. *It won't be his fucking lid. It'll be something wet and sticky.* He'd been so thrown by the idea of body parts through the post, he'd overlooked the army slang for helmet. Police slang too, so maybe he just hadn't registered it. Didn't prove anything though. This guy could still be a total wannabe. An army dreamer.

'Prudom gave you lot the run-around for 18 days, though. Reckon I can beat that. And his tally.'

His tally. Prudom had killed three, but injured or attempted to kill at least two more, leaving one woman with brain damage and no memory of her husband being shot whilst tied to her, and another, a pensioner of 75, tied up to be left for the bread-man to find. Will leant forward, pulling the sheets aside. He stood, spreading his feet and clawing the tiles with his toes, looking at the bigger man. 'You're a prick.'

The eyes flared for a second as Adam's body moved, arms spreading a little, but then his face cracked back into that wide grin. 'Ahhh, nice one. Squaddie. I like it.' The smile dropped away and Adam's hand flashed to the cord. He held the call-button out, towards Will. 'Call them. If you like. Bring nursie in.'

Will stared at him. 'What is it you want, Adam?'

He let go of the cord, nodded, an errant schoolboy finally ready to settle. 'Okay. Here's the plan. I've got Ryan buried.' His glassy eyes were impossible to read for truth. 'I don't show up to get him soon... he runs out of air. You come with me, now, if you want to see Ryan alive again. Or...' He glanced at the bed, the call-button, the room around them. 'Or stay here and feel sorry for yourself a bit more.'

Will said nothing. Of course, this was where it was going, stupid to think otherwise. And even though he knew he was in no shape for this, physically or otherwise, even if every cell in his body was screaming to be allowed to sit this one out, what choice did he have, really?

Adam was at the dresser pulling out Will's clothes. He turned, holding up Will's jacket. 'Good bit o' leather, that.'

Will sat on the bed and waited to be handed his clothes, every inch an invalid.

Will wasn't quite shuffling along behind, but the aching in his back and leg jarred and he couldn't match Adam's buoyant strides.

As they were about to leave the ward the round-faced nurse appeared with a flustered glance at Adam, answered by a toned-down grin. She gave Will an uncertain smile. 'What're you –'

'Checking myself out.'

'Oh, er…' She turned around, headed for the desk, shaking her head and looking Will up and down. She held up a hand. 'I'll have to get some discharge papers. Wait here.'

After she'd bustled out, Adam started walking again, in the other direction. 'Screw that! Come on.'

Will reached out as he passed the desk, fingers closing around a marker pen, pocketing it by the time he'd rounded the corner. He couldn't imagine alarm bells ringing over him leaving without officially signing himself out, but the doctor might at least raise some issues, and Samira would be coming here later. But how long would it take to figure he was missing? A day? More?

He had two choices, the way he saw it. Incapacitate this bastard; unlikely, in Will's current state, and even at his best. Adam looked too able. But even if he somehow managed it, would Adam crack and tell them where Ryan was buried, if he truly was? Leaving aside whether he was or wasn't army-trained, you don't survive an orphanage with two psychopaths in control and grow up to be someone who rolls over easily.

Plan B then. Somehow get a message to Samira or Price.

They were through the double doors, then a left. Adam moved with purpose, looking like he belonged. Another set of doors. Nurses were busy with clipboards and blankets. A passing doctor glanced at Will's bandages, but didn't seem overly concerned. At the staircase now, and Will was a little out of breath. Down they went, coming out in what looked like a side entrance, quiet. Adam had clearly recced this place out.

Outside now. The air of the carpark was cool. Adam swept his arm towards a pedestrian walkway. But halfway along it to the exit, he took a left, glancing at his watch as they passed the row of portacabins probably for cleaners and other contractors.

Adam stopped, held up his hand, motioned Will to one of the cabins. The cover of a doorway, not visible from the walkway. Adam had put his beanie back on and pulled it down close to his eyebrows.

Behind the cabin, Will could see the road, the green roof of a bus working its way down towards the town. He had the strongest urge to run for the wall, scramble over and jump on that bus. Not even back to the station, he thought. Just to sit on it, all day, nodding off upstairs, vaguely aware of this little northern town bumbling past. Free from this. Enough.

Pointless. He'd agreed to come along. Ryan's life wasn't something he could take bets on.

Adam's expression had softened. Will followed his gaze. Two nurses, one quite striking, slim, strawberry blonde hair fiery against the white in her uniform, pushing a trolley across the concourse, pace brisk, laughing with her colleague at some shared titbit.

Adam turned to him, handed him the beanie. 'Put it on. Cover the bandages. Do anything to raise the alarm, I double time it away. Just stay put, if you want Ryan to keep breathing.'

Will nodded, put the hat on. Adam hesitated a second, looked like he was gathering his nerve. He straightened, jogged across the concourse. Will was vaguely aware of the strawberry blonde nurse stopping, turning and dropping her smile, but no time to see what unfolded between them. He pulled back into the doorway, took out the marker, found a scrap of paper in his pocket.

Less than a minute and he'd finished writing. Adam was alone with the nurse; her friend had clearly given them some space. Will looked around him. No letter box; well why would there be? Just cabins for cleaners and caretaking staff. The door-handle? As long as Adam didn't come back here...

He folded the note lengthways, tried tying it around the handle. It wouldn't work. He unfolded it, tore a hole in the corner and slipped it over the doorknob. Okay. He turned, just in time to see Adam walking from the nurse, back towards the cabin.

Will walked towards Adam but ignored him, staring boldly at

her. She was gazing after Adam, complexion drained, but she must have felt Will's look, or maybe she was just curious, and she turned a little. Will thought of putting some clue into his expression that he was in desperation, that Adam here, whatever he was to her, was on the brink of carnage. A lot to pack into a single look. In the end he held her gaze a few seconds and shook his head very slightly, before Adam moved into his line of sight.

'Stop looking at her, squaddie. She won't help you.'

Will gave him a grin. 'Girlfriend?'

'Nothing to you.'

'I only ask because your little chat clearly made her so happy.'

Adam turned and glanced back. Again, a moment... a few days ago Will might have taken it, launched himself at him, but...

But, but, but...

Adam turned back to Will, the nurse's retreating back just visible, the trolley rattling along in front of her; a millstone on wheels. No, Will thought suddenly; this girl's millstone was standing in front of Will.

When it came it was vicious, but hardly unpredictable; Will's hands were up and deflected the force a little, but the jabbed fingers to his sternum made him stagger backwards and almost lose his feet. He managed to control it though; he'd started turning before Adam's blow landed, away from the portacabin and that bloody door-handle; that was the thing. He bent double, exaggerating his cough and splutter, but only a little. The top of his bandaged, beanie-covered head was to Adam, completely vulnerable now. Would their proximity to people stop this from escalating?

Some heaving breaths and then Will straightened up.

'Told you not to look at her.' Adam was opening and closing his fists, but his grin was only a little stretched. He moved off, towards the concourse, blessedly not giving the portacabin a glance. He stopped and turned to Will. 'You coming, copper?'

Better than *squaddie*, at least. Will walked, rubbing his chest and keeping a wary distance. He looked back at the hospital as they reached the road, a pang of yearning for the safety of the crowd making him shiver.

44

The address from the foreman was for a shared house in a backstreet off Manningham Lane in Bradford, about 12 miles from the valley. She watched Naylor bending to peer in the letterbox after his knocking was unanswered for a couple of minutes. She looked at her watch. The landlord was probably still at the mosque.

It was less than an hour since she'd watched Price and the rest of the crew roll up at the half-dismantled festival. While the DCI hadn't quite clapped her on the back and jumped for joy, she thought there was a glint of grudging respect as she'd talked him through the steam-cleaner and how she'd come there in the first place. He'd had good news about Little Kenny too. 'He couldn't run very far. We brought in his brother too. That bit wasn't so easy. Lucky we had our own big boy with us.' He'd winked at Turner and Samira had avoided catching his eye.

'Anyway, I've spoken to Drugs Squad. They've agreed to turn over the Ramirs' place. See if they'll name Kenny for a reduced sentence. So, it looks like even if he manages to wriggle out of assault charges for Ashcroft, Kenny's going down.' He showed his teeth again. 'Either way, the Super's chuffed with you.'

She was blinking, not quite knowing what to say. She opted for nothing, asking if she could come and check on Adam's address. Price had smirked and said, 'Accompanied, lass. Accompanied.'

Now, in the car, there was a fairly uncomfortable silence as they watched the murky green door. Finally, she told Naylor she was nipping to the shop on the corner.

'Oh yeah? Need some tampons?'

She smirked. Let him have that one, she thought.

She came back with a pocketful of ten pence pieces and gestured at the phone booth on the corner. Naylor gave her a sulky nod.

She'd just opened the phone booth door when a man in faded jeans and anorak, fortyish, hairline beating a retreat, ambled between the car and her and turned to the green door, keys in hand, yawning wide enough to close his eyes so that he seemed to have completely missed her advancing behind him. He jumped as he turned. 'Jesus!'

Adam's room was bare. He'd left the drawers empty and the bed made up neatly.

She crossed to the sideboard and perched. 'What can you tell us about him, Mr Harris?'

'Not much.' His eyes were tight. 'Like I said, I work nights. Occasionally bump into him on the stairs.'

Naylor sighed. 'You and him the only tenants?'

'Yeah. Always people coming and going though. Landlord only ever takes working people and you know what it's like, not that much work to go around.'

She nodded. 'So, when you bumped into him on the stairs, what did he seem like?'

Harris's eyes focused on nothing. 'Well, he seemed a decent guy. Friendly enough. Sort of.'

'Sort of?'

'Well I mean, he's not someone you'd mess with. You know he's ex-forces, right?'

Not news, but nice to have it confirmed. Naylor piped up. 'Did he tell you that, Mr Harris?'

'Didn't have to. It's written all over him really. Way he moves, talks.' He looked around the room again. 'And he's so neat. What's the word?'

'Fastidious?' she offered.

He raised his eyebrows. 'I was going to say disciplined. Like it's been drilled into him.'

It could as easily have been the product of early years in an austere children's home. Especially one tended by a sadist. But she nodded.

Harris glanced at the empty wardrobe and the neatly made bed. 'Tell the truth… I'm not sorry he's gone. Not that he ever did me any harm… but he was… scary.'

'Mr Harris. I doubt he'll be coming back.' She spread her hands. 'He's not going to hurt you.'

He gave a small smile, took off his glasses, breathing on them and wiping the lenses on the bottom of his shirt. He replaced them and looked at Samira, chin jutting a little. 'I know. I saw him two days ago when he cleared out. I think... think it was the first time he'd been back in a while. A week, at least. I watched him before I went to start my shift. From... my back window.' He pointed, a small ashamed gesture. A lonely man working anti-social hours and peering through curtains before his time. They walked to the back of Adam's room, the window presumably sharing Harris's view of the overgrown garden at the rear.

Naylor noticed it before she did, pointing at the browned circle of grass in the middle, ashen clumps sodden by the rain. 'Had a bonfire?'

'Yeah. *He* did.'

'What did he burn?'

Samira answered Naylor before Harris could continue. 'His own stuff. Right?'

Harris blinked, glanced at her, then nodded. 'He didn't have much. But enough for a blaze. I was worried it'd spread to the trees but he... controlled it. Hosed it out. Then he just left.'

Samira shivered. A cold gnaw at her stomach. Plenty of people talk about burning their bridges. Few actually do it. Adam had, after killing the two people who'd messed up his life. Question was: what was he planning for an encore and how did the Byfords fit into it?

'He didn't burn everything though.' Harris puckered his lips slightly. 'I'm not sure but... he might've...think he might've had a gun with him. A rifle.'

She and Naylor exchanged glances.

He pointed at the window. 'I mean, from here, it could've been a fishing rod for all I know. In a long bag, you know?' A laugh that trailed off. 'But it looked like a rifle. Yeah. I think it was.'

No firearms licence had been issued to any Adam Smith. Price had run the check by the time they got back to Spinnerby, surprising her, then she remembered what Will had said about Price being firearms trained and a little bit gung ho. Probably the closest thing to any action he'd seen in years, so an alert was out to stations in the North with a description of someone answering to the name, carrying a deadly weapon.

'What if he goes crazy with that rifle?' Naylor asked. 'Starts taking pot-shots in town?'

It was possible, of course. It was only five years since Barry Prudom. Adam didn't seem to fit the same mould but what did she know really? Years of abuse and at least two murders behind him. Who could predict what he'd do, especially if he felt the net closing?

The incident room was bustling; Price and his favourite crew; namely Grundy, Turner and Sturgess, huddling around cigarettes, Naylor joining them with a swagger that just didn't become him. Amazing how quick he changed around the others. He gave her a *man's talk* look. She clicked her tongue. Brandy and cigars in the drawing room, just like that. What was she supposed to do, talk crochet and make-up with Clarke?

She walked over to them, their bravado hollowing the closer she got, then they stopped talking altogether, Grundy sneering, Turner's rugby ears seeming to stiffen. Price looked at his cigarette-end poised just over the map they were clustered around, but his voice was pitched for her. 'Aye. What is it?'

'Just wondered if anyone has been out to see the Byfords yet?'

A couple of genuinely confused grimaces and a shake of the head from Grundy. Price looked up at her. 'Doubt this Adam's going to go there. So don't worry yourself...'

Incredible. Even Price still wasn't putting the pieces together. Samira's mouth had opened to ask whether anyone had considered what the name Adam Smith might mean to Sean Byford. Because just maybe Byford could give them something that would lead them to Adam; something he might remember from whenever he'd treated him or refused to treat him or whatever else it might have been that caused Adam's grudge.

She closed her mouth, gave them a *silly me* smile and turned tail. Some little aside from Grundy, a little coughing and spluttering and she could feel their collective stare on her rear as she walked away.

It didn't matter. They'd sit here and pore over that map of the moors for another twenty minutes, waiting for some report from one of the red and whites already dispatched from here and from Halifax, and then they'd talk about possible scenarios a bit more and then hope for an incident where they could swan around looking hard. But only until the armed response unit from Manchester could be called in, and then these five could shrug, step back and complain how they'd do a better job if they'd had the training for it.

She dawdled at her desk, just in case they were still looking at anything other than her bum. Her fingers went to a loose sheaf of part-yellowed papers, all she'd been able to add to what Roland had given her on Right Choice, the adoption agency that had presumably attempted to place some of the Moorhaven children. Now closed, of course; Social Services and a couple of bigger agencies handling all of that since the late 70s. She brushed the top sheet away, her forehead crinkling a little. There was something she'd noticed earlier without really registering it… and it could be nothing but…

Moving slow, forlorn and disgruntled, shoulders low like she couldn't quite decide what to do, she headed for the back stairs. Soon as the fire-doors were shut she started running, taking them two at a time.

45

'What do you mean: he's gone?'

The round-faced nurse gave her a look someway between boredom and annoyance. 'Signed himself... no, actually didn't bother to sign himself out. Couldn't even wait for me to go and get the form.'

The hospital was en route to Gammerton and Samira had wanted to check in, part of her hoping Will would be miraculously well enough to come with her to the Byfords', part of her in need of some support... and part of her...

...part of her just needing to see him.

She stood in the corridor, tempted to push past the nurse into the room Will had been in. But even from here she could see the bed being made up.

'Doctor's furious. He'll be having words with your boss, I reckon. Not exactly professional behaviour is it?'

No, not exactly.

'Sorry. Busy. *Patients* to deal with.' She bustled away swishing nylon, nose high.

Samira stayed where she was, chewing her lip. Had he just gone home? Back to that cold house on the moor he was calling home, more accurately. But they'd agreed she'd come get him and he'd stay at her place a while. That was their pact. Unless... what? Unless there'd been no pact, and she'd seen things he hadn't.

But she remembered the look in his eye as he'd fumbled at that silly bloody hospital smock, his other hand not wanting to leave the curve of her hip. No. She hadn't imagined anything. He'd have waited for her. Or he'd have called the station and told her.

So, where was he?

She walked, mind only half on her surroundings. Maybe he'd had one of his attacks, paranoid about the doctors probing into his condition. She looked around her. There were phones in the foyer.

She dug out her notebook and flipped to where she'd put his number a few days ago, *just in case*. She went to the kiosk, picked up and dialled, letting it ring a minute. Nothing.

She headed outside, still-damp air carrying a welcome sharpness, sunlight beaming off wet car-rooves. She ambled, hands in jacket pockets, vaguely towards the Fiesta. She found herself stopping, leaning on the railing and staring down at the carpark. Much as she knew she needed to get to the Byfords' place, her legs just didn't want to take her that way.

The outpatients building was separate, and she marched there as if pace would give her purpose. Maddie would be busy, probably wouldn't be able to tell her anything anyway; different ward, different problems. But still, as Ward Manager, Samira's old college friend had some clout; she might get Will's nurses to be a little more forthcoming.

The doors slid apart and she barely recognised the figure leaving just as she entered, wouldn't have in fact, if not for the way it turned half away from her as it moved; an unnatural movement. Samira wheeled around, walked back into the open air, taking a second to remember her name, half-shouting 'Karen!'

It was in the shoulders, the way they slumped slightly as she stopped, hesitating before turning, finally the grudging nod, a smile of pretend *only now* recognition. Karen's strawberry blonde hair was almost all covered, just a few strands whipping around her face from the hooded anorak. 'Oh, hi.' She'd already half turned away, but Samira saw her face long enough to see she'd been crying, something desolate under the tiredness.

'Just finished your shift?'

'Yeah. Really knackered… sorry, didn't recognise you.' Karen was walking, Samira matching her stride.

They'd only met the once, Samira pressing her for her knowledge of PTSD, so it was plausible she hadn't recognised her, but bullshit all the same. Just being blanked, Samira could handle; it wasn't as if they were friends. But there was something else in this. Karen had panicked as she'd seen Samira. Call it police intuition… no, police*woman*'s intuition. Even better.

She reached out, hand on Karen's sleeve, gentle but firm. 'What's happened, Karen?'

229

'Oh… nothin'… I'm just…'

'Karen.' Samira stood in front, had both of her sleeves now, forcing her to stop and look at her full on. 'What is it?'

A tug of both arms, but half-hearted, and gritted teeth for two seconds, eyes filling like bar-optics ready to gush.

Some kitchen-sink domestic? Her ex, causing her grief? Something about Karen's face said there was more though. She was distressed, yeah, but scared too.

There were very good reasons for Samira not to care, but something was telling her she ought to. 'Let's get a drink.' She turned her, arm around her shoulder and walked her back to the sliding doors and inside, gesturing at the coffee machine in the entrance, the small seated area with a couple of empty tables presumably for waiting outpatients. She thought about getting them some cups of steaming froth from the machine, but worried Karen would bolt, she just sat in front of her. 'Is it your ex, Karen?'

Tears in earnest now, hand over the eyes. Samira gave her a hankie. She'd nailed it with the kitchen sink domestic then. Okay. She glanced at her watch. Let her get to it her own way, in her own time.

As Karen sniffled some more, Samira glanced out the window. There were a couple of patients smoking around the side of the building. But she looked behind them, down the narrow walkway that joined one concourse to another. It was unmistakeable really, the orange stripe with the chequered lines above and below that ran the length of the car. A police Sierra.

Nothing strange about that. This was a hospital. All sorts of reasons to be here, accompanying someone to Emergency maybe.

'He… paid me a visit earlier.' Karen sniffed.

'Your ex?'

A nod.

Samira breathed out, her attention still half on the car. That area was where the contractors came and left, the row of portacabins used by them; cleaners, builders, maintenance. Nowhere near Emergency. Why park down there?

'Hadn't seen him for a bloody year. Then he just shows up out of the blue. Looks terrible.' She tried a smile that didn't really take. 'I couldn't believe how far downhill he's gone. But it's okay.' She dabbed her eyes again. 'I mean it's not like he came here for me. Visiting some mate, poor bloke.'

'For being a mate of your ex's?'

A breath that could have been a laugh. 'That too. Actually, I meant he looked in bad shape. Head trauma maybe.'

Something in Samira gave a little jump.

'Anyway, I'm sure they won't be mates for long.' Karen was saying. 'Doesn't know how to keep friends, our Adam.'

The jump turned into a rollercoaster swoop. Samira actually gripped the table. 'What did… can you say that again?'

'Which bit?'

'Both bits. All of it. Who's Adam?'

Karen gave a *duh* look. 'My bloody ex, who do you think?'

Jesus. Samira put a finger to her head. What had Karen said about him a few days ago? Falklands vet. Traumatised obviously; that's why they'd talked. Alcohol problems. Other issues stemming back to childhood. But as far as she could remember, she'd never mentioned his name. 'So, what did Adam say to you?'

'Said he just wanted to say goodbye.' Her voice cracked on the last word and she looked away.

Brain fizzing. Samira took a few seconds to get her thoughts in order. 'Okay.' She chewed her lip. 'Any time when you were together, did he mention anyone he felt he'd been wronged by?'

Karen's face had frozen, eyes narrowed. She seemed to deliberate, then started to move, zipping up her anorak, bag back on her shoulder. 'I've really got to –'

Samira put her hand on her forearm again. 'Sorry Karen. This has just escalated. We either talk here or down the nick.'

Her freckled skin was pale. Movement stopped.

Samira released her forearm. 'If he's gonna top himself, that's one thing. But you know he's planning more than that. That's why you blanked me.' A quick glance out the window for the Sierra. Gone. She turned back. 'Tell me everything. Exactly what happened earlier. Everything he said.'

It took a few minutes, a lot of glaring and folded arms, but when Samira mentioned the rifle and Adam having burnt all his possessions, she started talking, answering Samira's question about who he'd been wronged by. 'Two women and a man. Sheep for the shearing, he always said.'

Brenda and Smiley had to be two of the three. But if the third was another woman... Samira sat forwards. 'Two women and a man? Not the other way around?'

Karen opened her hands. 'That's what he said.'

Samira thought of the snippets she'd got from Roland on the adoption agency, and what she'd spotted earlier. It made sense. But it meant she and Will had been on the wrong track. 'The man you saw with him today, with the bandages. Did you speak to *him*?'

She shook her head.

'When and where exactly did you see them together?'

'Over there.' She pointed at the walkway between the buildings, the side road where the police Sierra had been. 'About an hour ago.'

The security guard turned from the porter he was chatting to as she approached. Samira had her warrant card out and the porter looked down, took a drag on his cigarette. The guard, grey hair combed back, pot-bellied, gave her a nod, almost familiar, so she wondered if she'd met him before. 'Another of you?' He laughed. 'Overkill, isn't it, for a LOB?'

She raised her eyebrows. 'You police?'

'Used to be. Seven years in.' He looked wistful.

She nodded. It *could* be helpful. Question was, had he decided for himself that whatever the Sierra's occupants had been called out for was a *Load of Bollocks*, or had the answering officer told him that. 'What makes you think it was LOB?'

'Well, your two lads seemed to think so. The Sarge anyway. That big lad wasn't so sure, I reckon, but not wanting to contradict his senior,'

Okay. She nodded, keeping it routine. 'Yeah, PC Turner and Sergeant Grundy, right?'

'Aye, that was them.' He glanced to his left. 'This lad was the RP.'

The reporting person. Samira found herself starting to grit her teeth. No wonder this guy hadn't got past seven years in. Too fond of the jargon by half. She looked at the porter, taking out her pad and pen, about to talk when the guard started again. 'I only got involved when I saw the jam-sandwich roll up. Only then I heard about the note.'

Samira's heart leapt but she covered it with a scribble on her pad. 'Yeah, the note.' She looked at the porter. 'Where did you find it?'

The porter was around thirty-five. Hair unfashionably long, pony-tailed, a couple of heavy metal type rings on the fingers of one hand. He walked to the doorway, pointed at the handle.

'Sergeant Grundy took it with him?'

The guard cut in again. 'I never saw the contents of the note. Your Sarge reckoned it was LOB though. Someone having a laugh.'

'Yeah, good old Grundy. How did he suss it?'

The guard did that wistful look again. 'An officer-number and name on the note. He said it didn't match any copper round here. Someone playin' silly buggers.'

She did another scrawl on her pad and tried to make it look final and decisive. 'Right.' Looked at the guard. 'You've been really helpful, thanks.' She glanced at the porter, as if it was an afterthought. 'Oh, just need to ask you another couple of questions. Walk with me?' The porter hesitated a second, then stubbed out his cigarette.

So far he'd been mute. Was he just naturally quiet, or witless? Former not latter, she really hoped. She watched him glance over his shoulder at the strolling security guard. 'Bob tries a bit too hard. But he means well.'

'I know.' She smiled. 'Thing is, that note. Between you and me, it wasn't a fake.'

Just a slight nod, like that was no big surprise.

Suddenly she started to like this guy. 'If you could remember anything at all about what was on it, that could really help.'

He looked at her levelly. 'I'll do my best.'

46

Grundy's cheeks were reddened and cleft with the smile of a man happy with his lot. He was alone, on the bench, bending to put his socks on, vest and y-fronts grey through steamy air, locker door wide, uniform hanging behind him, civvy clothes spread and ready. His arms and chest flexed and despite his wide middle, Samira saw something of a nasty granite hardness in him that she'd never quite suspected, and it almost made her rethink her intentions and turn and close the door. Too late though; he'd seen her.

His jaw hung, eyebrows stretching upwards. Another day, it might have been comical. His face suddenly contracted. Fear? She thought so; just for an instant, covered by that slack grin of his. 'Wahayy, come on in, Lass!'

She scanned around the showers; no one else. She stood at the hooks opposite him, arms folded. 'How come you're not out prowling with the others?'

A shrug. 'It'll all kick off when it's ready to. Anyway, I'm on the night shift later. Need a few bevvies and a kip.' A wink. 'Come join me if you –'

'Where's the note?'

The blood didn't quite drain from his face, just something in the grin that hardened. He stood up. Stared at her. Shrugged. 'Fake.'

'Oh, right. Can you tell me how you happened to know DI Ashcroft's officer number off by heart?'

The grin again. 'I blew in, checked it.'

'I've already checked with switchboard.' She didn't mention the porter's certainty that Grundy hadn't. 'You made no such call.'

His lips were drawn now. 'They're always forgetting to log stuff. Sometimes that bloody 6-track is switched off for days on end.'

The cumbersome recorder, a leftover from the 60s that Samira had been appalled to see was still used in Spinnerby. Dispatch were constantly talking about getting it replaced but hadn't got around to it yet.

'I don't get it. I really don't.' She looked him up and down. 'Me, I can understand. You don't like darkies, right? But Ashcroft? He's one of your own.'

He laughed. 'Darlin', he's blacker than you.'

'That why you didn't respond to his distress call the other day? Left him on the crags to get the crap kicked out of him?'

A shake of his head. 'The signal's garbage at that end of the moor.' The grin again. 'I can recall no such call from inspector Ashcroft.'

She gave him a cold smile, leaning forward a little. 'It's one thing to let him get beaten up. Something else to ignore a distress message from an officer held under duress by a double murderer. One who is also very likely holding Ryan Byford, the kid everyone has been looking for the past week.'

Grundy's eyes trailed down along her body, then to his own. 'You know what? I think I'm getting a hard on.'

'Really?' She swallowed in a suddenly dry throat, but she looked down at him, looked up again, doubtful, almost pitying. 'By the way, I logged an allegation about serious misconduct –'

'Bollocks!' He advanced on her, just a little. 'Price is out and about. No way you could've –'

'Who said anything about Price?' Her blood was roaring now but she stood her ground. 'I talked to Stratham. He's on his way over.'

He squinted at her and she held his stare.

She glanced downwards. 'Still frisky?'

'Fuckin' bitch!' He turned sideways and she spread her feet slightly, hands ready. But he picked up his trousers and held them over himself, shaking his head and breathing loudly. 'Okay. Report me. Do what you want. Your word against mine, sweetheart.' A cold grin now as he stared around the empty changing room. 'A sergeant, thirty years in… against a nobody. Less than nobody… a *split-tail jig* nobody. Let's see how that comes out.'

She nodded, backing away, turning when he had one leg into his trousers, quickening her step until she was up a flight of stairs, and only then realising how hard she was shaking.

47

The roof was the one place you could sometimes get a signal through to the moors with a walkie-talkie, if you didn't fancy negotiating with whoever was on dispatch, and she didn't. Right now, she didn't trust anyone in this building.

She thought of Will as she climbed the steps, not quite allowing herself to contemplate what might happen if she couldn't help him, because that way lay panic. No. She had to be calm. He needed her to be calm.

Will had said something yesterday about Price in the hospital. How had he put it? That when you got right down to it, the DCI was a lot of things, xenophobe, sexist, old-school and hard-arsed, but beneath all that, a straight arrow.

What about Stratham? She stopped on the steps. She could go back down and call him, like she'd pretended she had to Grundy. He'd already been informed about Adam so it wouldn't take much to bring him over here. So why hadn't she?

She let out an annoyed groan.

Respect. It was that simple really. She couldn't let the stench of this clung to her; she had to win these idiots over. Price, first of all. Only if that didn't work would she go near Stratham.

She nodded. Took the last flight of steps in a few strides.

She heard movement before she saw it. Shuffling, a sniff. The landing was murky, she stood at the top step blinking around her. She squinted. There, in the gloom next to the roof-door, under the fire hose. A slumped figure. The head raised itself, large wingnut-ears freeing themselves from shadow. Turner.

Ice floes in her blood, limbs stiffening. Enough, already, enough. Grundy was mean, but past it. But this big bastard… she put a hand on the wall, the other feeling for the baton in her belt. But then she saw the line of his shoulders, features shaping themselves as her eyes adjusted. He wasn't crying but… eyes hidden, a hand over them.

'What you doing up here, Turner?'

A dull shake of the head. Something muttered.

'What?'

The hand came away from his face. 'I said *I'm sorry.*'

She said nothing. Stared at him.

He glanced at the door next to him, head dropping again. 'For leaving you on top of those flats. Wasn't what you think.'

'So what, Grundy put you up to it?'

A puzzled look. A shake of the head. 'He eggs me on sometimes. All them darkie jokes and stuff. Just a laugh. But... that wasn't what that was about, on the rooftop.'

She shrugged, hand tightening on the baton. 'How about the note? The SOS from DI Ashcroft. Did Grundy egg you on with that too? To ignore it? Destroy it?' Hard to tell in the gloom, but maybe he paled.

She grimaced down at him. Hand still on the baton, she sprung the door, swung it wide, sudden daylight making him cringe away.

A few minutes, and four tries on the walkie. Nothing. The door creaked wide and gravel crunched behind her. She snapped the baton out, extending it fully and turning in one sweep.

Turner was shaking, hands splayed on the wall behind him. No, not splayed, too gentle a word. His eyes screwed up tight, face stone-white. He was shuffling along the outbuilding wall, but two more paces and he'd have nothing but the low wall of the rooftop itself to cling to. She almost wanted to see what he would do. But she wasn't so cruel. No need, now, anyway.

She walked to him; put a hand on his beefy arm. His eyes snapped open and he grabbed her, tight, but a life-raft, not a victim, she already knew. His BO was bloody terrible, but maybe with reason, she thought. Vertigo, or more accurately acrophobia, can open the pores like nothing else; she'd heard that somewhere.

'You're still a redneck rugby-brained bastard.' She eased him back towards the door and sat him on the step. He was panting. Close to hyperventilating, she thought. She glanced around. A paper bag would be too much to hope for. Then, her eyes went back to his hand. He was clutching something. He held it out to her.

His notebook, open. He nodded, his breathing slowing a little. 'From the note. Wrote it after... Grundy burnt it. From memory.

Might be… some bits missing… best I could do…'

She nodded, scouring the pages. It gelled with what the porter had told her; mostly Will identifying himself and that he was with the abductor of *Willow*. Jesus! Grundy would go down for this. She stopped on a single phrase, her finger jabbing at it. 'You sure about this?'

He grunted something vaguely affirmative. 'I need to get inside.'

She helped him up, wondered for a second about asking him to come with her, but considering what she'd just read, there'd probably be heights involved. She looked at him. 'Want to help me?'

'Aye.'

'Go find Price. Tell him what's happened.'

His face tightened up.

'I know, it'll mean squealing on Grundy but –'

'It's not that.' He grimaced. 'I just hate the bloody moors.'

She grinned. Turned it onto a questioning frown. 'Turner, why the hell did you join up in the first place?'

He panted, either laughing or on the edge of tears.

She raised the notebook. 'I'm keeping this. Evidence. Not that I don't trust you but…'

'Okay.' More colour in his cheeks now. 'Hey. All that black stuff… just jokes, you know?'

She let out a breath. 'Walk me, yeah? And if we see Grundy… don't you flip on me.'

He blinked. Shook his head. 'It's alright. I'm a bit sick of the old bugger to tell the truth.' He gestured at the notebook. 'He went too far with this, anyway.'

'Okay.' But it wasn't really. She looked at Turner's huge neck as he led the way down the back stairs. Like so many men, allowing his size to dictate perceptions. Laughing far too loud and all the while crying inside; because it was all he knew.

48

The snicket was slippery from all the recent rain and Will stumbled as a sudden gust shoved at his face. There was no Samira to grab his hand this time. The relentless figure of Adam was above him at the top of the slope, not noticing or not seeming to. Will stood, hands on the drenched stone of the wall, head pounding, throat burning. The bandage was flapping loose and he tried to tuck it back under the hat.

Adam hadn't stopped once since the hospital. The occasional glance to see Will was still behind him but other than that, no quarter for Will's state at all. The implication was clear; keep up or it's bye-bye Ryan.

Will looked up at the long sliver of late-afternoon light glistening off the stone slabs just as a yapping bark echoed down at him. A pensioner with a dog rounded the corner. Adam slowed his pace a little and gave the chap a nod, even petting the dog as he passed. Then, as the old man pulled on the lead, planning his footing on the slippery path, Adam stopped and turned behind him. For an awful second, Will was sure Adam would lean forward and give a little push or kick the dog-walker's legs out from under him.

Adam stood and watched, giving Will the finger across the throat gesture and pointing at the old man. No doubting the message. Say anything stupid and the old man would pay for it.

The dog-walker's brow crinkled at the sight of Will. Not surprising; he was a mess even apart from the ragged bandages; sweating, shaky, out of breath. The old man looked as if he was about to speak when Will crouched to his haunches and let the spaniel sniff the back of his hand and stroked under his chin. He gave the closest thing to a smile he could manage and answered the man's 'Afternoon!' with a nod.

Adam was still staring as the old man and his dog ambled away. He glanced at Will, a grin of disappointment or relief flickering before he turned and fell back into that fast, persistent rhythm.

Coming out at the top of the passage opposite the school, Will bent double, heaving. Adam was sitting on the drystone wall, ankles crossed, arms folded. Will was vaguely aware of him reaching into his pack and tossing something over. Will caught it, just, fumbling a little. A plastic canteen of water.

'You don't look so hot, copper.'

Will took a sip, rinsed it around and spat, then took a longer pull. Brackish, but no matter. The scenery stopped swimming and his head pounded a little less; not much help for his back, ribs and legs, of course. But he nodded at Adam and took a little more. He tossed it back, glancing down at the stone path they'd just climbed. 'Last Monday.' Will's breathing was just about regularising. '… you arranged to meet Ryan here? Or down by the canal?'

Adam's eyes narrowed a little over a slow smile.

Will coughed again. 'The kid idolised you, right? Ever since you were here working with that building crew eighteen months ago.' A guess, but it made sense. Will nodded over at the new block of the school, thinking of the metalwork teacher he'd taken an instant dislike to, when he should have been paying more attention to what he'd been saying about Ryan's sudden interest in builders. Will looked at Adam squarely. 'Eighteen months. You played a long game, right?'

Adam still smiling.

'Did he fancy you? That it?'

The eyes glazed, the smile freezing. Will's body tensed, his arms ready as he could make them, but Adam just shook his head. 'Now who's being a prick?' He put the canteen away and pushed off from the wall, strolling toward the school.

Will caught up. 'Okay. But he idolised you, yeah?'

A grunt.

It wouldn't be surprising. No competition but an expert on human behaviour who didn't notice his own son and a mother more worried which ankle bracelet to wear to the office. 'I bet all you had to do was take an interest. Talk to him a bit. Tell a few stories about the Argies and Mount Longdon and the –'

Will almost blocked it, could have, on a better day, but suddenly Adam's forearm was against his throat and he was in some sort of choke hold, being rushed backwards. A low growling, an instant to realise it was his own, but then something drowning it out. A car engine, not too distant. Adam pushing again, Will's heels skidding, something behind his knees and a tumble backwards into long grass and heather, Adam's forearm forcing him down, the choke hold eased, but only a little. 'Fucking still!'

A splash of tyres, the engine's tone sinking. Adam was up on his knees, forearm pulled away. Will breathed and rolled onto his front, spitting into bent reeds.

'One of your jam-sandwiches.'

Will sat up.

'Just cruising'? Or looking for me?' Adam winked. 'Doesn't really matter, either way. They won't find anything until it's too late.'

Will didn't like the sound of that but said nothing. He reached into his jacket, other hand up defensively, but Adam just shrugged. He'd already been through his pockets back at the hospital, taking out the walkie-talkie, his cuffs, the *Leatherman* tool. He'd know there was just a sheet of paper in a baggy he'd ignored. Will unfolded it, passed it to him. 'This is how I knew about Mount Longdon.'

Adam sneered, eyes darting back to Will as he started to read, but then stayed with the page until the end.

It was hard not to see the boy in him. The angelic face on the torn photo Will had passed to Samira, thinned by manhood, but much of the thirteen-year-old frozen there by whatever torment and abuse. Ironic, really. When he wasn't looking at you, or talking to you, it was possible to feel sympathy for him.

'Clever lad.' He said. 'So?'

Will shook his head. 'For a twelve-year-old, getting inside your head like that goes way beyond clever.'

He snorted. 'I've told you, the lad's no fairy. It's nothing like that.'

'I know.' Will let out a breath. 'He actually gets you. Did you tell him about the orphanage?'

Adam's eyes went straight to Will's neck, but he flexed his fingers and shrugged. 'Some of it.'

Will leant forward. 'Twelve years old. No one listens to him. Then you come along. He trusts you enough to defy his parents, skive off school, hang out. And how do you pay him back? Kidnap him and bury him alive, *if* we're supposed to believe that.' Will saw Adam start to speak but cut over him. 'Even if he gets out of this in one piece he'll be scarred for life. Just like you were.'

Adam's face was drawn, the smile gone.

'All for what? To get back at his father for letting you down when he had you on his couch or –'

The change in Adam's expression was sudden. He laughed, shaking his head. 'Nah, nah, nah... you've missed it, Sherlock!'

Will was reeling. If it wasn't about getting back at Sean Byford then what the hell was it about? 'So, you weren't a patient–'

'Alright. Enough. You've had your chance.' Detachment again in the set of the mouth and the not-quite-there eyes. But as he stood, Adam, aware or not, folded Ryan's story with careful fingers and put it in his inside pocket. 'Get moving!'

This time, Adam directed from the rear. Tempting to believe it meant he was rattled. Will was approaching the side wall of the school and Adam waved him over it. An easy climb; just as well. His legs were rubbery after their trek up the valley.

At the treeline, there was a sudden tug on his collar. 'Down!' The school's main building was opposite.

'Let's see who's about.' Adam was somewhere behind him; close enough to speak quietly, far enough to risk nothing if Will was to swing an elbow backwards.

Something whizzed past Will's ear, then the crack of pebble on glass, another in quick succession as the first skittered away. 'It's Sunday.' Will twisted to look at Adam. 'There'll be nobody –'

Adam grinned, nodding towards the window. There was movement beyond the glass. A boy, early teens. Ryan? Had Adam been bold enough to keep him hidden in the school he'd supposedly abducted him from? But no, a Caucasian face. Another, slightly smaller head appeared, this one undoubtedly female. Both grinning, checking driveway and carpark. Then an adult face, not so cheery. A shake of the head and the three figures moved back into the dullness of the room.

Sudden clarity. Today was May third; tomorrow bank holiday. Mayday. They'd be preparing food or a float or carnival goodies. He glanced in the direction of Shockley Beck, the roundabout and central Maypole that had seen rushes bourn and dancers in bells, ribbons and clogs wobbling around it for centuries.

'They'll all be in there,' Adam said. 'The neighbourhood dads. Proud as punch. Community spirit. All that shite!'

Will swallowed in a dry throat. 'Did Smiley bring you here?'

'Not here.' Adam glanced up the hillside, the orphanage not quite visible from here but the old Junior and Infants' was. 'Marched us all down to his school, not that it *was* his school. Student-teacher wasn't he? That's all. Acted like he was running the place. Had us all making bunting. All the parents and teachers there… chat, jokes… as if everything was normal.'

The quiet hung there for a few seconds. 'Well, none of them could have known what was –'

Adam's hand clasping the bandage, arm over his eyes and unmistakeable sharp edge of a blade at Will's throat. 'Say that again. Say it.' Adam's voice was mausoleum-cold, close. 'This village is tight as a gnat's chuff! Really think no one suspected? Bollocks!'

Will's heart thumped, his breath held. Then, as quick as it had appeared, the knife was pulled away, his head released.

'Wanna know why they never said anything?' Adam had moved away again. 'Cos it wasn't that different to what went on behind their own fucking doors.' His hand gestured into Will's line of sight for an instant. 'Like right now. Probably a dozen families in there. Interbred little one-horse dorp like this place, what's the ratio? How many normal families? Where the kids aren't living scared. Then there's the teachers. How many of them above suspicion? All part of the same game.'

Will found himself seeing the world through Adam's eyes. A cold, bone-dry place, childhood nothing but some perverse game of survival where parents abandon or abuse, and authority figures are never to be trusted.

Adam showed himself on Will's right, the knife-pommel balanced on his palm. 'You know what game I'm talking about,

Mr policeman. You're part of it too.'

'What you talking about?'

'Five years Brenda ran the orphanage. All that time, your lot never heard a fucking dickie-bird?'

Will's eyes tightened. His time as a PC, a few years after Moorhaven was shut down. There were rumours. Nothing specific; just the place having generally had a bad rep. But rumours should have been enough to start somebody asking questions, either at the time or afterwards. Adam, for all his paranoia, had a point.

'So, I don't know, maybe this should be where I start.' That empty smile again. 'What d'you reckon? Should I head in there? Start mixin' it up a bit?'

Will swallowed hard. No sign of any gun yet but Adam could easily have something tucked away under the combat jacket, and even if not, the long-bladed knife in his hands was enough.

Adam had started singing, voice gravelly but strangely tuneful. '*Tell me why… I don't like Mondays… tell me why…*' He broke into a laugh, tossing the knife from one hand to the other with deadly speed, eyes on Will the whole time. 'Tell you what, copper. You can save 'em. Easy. All you've got to do is exactly what I say.'

Will let out a long breath. Said nothing.

'Go in there, pick one bloke. I don't care who it is, daddy, teacher, whatever.' A real glint in Adam's eye now. 'Get him outside, and then… drop him.'

'What d'you mean, *drop him*?'

A shrug. 'Punch his lights out. Or throttle him or whatever takes your fancy, I'm not fussed. I just want to see him unconscious.' He raised his wrist. 'You've got three minutes. I'll be watching from right next to that window. No time for any phone calls anyway. And remember, Ryan's air won't last much longer.'

Will was shaking his head. 'You can't be… I mean, if I deck someone they'll phone my lot anyway. Thought you didn't want attention.'

'Well, you'll just have to do it quietly.' He pointed at his watch. 'Clock's ticking. Oh and by the way, just for an extra challenge, make sure it's someone bigger than you.'

Will grimaced, a low growl of frustration. He started walking, turned it onto a jog. His mind raced; some way he could turn this to his advantage? A message to Samira and the others? But what could he say? Adam was dangerously unpredictable and quite possibly ready to go Barry Prudom all over this district? Nothing he hadn't already pinned to the door handle at the hospital like a wish flag.

He was inside now, digging out his warrant card. Adam was right, ten or more families, by the looks. No teachers he recognised. A few people looked up as he came in and Will walked over to the nearest, fiftiesh, frail, jaw dropping presumably at Will's state of dress. 'Can I help you?'

'Just want a word with...' He scanned the small group at the other side of the long tables. A stocky guy, annoyingly young and fit-looking. Looked like he worked out more than a little. Jesus! 'That fella, what's his name?'

'That's Damien. Damien Vaughn.'

'Right.' Will walked around the table. 'Mr Vaughn.' He held up the card again. 'I'm afraid I'm going to have to borrow you a few minutes.' He smiled at the two little girls suddenly clustering around Vaughn's stocky legs. Was he really going to punch someone while his daughters were in here waiting for him? He glanced around for someone else. All either shorter or slighter than Will or looking infirm or just plain non-deserving of a punch in the face from a stranger. It would have to be Vaughn.

'What's this about? Stay here, girls.'

Will started walking and Vaughn fell in step. 'Nothing serious, sir. Just need your help with something. I'll tell you outside if that's alright.'

'Is Sarah okay, yeah?'

'Yes, don't worry. It's nothing like that.'

'Oh shit! It's not my Saab is it?'

Nice! Always possible Will had chosen a complete arsehole at random, which might make this easier. Outside now and Will turned so Vaughn's back was to the wall. He could just see Adam's army-issue boot sticking out from behind the buttress.

He turned. Vaughn in the right position, leaning forwards from the hip to hear whatever Will had to say. They couldn't be seen from the window. It was perfect. Now or never.

Vaughn looked down suddenly at Will's right hand, a laugh releasing itself. He took a little step away, re-assessing, the dirty dressing under the beanie, Will's strained eyes, the sweaty and muddy smell of him. When Vaughn spoke it was the drawl of someone not used to showing much concern, or not being able to mean it when he did. 'Err… you alright?'

The tremor was threading up Will's arm, biceps stiffening.

Vaughn was laughing quite openly now and Will would gladly have punched him if he could. 'Errm… think I might wanna see that ID again, Sergeant. It *was* sergeant wasn't it?'

Will made no move for his warrant card. All he could do was stand. Probably his eyes flickering as well, thoughts crowding around his skull, trying to stay in this moment here. But what had triggered it? There were no dripping pipes, corrugated iron or blue flashing lights here. He thought of the two girls inside, and what he'd been about to do to their father. Was that it? Children abandoned, in peril, to some extent.

'He's a detective inspector, you dickhead.' Crunching gravel under army boots. 'Show him some bloody respect.'

Vaughn was against the wall now, hands up. 'What is this?'

Adam's smile was deadly, and Will saw him reach behind himself, but Will's good hand closed on Adam's forearm. 'Not… it's not…' Will licked his lips. '… not…the man we're looking for, Sergeant!'

Adam's face caught somewhere between rage and mirth, staring at Will, down at his hand then into his face. He spoke quietly, for Will's ears alone. 'Full of surprises aren't you, Squaddie?' Then he shook his head, turning to Vaughn, putting on what Will had to admit was a pretty good policeman's tone. 'Sorry, sir. Our mistake. Please go back inside.'

Vaughn had turned away and what he said next was muttered, but loud enough for Will to make out. 'Bloody *defective* inspector, more like.'

A single moment stretched; Will rigid, legs in a swamp, no sound but the twisting of his sleeve. Then, everything zipping;

Adam springing onto Vaughn, something skilled with knee and elbow, bringing him down, then arm raised, flash of the blade clear in the crisp air ... Will stumbling to his knees like a broken string-puppet, head shaking from side to side, a repeated 'No... no... no...' freezing on his tongue... then skittering stones and light footfalls, ankle socks and pink shoes. 'Daddy, Daddy!'

Adam staring at the girls now, shaking his head, mouthing something. He drew the knife back up and Will could see it was un-blooded. It hung in the air above their little tableau until he slipped it back into his belt, stood, turned and looked at Will.

An arm, rigid fingers under Will's armpit. Boosted up.

The two girls running to Daddy, tears flooding, covering him with their bodies and kisses, Vaughn's half-conscious, apologetic mumbles fading as Adam swerved both himself and Will into a ragged run across the field.

49

'Get out of the bloody…!'

Samira stomped the brake, steering into a skid at the tall, hunched figure of Sean Byford and his hands clawed in almost comical recognition. The seatbelt bit as she lurched, Byford suddenly splayed on the bonnet, eyes fixed on hers, inches of air and glass between them.

'What're you doing?' She was out, snapping her seatbelt back, slamming her door. 'Could've killed you!'

'It's Cathy!' He shook his head. Samira glanced at the cottage. Had he run out in a panic, Cathy hanging from the rafters or sprawled in a bath, razor in hands? No. He looked distressed; not traumatised. 'She's gone!'

'I'll follow you in, okay?' She waved him into the house, glanced around for Clarke's car. No sign. Had Cathy commandeered her for a little adventure? Or had Price called her up to the moors so he and the lads had someone to strut for? Samira reverse-parked quickly, locked up and ran up the drive. He'd left the door wide and she snapped it shut behind her.

He was in the kitchen. Looked as if he'd just made a decision, standing, putting something into his pocket. 'She's gone to find Ryan.'

'Did she leave a note?'

Slow nod.

'Can I see it?'

An equally slow shake of the head. 'Don't think so.'

'Why not?'

'There's nothing… nothing relevant other than what I've just told you.'

She tilted her head. 'But there might be, mightn't there?'

He pursed his lips, said nothing.

'Because you're not seeing things clearly right now, are you, Dr Byford?'

A defeated sigh. He pulled the crumpled note out, handed it over.

No *Dear Sean* or *Sean* or even *Husband.* Just straight to it.

I'm going to get our son. Then we're coming back here and I'm packing our things and leaving you. It's not about the age difference before you start on that. I never cared about that and I don't care now. And no, I haven't found anyone else. Truth is, I just don't understand how anyone can know so much about people and absolutely sod all at the same time. It's frightening. You are a complete automaton.

Good luck.

P.S. *You'll think this is another of my little* episodes, *but it isn't.*

Samira re-read it, passed it back. *Little episodes?*

His tone was calmer, but embarrassed. 'So… there we go. No hint where she's looking for Ryan.'

'She doesn't say *look for*. She says *going to get*. I think she *knows* where he is.'

Byford's jaw had dropped, which Samira would have enjoyed a little more if she had time. She looked out the window at Gallerton folly. 'She say or do anything else out of the ordinary since Friday?'

Byford screwed up his face a little. 'Well… last night I hypnotised her again. It wasn't –'

'Woah! Hang on. You did what?'

He frowned. 'Her idea, not mine. We've been trying all week.'

Samira took the chair opposite.

'Cathy's actually fairly highly strung. I mean she's the worst type of subject for hypnosis. Anyway, it can take months to get a result. People think it's just *swing the watch* and away you –'

'You got nothing then?'

'Nothing useful.' He perched on the high chair, wise owl suddenly. 'I tried to probe whether she remembered anything leading up to Ryan's being snatched. Like whether we'd been followed or watched. Cathy just started talking nonsense.'

'Like?' Samira glanced at her watch. 'What nonsense specifically?'

'Well…' If Byford picked up on her impatience, he didn't show it. 'Towers, shapes. Surreal images. I mean, classic

249

Freudian stuff really.'

She thought of the two words she'd circled in Turner's notebook, words from Will's message: Maynard's Tower, the other name for Gallerton Folly. She stared at it through the window again before she realised Byford had stopped speaking. 'What kind of shapes?'

'Green triangles.'

She felt a smile spreading and knew it would look wrong but couldn't stop it. The logo on one of the Events services vans that Adam had had access to. Had Cathy remembered seeing it around here, more than once? Near the folly? Logged it away in her subconscious? 'What about the voice on the tape? Any luck with that?'

He grimaced. 'She didn't articulate anything, but that doesn't mean she didn't make a connection later. Hypnosis stirs things up, you see.'

Certainly did, if it had sent Cathy up the hill as a one-woman task force. Still, she'd been equally pro-active about finding Brenda Terrell and getting her up to Moorhaven a few days ago. A tigress under all that Louis Vuitton fleece. Samira gave him a levelling look. 'All this time, we thought it was you being targeted. It's Cathy, right?'

'I'm starting to think so, yes.' He looked up from the floor, then away. A tight smile. He stood wearily, turned, reached up for a high cupboard and pulled out a couple of tubs of pills. He laid them out on the kitchen table.

Samira couldn't make much sense of the labels but they looked pretty strong, whatever they were. Antidepressants? No, heavier.

'When I said she was highly strung that wasn't entirely...' he laughed, though it was thick with feeling. 'Cathy's actually schizophrenic.'

Samira sat down again, shaking her head.

So many things were slotting into place. Cathy's behaviour. Byford's too. His taking so long getting back from Bern, for one thing. He'd probably thought Ryan's disappearance one of her delusions. Then, as he'd realised it wasn't, his apparent coldness, while underneath, paddling like a bilge rat to keep the little boat of his family afloat. Except it had sunk already. Didn't he see that? 'Does Cathy hear voices?'

'No. She… believes things that aren't real sometimes.'

'I'm truly sorry.' She frowned. 'But you should have told us about this.'

'Oh really?' He flushed, his jaw working. 'To cope with it, raise a child, hold down a job. You know how Cathy has handled it so long? Because she's brilliant enough to think her way round it!' He snorted a laugh. 'If I'd told you on Friday after you'd found her on that moor with a gun…' He shook his head. 'She'd be in a secure unit somewhere by now. Right?'

Might be better than wandering the moor in search of Adam. Though from what Samira had seen of some secure units, maybe not.

'Anyway, I didn't see how it had any bearing on Ryan.' He looked down, his voice calming. He rubbed the bridge of his nose. 'Maybe that was stupid of me.'

Samira chewed her lip. 'Cathy's illness, that's how you two met?'

'What? Oh, no. She was never my patient. We met at a conference. She was a student. Clearly had some issues, but the schizophrenia didn't manifest until later. After we'd adopted Ryan.'

Samira nodded. There were two questions had brought her up here. Time to ask them. 'Does the name Adam Smith mean anything to you?'

He shook his head.

'We're pretty sure he's got Ryan. He was one of Brenda Terrell's orphans.'

His forehead creased a little more, along with another headshake.

'Okay. Something else. Cathy. What was her maiden name?'
'Martin. Why?'

There it was. Samira let her breath out, stood and looked at him. 'Did you know she worked for an adoption agency about 14 years ago, Right Choice?'

He spread his hands. 'Yeah, I mean Cathy tried various things before she got back into education. All sorts of jobs. She's from money, so it was about finding direction. I think that's why she wanted to adopt. Working with adopted kids had planted a spark and when it turned out we couldn't... conceive –'

Samira held up her hand. 'I'm more interested in how she said she didn't recognise Brenda Terrell. How's that possible?'

He blinked. 'It's something people don't realise. Schizophrenia affects episodic memory. There're whole chunks of her past she can't recall the same way you or I –'

'But what about you? You heard the tape. Why didn't you connect the name Brenda Terrell and the orphanage with Cathy's having worked in an adoption agency?' She shook her head. Will hadn't been wrong about Byford holding back.

His jaw flopped around like a loose lie. 'I didn't... think it could be...'

All those years, covering for his wife, consciously or otherwise. A habit he couldn't break, even for his adopted son? Samira shook her head at a sudden jab of pity for the man, not sure it was warranted.

She turned, shaking her head as Byford stood. 'I'm going to find her. You call the station and ask for –'

'No way. I'm coming too!'

'I can't let you do that. This Adam Smith... he's armed and dangerous.' Her voice cracked a little. 'And he's got DI Ashcroft as well as your son.'

Byford was ashen, hand frozen halfway into his jacket. 'How?'

She shook her head, gave him the bare bones of Will's abduction from the hospital. Byford's complexion was beginning to match the off-white Formica worktop next to him. He straightened, managed to push his arm through his sleeve, then slumped again. 'I should have...' His eyes dipped like shamed children.

'Should've what?' Samira tightened, a sudden lava swill of anger flushing at her temples as Byford did his guilty stare some more. 'Okay. Enough. Just stay here. Try following me, I'll cuff you to that bloody table.'

She could hear him shuffling behind her into the hallway and she turned, mouth open to speak, hand actually moving for her cuffs and then there was a sudden distorted flurry through the bevelled glass of the door. Someone was walking up the driveway. She almost reached for the handle, thinking Price might have got the message from Turner, or maybe Clarke had come back and...

No. Not Clarke. Male, tall, Khaki jacket, jeans. Cradling something that glinted.

She pushed Byford back into the hallway, manoeuvring him fast, blessing the fact he didn't resist, just let himself be manhandled. They were through to the kitchen and she shoved him through the doubled doors then out to the back door of the cottage. 'Keys?'

He nodded, scrambling in his pocket. 'Is it...?'

'Yeah it's...' A strange stillness snatching at her words as Byford got the key in the lock, things seeming to slow. Then it came; more massive than she expected, yet less hollow. The thudding of a single rifle shot at the door at the front of the house, wood splintering, glass breaking, sending both she and Byford into an instinctive crouch, hands over heads, Samira's unfinished sentence tolling in her head like an echo. *It's Adam. It's Adam. It's Adam.*

50

Pain crept through his head, nudging him awake like an old friend.

Around him it was grey and muggy, what was left of the drizzle-filtered May daylight catching the edges of hollowed-out rock. Long drips of stalactites were just visible, telling him what he already knew. The caves. Adam had brought him to the caves.

Things had been a blur earlier. There had been a van with a panel door though, he remembered that much. Will rolling over its greasy carpet, hands jittering like two snared rabbits in his own cuffs, the van's climb a sharp gradient. He was let out into the light and left clawing at the van's side, his hands sticky and he'd stared at them, expecting blood. No. White paint, still tacky. Was that why Adam had walked to and from the hospital? Worried the police had the registration?

Then Will had looked up at the brow of hillside. Above it, jutting from the trees, the familiar silhouette of the half-ruined building, and with it a sudden flare of hope. Maynard's Tower.

Samira. I was right.

It was the only place with vantage over the whole valley. The only place anyone could have watched both the orphanage and the hillside where he'd been ambushed by Little Kenny.

But there hadn't been much after that, Will finally fading out.

And now, coldness around his body, his neck and the back of his head. He sat up. Water splashing, trickling around him, but not deep, mercifully. Jarring pain in the side of his face to match the duller ache in his head. He breathed. Looked down at his hands, the glint of his handcuffs. He flexed his fingers, staring around him, scouring his memory.

The landslip had been maybe twelve years back, a sudden storm and rain deluge sealing off the shakehole, the 'entrance chamber' to the cave-system, swallowing up a small stream. Hadn't there been talk of cavers from the Pennine club wanting to dig their way through a few times? But it had come to nothing. Too much work. Too dangerous; the risk of flash-flooding.

But not for Adam, clearly. He'd done it himself, forcing his way through with sheer brute will and focus. What's the best place to hide out with a kidnapped boy? Somewhere no one would think of looking. How about a supposedly impossible to reach network of holes in the ground about five hundred metres from the boy's house?

Scary really, what it said about Adam's determination.

Will stared at the space just beyond the large drips of rock; a natural recess. Something in the dark there, a squat box forming out of the shadows as his eyes adjusted. Wires at the top? A generator.

Coldness eating through Will's guts. Adam had tortured Peter Smiles here; no one to hear any screams. Oh God! Was that what he had in mind for him?

It made him try to stand, but dizziness swayed him back to his haunches. He took some breaths, something like logic quietening his crocodile brain; he couldn't do a thing with these cuffs on!

He looked down at his wrists.

Will had two pairs; one new, one probably predating Houdini. There was one thing that might work with an older set. It was the only way he'd heard of to open cuffs without a key, apart from using a bobby pin. Not much chance he'd find one of those in here.

He lifted his hands, squinting in the grey light. Okay. He leant backwards. Stretching his arms to get as much leverage as he could, he brought the sides of the two bracelets together moving them carefully until they slotted into each other. Instead of a sharp turn he gradually increased the pressure, twisting his wrists in the opposite direction. It hurt, of course. That was the trade-off. His lips drew back as his arms shook and his muscles bunched against his shirt and jacket. His head was pounding, earlier pain swelling up again. Deep, carving pressure at the sides of his wrists and then... a sudden tingle of air as the handcuff's toothed arm popped from the weakened slot.

Breaths, in and out for a minute. He moved, crouching, wary of the overhanging rock ceiling, dips, troughs, uneven footing.

He thought about shouting Ryan's name. Was the boy here somewhere? But what if Adam was close by as well?

He was at the edge of the light now. Moving onwards would be into total darkness. He swept his hands around him, trying to cover every inch of ground, sudden stickiness in his eyes, a trickle, but fresh blood all the same. He wiped his eyes, tried to tuck the bandage in again. Hopeless.

He took off his jacket, fumbled his shirt off, buttons popping in the dark. He tore the shirt into the longest strip he could manage, tied it to the trailing end of the dressing and wrapped it around his head, firm as he could, material dangling like a bandana. He turned, pulling his jacket back on and fastening it up... then stopped. From this angle...something... the dimmest of memories. Himself and his Dad; that one visit they'd made here, so long ago.

His stretching hands found a low lip of rock. He swung under, feet first. Lying on his back now, he squirmed through the narrow gap, feet able to go no further, sudden claustrophobic panic speeding his breaths. Air, a faint breeze to his legs from the left, a slight greyness amongst the black, like an after-image. There was light that way.

Santa's letter-box. That was it! That's what cavers had called it. He'd squirmed through it with Dad. You had to roll and twist, make an L shape.

He turned, his hip within inches of the rock ceiling, wriggling feet and lower legs out sideways through the gap and shimmying through after them. The air changed, the sounds of his movement echoing wider. He went to his knees, head up towards cracks of daylight. There, set back, a blob of grey, too regular against the rock to be natural. A tent. He moved in, pulled at the flap, found the zipper, half expecting Adam's hand to pop out and grab his wrist. It was pretty dark inside there of course. An empty water bottle; he shook it, suddenly realising how much he needed a drink. He sipped at the dregs. Reached around again. Rope. He pulled at it, knots here and there, a loop at one point, some frayed ends, knife-cut? Another bottle rolled and he fumbled it up, unscrewing the top, the sudden whiff of urine. He threw it behind him.

But then he sat back. Ryan had escaped, somehow, that's what was important. The scent of maleness, nights of being trussed-up here, stale breath and clothes; him and Adam. But from the other end of the cave, he thought, cigarettes. Something else though, in the cramped air of the tent. He leant forward again. Something fresher. Just a hint of it. Perfume?

He stood and went back to the darkness. He followed the rut of the chamber down as the gradient dropped away, walls bottlenecking into a narrow passage. His chin was right down as he edged along on elbows and knees. There was a sluicing, echoing wash of noise around him, his sleeves wet already. More light too, greyness welcome as any 100-watt bulb. He began to slide a little, water up to his chin as the smoothed rock beneath him sloped downwards. The gap narrowed to a mouth and he bowed his head, breath held.

A sliver of open sky, earthy water streaming into his face. A chimney, straight up, so much smaller than the last time he'd seen it. He stood, feet slipping and skating around.

Santa's Chimney. Tough for adults. Will's twelve-year-old body had squeezed up into it all those years ago easily enough until Dad had stopped him, called him back down. Deceptive, he remembered, and he could see it now. The undulating rock chimney, wide enough for the most part, but with some narrow parts where you'd have to bend, and where if you angled your body in the wrong direction or lost your head, you'd be wedged tight as a nut. There'd even been talk of closing it up, before the landslip had done the job for free. He remembered Dad being dubious and giving up in the end, and they'd gone back the way they'd come. But that wasn't an option here, because Will had no torch. Back beyond the passage where Adam had left him was only darkness.

This way, or nothing.

51

The Byfords were isolated out here, maybe quarter of a mile to the nearest cottage or farmhouse, and rifle shots wouldn't be unheard of with the moors so close… but still. Adam must have seen her car and known it for police-issue. Clearly, that didn't bother him. He was into his endgame, she thought.

A smash of glass and wood splintering. He was nearly in.

It was a split-second thing really, leaving the back door open and hustling Byford back through the cellar door, resisting the urge to put some distance between them and the cottage. But there was something about the steepness of the slope from the back door, the condition Byford was in, the open expanse that would leave them without much cover until they reached the fence.

Byford reached for the light-switch and she let him flick it, something like an idea forming. She eased the door closed behind them and they moved down the stone steps fast. If Adam fell for the open back door, believing they'd made for the slope, they could double back out the front way to the car. She listened for footsteps overhead as she scoped the cellar around her. Damp, walls glistening. Boxes, sacks, abandoned bicycle pieces, rolls of old carpet and underfelt, an alcove around the side with an old coal chute. Nothing to defend them with, nowhere to hide. She took out her baton, extended it, listening again. She grimaced at Byford. Then she pointed up at the light, moving close and cupping her hand to whisper. 'You're taller. Take the bulb out. It won't be too hot yet.'

He blinked and did the jaw-hanging thing a little, and she thought of how he'd been at the tower block with Little Kenny. But he reached up, trying to twist the bulb out. He snapped his fingers away, blowing on them. She'd already found a hanky in her pocket and she gave it to him. He tried again. 'I think it's stuck.'

Movement from upstairs. The back door opening wider. They were both still, Byford's hands poised near the lightbulb, Samira's on the extended baton.

The door slammed, and Byford looked at her. Bootsteps,

inside the hallway. Adam was still in the house. He hadn't gone for it.

She held her breath. More footsteps, creaking boards. She cupped her hands at Byford again. 'Hold the hanky around the bulb.' She stepped back, hefted the baton. He gathered the silky material up from the top of the bulb. She swiped at it. Once. Twice.

It was a dull pop and the tinkling of glass was muffled, but certainly from here, it was audible enough. She managed to grab Byford's wrist in the sudden pitch black and manoeuvred them both into the alcove.

Byford's breath was close to her ear now. 'DI Ashcroft... he shouldn't have been on active service. I should have advised him to seek professional help... I didn't. Because... I wanted him to find Ryan. I'm... sorry.'

She swallowed hard, shook her head at the darkness. No time for this.

With a rattle, the door at the top of the steps opened.

Quiet for a few seconds. Then the clack of the light-switch being flipped. Flipped again. Stillness now, just their breathing, monstrously loud in the dark. The sound of fabric rustling. A zipper being pulled. A smaller click and then light filtering and flashing from the steps. A torch! Her heart plummeting. Of course, the bastard *would* have a bloody torch with him! Bootsteps on stone. She tried to ready herself.

A figure passing in front of her, another whisper, a hand touching her arm. 'Hide.' Byford walking toward the light as she clawed the air behind him. 'I'm coming out! Don't shoot!' What the hell was he doing?

Too late to stop him now. She backed away.

Byford was at the bottom of the steps, his front in sharp relief from torchlight.

Laughter from the top. 'Some balls, pacifist! Where's the wife, then?'

Byford's voice was quieter, but for a man facing an automatic rifle, she thought, some resolve there. 'She's gone. Up the hill with that policewoman. Gone to... find Ryan.'

Samira felt her own jaw hanging in the dark. A barefaced lie mixed with truth. Would he swallow it?

Silence and then Adam's voice again, subdued this time. 'Come up here.'

Samira used the cover of Byford's footsteps on stone to move herself directly under the vague grey outline of the old coal chute. She felt around the lip, crouching and sticking her head inside. Hard to tell, but she could probably squeeze her body into the bottom part, tuck her legs up, hold herself there with her back and feet wedged on either side, if she had to. She waited. What would Adam do?

Some more talking, too quiet to make out, then a sudden grunt from Byford that turned into a juddering cry, the sound of flesh and fabric sliding and rolling, she thought, and a final sharper cry as Byford slapped against the cellar floor. Adam had pushed him or prodded him down the stairs, probably with the rifle. Should she just step out there? Something told her it was the wrong move.

'I've ga… got a… note… here.' Byford was half choked.

'You what?'

'From Cathy!'

Adam's bootheels coming down.

Enough. She hoisted herself up. It was slimy with old coal and moisture, her boots slipping against the opposite side of the chute, her legs almost straight, knees bent enough for it to be bloody painful. How long could she hold it?

Adam must have reached the bottom, the sound of rustling paper, the light changing on the ground beneath her as he moved his torch to read. About ten seconds before the laughing started. She used it to shuffle her body upwards, some relief as her legs locked straight, her back and bottom paying for it though.

'She left you? Aww!' Another bout of laughs. 'Priceless!' A colder quiet for a few seconds. 'Stay here!'

The torchlight brightened under her legs. The sound of boxes being prodded and kicked over, the bicycle's wheel spinning. She looked down, between her shaking thighs. The light moving, changing as Adam flashed all around the room, then steadying and getting brighter. He was coming!

She tensed, closed her eyes. When he shined that torch up

here, he'd have to stick his head under to see anything. When he did, she was going to swing her boot backward and try to stamp a heel in his face. A cold resolve. Whatever happened after that, let it happen.

'Did Cathy work on getting you adopted?' Byford's voice was full of blood and he coughed before continuing. 'She let you down. Is that wha – ?'

The light moved away, Adam's boots crunching over cardboard, that rolled carpet, at a run. No sound from Adam now, no words anyway. Muffled grunts of pain from Byford, air and a strangled cry exploding from him at one point. Oh Jesus! He'd kill him. She felt her eyes screwing up tight as she shook her head. She couldn't let this go on. She shifted her boot, ready to collapse out of the chute.

It was distant, but clear. A siren. One of theirs. Turner and Price?

The sounds of Adam's exertions altered. Byford's grunts too. 'Come on!' Adam's voice labouring. Torchlight flashing madly now as they scrambled away, Adam probably half-carrying, half-dragging Byford. 'Come on, squaddie, easy does it,' she thought she heard from the stairway.

The pain in her thighs and knees was sharp but still she couldn't quite let her legs down. Not yet. Then the stutter of a car ignition, more like a van, she thought. With green triangles on it? A bizarre mental note to make sure that she gave the Event Services foreman a good slap as well as charging him for withholding evidence, if she ever got to pay him another visit. Adam hadn't just borrowed one of the vans occasionally. He must have had one right now.

Behind the sound of the van, the siren doing a doppler thing. Going somewhere else. Amazing. *The show's over here, boys!* She was giddy, sudden ragged laughter tearing from her. She let one foot down, straining for the ground, a basking flamingo, until the other leg gave with a quivering slip and she crashed down onto her backside, jerking her head to avoid the lip of the chute.

A grunt of released tension, some tears, hands massaging life into her thighs and calves, some long deep sobbing breaths.

261

Then she bent and retched, everything coming up, until there was only a dry hacking in her throat.

52

Afterwards, Will couldn't even remember the climb. There was just a vague sense-memory in torn fingers and empty, hollowed out exertion in his shoulders, arms and legs. He lay near the cracks at the top of the rock-chimney and basked in life, the wet rock around him, the tufts of wild heather brushing his skin, the skies darkening blue.

The cold of his wet clothes was soaking through, along with the pain of his injuries. Reality. He rolled over and dragged himself to his knees.

The crag he was on was high, a good vantage, but he'd be easy to spot. He crawled to the edge. It didn't take long. Something was out of place in the heather and scarps down there, about a hundred metres towards the setting sun. Movement. Hard to be sure with the light glistening off the wet rocks, but there, heading west, two figures. Suddenly some low cloud helped him out. Blonde hair, an exquisite neck, unmistakeable. Cathy. Next to her, his head almost to her shoulder, a boy in school uniform with a kagoule.

Will laughed out loud.

But as he watched, his smile faded. They were heading into the sun, away from the caves. There were about two miles of bogs and heather; heavy going before they'd hit the Manchester road. About half an hour of daylight left, he figured.

He could shout, they were within earshot. But Adam might be too.

Will started to work his way along the crag. He could move faster up here than they would, bringing himself more or less adjacent to them. Okay. It was a plan.

He scuttled along the crag and then picked his way down onto the heathery scrub, progress slowing. After the rain, each step needed judging and he was hot and sticky in the leather, the tattered remnants of his shirt already dry from his body heat. He crouched, caught his breath.

Something was wrong. He couldn't say if it was the sound of movement behind him, small stones freeing themselves and trickling, or the sudden cawing of some bird fluttering to flight.

He swept around, staring back the way he'd come. There were two figures on the crag, forty feet up. A sudden shout, strangled. 'CATHY! RUN…'

Byford? A clattering noise of limbs scrambling against rock. Byford's legs were kicking, his hands up at his neck, Adam above taking his weight.

Will could hear the distant sound of Ryan's cries, between gasps of wind. 'Daddy! Daddy!' Then louder, Cathy's voice. 'STOP! WE'RE COMING BACK!'

Adam didn't react, that Will could see. From here he looked to be grinning, but it could as easily be the exertion of dangling Byford below him.

Another cry, wind snatching words away, but he made out a *stop* and a *don't*. Ryan again.

Adam's knees bending as he hauled, Byford's heels scrabbling, hands flailing. like a broken kite coming to rest on the rocks.

Adam straightened. Stared straight at Will. 'You too, Squaddie. Get up here!'

Byford, poor bastard, panting and wheezing on the ground, Ryan hugging him back to some semblance of life, as Cathy and Adam ranted away above them.

Will had been so wrong. The connection had been with Cathy all along.

But something else was wrong here.

As a boy, Will had had a Muhammed Ali glove puppet, levers inside the glove; you pressed, Ali punched. Dad had bought the Joe Bugner model so they could give each other a good pasting. It was great. A cartoon-like violence about it because you could go for hours. Somehow that's what they were like, these two. An unreal quality to their verbal jabs.

An adoption agency? Was that what they were talking about? Cathy had been young, a new job, important to her. But something had gone wrong; reading between the lines, she'd exceeded her brief. Hard to be sure; Cathy's every word was fraught, as if her story was laden with some cosmic significance that nobody could ever possibly comprehend. Her eyes glinted with the drama of it, and he thought of her flirtatiousness when they'd first met, and realised he'd misread that too.

'She wasn't well...' Byford interrupted, hoarse, gulping, and voicing what Will had taken until now to realise. 'She *isn't* well!'

Adam pointed the rifle at him. 'Zip it, pacifist!'

Cathy was still talking, her head shaking. '... because they didn't understand me, didn't know what I could do. They all had it in for me anyway...' Her tone suddenly warmed. 'So I... I visited Moorhaven a few times. I wasn't supposed to. I knew I had to help. I *had* to...' She smiled through teary eyes at Adam.

Would Adam see her paranoia, through the filter of his own? His voice was cracking. 'You promised me! Said it was all arranged!'

Cathy's smile vanished. 'No... it was *them*... they made me leave the agency. They told me I was sick but I wasn't... I was *fine*...' She sounded petulant, fifteen all of a sudden.

And in the weirdest way, Adam's eyes seemed to match her adolescent strop, plaintive, wide. 'Nah. You stopped coming, dropped me flat!'

The sudden feeling everything was reversed, reality upended. Even Byford hanging on every word, as if Cathy and Adam were the ones dispensing logic. Will looked at the boy. What if Ryan was the only truly sane person on this crag? A weird epiphany, spreading a slick of oily sickness in Will's throat. He got a hand up to his mouth, swallowing.

Adam's eyes were still only for Cathy. 'I could've been alright. I'd have been a good kid, whoever took me.'

Will swimming in mad umber, the crags seeming to tilt under him. No crash of past reality this time though. None needed. The *now* was messed up enough.

He thought of the orphanage. There would never have been any adoption, Adam must know that. A good bet that Brenda had teased the kids with the idea of it, just to snatch it away. Which meant Adam was rationalising his motives, making these people suffer over nothing. Fast forward ten years: Adam had probably seen Cathy, recognised her on the street, in the supermarket, whatever. This woman who he'd decided had let him down. He'd followed her. Seen her posh little life with her respectable husband and, in an ironic twist of the bayonet, a clearly adopted son.

Adam wouldn't have been able to stand the fact she was so apparently happy.

And the irony, the ultimate irony of it, was that she was anything but. No wonder Ryan had been so troubled at school. This little family was just as fractured as Adam. Or as Will himself.

Will started laughing.

Adam twisted to him, forehead warring with emotion. 'You don't... you've got no idea what this –'

'Just grow up, Adam, for Christ's sake! Look at her!' Will's voice had found its strength. 'She's no Brenda. No Peter Smiles. Just someone who tried to do more than she could.'

Cathy flinched away, eyes searching her husband's suddenly, then to her son's.

Adam straightened, the blank veil descending again. 'Doesn't matter, Squaddie. Not now.'

No, it didn't matter. Will knew it, well as anyone.

Stoke the engine, delusion will feed itself. And then all you have to do is ride.

'Okay.' Adam dug in his back pocket, tossed the handcuffs at Will's feet. 'Don't know how you got out of these. Bet you can't do it with one hand though. Put them on, right wrist.'

There was a choking in Will's throat he couldn't quite swallow past. He looked at the cuffs. Then at Ryan, head buried in his mother's arms now. The rifle was steady, hadn't wavered from Ryan's head for five minutes. Will bent, picked the cuffs up in his left, managed to keep his right still enough to get them on, after several tries.

'To your belt,' Adam said. 'Should even things up a bit. I know you're banged about and you've got *problems* but you and I both know you're a bit handy.'

Will did as he was told.

Adam turned to the couple. 'When I say *go*, Cathy, you're going to bring Ryan to me. Then, you and pacifist there... you're going to kill this copper.'

266

Byford gave a choked splutter. 'You're crazy.'

'Professional diagnosis?'

'You can't...' But Byford was looking at his son.

'Treat it like an experiment. Some of your lot have done worse.'

Byford's head was shaking.

'If you do it, you, Cathy and Ryan can walk down that hill and go home. Shut yourself away, take long baths, cosy up, forget this ever happened. Well, the last bit might be a toughie but, at least you'll know you've saved your son. Because if you don't do it...' He looked at Ryan. Then, the rifle held in one hand but still steady, he reached around and pulled a large bayonet from his belt. He let it catch the light. 'I'll do him by inches.'

Ryan let out a howl and his mother's eyes had closed. Byford was crying too.

It flashed over Will again, the black water, the boy on his shoulders. Something almost welcoming about it this time.

If he spoke, if he'd been able to speak, he might have told Adam that Smiley and Brenda had been monsters, that the game they'd passed on had done nothing but ruined lives, and yet all Adam could do was keep playing it. But he didn't, because it was futile, and anyway he'd known from the moment he'd walked out of the hospital how this would end.

Truth was, Will had been on borrowed time since the pool. Part of him wished he'd never left it, and another wasn't entirely sure he ever had.

It took a little while to get going.

Will waited. When it came, it would come from Cathy first. He would have to hurt her, and then Byford would rouse himself. When they finally started working together, he'd be in trouble.

Cathy stood, moved Ryan over to Adam, the boy's cries stopping now. Will caught a glimpse of his eyes, and they were somewhere else, he thought. No harm. Adam just nodded. Byford's head was in his hands. Cathy's voice was shrill. 'Get up, Sean!'

His head shook. 'This is...'

She leant in, grabbed his lapels, and screamed in his face. His head jerked up, his eyes sallow holes, darting everywhere, everywhere but at Will. Cathy screamed at him again, slapping his face. Halfway through the scream, her body span backwards and she threw herself at Will, arms flailing.

He knocked her hands away a couple of times. She backed up a little, delicate ankles, a moorland doe staggering, and he thought of that first moment he'd seen her stepping from Grundy's car. Something, as a man, he couldn't help reacting to; that flutter of eyelids, the tears and pleading. Now, she lashed in with her foot, almost catching him, fingers raking for his face as he bent to avoid her and she was on him, wild, tearing, biting.

He backed away. All he could do was postpone the moment of hurting her as long as possible. He knew he had about seven feet of the craggy surface behind him before it dropped away. He took a few backward steps, her nails catching his face and her knee just missing his crotch. He bent, shoulder nudging her back and his arm swiping again. Fury behind the tears, she screamed and he was just aware of Byford getting to his feet as she surged at him again. This was it. No choice now. He stepped back, grabbed her wrist and spun his body, tripping her and using her weight to whirl her down the slope.

She was scrambling, half-rolling, a cry of frustration.

Byford's face was sudden anger as he charged, head down. Will sidestepped and got his arm around his neck. As a fight, that's where it would have ended if his other hand were free. Maybe it could end here anyway though. Will tightened his arm, angling his body over Byford, grinding him down into the dirt, tightening. Byford's hands were frantically scraping at Will's back. A little more, Byford would be unconscious.

'No holding, Squaddie.' The bayonet flashed and Ryan screamed. Will caught Adam's eyes. 'Unless you're going all the way?'

He gave one more squeeze and let Byford loose. He glared at Adam, knowing that this was hell, and that Adam was the king of it, whatever he'd been through, whatever he'd suffered. No words for any of it.

There it was then.

Will rocked back, stayed on his knees, only half-aware of Byford coming closer. Will stared at the boy. Not the boy he'd had on his shoulders. Another one.

More footsteps behind him, Cathy, not crying or screaming now as she reached for his free arm and put her knee to his spine. Byford was panting, close by, suddenly not committed again, hovering.

'Help me!' she said.

This time it was all it took. Byford pushing Will down, his hands at his neck.

'Hold him!'

'He's not…'

'Just hold him!'

They were tearing at him, pulling scratching, squeezing. No expertise in it, but only a matter of time until they figured something out. Cathy's knee pressing hard at his spine. Then she put more weight onto it and he let out a dull grunt, air rasping between his teeth.

The pool again.

Fuck the pool though. Just fuck it.

Cathy's voice, through panting and tears. 'He's stopped fighting. He's…' The shrill edge gone now. 'Oh, this is… we can't just…'

Byford's weight on Will's back now, his arm slipping around his neck drawing his head back and up. 'We have to.'

Something like serenity pouring over Will. It felt warm. Like a lagoon.

He saw Adam lifting the bayonet over the boy. 'Better fight, Squaddie! No pacifists here. Not while we've got –'

Strangest thing. The thud of something loud, Adam's face a wash of surprise, his arm jerking backward, the knife spinning out of it, Ryan crawling away, Adam up, stumbling, tottering, his other arm lifting the rifle but then another thud and this one turned him and tumbled him off the edge, the rifle letting out a shot high into the air as he went.

Byford still squeezing though, and everything seemed to redden. A scream, less shrill, a voice warm with stifled rage.

'Off him!' He felt Byford's body sliding. A pistol appearing. A Luger? A gentle hand suddenly on Will's back.

A face he hadn't looked to find here. Samira on her knees next to him. 'Jesus Christ, Will!'

He grunted something.

She was shaking her head at Byford and Cathy. 'What the fuck's going on here?'

Will had a hand on her arm. He looked at the edge. 'He's still got that rifle.'

She nodded, fished her handcuff keys out. He twisted his waist and they got him free.

They crept to the edge of the crag, leaving the Byford family, huddling now, a single organism with a wracking sob running through it.

He was looking for a word to describe it. 'Under duress.'

'Didn't bloody look like it.'

Will pointed at the moving bushes below, the drop beyond that led back to the caves. 'There.'

'Gone to ground.' She sat back, looking at her hands. 'Oh Lord, Will.' She was shaking, he realised. Not quite the mad quiver he was used to seeing in his own limbs, but shock at least. 'Feel sick.' She almost dropped the Luger, but he took it from her. 'I wasn't even going to fire… I was going to shout a warning… but it just went off. Then when he raised the rifle I had to… I mean I had to…'

'Samira. Look at me.' He gave her a few seconds. Glanced back at the Byfords. 'We need to walk them out. And we need backup.'

Her eyes seemed to find focus. 'Ha! Good one. Been trying for hours. Price is swanning around like a…' She trailed off as sirens echoed off the rocks, then shook her head and gave a brittle laugh. 'Oh great.'

They started moving, Will giving an unceremonious 'Come on!' to the Byfords.

It was the longest five-minute stroll Will had ever

experienced. He was pretty sure Adam wouldn't come after them, but pretty sure is meaningless when the stakes are so high, so he took up the rear, the Luger pitifully small in the fading light of sunset. Every step, he was waiting for a distant cough of bullets. It wasn't as if they could run, over this ground.

Finally, they were past the rocks and under the natural cover of the treeline. Invisible now, to anyone on the crag. Will sped up, got a hand on Samira's arm, pitching his voice for her alone. It took him a while to be sure she was actually hearing him. He revealed his thinking from a dry throat. She didn't argue, just looked numb. That would have to do. 'We agreed then?'

No reaction for a few seconds. Then she nodded.

Will turned to the Byfords. None seemed able to look at him, though Ryan could hardly be blamed. The boy was traumatised, clearly, and Will was reminded of Tim Havilland so much it actually hurt. As they approached the dark brooding outline of Maynard's Tower, blue lights flashing on its side from the gathered red-and-white cars, Will moved from Samira's side and grabbed Byford's arm, held him back.

'Inspector I... I'm so...'

'Shut up and listen to me. What happened up there... it's not important. But before everything gets chewed up in paperwork, I want to say something.'

A perplexed stare at the ground.

'Talk to your son, every night, every day, as long as it takes.' Will held up his hand. 'I know, you're a psychiatrist. Talking's what you do. But you can be good at your job and miss what's happening right under your nose.'

His chin jutted a little, that arrogance of his about to surface, probably an indignant shot of professional pride thrown in too, and Will gripped his arm, none too gently. 'Take it from someone who knows. This could ruin him! Don't let it!'

Byford winced, staring at the boy. Finally, he nodded.

There was a flurry of movement as the uniforms saw them coming. Price appeared with Turner alongside, then the others; Benson, Naylor. Price was edgy, hands not sure what to do with themselves. He blinked at the sight of Ryan Byford, then turned to Will. 'Manchester armed response are on their way. Twenty

271

minutes. We'll get everyone down to the station and set up a watch here so his only way out is –'

'You need to watch the Manchester road too.' Will glanced at Samira. 'But I think he's holed up in the caves, and he's got at least one bullet in him. Arm or shoulder.'

Price stared at Will, was about to speak when Samira stepped forward. 'Took your time, sir!'

Will was expecting something sarcastic in reply, but instead Price just nodded and motioned her and Will away from the others and then at the Byfords. 'Will you go with them, lass? They need someone with a bit of understanding and, well...' He glanced at the uniforms and plain-clothesmen around him.

She stiffened, and Will didn't know if it was the *woman's job* she'd just been given or the fact that ten minutes ago she'd been pointing a gun at both Byfords in turn. Really, she should be in blankets herself, being checked for shock in the back of that ambulance. But that would mean admitting she'd shot Adam, exactly what she and Will had hastily agreed she wouldn't do. She loosened her shoulders, gave Will a quick unreadable glance and walked towards the Byfords.

'So, you shot the fucker?' Macho admiration in Price's grin.

Will watched Samira's retreating back. She'd just saved his life, probably the others too. But she'd used a weapon that shouldn't have even been in her possession; left in the glove compartment of her Fiesta, presumably, after she'd taken it out of his car for fear of what he might do to himself with it.

An enquiry, and there would certainly be one, would uncover that fact, and though Will couldn't give a shit about what it revealed about him, he did care what position it put Samira in. A detective constable using an illegitimately obtained weapon that should have been put in storage days ago. Spun the right, or more accurately the wrong way, it could end her career.

The gamble really, was with the DCI.

Will looked at Price steadily. 'Yeah. He had a second gun. A Luger. I managed to get it off him.'

Price nodded, lit up a cigarette and blew the smoke through his teeth.

A second ambulance rolled up the hill and Will headed for it.

The boot of one of the red and whites was already open, equipment at the ready. Will bent into it and took a torch, as well as a rainproof jacket. If anyone asked, he could say he felt cold. Natural with shock. He closed it up around himself, the torch under his arm. He glanced around; Price was rounding up the others and setting up a barrier. Will headed for the ambulance again, then stopped, watching Samira putting Ryan in the back of the other one, Clarke dealing with the Byfords behind her. Samira was talking to the boy, and though he was far from ready to throw a house party, there was the beginning of something like connection in eyes that had been dark holes into hell a short while ago.

And Samira herself? She looked amazing, as always. Unaware he was watching presumably, being good at her job, even after everything, a natural with the twelve-year-old boy.

And then she did see him, her face filling with passion. The perfect moment to walk to her, forget propriety, forget protocol, forget what he was about to do and just grab her.

The warmth in her face reformed. Annoyance as he stood frozen, a minor shake of her head before she turned away and shut the door.

Will walked to the second Ambulance, glancing back again. He moved to the back doors, gave the medic a nod and then walked down the road a little way, letting the vehicle shield him. After about twenty yards he ducked into the heather and hunkered down. He waited for some of the vehicles to leave, then he crept as far from the road as he could.

He took the Luger and the torch from his waistband and started working his way back up through the long grass. Finally, he swung around to face the tower and the crags and caves beneath them that would be as dark as any grave by now.

53

Back into darkness, by choice.

It was a yawning mouth of rock and he hung back in the heather. He was breathing heavy, pain in his head and a numbing tiredness that had him lolling. He went to his knees, checked the torch, keeping it low, hand cupping the bulb, staring at orange-yellow transparent fingers. He remembered what Samira had said about the first time she'd met him; he'd been checking them as if he didn't believe he was actually here.

He turned it off, standing, gauging the dark lip of the hole. Always possible Adam was just inside, the SA80 ready to sight on him. He glanced at his watch. Armed Response would be within a few miles by now. He could either wait here for them, though they were as likely to shoot him as Adam, or take his chances crossing the 50 yards of open space between the heather and the cave.

He moved. The May evening-sky light enough to expose him. The expanse of rock was lunar and unforgiving. Clamber, stumble. A ricocheting spread of bullets, the whump of his guts exploding onto the rocks in front of him; he'd probably see it before he felt it.

The lip of the cave, ducking around the side. A patch of relative safety. Panting, lapping at life. Okay, Okay. Passing inside, Luger in one hand, torch in the other.

No sign of light, no sounds other than his breaths and the steady blather of water. He moved in as far as he could, extended the torch at arm's length and turned it on for a second, memorising the scene.

Steady going for a while, though the watery footing meant he'd be announcing his presence. No way around it. Dark enough now for him to need the torch every few seconds anyway. If Adam wanted, and was able to shoot him, there was nothing he could do about it.

Tucking into the letter box opening was easier this time, but he still needed a flash of the torch and knew its light would filter through. Curling his body, the police raincoat swishing. He jack-knifed out and stood, flashing around again. The grey blob of the tent as he'd left it. Adam dragging himself into a canvas canopy to nurse his wounds, did that sit right? No. But he checked it anyway.

He set off down the furrow of water, not looking forward to how it would have likely swelled at the bottom, enough for him to have to submerge himself.

Then there was sudden white torchlight like tracer fire, through cracks further up the rock wall, from what must be Santa's chimney. Cracks he hadn't known even existed. He stumbled to the rock partition, hugging it, holding his breath, listening hard.

Breathing, rough and wet, and a tangy offal smell. Not pleasant. He had some idea what it was. He started up the gradient, boots on drier rock now. He held the Luger high and ready.

'In here, Squaddie!'

Will flattened, still.

A groan, the sound of something slipping. Light through the cracks fading, stronger, then dimmer again. A single word. 'Fuck!' Another gurgling groan. 'C'mon Squaddie. I've…' an agonised laugh that couldn't be faked. '… dropped the torch.'

Will shone his own torch through the nearest crack. Waiting for answering gunfire. Nothing. Put his face to the hole.

The rifle was on the ground. The torch was dangling from its strap above, its short swing slowing, shadows in a rocking dance, but alive, like this was the inside of some leviathan's belly, not a cave.

Will squeezed through the larger of the cracks and out into the chimney passage, the Luger pointing upwards. His shoulders hunched as he sat himself not quite directly under the rock-chimney and looked up at the partly blocked slit of daylight. Streaks of blood and faeces were on the rock beside him.

Silence apart from Adam's rasping breath for a good half-minute. Will finally broke it. 'Santa's chimney. Tricky climb.'

Adam's cough was awful, and the spittle that dripped was dark.

'Can you move?'

'Wedged… good and tight.'

Will nodded, at no one in particular. Doubtful Adam could see him anyway. He aimed the torch, staring up at the trapped body, trying to make out the angle, what limbs were visible. Futile. It would have taken a real effort to climb up there; but deliberately pressing yourself into a space too narrow, making yourself stuck, that would take a special kind of madness.

Will's nostrils flared, stomach churning over. 'Gut shot?'

'Aye. Your lass got lucky.'

'Doubt she'd see it that way.' Will looked up at the crack and tried to think of sand under his bare feet and Samira smiling. 'Anything you want?'

A laugh, ending in a grinding cough.

'That girl at the hospital. You want us to bring her –?'

'No fucking way.' Then gentler. 'She's had… enough crap… from me.'

Will glanced at the rifle. 'Why like this? Why not just another bullet?' He knew the answer before he heard it, but still it made him angry.

'The game's… got rules!'

Utter quiet now. Stretched. Adam's breathing seemed to have stopped. Then a sudden coughing fit, the worst so far. Will waited, then said, 'That Barry Prudom crap! You never had any intention, did you? Moors massacre my arse!'

Something like a laugh. 'Sorry I had to involve you, squaddie. Wasn't personal.'

Will thought of saying that actually, he'd taken it pretty personally, all things considered. 'Out of interest, Brenda seemed a bit rushed. Was that because we were getting close?'

'I had… bigger plans for her, yeah. Didn't matter though… dead's dead.' Words in gluts now, like lifeblood. 'Back at Moorhaven… before… all that adoption bollocks… there was a copper… came to the school opposite. A talk on… road safety or summat. I jumped the fence. Went to see him.'

Will put his head back out of the torchlight and grimaced at the darkness.

'I talked to him. Told him what was going on at the orphanage.'

1970s. Some small-town copper confronted with the

incredible. Would it really be any different now, though? Will cleared his throat. 'Didn't believe you, right?'

'Pretended he did. To shut me up. Took me back to Brenda. They had a good laugh about this lad... making up stories.'

Will pulled his waterproof close around him. He'd thought it might be something along those lines. He thought about asking if Adam remembered the officer's name. What did it matter though?

'Oh...' Shifting and groaning, more spatters from above, Will drawing his legs back in time to avoid them. Panting breaths, until Will almost told him to take it easy, that it was alright, to let it go. But he found he couldn't. Or didn't want to.

A wrenching grunt now, like Adam was making a supreme effort, and then from the narrow slit, a hand, blackened with blood, straining down between his legs, the torch dangling lower. 'Ashcroft!'

Will thought of denying him, but what was that worth really? He stood, reached up and held his shaking hand with his own.

When the shaking had stopped, along with the laboured breaths, Will checked the rifle.

He looked up at the body, or what he could see of it. They'd never get Adam out. So there'd be no autopsy.

He put the SA80's stock to his shoulder and squeezed off a shot into the deeper water at the bottom of the passage. It was thundering loud in the cave, but he doubted anyone outside would have heard it. He stared at the rippling water; he could think of no reason even the best SOCO would go looking there for a bullet, and Booth, Spinnerby's incumbent, was anything but. He put the rifle down and spent the next few minutes wiping it down where he'd touched it. There'd be at least a cartridge missing. Will would tell them Adam must have turned his rifle on himself and then somehow managed to climb up into the crack, for reasons known only to himself, the mad bastard, and so on.

With any luck, Samira, or anybody else would never have to know it was her bullet that had killed him.

54

She knocked on the door and Karen Donahue's wild russet hair, eyes just as inflamed, the matching spark of a cigarette clenched between tightened lips, peeped around the jamb. Karen walked back inside her flat without a word or backward glance, leaving Samira to close the door behind her.

No eye-contact. 'What d'you want, then?'

Samira talked through the necessaries, the paperwork, the detail. Mainly dates and cross-checking. Karen blew grey smoke around the occasional monosyllable. When she was finished, and Samira had started making her apologies and was about to get up, Karen cleared her throat, stubbed out her second cigarette and looked at her steadily, though her voice shook. 'They've started concreting.'

Samira nodded. 'No choice, Karen. They couldn't get Adam's body out.'

'So, they'll just seal it up. Put a skull-and-crossbones there. I get that, yeah. What I don't get is why they're not going to mark it with his name or his commendations for bravery in the Falklands and Ireland. Something. An unmarked bloody grave. Why?'

'Because of what he did, Karen.'

'Because of what he did.' She repeated it quietly. 'Getting rid of two complete monsters.'

Samira chewed her lip. 'Yeah. He did that. But then he also abducted a twelve- year-old boy, terrorised his parents and almost killed… one of our DIs.'

A cold smile. 'Yeah. How's *that* going for you anyway?'

Samira got up, was heading for the door. 'Thanks for your –'

'Thanks for what? Helping you lot shoot my ex-husband?'

There was a chill in Samira's stomach.

Karen moved closer, and it struck her that this was a kind of cruel parody of the first time they'd met, when she'd asked for advice on Will's condition. A sudden idea Karen might be about to slap her, or rake at her face. But instead she just stared; a straight, piercing look. 'I used to think it was about men and women. Y'know? Like, *we're* born to pain, so we just curl up and take it. Men? They have to spread it around, even if they don't mean to.'

Samira edged for the door. 'Look, I really must –'

'It won't work out.' She winked at her. 'You and your copper. But you know that already, don't you? Smart bitch like you. Got it all figured.'

Samira backed to the door. Everything from this woman was drenched in pain and bitterness, and she knew nothing. She had let her vent because on some level she probably owed her. Crazy to take any notice. But Samira stood at the door, turned and spoke when she knew she didn't need to. 'Why?'

She snorted a laugh. 'Men are selfish bastards at the best of times, right? But when they're damaged, like your copper... like Adam...' She shook her head. 'It goes beyond selfish. They don't... even... fucking... see you!'

Samira smiled. 'He sees me alright.'

'No, he doesn't. He sees a cure, and when it doesn't work, what d'you think he'll see then?' She turned to head back into the room, lighting another cigarette. 'Let yourself out, copper.'

Bullshit. Wasn't true at all. But it was still rattling around her head as she sat down for her meeting with Stratham and Price a few hours later, making it tough to concentrate.

The pleasantries went on a while, compliments over her work on the Byford case, Price offering something about how if he'd made it hard on her at first, that was just his way of making her resilient and testing her loyalty. She took it all with the best grace she could manage, drifting a little as talk turned to Moorhaven, the bodies found there in the last few days, the promise of more to come over the next weeks. Nothing to say to any of that really; *too little too late* coming to mind, but not to her lips.

She tuned back in as Grundy's name was mentioned. 'He's requested early retirement. Effective immediately.'

She nodded. 'So, he gets to keep his good name. No headlines. No tribunals.'

Price opened his hands. 'Ashcroft decided not to press charges, so there we go.'

'Grundy's finished as a policeman.' Stratham steepled his

fingers. 'Whereas you can go on to take the sergeant's exam a month from now. Statistically that's about two years earlier than most female officers –'

'About six times quicker than *any* black officers.' She said. She noticed Price stifle a grin. Stratham was suddenly quiet. Re-evaluating, by the look of him. She took a deep breath. 'Grundy's just a little cock... on a very big dunghill.'

A snort from Price, Stratham still blank. 'What do you –'

'It's everything, sir. Every joke in the canteen, comments under the breath in every bloody briefing I've ever sat in.' She glanced at Price. 'It's about blowing in for backup and knowing the chances of it arriving are worse than shit.' She watched his eyes flicker. 'It's about being given all the crappy jobs to do while watching people with less brains and less talent get further along, quicker than –'

Stratham's steely buzz-cut inclined itself towards her, his hand held up. 'Detective Constable Byrne, you're a very intelligent woman. I wouldn't be surprised if twenty years from now, you're sitting where I'm sitting right now. But because you're intelligent, you know change happens slowly. And it has to start somewhere.'

She chewed her lip.

55

He'd been anything but sure she'd agree to dinner; the five days since Adam's life had seeped into the Pennine crack had been tough; his lifeblood tainting everything.

His few attempts to explain his heading back up to the crags to find Adam, she'd ignored. A rift he thought he'd never heal. The more he thought about it, the more he realised how it must have been to her. He'd turned his back on her, after everything. That's how she'd see it. But he couldn't tell her why. He'd had an idea that one of her shots might have been fatal the moment he'd seen Adam spiralling off the crags. He hadn't known if he'd be able to do anything about it, but that hadn't been his only reason. He'd wanted it over. He'd had to see it through.

So, the next time they'd spoken, he'd dived straight in; asked her to dinner. She'd blinked a few times, looked at him like he was someone vaguely familiar, chewed her lip the way she did and said nothing. Walked away shaking her head.

A few hours later as he'd moped around the incident room, she'd stuck her head round the doorway and nodded at him. 'Seven thirty. Paulo's.'

'I shouldn't have left you. After what had happened. I just…'

She wafted a hand over her food. 'I didn't need hand-holding. That's not it.'

'What then?'

She sighed, head on one side. 'When I arrived at the scene, when the Byfords were doing their best to kill you… you were going to let them.'

Will felt a wash of cold in his guts.

'It's how you've been since I met you. All of two weeks ago…' She put down her starter fork, took a sip of wine. Rolled it and swallowed, her chin setting. 'You don't think you deserve to be alive.'

Truth like bullets. He shook with the impact.

He did something then that surprised him. He leant forward, took her hand and started speaking. He didn't stop until he'd told her about Creasey and the pool. He broke off only as the waiter approached with their main course, to hold it off another ten minutes. It wasn't a story to go with food.

Fairly broad strokes, because in conscious memory that's all he had, except when it was upon him, crashing over him... then it was all there to see... in all too perfect detail. But here, at the table, he told her how Creasey had snatched the Havilland boy, nine years old, and how Will had tracked him to London Docklands, and how he'd been jumped by Creasey, dumped into a pit of slowly filling water with the boy. Thames water rising, Will had kept them standing, later the boy on his shoulders, later kicking. Hours like days, both sure they were going to die, at some points Will convinced he was dead already.

There was more to it, of course. Much more. Something he couldn't look at yet. But for now, it was something to talk about it at all.

When he'd finished, Samira dabbed at her eyes and took one deep breath, letting it out slowly. 'How do you feel after telling me?'

'I don't know. Freer maybe. Lighter.' He blinked. 'After dumping it on you.'

'I asked. Repeatedly.' She was looking up at him, the line of her body and neck fine as any sculptor's dream and he wished he could step inside the open grace she seemed to carry in abundance. She leant in. 'But know what? I don't think it's *me* you need to talk to.'

'You don't mean bloody Byford.'

'No. I don't.' She squeezed his hand.

It was so obvious, it didn't need articulating. So obvious it had only occurred to Will as he'd told her the story. He nodded.

Quiet, measuring looks. He stared at his hands, then at hers. 'First time you've ever fired a gun?'

She stiffened. Nodded.

'You shot someone. Your bullet didn't kill him but –'

'Are you sure though? That second shot –'

'No.' Will held her gaze, making a sudden silent vow that if he could help it, this would be the only lie he'd ever tell her. 'Adam squeezed one into his guts. He'd had enough of his

282

game. That's it. Over. You saved my life. Saved the Byfords.' He looked at her shoulders. 'That's a killer dress. But you're not a killer. Okay?'

She looked away, a smile at the corners of her mouth, eyes glistening.

'Samira.' He felt his heart hammering. 'Come away with me. Tomorrow. We deserve some light. Spain, Italy, whatever. Paris. Will you come?'

She touched his hand again, then she stood, picked up her bag, motioned at the bathroom.

Ten minutes and it hit him. She wasn't coming back. The waiter walked over with a folded napkin, put it on the baize in front of him.

As he reached for it, his hand did its thing. First time in days. He used his other hand, spread it open.

Three words at the top. Simple and true.

We're not ready.

He almost stood, ran to the door. Maybe he could catch her.

He shook his head and read the rest.

We're not ready and we can't wait for each other. It's a weight we'd never shoulder.

You've got your pain. I hope you can sort it out. But there's something you might not know about me.

I'm angry, Will. Every bloody day, I'm angry as hell. At the world. At the system. At myself.

So, this isn't just about you and your pain. Just so you know.

I hope one day I'll see you again.

I wish you the world.

S.

He pointed the car at the dirge of tarmac and grime, the blackened hills beyond.

He shook his head. Direction. Small steps. Right now, he needed to know where he was heading. He tried to visualise it, the large semi in Guildford. He'd been there once. His hand on the bell, the crisp home-counties accent carrying. 'Back here.'

The stiff line of Haviland's shoulders. His wife more hopeful and fluttering. Will stifling a shudder at the devastation blasting through the lives of another family.

Would it still be that way? Or would he walk into the spring-warmed garden and find a healthy boy playing with his parents? Would Tim Havilland turn and recognise him and if he did, would he want to talk to him? Maybe not straight away, but would he feel the same need to... depressurise?

And after that? AMIP? A full disclosure from Will though. Three more words he'd always had trouble with, if truth be known. 'I need help.'

Later, maybe an hour, when he'd wormed his way out of the black Pennine hills and the horizon had lost its menace, he felt a certainty of hope again. He'd be back here.

Back for her, one day.

THANK YOU FOR READING

I hope you've enjoyed it. For updates and occasional goodies-
contact me:
info@writerjohnkennedy.com
website:
www.writerjohnkennedy.com

Printed in Great Britain
by Amazon